THE MYSTERIOUS WOMEN OF J ROAD

a novel

allison cundiff

APRIL GLOAMING

This book is a work of fiction. Names, characters, places, and incidents are the product of the author's imagination or are used fictitiously. Any resemblance to actual events, locales, or persons, living or dead, is coincidental.

©2026 by Allison Cundiff
Design ©2026 by Theo Hall
-First Edition

All rights reserved. No part of this publication may be reproduced or transmitted in any form or by any means, electronic or mechanical, including photocopy, recording, or any information storage or retrieval system, without permission in writing from the publisher.

Publisher's Cataloguing-in-Publication Data
Cundiff, Allison
The mysterious women of j road / written by Allison Cundiff / designed by Theo Hall
ISBN: 978-1-953932-43-3
1. Fiction – Southern; Fiction – Horror: General; Fiction – Thriller: General I. Title II. Author
Library of Congress Control Number: 2026934002

Praise for *The Mysterious Women of J Road*:

"Using the darkest of Vance Randolph's romantic folklore as a jumping-off point, Allison Cundiff reimagines a rural Ozarks unlike anything you've ever encountered, a hidden and haunted society deep in the hills. Anyone who travels the dirt trails to meet *The Mysterious Women of J Road* will think twice before their next twilight walk in the woods."
 – **Dr. Brooks Blevins, Noel Boyd Professor of Ozarks Studies at Missouri State University**

"*The Mysterious Women of J Road* is an Ozark horror story filled with spells and strange beasts, demons and dark magic. But Allison Cundiff's genius as a storyteller is to ground the tale in even stronger, if far less fantastical stuff: family bonds, the handing down of traditions, and the human imperative to protect those we love. Witches and healers. Vines that sting and vines that soothe. Red-eyed Ozark howlers and good, loyal dogs. Here's a novel to disappear into. You'll come out the other side more aware than ever that the world is a strange and woolly place, and grateful for the guiding hands of the gifted storytellers who help us better understand it all."
 – **David Williams, author of *Come Again No More* and *Everybody Knows***

"From yarb-doctors and granny-women to snake-handling and animal-omens, hexes, howlers, and hoodoo, Cundiff's novel fishes the deep dark pools of Ozarks lore. More, it captures the history-haunted psyche of that landscape: those cricks no sensible person dares cross, and the half-seen things that wander the woods. There are things in the woods that wonder what you taste like. The Thing you can't see is worse than the Thing you can, but worst is the Thing caught fleetingly, out of the corner of one's eye. Cundiff's novel grows from deep folkloric roots, a world where what we're talking about isn't really what we're talking about, where a little girl told the famous field collector Vance Randolph, 'We always lie to strangers.' It works from suspense, but also that emotion's more serious sibling, dread. It joins the growing library of Missouri noir."
 – **Dr. Adam Brooke Davis, Professor of English, Truman State University, and Editor of GHLL**

"This book scared me so much at first that I locked the doors and went to bed with ice cream. The next day, I started thinking about how well this author knows the place she writes of and the cultural fault lines there. Though she does scare us, she also has a tenderness toward life that I find powerful."

– Dr. Monica Barron, author of *Prairie Architecture*

"Shifting effortlessly between page-turning thriller and the legend-making of regional folklore, *The Mysterious Women of J Road* is literary fiction of a high order. It is a highly entertaining novel that also probes the way the past cuts deeply into the present. The book is a chilling master class in character study, tension-building, and the particulars of place. It is both a supernatural and realistic tale that adds important layers to the recent wave of stories set in the Ozarks. The writing is sophisticated, the characters are vibrant and intriguing, and surprises await readers in every chapter. The novel becomes a thoughtful and, at times, violent demonstration of the power that a home place holds on us. A thoroughly satisfying—and frightening—narrative from start to finish."

– Dr. Brian Hardman, Professor of English, University of the Ozarks

"Cundiff's latest novel includes, in addition to a sense of building mystery, fascinating contrasts: the old ways and the new, folklore and technology, the supernatural and hyperrealism. The concrete details keep the reader grounded in a sense of reality, even when fantastic situations occur."

– Keven McQueen, author of the *Offbeat Kentuckians* series and *Murder in Old Kentucky*, Instructor of English and Theater at Eastern Kentucky University

"More than a mere horror story conjured from the darker shadows of Ozark folklore, Allison Cundiff's *The Mysterious Women of J Road* is an intensely imagined tale of courage, conscience, and identity that unfolds against a backdrop of lurking, invasive evil. When protagonist Lillian Black is hurled into a maelstrom of malevolence incited by a family member, she calls upon her faith and an extended family of Ozark granny women to defeat a force bent on robbing her of all she loves, values, and believes. Her defense against this force proves as costly as true heroism always is, and readers come away from this book sufficiently warned that, for good or ill, 'It's all our choice who we're going to be.' "

– C. D. Albin, author of *Hard Toward Home: Stories*.

For Lyla, who loves a scary story. And for Camille, who reads them to her.

"Sophisticated visitors sometimes regard the 'hillbilly' as a simple child of nature, whose inmost thoughts and motivations may be read at a glance. Nothing could be farther from the truth. The hillman is secretive and sensitive beyond anything the average city dweller can imagine, but he isn't simple. His mind moves in a tremendously involved system of signs and omens and esoteric auguries."

–Vance Randolph, *Ozark Magic and Folklore*

"Behold Dis, and behold the place
 Where thou with fortitude must arm thyself."

–*Inferno*, Canto XXXIV

1

Sam Ebbons' pointer was his pride and joy. With a solid liver head on a pure white-ticked body, the dog, bred from a bloodline of champion hunters, was a gift from Sam's father, Brutus, a man of rigid convictions who rarely indulged his son. The pup had been the largest male of the litter, eager to obey and alert, taking to Sam as soon as he had lifted him from his mother's teat in the den's cedar warmth. Sam turned the pup around in his big, nicked-up fingers and announced he was the finest dog he'd ever laid eyes on. After the pup was weaned, he never left Sam's side. That is, until he was taken from Sam by the southerners of Lick Creek. The dog was never found, but his collar washed up, tattered and faded, on the north shore of the Lick one week after Sam was found dead on his bathroom floor, the cause being respiratory failure from elapid envenomation.

 The collar had been found by a local by the name of Althea and turned over to Camden County sheriff Gideon Underwood one week to the day after the dog had been reported missing, and six days after Sam Ebbons was discovered unresponsive, having aspirated on his own vomit. The tight-knit community was particularly interested in both the missing dog and the details surrounding the owner's death, but Gideon Underwood wasn't talking. The medical examiner initially suspected overdose, then poison, but there had been no other signs of distress, and toxicology had yet to come back from Columbia. When Gideon saw the collar on his desk, sitting in a clear evidence bag, he felt a chill spread through his groin. He took it upon himself to pay a visit to the dead man's father as he felt badly for him, having buried both his wife and only son, and seemed committed to living out his days alone in his double-wide behind the Dollar General off Highway 7.

 Gideon turned down the CB on his way over, thinking in the silence about Brutus and his particular ways. He wondered how the man would take this new detail and thought he'd try to convince him once again to come down to the station to provide an official statement. Gideon pulled off 7 and onto the gravel rural route, parked a ways off from the handicap accessible ramp, and killed the motor, listening to the arching ticks of the grasshoppers that had arrived in a fury that week in the midst of some sort of electrical storm that had turned his jurisdiction upside down it seemed. The town had lost power for a few days, the hospital running on their generators, and the local airport shutting down for a day and a half. The governor had called twice, not bothering to come in of course, but there had even been talk of the National Guard. Gideon had been fielding calls from the local college's agricultural department, something about the supposed climate crisis. Gideon didn't mind the locusts much. Good for his bird watching as they fed on the glut.

The sheriff stood to stretch his legs, taking his time with his knees, then walked slowly to the door, giving Brutus, a veteran of the Gulf War, plenty of time to discover him before he rang. Gideon knocked three times and squinted in the soggy afternoon heat. Brutus answered in his own time, holding his Mark V Weatherby, as he was wont to do, exhaling smoke to the side of him as he opened the screen door with a curt nod.

"Gideon," Brutus said coldly.

"How you holding up, Brutus?" Gideon asked, looking him over.

"As well as to be expected," Brutus said slowly, lifting his hand to block the sunlight. A tuft of gray hairs poked out from his undershirt. "You got some news for me?"

Gideon shifted his weight, glancing behind Brutus into the trailer's darkness. The light from the television illuminated the corner of the trailer where an overflowing ashtray sat beside a sweating Big Gulp. A chorus of barking echoed from the dog pens behind the trailer.

"Sam's dog's collar washed up on the north side of Lick just yesterday," Gideon said, pulling the wet stub of an unlit cigar from the corner of his mouth and spitting into the dirt. "It's gone into evidence, but I wanted to stop by to tell you," he finished.

Brutus' sagging face tensed as he looked down at his gun, adjusting it needlessly. "Mhm. Anything else?"

Gideon returned the cigar to the corner of his mouth. He pulled a glossy photograph of the dog collar from an envelope and handed it to Brutus.

Brutus looked it over. Tags were attached. No signs of distress. Gideon watched him examine the photograph. For a man who had just buried his son, Gideon reckoned Brutus looked about how he should.

"How the other boys doing?" Brutus asked.

"Alright, it seems."

"You hear anything?"

"Nothing since the day we found Sam."

"Kurt?"

"Back filling gas at the Red Fox." Gideon hitched up his pants. He knew what Brutus was thinking. Why was Sam the one of the four to die? Why *his* son?

"I wish those boys would give you something useful," Brutus barked, his face looking very old in the sunlight.

The sheriff nodded. "You sure *you* don't have anything useful?"

"Told you everything I know, Gideon. But you won't listen worth a damn."

"We've been over this, Brutus. South of the Lick is out of our jurisdiction. Their people are looking."

"Their people. So they say," Brutus mumbled before raising his voice again. "Who in the hell are their people anyway?"

Gideon had followed up with the precinct in charge of the south of Lick Creek two days after Sam's death. They had reminded him they had no intention of combing those parts beyond what they had already found: nothing. If he wanted more, he'd have to escalate it himself, which was not within his budget.

"Well, if anything comes to you, you know how to get ahold of me," the sheriff said.

"I told you," Brutus said, stepping a few inches closer to Gideon and lowering his voice, though no one was around. "You're asking the wrong man. The law needs to comb south of the Lick. It's where my boy got bit. You know as well as I do that things aren't right down there." A gust of hot wind lifted a spray of cottony blooms over the men.

"Aren't right?"

"That's right. Those hill people and their snake medicine—well, they got my boy, and you know it."

Gideon stiffened at the man's tone. "There is no evidence of any foul play, Brutus."

"Ah, that's horsehit and you know it," Brutus said in exasperation. "Someone had to see something, Gideon."

Gideon tongued the sore that had been lingering in his mouth since spring and said nothing, thinking over Brutus' claims. He took the photograph back from Brutus and made a show of looking around the property as he fit it back into its envelope.

"Let me think on it," he said finally. "I'll be in touch if anything else comes up."

Brutus limped backward, grunting something incoherent before closing the door between them. Gideon lingered on the trailer's shoddy porch for a moment, the smell of Marlboros lingering. He took his time walking back to his vehicle, noticing the security cameras, one out of order, along the perimeter of the property. Aside from the rhythmic ticking of the insects, he found it unsettlingly quiet.

The Gascon River and its tributary, Lick Creek, were the heart of the Department of Conservation's current legal snafus in Camden County. Primarily spring-fed and running through the westernmost part of the county, the creek once drew a plentiful amount of visitors, which heartily contributed to the hunting and fishing industries in Camden County. Lick Creek, or "the Lick" to the clans around those parts, was beautiful flat water with postcard-perfect coastline full of active wildlife. But beneath those images was something much darker. The problems started with the old coal mines in the area who leached acidic drainage into drinking water around the turn of the 20th century. Illegal dumping of industrial waste, mostly from Bryson Foods in Pettis, had accumulated with such intensity that by the time Reagan was in office, bacteria levels were over eight hundred times what was federally allowed in drinking water. Gideon's office had a yellowing framed letter from the White House expressing concern and ensuring their commitment to supporting the great state of Missouri in its clean-up. In his tenure as sheriff of Camden County, Gideon had seen some of that, but not enough to keep the men in their white suits and test tubes away. Dead Zones popped up nearly every year. Boil orders were a regular occurrence. Babies were born with problems, the hospital said. Beyond that, there was the current, to boot. In short, the Lick was trouble.

To avoid the runoff problems, most of the locals moved upstream to where there were improved conditions, but a cluster of old-timers had stuck around. The south of Lick Creek was one such cluster. They fell under the care of Shale County, just south of where Gideon presided, but according to public records, the law hadn't been called to those parts in nearly thirty years. Hell, no electricity or septic were even set up on the two thousand or so acres of timber on the south before it met the highway. They were old-school hill folk. Traditional types, with their own churches and medicines. The folks on the north side, they paid their taxes and used the roads like anyone else did. On the south side was a different sort of folk. Deeply distrustful of the government, they lived wholly off the grid. They birthed and buried their own, grew their own provisions, and caused no disturbances to speak of. They kept to themselves, to the point that some even talked that there were few of them left. For nearly a century. Around the time Jimmy Carter took office, they stopped paying taxes. Their interaction with the city continued to dwindle. There were no registered births or deaths on the south of Lick after 1985, no schoolhouse, and no fire station. No electricity ran on their land, and there was no use of the roads. Hell, no people were even spotted by the law, though most of the private properties were uncombed by the sheriff on the south side. For all Gideon knew, there were simply private people who affiliated only with their own clans. If there was anyone left, no one had seen them in years.

The northerners were the last true hill people of the Ozark valley in touch with the outside world. The population consisted of families whose people had settled in the territory hundreds of years before. Largely isolated before the technology, they had learned to rely on themselves, developing superb carpentry methods and skilled building techniques whose work could be seen all throughout Camden County. They primarily home-schooled and treated their own maladies using their own Yarb doctors and granny-women whose medicinal techniques relied on Indian medicine learnt from the Osage tribes that once inhabited those parts. Occasionally the northerners would venture into town, finding their crafts or tinctures would fetch a pretty price at the farmers' markets, or they'd sell their produce on stands or covered wagons pulled off into the tall grass off the highway.

The northerners kept on their side of the Lick. If asked about the south, they averted their eyes or crossed themselves, pressing their lips into a line. Highly superstitious people, they avoided gossip, but if encouraged, they might speak snatches about the Devil or his work. They had their own beliefs and stuck to them and that included not running their mouths about anything that could follow their folks home.

Brutus' boy had died the day after hunting frogs on the Lick, and folks had been on edge. How does an otherwise healthy twenty-four-year-old man suffocate after drinking two beers and whose blood alcohol level was well within limits? And how to explain that the two other men in the party had been hospitalized and treated with antivenom, but, and here's the kicker, had no snake bites. Even if they had been bitten by one of the common Missouri snakes, most of those bites don't extend beyond some nausea and dizziness.

A resident doctor from Rolla had come up to inspect the body. Found evidence of distress, signs indicating a possible struggle, but the cause of death was asphyxiation. Took samples from the leg wounds back to the city to their labs. Doc even took a look at the two men who'd been with him that day. The dead boy had been cut pretty bad, but the other two—not a bite on them. Johnny Cedars has a puncture wound on his hand, but that would not have caused his symptoms. Then there was that missing dog. Tire tracks all askew on the north side, but nothing from anyone on the south. The doctors were as stumped as the law.

In the days since the incident, there had been talk of poison, of drug deals, of witchcraft. No one from the north said they'd seen anything. There were no trails for Gideon to follow, no one left to question. Something in this case felt off, like the light at the wrong time after waking up from a nap.

This community always locked their doors at night, but since last week, church attendance in town had doubled. When there's talk of the Devil, no one sleeps in on Sunday.

2

Brutus Ebbons and his three siblings had been raised up on the family's dairy farm in the boot heel of the state. Their parents were veterans of the Vietnam War turned homesteaders. Joan, who had worked in intelligence, intercepted radio transmissions. She was a sensible woman of slight stature who, in her retirement, cultivated heirloom tomatoes and bred Yorkshire Terriers. Jack, a retired Army Sergeant, and a recipient of the Purple Heart as a result of sustaining a gunshot wound to the abdomen during the Tet Offensive, raised Holstein dairy cows and studied Roman history, specifically the late Republic under Augustus. Working the cows taught Brutus, his two brothers and his sister to respect the end of a long day and to understand the exceptional value of quiet.

Brutus had been a sturdy and focused child who gave his parents little trouble aside from a childhood stutter which had been corrected by the military in his first year of service. His self-reliance was the central source of his family's pride. After passing a special state exam that allowed him to enlist in the Army three months shy of the required age, Brutus went on to complete two back-to-back tours in Iraq as part of the 4th Stryker Brigade, doing his part to save the world from rising oil costs. His career was cut short when he almost lost his leg to an IED, though he'd tell you his long-term disability was due to a combination of Gulf War Syndrome and anthrax injections. Not even thirty and home on disability and an honorable discharge, Brutus settled in Camden County, married a local girl almost immediately, and produced one son, Samuel, someone he had hoped would serve his country as he had. However, that was not to be. After losing his wife to a quick and painful bout of a rare esophageal cancer when the child was still a boy, Brutus turned his energy toward raising champion German short-haired Pointers, lugging around an old hunting rifle which he kept (usually) unloaded and which helped him with his bad leg. He used this to direct the dogs, discipline his son, and dissuade visitors to his property as he was deeply distrustful of his fellow man, especially their elected officials.

His boy Sam had been a child without direction. Slow speaking and quick to anger, he had been held back in school, struggled with petty crime, and was generally unfit for service. He gave his mother a nervous disposition and his father fits of fury. In manhood, Sam had neither wife nor children. His father worried he'd amount to nothing but a slow accomplice to one of the local gangs of stick-up boys, but Sam was simply a boy who preferred his own company. About four years before Sam's death, Brutus and his son engaged in a shouting match that ended with Brutus putting his fist through the walnut paneling in his double-wide. Angry and ashamed at always disappointing his father, Sam stormed off while Brutus made a call to the mill about honest work for his son. The manager was the former private whose life Brutus had saved when their Humvee was hit by the aforementioned IED. Brutus had reached into the vehicle as it burned, pulling him from the gunner's hatch seconds before it blew. He received the Gold Lifesaving Medal as a result, which he kept in an old footlocker under his bed, and the very grateful private Skip Henry III was able to return to his wife and children with only third-degree burns which he proudly displayed during his rounds of inspection at the mill. Skip was happy to hire Sam on third shift. His hours meant Sam clocked out around when Skip arrived for the day. He'd greet Sam as the sun came up, never missing an opportunity to remind Sam that Brutus was the great hero of his life, a detail that quite profoundly contradicted Sam's own experience with his father.

The mill was repetitive, exhausting work that required physical strength and sustained focus, but it was ideal for Sam, whose quiet, heavy-bodied disposition preferred such an environment. After two years without incident, Sam was promoted to operator, and Brutus, feeling pride for his son for perhaps the first time ever, called him over for beers he had cooling in the icebox. Sam followed his father to the pens where a mound of eight-week-old puppies tumbled over one another, their cries filling the air between them.

"Pick one," Brutus said, nodding toward the litter, not quite smiling.

"What now?" Sam asked, astonished. He looked over at his father, mouth agape.

"This one here's the runt." Brutus pointed at a smaller female. "But she's robust. Liver-headed ones are all male."

Sam crouched down, feeling almost as though he could cry. He watched the little bodies tumbling over one another for the teat and thought maybe he might try to work a little harder to be a better man. He spied a larger one, chubby but quick. He reached for him, holding his face up to his. The dog looked at him straight on as though he'd known him forever. *This here's my dog*, Sam thought. After he had selected his pup, in a moment of warmth for his father, he asked if he could name him Brutus Junior. Brutus looked over his son, thinking at that moment how odd of a boy he was.

"Well, seeing as I'll not likely have any grandchildren of my own, I s'pose that would be alright," he answered awkwardly.

So Sam called the dog BJ, and he trained him up right.

3

Sam knew he disappointed his father. It didn't bother him much. He wasn't interested in going all the way overseas to serve his country when they weren't even at war. Anyway, he figured he could make his pension just as easily right there in Camden County. His father had insisted he talk to the recruiter, though, not heeding his son's nearly muted protest. So Sam simply refused to take the ASVAB, staying out late with the boys the night before and sleeping through the two scheduled tests, feeling halfway sick inside because of it. Truth of the matter was he didn't think he could stomach killing anyone, even an enemy. Furthermore, telling his father his thoughts on the matter felt like standing in an unsafe place, as Brutus wouldn't hear of any show of weakness and would surely call him yellow. Sam had never been one to fight, even though his size could have backed him up, so he fell back on being too slow, too drunk, too dumb instead of just speaking the truth. The charade made him feel all wrong inside, as lies never quite sit right in an honest man, and when he told his father he had missed the test, Brutus kicked him out on the spot.

Sam called up his friend Jess, who helped him load his things into his truck while Brutus watched from the window, leaning on his big, unloaded gun. Sam had found a small room to rent adjacent the Mexican restaurant along Highway 5. The place had fluorescent lights in a popcorn ceiling where water stains collected, but he'd have his own garage space with a padlock and it included a little grassy patch out back where he could stash his Weber. Time passed and he worked his job at the mill. His father gave up a bit on his resentment, and after a few months they started meeting for chicken dinners, never talking much about anything aside from the mill and the dogs. To Sam, life felt thin. Void of color.

Sam kept a family photo album full of pictures of his mother, Rosie St. Germaine, on his kitchen table, which he looked over every morning over his bowl of cereal after his third shift ended. She had been a frail sort of woman who bottled every feeling she ever had deep inside of her and so love, to Sam, grew to mean quiet obedience. She had died of cancer before he had finished high school, the illness taking her quickly, over within a full season. She had never smoked a single cigarette in her life, never complaining when Brutus smoked in the house, which he continued to do after her diagnosis, yet she was the one who caught the cancer. Her death left the house even quieter than it had been before. Sam, of course, wished it was his father who had died, and Brutus knew this as well, the unspoken unfairness of life hanging like a cloud between the two men. Sam looked for his mother in every barfly he bedded down with, but all he ever seemed to find was the ones who had been hardened cold by whatever they had seen before him.

After BJ, though, things changed. There was a creature who needed him. Who wanted to be with him. The dog was never disappointed in him, never cold to him. In fact, he thrived from the commands Sam issued, delighting in his owner, despite Sam's many failures. Didn't see him as too heavy, too lazy, too goddamn dumb. What is this if not the most perfect form of companionship? Sam would take him out back to the grassy spot beside the commuter parking lot to work on obedience, spending hours on commands, rewarding him with kibble and all the encouragement he had never received in childhood. He had eyes on every bird Sam directed him to, running hard and fast to locate upland game. The dog lived to please. After a full year with the BJ, Sam felt his body filling out a bit with honest love. It felt sacred.

Sam spent as much time as possible in the grassy fields adjacent the highway around dawn after work where he could wait out pheasant. Sometimes he'd be there to shoot, sometimes just to watch. After he got BJ, the dog would accompany him to the field. He trained him to step quietly as the pheasant spook easily. BJ would tiptoe on freckled legs, the little muscles around his hindquarters twitching with eager obedience, nearly silent in the big bluestem until Sam gave the command, and then there was the flurry of it all. The startled pheasant, bursting to the sky in a rush, the gun's crack, BJ's blissful retrieval on his whistle. Under Sam's tutelage, BJ showed a natural aptitude for locating fowl. He waited on his owner's direction, was quick as a dart, using his strong legs and endurance only when called to.

Sam liked to wait out the male birds, tracing them as they moved trustingly in their arcs of heavy flight. When he'd shoot, he'd listen to the sound echo back, rolling across the grasslands, and he'd feel at peace. But mostly he went to the fields to sit in the silence. In muted light, the birds would migrate slowly from their comfortable loafing spots, their colorful, pear-shaped bodies moving slowly, enjoying their little lives. No one bothered him there with their talk, their disappointments.

For Sam, his dog beside him in the last of the day's light was church. He was unlike any other gun dog Sam had ever known. He never made mistakes. The hours spent training BJ for the hunt lightened him, and he began to shift into a man with something to live for. He began whistling at work. He even got up the courage to smile back at Gayle Clooney, a curvy little thing with two kids and no husband who worked the books at the mill.

On Fridays, Sam walked across the street to the Watering Hole and looked for a lonely woman to buy a drink. And on the last weekend of each month, he met the boys for hunting whatever was in season, which was more just an excuse for the men to drink cheap whiskey and get away from their wives for the weekend.

On the last Saturday of July that summer, Sam loaded his truck at dawn, his dog chewing hide on the porch. It would be the last trip Sam would ever make as he would be dead by the next day. He'd packed enough for two full days of shooting. His one-man tent, a tarpaulin, his sleeping bag, lantern, camping stove, and two days of food, just in case, though he knew Jess would likely head back that first night. Jess' wife had just had a baby, and according to Kurt, the delivery was a tough one. Jess had called him up Friday afternoon to tell him the good news. Out of the four, Sam trusted Jess the most. They both had come up in town without mothers, a sort of brotherhood the others with whole families could not comprehend.

"Lillian had the baby," Jess said, with a brightness in his voice which irritated Sam. "Little girl."

Sam didn't care about such things. He wanted the hunting to go as planned with no disruption. "Good to hear," he had mustered, feeling the anger rise from his chest to his neck as he held the phone to his ear.

"I was thinking I'd sit this one out. Youse can have the whole weekend without me slowing you down."

"Naw," Sam had said with a sniff, feeling proud of his even tone. "Kurt said he's done in from his week. Says an overnight is plenty for him." Sam ran his hand across his dog's brown spine and breathed in deep, like the head shrinker at the clinic had taught him.

"Well, alright then. Maybe I'll join you for the day," Jess said.

"Mhm," Sam said, and waited.

"Sounds good." Jess said after a minute. "See you at my place at dawn then."

The closest creek for bullfrogging was the Lick off J Road about twenty miles outside of town. The Lick wasn't ideal by any means. It was rocky and full of runoff from the Waste Management Plant, plus it was only accessible from the very rural north side as the full south side was private property. But it was a creek full of frogs, and they were in season, so in addition to his camping supplies, Sam packed his net, his crappie rod, and his cooler. He looked at his .22 but thought better of it. He planned to keep BJ in the house since it would only be a day away, but he worried he'd chew the couch again, so at the last minute, he whistled him into the bed of the truck, and the dog happily obliged, leaping from the porch to Sam's side. Maybe if he knew it was the last day he'd ever have with BJ, he would have given him part of his breakfast instead of making him stay in his crate, or he would have kept him off chain during his run for gas or let him in the cab instead of riding in the bed. But it was just another day, and people tend to waste those away unaware that fate is coming for them as it comes to everyone. It was, for Sam Ebbons, the last day he'd ever make his instant coffee, the last day he'd look through his mother's photo album, the last day he'd lace his boots, the last day he'd take a breath on this earth.

4

Sam spent the ride to Jess' with the windows down, feeling the warm wind against his face, the trees full of the sound of high summer. BJ lay in the bed, his head raised in the wind, snapping at flies in the predawn light. Sam pulled up to Jess' gravel driveway, slowing as he spotted Jess down by the cove. Jess' wife, Lillian, stood on the porch packing what looked like biscuits into paper bags.

Lillian was a pretty thing with mouse-colored hair all tied up in a knot on top of her head. She had big eyes that were always looking you over it felt like. That morning she was wearing a little smock that showed her legs, which were covered in bites. She squinted when she saw Sam's truck, moving toward him as he pulled in beside Jess' old Chevy.

Lillian and Jess were both hill folk, but she was even more backwoods than Jess. She hadn't done proper school at all. Not even one day. Hadn't had any vaccination shots neither. Jess said she called them "government pinpricks." Kept to her people and away from town mostly. Her grandmother had schooled her in hill medicine, so their cabin was covered in old shards of things, antlers, little vials of herbs and such. Even a snapper shell that sat right on their kitchen table, held the butter and the napkins. Gave Sam the creeps. When Jess had first told the men he planned to marry her, the men suggested he had been bewitched. Jess laughed so hard at the Watering Hole he spit out his Budweiser, right there on the ground.

Kurt had put his arm around Jess, told him he was worried that things were moving too fast, that he needed time to play the field before settling down, but Jess shook his head at that. Said he had known since he first laid eyes on her. Said she was good to the core. Kurt countered that she was just the only nice girl Jess had ever bagged was all. Jess said over the jukebox that she was pure of heart. Said his mother would have liked her. Sam took Jess' side then. Dead mothers always have the last word.

Lillian didn't doll up like the girls in town, but you could tell her figure, even through her shapeless clothes. Long and willowy like a weasel but strong in the wrists. She and Jess had met at country church, some form of primitive Baptist congregation Jess' mother once belonged to before meeting his father. Sam had first seen the church when on a delivery for the mill and wondered what sort of people gathered there. No structure, no missals. Just an altar made of stones and a collection of haphazard stumps for seating. They didn't even read from the Bible. Preacher just barked at them about hell for an hour each week. Sam had stood up at their wedding in his only good shirt and watched in awe as the pastor, a small, stooped man dressed all in black, joined his best friend and this hill woman in matrimony. They weren't even to kiss when it was over, but get onto their knees before the stone altar and recite the Lord's prayer, the pastor's hands on their heads. After the ceremony, Brutus whispered to Sam that Lillian's grandmother kept a pet rattler in her quarters. Sam had said that was a damn story, but Brutus insisted it was true.

Lillian lifted her hand in a wave as she walked to Sam, shielding her eyes against the rising light. She was pretty in a sort of clean way, but something about her unsettled him, as though she knew of things but kept them secret. Most medicine women, called grannies in their parts, were long gone, but the high country relied on them still, and Lillian had a steady stream of clients. She and another woman had delivered two of his coworker's babies. Her grandmother had sold vials at the markets. He'd fingered one when he was a child, but his mother had pulled him away, telling Sam country medicines caused the icy hands.

Sam would see grannies sometimes in general stores or on his way somewhere in the deep country. They were the ones hill people called with their urgencies. They were superstitious women who spent their time in rockers or collecting berries to address injuries that town doctors couldn't quite cure. Stooped and wrinkled, they quietly carried around their bags of tinctures and walked barefoot straight into your home. They handled child birthing and presided over burying the local dead, though they didn't dig the graves. The last Indian property in Camden County abutted the south of Lick off J Road where the grannies practiced, and he'd often see them together in their old pickups or in the hardware store, their heads bent in low conversation. The locals whispered that people in their parts even dabbled in witchcraft.

Lillian rested a pale forearm on Sam's door side, her own dog following her. Wendy, she called her, was a good-looking shepherd mix who stood unmoving at her side watching BJ as he paced nervously in the back of the truck. Sam meant to ask Jess about how he trained her up to be so steady, as he was working on BJ's jitters.

"Little something for the road," Lillian said, handing him the biscuits then reaching in the back to pet BJ. BJ licked her hand.

"What have we got here?" Sam said awkwardly, looking in the bag as he killed the engine.

"Ham and biscuits. Hope you like mint jelly."

"Mighty kind of you," Sam said.

"Can yer dog have a bit of ham?" she asked, reaching into her apron as BJ watched her.

"He'd love you for that," Sam said, warming to her completely. It was then he noticed the baby, just a bundle in a gray slip against her chest. It was brand new looking with a shock of black hair the color of Jess' and pink all over. He wondered briefly if he'd ever meet a woman who'd have his baby. He wondered if he'd have to go to the hills to find one uncut by the world and its cruelty.

Sam got out, moving to hold BJ at the collar and noticed her dog's stillness as it watched him. "Your dog sure is trained up, Ms. Lillian," Sam said,

"Mhm. Wendy's a good one," she said, turning her odd eyes toward Wendy. She panted as she nosed Lillian's ham, wholly uninterested in BJ.

"You feeling okay after the baby and everything?" Sam asked awkwardly after a moment.

"Just fine now, Sam," she said, keeping her face even, as though she was just being polite.

"That's a healthy-looking baby. Girl or boy?" he asked.

"Girl," she said, peeking down and lifting the fabric to show a small pink face all scrunched up in sleep before covering her quickly again.

"She looks so tiny, don't she?" Sam said without thinking, trying to avoid looking at the outline of Lillian's swollen breasts under her thin dress.

"She sure does," she said, without thought of Sam's oddness. "Day and a half ago she got here. Truth be told, I'm taking her in to lay her down. Just wanted to see y'all off proper."

"You sure you're okay all alone?" he asked, thinking he sounded weak as he said it. As though under some kind of a spell.

"Sure thing, Sam. Jess has been looking forward to this trip all week. He knows I love frog legs," she added, her odd eyes turning up to lock again onto Sam. To him they looked like animal eyes. All yellow-colored, like muted balls of sunlight on an overcast day. "Thanks for thinking of us." Her dog inched closer to her as she spoke, her muzzle brushing against Lillian's bare legs.

"Yes, ma'am," Sam said, turning to lower the tailgate to break away from her gaze. "I'll make sure we get your hundred."

"Good man. Y'all be safe today," she said smiling, as she turned to look for Jess, her eyes finally resting elsewhere, the heat of her hand leaving a print on his top railing. A part of him longed to touch it, to touch a piece of her, and he watched her move barefooted toward the cabin, crossing the briar patch with ease. He considered her long, bit-up legs, and felt a mixture of hard lust and fear before turning back toward the truck, grateful to be done with the pleasantries. She left him both stirred and discontented. He wondered soberly how Jess and Johnny could stand being around women all the time.

Jess came up around the side of the cabin, raising his hand to Sam, and Lillian's face landed warmly on her husband's. Sam was not used to that sort of affection from women. Sex was something he had experienced mostly in low lights after a brief courtship over the noise of a jukebox. Women looked something different to him the next morning. Something he didn't like. He liked seeing when a woman was warm. His mother had been warm.

Sam caught himself staring as he leaned against his truck and pulled his gaze away. Wendy lay on the faded timber of the porch watching him in the silence. He felt a chill move through him as he transferred his gear into Jess' truck.

5

Jess' truck was beat to hell. It was a 1995 Silverado with a small-block V8 that he had saved up his whole life for, and it still ran good as new despite everything it had been through. He'd been driving it to and from his worksite for years, hauled thousands of pounds of lumber in it, collided with a handful of whitetail in it, and even rolled it once when he was cut off by a Lincoln with Illinois plates. A real beater, it pained him to look at it most mornings. Johnny had affectionately nicknamed it "hammered shit," told his brother he'd never seen a truck live through as much as that one had. Jess loved it nonetheless. It fit all four men and Sam's dog, and it was the only vehicle in the bunch whose suspension could truly handle off-road.

Jess was used to worrying over things. He'd ache over anything he didn't have the time to tend to. He worried over his truck, the stain on his cabin's beams, his wife's birthing, the new baby's breathing. The baby, sweet as she was, about gave him a goddamn heart attack. But despite his aching, his truck always started right up, and his woman loved him as though he were the only man in the world. And the morning he drove his friends to the Lick for gigging, the last morning he'd ever have with Sam, the morning that would almost kill him, it was the one morning the truck didn't nearly start. As though there was something stuck inside the starter, Johnny had said. As though someone or something was trying to tell him something. Jess didn't understand it. Looking back, though, he thought maybe it had been some sort of sign.

After Jess' third try at starting it, Kurt told him to pop the hood. And since Kurt could fix anything on God's green earth, Jess did, wondering again if it was best he sat this trip out, and almost said so, until Kurt adjusted the relays and dropped the hood, telling Jess to try it again, when it started straight up. They laughed it off then, and Jess backed out slowly, the sound of the gravel beneath the tires, the sun taking its sweet time coming up, and Jess soon forgot all about his worries as they turned onto 7-13.

Johnny never drove, as he didn't want to dirty his truck before his kids' soccer practice, and Kurt couldn't even drive, due to his DUIs. Sam didn't have an extended cab, so it was always Jess. They always tossed him money for gas, so he was happy to do it. He was just eager to get on the water after two terrifying days of watching his wife give birth. She was up and around though, and she wouldn't hear anything about him staying home. Claimed she wanted some quiet to sleep with the baby and his piddlin' would keep her up. He protested but down in his belly knew needed the time away from women-things, and he knew she knew it. It would just be for a few hours. He'd asked their neighbor to keep an eye on things.

The men had come up in school together, Johnny a few years behind them. None had gone into the service. Jess had thought of the military, but his migraines gave the recruiter pause. He'd always been good with his hands, so he worked construction. Sam was at the mill. Just promoted that year, actually. Johnny worked in operations at the plant. Kurt lived over behind the Grey Fox Tavern and did odd jobs for the owner, who paid him in liquor, which kept him bound in servitude. Kurt was divorced from a big blonde who came up outside Onondaga. She gave him two boys before leaving him for the bug man. The bug man, a fella named Mike, came to spray for brown recluse spiders one morning after Kurt had left for work. When Kurt got home that night, a truck was parked in his spot in the driveway, his family was gone, and Mike Alafort was sitting at his kitchen table drumming his fingers. He told Kurt his wife had left him, told him to let them be, that he could provide better than Kurt ever could. Told him they were his family now. Mike said he had stayed behind to tell him the news, man to man. Kurt, however, had a few at the Fox after quitting time, so when he heard this news from Mike in his own kitchen to boot, things came to blows and Kurt ended up with a broken nose. When the law came, Kurt cried big tears to the police, which he later regretted. He told them Mike was breaking and entering. Said Mike had sat there waiting for him in his own home, had even made a pot of black coffee. Coffee Kurt had paid for. This man had even offered him a cup from his own set of coffee cups.

The law took Mike's side, on account of Kurt's drinking and arrest history. They found Kurt guilty of attempted assault, but Mike dropped the charges. Kurt's wife lived in Springfield now, and Kurt didn't see them much. It was a subject the men knew not to discuss. They rambled down Lake Road 7-14 to the highway, the Chevy roaring into the morning.

"This truck's endurance is a modern miracle," Kurt said from the backseat, looking over BJ to Sam. Sam chuckled, tonguing the chew in his bottom lip.

"It's indestructible," Johnny hollered over the wind from the passenger side.

"Tell that to the floodplains," Jess said, looking both ways at the stop before turning left onto Highway 7, heading west past Climax Springs toward 65.

"Right over there," Kurt said after a minute, pointing across the highway to the field before the stretch of woods beside the Harry S. Truman reservoir. "That's where he got away."

Johnny spit a shell into his cola can. "Here we go."

"I'm not shitting you. Biggest buck I'd ever seen. Just a monster," Kurt said, making a space of a few feet between his hands. "Ain't never seen a rack that big."

"What happened?" Sam asked, egging him on. BJ scratched at his ear. "Why'd you let him get away?"

"Couldn't get my shot," Kurt said wistfully, peering out the dirty window into the distance. "I was getting my aim right as he snorted and ran off."

"That's what you say every winter," Johnny chided.

"I'm serious. I couldn't get a shot. Wasn't going to waste the bullet."

"Our grandfather has this thirty-aught-six. Real beaut," Johnny said, looking over at Jess, who navigated the uneven road, the worry sliding off him as he continued west.

"Where'd he get it?" Sam asked.

"Bought back in the day from the Sears Roebuck. Still works like a dream," Johnny said. "One day I'm gonna take it out and get a deer with it."

"No way daddy will let you have it. That man will probably want to be buried with it beside him," Jess added, laughing.

"Then I'll rob his goddamn grave," Johnny said, cupping his hand to light a cigarette.

"I'd rather a Winchester," Sam said.

"270?" Jess asked.

"Yep."

"Now that's a good gun," Jess said.

"I like the shorter case length," Sam said.

"You should clean up your pop's gun," Jess said, eyeing Sam through the rearview mirror.

"No thanks," Sam said, laughing.

"Shit, that's a gorgeous pistol," Kurt said.

"If you can pry it from him," Sam said, lowering his sunshades as he spoke. "It's like his baby."

They pulled off onto J Road just as the sun was full in the sky. They took on the quiet of the lesser highway, the canopy taller, the shoulder less maintained, the humidity stuck on their bodies. Sam looked at BJ as he stirred in the cab, feeling the fullness of pride in his belly. Kurt spotted a doe with her two babies in the clearing in the south and thought again about deer season that November. Johnny hoped to get back in time to catch the ball game but didn't say it. Jess thought of his wife as he fought third gear on the uneven terrain. He thought of the baby clinging to her breast, and a weak stab of guilt at his pleasure for being away, though she practically had to push him out the door.

There was an easy, familiar energy between the men and the highway, which they had all to themselves, and each of them, for the last time that day, would forget about the heavy things that worked their way through their days. They were all, for just a moment, in their right places. Even Jess as he looked into the swaying prairie grass, the turkey's foot and big blue stems reaching up, he forgot about his mother and her gaping absence, forgot about his wife and all the blood he had seen, and in their absence, the absence of the wounds of womanhood, he felt peace.

It was three miles from J road to the rocky turnoff to the Lick, and the men rode in silence, taking in the hills which rose and declined with a sort of unnatural motion on the south end of J. The place was quiet. Too quiet, even in the thick of the acoustic dawn of summer, ripe with the warbling songs of the robins, meadowlarks, and sparrows drowned out somehow by the stillness of all that timber and the absolute isolation of the place. A place where you could cry out, and no one, not a soul, would hear you.

They got to the turnoff in about ten minutes, pulling over in the dirt shoulder to the Lick, whose rusted gate, surrounded by overgrowth, was closed and locked. Kurt jumped out to inspect, fingering the Russwin.

"It's locked," he hollered over the truck.

Jess cut the engine.

Kurt reached around the gate to fiddle with the back side of the lock.

"This is common ground," Sam said, hopping out of the cab. Johnny checked his phone. No bars.

"You got bolt cutters, Jess?" Kurt asked. Jess felt his guts turn. Just a little.

"Not sure we should be cutting locks, boys," he said, leaning his elbow out the window.

"Awh, don't be yellow," Sam said without looking at him, rustling around in the bed of the truck until he found it. "Ain't no one out here but the crows, and I doubt they'd even care."

"No service," Johnny said, holding up his phone.

No service—how will Lillian call if something happens? Jess looked up to see Sam hop the gate, angling the cutters toward the gate.

"Should we be doing this?" Johnny asked the boys.

"Doing what?" Kurt squinting. Jess looked out the window at the oaks and hickories, their branches rustling from the squirrels' jumps between them. The coneflower grew over waist high, wholly uninterrupted in these parts. There wasn't a cabin for as far as he could see. They were far out, and from what he could tell, they were alone.

"I guess it's alright," Jess said, more to himself.

The lock fell apart, and Kurt pulled open the rusted gate with a rusty protest. Before long, the men were back on their way, Jess pushing aside his momentary anxiety.

"Alright, let's do this," Jess said, turning under the canopy, the temperature dropping at least five degrees. The one-lane road was bumpy, and Kurt suggested they walk the last half mile to the camp, but Jess claimed the Chevy could take it. They drove until they passed Lillian's old homestead, sitting abandoned since her grandmother's death last spring. Jess stopped the truck, thinking how the little cabin had changed since he first pulled up to ask Celeste Black for Lillian's hand. His tires crunched as he slowed. He pointed off toward the sagging one-story structure, the mortar between the logs crumbling, thigh-high weeds and a dirt yard. And somehow, in the middle of all that, a clearing of Cardinal flowers.

"See that? That right there is Lillian's family plot."

Sam leaned forward to get a better look. BJ whined in the backseat.

"Jesus H. Christ, that is bleak," Kurt said.

"No one's been there for almost a year," Jess said.

"She should be mighty grateful to you for getting her the hell outta here," Kurt said, lighting a cigarette.

"She owns the land still. Might be worth something someday," he said.

"They'll throw a strip mall in here in no time," Johnny added.

Jess drove slowly forward, considering his wife's simple roots. He'd always felt a little guilty at how he had plucked her from the hills. He liked her people well enough, but he was steadily against settling anywhere as remote as J Road. So he had taken her back to his cabin, across the highway and up the mountain to settle coveside at the fourteenth mile marker. She had brought along her tattered hope chest, full of heirlooms, practical dresses, and vials of tinctures. Potions, he called them, making her laugh. Some part of him worried, though, that he had chained something exotic and taken it out of its natural element.

"She really grow up in there?" Sam asked, peering through the back window as they passed.

"Till the day we were married."

Sam saw the rot creeping up the length of the side, the tall weeds, the debris heavy on the limp roof, and felt a slight slinking dread. As he turned away to watch the road, he instinctively moved his hand to BJ.

6

Marjorie Leftbone was the Camden County granny-woman who presided over all things childbirthing. Her jurisdiction stretched from the intersection of J and Highway 7 all the way west to Curtis. She had delivered over seven hundred children in those parts, and her work was steadily booked even though Mercy Hospital had been erected at the fourth mile marker some twenty years before. Many women in their parts preferred one of their own to usher in new lives. It was tradition, tried and true. Though Marjorie had not been present at Lillian's unusual birth, she did deliver Lillian's child when it was time, arriving with her suitcase and tinctures after the contractions began and having it all over within a day, which was her custom.

After the baby's safe arrival, Marjorie had issued the traditional after care: she insisted Lillian stay as still as possible after the delivery. Lillian had made it through without any extraordinary measure, but she was pale, Marjorie had told Jess, a common yet concerning complication from childbirth, according to granny-women, and therefore, the girl was only to do what was absolutely necessary, which was nurse, sleep, and drink red-pepper tea simmered in butter and made sticky with honey. No sweeping, no chopping wood, certainly no lovemaking. For the first week, she was to avoid leaving the bed if possible, taking only sponge baths and sleeping when the baby slept, though most mothers knew that was wishful thinking.

Marjorie had left Lillian a tube of lanolin and a book of matches for the bedroom, but there was nothing she could give her for the pain. It came in surprise bursts from inside of Lillian's core, the cramps so severe she was passing clots, aching every time she had to use the bathroom. Marjorie had never had her own children, choosing to keep a series of animals as familiars, she called them, including crows, two donkeys she lodged outside of Celeste's, and a blind cat named Lefty, but she knew enough about labor and delivery to know Lillian's birth had been thankfully without complication. Alice, the neighbor, nodded knowingly. Jess was to call up Marjorie if there was any fever or listlessness.

Lillian took it extra easy, following all the granny's instructions. The baby's coming left her tired in a way she had never felt before, like her spirit was bruised up something fierce. So she spent the first day after delivery sleeping alongside the baby, extending and inspecting each finger and toe until she'd spring her little arms and legs back close to her body, back in the fetal position she knew so well. Jess stayed close by, wary and grateful, leaving the room only to warm the water or put a log on the fire, watching his wife nervously as she nursed or slept, her breasts swollen in a way that both aroused and appalled him. The bedroom had been a place of maternal comfort he had remembered way back when his little brother was born. All warm with their bodies and their love. Even the three dogs stayed close. Wendy slept so close that Jess nearly tripped over her twice in the dark. And Lillian was happy, but her man and his nerves were crowding her. So when her husband mentioned he was going to pass on his monthly hunt so he could watch over her, Lillian insisted he go. The day would give her time to relax without worrying about his worrying, and she could spend the day lying still, running her finger over her baby's small features, listening to her tiny breaths.

Lillian didn't understand all the fuss. As a granny-woman in training, she'd seen far more difficult births than the one she'd had. She was grateful for the labor she'd been granted. It had come on suddenly on Wednesday morning, her water breaking as she swept the porch. Marjorie had arrived within the hour and helped to speed the delivery. Most government hospitals have women pushing on her back for days at a time, but all grannies had women in the position of their ancestors, on their knees or squatting, which uses gravity to the woman's advantage. So that's what Lillian did, and her baby had been born healthy as a hog. First time Lillian saw her baby, she was sitting upright in a squat for the final push, spying the baby's face as it appeared between her legs in a rush of pain. As the head appeared, she couldn't believe it. Was this her body that grew a whole person? Was this her child? Lillian thought, *I know you. I dreamed you.* Then she reached for her as she lay back, pulling her slippery body onto her chest, the granny there with her arthritic hands poised under their bodies. The child looked up at Lillian then, her eyes clouded from birth, before letting loose a furious cry that brought Jess to the doorway, his hat in his hands. She was the spitting image of Jess with a mess of wet, dark hair and a crease in her brow. The three of them sat together beside the bed watching her cry, stretch her arms, and take her first breaths in this world. Jess was beside himself, kissing her sweaty brow and thanking her over and over as Lillian tried to catch her own breath. She told him she thought maybe they should call her Jess Jr. on account of the likeness, but Jess wanted Gloria after his mother, so they went with Glory Be.

Thirty-six hours postpartum, Lillian had her first itching to get up and get moving. Her favorite morning chore had always been chopping wood for the fire. She loved the feel of the ax's smooth handle in her hands, the sound of the hickory splitting beneath the blade. It made her feel she was connected to some earthly power. However, splitting timber was out of the question, at least until she was more healed up. So after Jess had left that morning, she asked Brody, the neighbor boy to take care of it, paying him from her canning petty cash, which he passed over to his mama, straight away. Alice watched him work from the porch, a home-rolled cigarette in her fingers, nodding at his labor. Brody was around twelve, the younger of Alice's two boys but was the taller one, "having shot up like a bean pole," Alice told Lillian over the boy's head, her chin lifted in pride in the late morning sun as the heat beaded up on their lips, down the line of her boy's spine as he worked.

Alice was her one neighbor; they were the last cabin off that rural route. She was the daughter of a miner from Sweetwater. Her pa had moved them to the country after his silicosis confined him to bed, but Lillian's grandmother Celeste had treated him with a licorice tincture that gave him another ten years beyond what the government doctors had predicted. His coffin had been built by Jory

Nettles, Camden County's blacksmith. When he delivered her father's coffin to his final resting place, he took one look at Alice and was in love. So some good came out of a sad day, is how Alice remembers it.

On the other side of them was four hundred acres of Ozark forest, tended to by Jess' family for nearly seventy-five years. The acreage was vast, the height of the trees creating a nice shade through which streaks of sunlight illuminated the undergrowth of spurge, lungwort, and bugle, fragrant in the early morning. Their parts were mostly safe, but there were the occasional black bears or bobcats, and coyotes were regular visitors around their chicken pens. It was the rattlers or the occasional copperhead that kept Lillian to the paths. The old timers said their parts had things that would eat you if they could, but Lillian was more worried about the people who could freeze you up, despite you being good-hearted. Animals were her preference. You grow up understanding it's not personal with them. It's just life.

Alice's older boy by two years was called Eugene. He sat off along the property line, watching them talk. He was slower than the younger one. Didn't ever say much, and so Alice never sent him off to school. Townsfolk liked to talk about Eugene, saying he was born with deformities, but Alice denied it. Said he caught a fever when he was two and it "fell into his brain." It was bad luck in their parts to have a child who differed in any capacity. Lillian, with her unusual birth story, knew that firsthand. Locals were suspicious of anyone nontraditional. For Lillian, it was a mother who lived fast, as the neighbors said, and died young. Just days after giving birth to her.

Lillian liked having Eugene around. He was bright-eyed. Had an honest face that never hid anything. He was real good with the animals. One of the only folk Wendy would lie down next to. Could tell when there was a storm coming. Loyal to the women-folk, as though he belonged at the hearth with them. Lillian reckoned he'd stick around instead of moving off with a woman one day, and that was just fine with Lillian. She thought of him like kin.

"And how you getting on after Thursday?" Alice asked Lillian, eyeing the bundled child. Eugene looked over, his round face blank.

"As well as to be expected after a full day of it," Lillian squinted, feeling the itch of her healing.

"Granny-woman get her here in under one day?"

"Upon the hour," Lillian said as they locked eyes across the yard. A labor under one day was essential to Ozark hill folk, as anything longer signaled bad luck. Alice's mother had been a granny too, but Alice had chosen not to learn. These days she was happy to put the old ways behind her, though she checked in on Lillian's learning every now and again.

"God's word," she smiled into the air between them. "Jess on the hunt?" she asked as Brody brought the ax down onto the stump.

"Yes, ma'am. He and the boys. Now I can get some sleep."

"You sleeping when the baby sleeps?"

"Trying. But with Jess piddling around, it's been hard. Looking forward to a whole day of doing next to nothing."

"That's how it's supposed to be, girl," Alice said, laughing.

"All done, Ms. Lillian," Brody said, standing without pain. He collected the split hickory, one large cut per hand, and stacked the cords on the porch with a neat jute tie.

"Would you like me to clean the ax for you?" he asked, wiping his hands on his thighs.

"I'll take care of it," she said, bending gently to take the red handle. "Thank you, Brody." The boy wiped his face with his shirt and walked back toward his mother's shed. Eugene stayed where he was, pulling on his thumbs.

"I hope Jess gets a haul for youse," Alice said, standing to stretch. "Is he back tomorrow?"

"Before noon, I suppose."

"Well, don't you hesitate to ring if you need anything."

"Thank you for that, Alice. I'll fry up some frog legs for us next week."

Alice pinched out the end of her cigarette and gave Lillian one last knowing smile before moving back inside of her cabin.

Lillian walked the length of the porch, feeling the baby's warmth leave a line of sweat under her swelling breasts. The morning's heat had set in, and the forest was quiet. Even the wind seemed to hunker down. Ozark timber had always been home for her, but the morning felt off somehow. As though it was too—she couldn't finger the word. Still.

She shot her mind out, feeling for what was around. It was a little secret of hers, the sending out. She'd cast her mind out like a net, feeling for life, a sort of inner listening. She could feel heartbeats up to a mile or so away, their tempo too. The larger animals sort of pressed in from behind her body. The smaller ones felt like pulses under her feet. Her favorite was the little adrenaline hearts of the hares. She didn't mind the snakes neither. Feeling out for their hearts meant she knew where to step to avoid them. She liked that their hearts grew after a meal. Made the eatin' something less personal.

Celeste was the only one Lillian had told about her sending out, but she knew that all grannies had a sort of intuition. It just grew differently in each person. For Lillian, it started with spotting deer before they'd be in the sight line. Neither Lillian nor Celeste were ever hunting women, but Celeste would have Lillian give a send out in deer season before the neighbors would head out those mornings in winter. Lillian would stand on the north end of their property line, feeling guilty at first, so she'd scope for just the bucks. The older ones. The men would always return with at least one male for Celeste and Lillian to butcher for the winter. No one ever asked how she knew where the best stands were. Jess didn't know neither, though he and the boys always found plenty to shoot whenever they went out if his wife had hinted at a certain clearing. Jess always bagged at least one, claiming his wife could just smell 'em. If she suggested a clearing, he'd be silent as the dawn creeping up in his stand. His thoughtful disposition meant there was no adrenaline for the deer to smell. They can smell everything on us, what you ate for breakfast, the last time you made love to your wife. So Jess' stillness meant their deep freeze was always full of venison.

Celeste's talent was hand-on healing. She'd cup her cool fingers over a break or a wound, and the patient would calm immediately. Reckon it was some intuition too. Celeste always knew what Lillian had been up to. Marjorie's was birthing. She could coax any baby into this world in under one of the Good Lord's days.

    That morning there wasn't much Lillian could pick up on. Most animals seemed to have found someplace cool to wait out the heat. She could feel the pulse of some lifeblood lying beneath the deadwood in the next acre over. Squirrels, likely. She could feel the heart of the carp scumside at the corner of the cove. She could feel the heartbeats of her three dogs sniffing down by the water. She could feel Glory Be's heart in sync with hers and Alice and her boys next door, the biggest of them all. She was a new mother, so all hearts took on a slightly different shape to her. It was no longer just her body in the world. Her charge was the baby. She took one last look around, spotting Eugene in the trees above his mother's. Aside from that, it was quiet.

7

The men set up camp in a clearing about fifty yards from Lick Creek, each working in quiet efficiency. Jess had packed ammo, jerky, fuel, their sharpest knives for field dressing, chewing tobacco, and bug spray. Johnny brought his Little Wonder with its missing G string, and Kurt had brought Ten High sour mash whiskey. Johnny plucked a little of "Sweet Sunny South" as the men unloaded the truck, and Sam's soul relaxed a bit as he stretched into the subtle wildness of the morning's space.

All four were seasoned trappers from Camden County, all bred and buttered in those parts, and they didn't waste time. Sam and Kurt did an initial scope on the pond adjacent the north end of the Lick, but Sam was hesitant since he didn't see any frog eyes sticking out.

"This place got a queer smell."

"Stagnant here. Let's keep heading up the river," Kurt had said, and the men continued their walk, swatting at mosquitoes as they moved upstream.

"Greenbacks, 2:00," Sam said, using the end of his gun to point under a large rock where a cluster of bullfrogs sat cooling in the shade. Johnny's head popped up from where he had been eyeing the shallow water mudflat beside the cattails.

"I brought mice," Kurt said, pulling the freeze-dried bait from his bag.

"If you get in about knee-deep, you can lift the ferns where it's dark and blind 'em with your lights," Sam said. "I'll come up from behind."

"Should have brought the canoe," Jess said, pinching a finger of dip for his lip.

"Next time," Sam said as he unrolled his netting.

"I'm using my crappie rod," Johnny said.

"Tie this to the end," Kurt said, using his knife to tear a corner from his red bandana. "If you taunt him, he'll try to fight, and I can net him."

The men waded into the water to where their catch sat, oblivious. Jess stayed back, closest to the north side, eyeing the forbidden territory across the creek.

"Just remember to not cross over. Private property," Jess said.

The boys had been the same as they ever were, having come up together since infancy. Kurt had repeated a grade and barely made it to graduation. Johnny, the kid brother of the group, had always toddled around behind Jess and his friends, and since he had always been the best shot, was always invited out on weekend hunts. Johnny was the expert gigger. For a science project once, he had researched the difference between bullfrogs and green frogs, winning a state prize from the FFA. That morning he went into great detail about how to store the kills, pulling a potato sack from his backpack, giving each man a mesh sack. The goal was a hundred frogs. Johnny and Jess' other brother, Trevor, was on his second deployment. If he were in town, he surely would be leading the hunt. That boy could bag frogs with his eyes closed.

They started at the end of the creek, where the neck was shallow, growing only knee-length. As it moved farther west, the Lick rose to well above head level with a current that could carry the strongest of them away before they could think to protest. There would be no frogs there. So they divided into twos to spread out east for more game, Jess and Johnny going together as they had since they were old enough to walk. Kurt and Sam moved in the opposite direction, Kurt about twenty or so yards behind Sam along the north end. He issued a steady stream of complaints about the mosquitos until Sam told him to shut the hell up so he wouldn't spook the kill. BJ bounded about fifteen feet ahead, his feet nimbly stepping between rocks aside the light current.

As Jess trailed Johnny down the rocky creek bed, his thoughts moved back to the baby at Lillian's breast. He was grateful for the day away from women's things, like birthing and toiling. *Two of them are fine*, he kept repeating to himself, but in his heart was a sort of trouble. He looked up at his brother, considered bringing it up, then thought better of it. Johnny was seemingly unfazed by his wife's capacities. About midway through Lillian's delivery, Jess had called up Johnny. Johnny had asked about the labor, asked if he was watching the game. Jess had been honest, told him he was struggling. Thinking of Gloria, thinking the darkest thoughts. They were hard words for Jess to speak. But Johnny was all cool patience. Told him Lillian knew her body, suggested he wait it out. Maybe the midwife would let him watch. Jess said he had no interest in that, plus the granny wouldn't let Jess near Lillian. Said the delivery room wasn't fit for menfolk. That was A-OK with Jess. He had to come in once to deliver the ax, and once he saw the toiling, he felt his spirit leave his body. He did not tell Lillian this, but the sound of her labor had made him sick. Physically sick. There were moans, all otherworldly like. Quiet conversations between granny Marjorie and his wife that would stop when he stepped closer to the door. He had not been prepared for the amount of blood. Blood darkening his wife's body, blood covering the baby when she came, blood soaking through the towels and straight through onto the pine floor. It was dark, nearly black, not bright red like in the movies. He shuddered to think of it. And the sight of the room was something else. The granny-woman's black bag open on the bed, the espandi smoke billowing in the corner.

He had wanted to take Lillian to Mercy General, but she wouldn't hear of it. She had been trained up in midwifery and said she wanted the woman who knew her people to deliver.

Jess had felt the panic rising in his chest like a fist of burning fear and protested again, knocking on his bedroom door, thinking he'd run across to fetch Alice to help or call an ambulance. His wife had to soothe him then, patting the bed beside her.

"Here, Mr. Jess," the granny had said, pulling his hand to his wife's wrist where he felt her skin, warm to the touch. "Feel that? Pulse is normal. Color is good," she said, the folds around her eyes giving the impression of wisdom, though not enough to chase away his fear. "You're going to bring worry into this room. It's why I never let the menfolk around."

"Don't worry, honey," Lillian had assured him, her breathing all off. "Women been doing this for millions of years."

And so he bent to her. She had grown up on the Lick after all.

As his wife's labor lasted from day into the night, he forced his last memory of his mother from his mind. He had been just a boy when she died. The last he saw of her alive, she was headed to the hospital with his father. The next he saw her was three days later, stone cold in a casket, looking as though she were just asleep, her hands crossed on her chest with her bible beneath them. He had reached out his finger, hesitating over her hand, nearly touching her before his aunt snatched his hand away with a scold. That next spring their old beagle had gotten pregnant from the stray they'd taken in, some sort of mix. She'd delivered three stillborn pups before dying on the canning room floor. He had been the one to find her, her mouth open, and a fly on her flank.

You take care of Trevor and mind Aunt Dotty, honey. I'll be back tomorrow.

Jess learned the lesson and he learned it well: babies kill their mothers.

So Jess had just stood outside and paced and prayed, putting the same Waylon record on repeat to mute out the moaning and petting the dogs till even they got sick of him. The one bitch, Wendy, lay outside of the door, watching him pace. That dog had taken to Lillian since he brought the three pups home the week they were married. They'd been dumped behind the hardware store. Word was the mother had been hit by a car on 7. Jess took them off the owner, a half-Indian named John Jones who had been bottle-feeding them. One of the customers, a local drunk named Francis looked them over, calling them "junkers," but John Jones just laughed, saying as a half breed himself, he could see their potential for guard dogs and told Jess he could have them if he wanted. Jess brought them straight home in a cardboard box as a wedding gift for his wife who promptly named them, washed them in the cove, and dewormed them. He also bought her a new apron, a set of underclothes from the Sears catalog that he wanted to see her walk around in, and a rescued cast-iron pan that she scrubbed and seasoned before making a roast for them to eat the night after.

They conceived Glory Be sometime that weekend, as she was born nearly nine months to the day of their union. But the night Glory Be was born, Jess was too sick to even drink rye to celebrate. He sat beside the cold stove until the granny came out in the sliver of space from the door opening, asking for lavender for the pillow, and announcing that the baby had arrived. A girl.

Jess smiled thinking of that last part.

A girl. My own baby girl.

Just then, Jess stepped on something which split beneath his boot, shaking him out of his thoughts. He looked down expecting a hollowed branch but was surprised to see the bones of some sort of animal, a large one. He bent down, the bone-white pelvis of a calf maybe beneath the underbrush. He toed it with his boot and stepped back.

"Got you," Johnny said from a ways off, stabbing the water at its edge. He held up his long stick and bagged one frog, then another, their spindly legs twitching in their last moments. Looking around suddenly, Jess realized that they were at least a half mile from where they had parked, and fairly close to where the creek was shallow enough to cross to the south end. Lillian had sternly warned him about the south. Unsafe terrain, she had said. He glanced across, thinking it about the same as the north end, just with a thicker canopy.

"Let's turn here," he said to Johnny as he stopped, staring across the Lick.

Johnny was halfway across the creek, his jeans wet to the thigh. "No way." He held up his bag, halfway full. "They're moving like crazy here."

Then a series of yells from up above. Jess and Johnny looked up the creek to see the shimmering outline of Kurt waving his arms. He was on the south end of the Lick. Jess felt the sinking worry return to his belly. *The fuck? Why the hell did they cross?*

"Shit," Jess said, moving their way quickly.

"What?" Johnny asked.

"Kurt crossed the goddamn creek," he said, feeling real anger. "Remember I told y'all that's private property?" he hollered to Kurt. "God dammit."

"Ah, it's early, Jess," Johnny said, coming up behind him. "No old timers up yet," he reassured.

Jess moved quickly up the north shore, dodging rocks and sticks, his gear slowing him down. Kurt was hollering something Jess could not hear.

"Hold up," Jess said. "I can't hear you." Speeding up, Jess could see the thick, blackish foliage on the south side. He shielded his eyes with his hand. The timber was dark, looking like something that would grow in another zone, lush and thicker than the sun-streaked north end. It was oddly quiet aside from his mudders in the rocky shallow end of the north. He turned to check on Johnny just as Johnny waded across to the south end of the Lick.

"Johnny—"

"Get your ass over here, Jess. There's some sort of trouble."

Jess froze, his heartbeat in his throat. He scanned the treeline for movement. *It's still early morning*, Jess told himself, looking back and forth. There didn't seem to be anyone near this end to see them trespass. Johnny was standing on the bank on the south side, looking to where Kurt had emerged from the thick of the forest where vines trailed up the trees, blocking out the sunlight. The ground below the treeline was all lush darkness. He could see some sort of movement below the thicket. Squirrels, maybe, he thought.

"He ran that way," Kurt said to Johnny and Jess as he struggled to catch his breath.

"What happened?" Jess asked from across the creek.

"BJ," Sam said frantically, appearing a few feet inland from Kurt. Frustration had changed the shape of his voice. "Took off that way," he said, pointing behind him into the dark forest.

"When?" Jess asked.

"About five minutes ago. Won't come when I call for him neither."

"Through those briars?" Johnny asked, parting the limping willow's branches to squint into the dark of the treeline across the creek.

"Yeah," Sam said. "They're thick as all hell."

"Looks too rough for travel," Johnny said, following Kurt and Sam to the treeline.

8

"I don't know what the hell got into him," Sam said, taking off his hat and wiping his brow with the palm of his hand. "I called him. He started, froze when I called him. Looked back, like he was thinking on listening. But then he just bolted into that dark patch." Sam looked back into the understory behind where Johnny stood. Lillian's warnings circled in Jess' mind as he stood in the water on the north, her frantic face as she stood holding the baby. He had promised he wouldn't touch foot on the south side. He didn't want any trouble with the locals or any goddamn fines to follow him.

"He was running like hell," Kurt said. "Like he caught something's scent."

"Call him back again, Sam," Jess said.

"BJ!" Sam hollered, disrupting a handful of warblers above them. Then again. Sam's voice echoed back to them, but there was no other movement.

"I don't understand it," Sam said, turning back toward the men. "It was almost like someone was calling him away from us." He cupped his hands around his mouth. "BJ, come 'ere, boy!" he hollered once more, loudly.

The men stood frozen, unsure how to proceed.

"Jess, is this all private? Even the bank?" Johnny asked, gesturing over his shoulder.

"As far as I know," Jess said, watching Sam. "She just said not to touch the south bank."

"BJ," Sam hollered as he ambled up the shoreline. Nothing but the echo came back. "I gotta go find my dog," Sam said, climbing up the bank toward where BJ had run off to. Johnny and Kurt stood there on the south bank, looking back to Jess without saying anything.

"I'll go with him," Kurt said, patting Johnny on the shoulder. "Y'all wait here."

Kurt climbed up after Sam, taking slow, careful steps up the bank, his thick boots slowing his progress. Jess' stomach clenched as the two of them disappeared into the darkness under the odd canopy. The forest seemed to take them in, as though they were being enveloped as opposed to willfully walking into it.

Not twenty feet to their left, a tripline was triggered. Not having been signaled in nearly half a century, eyes, long closed, opened in the dark. And next, a gnarled hand, the rune of danger scarred on it, unclenched, blowing seeds ground to dust into the wind, carried to first the angry one, then the weak one, then to the brothers, first the adventurer, next the hesitator. The body so still it lay unseen, before it moved so rapidly it seemed to have no form, making a run to high ground where the old church stands boarded, to wake the others.

Jess could hear their footsteps for a minute or so, punctuated by Sam's hollering for the dog. His heart was pounding in his chest. What if they stumbled upon an old timer? What if they were shot at?

"Johnny, get back over here," Jess ordered, stepping knee-length into the water, beckoning his brother with his hand. "I said I don't want no trouble."

"You always worry," he said, peeking under the low brush looking for frogs. "You're going to give yourself an ulcer one of these days."

"Damn dog," Jess mumbled as he tried to get an eye on the men. Johnny took a step forward before losing his balance. It was on nothing really. The bank was even enough. He'd later tell his wife after being discharged from the hospital that he felt something had him by the wrist. That he'd been knocked off balance by something. His wife would look at him queerly but never mention it again. Johnny tripped forward over a log half buried in the sand of the bank and fell straight into the sand, breaking his fall with his right hand, which came down hard on a bramble of driftwood.

"Shit," he said, rolling to his side and pulling up his hand with a grimace. A red line opened up in the middle of the white palm. Jess bounded across the creek in three steps, forgetting his wife and her warning. He pulled Johnny up with his left arm and gripped his palm. Blood was pooling from a dark wound in the center. The white-washed stick he had impaled himself on jutted out of the sand with a tip of his blood on the end. It had cut straight beyond the taut callouses of his palm and into the meat of him.

"God dammit," Johnny said, pulling his hand against his belly.

"Here," Jess said, tearing off his flannel's hem to stop the blood. Johnny crawled to the stream to wash off the blood in the water, a cloud of blood collecting before the current carried it away. Jess helped him tie the flannel across his hand. They stood in the silence.

"We need to get you to a doc," Jess said.

"That branch went clear through my damn hand," Johnny said, holding his right hand in his left. The blood started soaking through the flannel bandage. One fat drop landed on his shoe, another into the sand. Jess moved closer to inspect again, a sickly silence between them.

"Christ, that stings."

"Let's wade back across here," Jess said, taking his brother under his arm and helping him across to the north end of the Lick. They sat heavily on the sand of the north side, swatting midges, Jess pondering what to do, Johnny rocking his body.

"You're gonna need to get that looked at," Jess said.

"Reckon I will. Hate to cut the day short," Johnny said.

"How many frogs you get?"

"About twenty."

"Trip's a bust," Jess laughed.

"Help me light this cigarette," Johnny said. Jess pulled a lighter out of his bag and lit his brother's cigarette. They stared across into the silent darkness of the south, feeling the breeze pick up across the water.

"How long they been gone?" Johnny asked.

"About five minutes. See anything?"

Johnny squinted across the water and shook his head. "Can't see shit it's so thick over there," he said. "Did Lillian say who lives over there?"

"Something about private land, old hill folk, but that's all she said," Jess said, feeling the tug of nervousness again.

"More hill than her people?"

"By the sounds of it," Jess said.

"Lookie there," Johnny said. On the south side, a large water moccasin coasted down the current.

"Pit vipin' bastard," Jess said.

Johnny exhaled to the side. "How's Lillian doing? Shae said it was a hard delivery."

"Both of them are fine, thank Christ," Jess said, thinking with a shiver of her body swollen and sweating, her belly alive with his child moving around inside of her. "But goddamn, I hated to see it."

"You get through it alright?" Johnny asked, holding his hurt hand above his head to slow the bleeding.

"Yeah, but it was awful, man."

"It's good to have something to do while they're laboring. Like shooting cans. Or old episodes of COPS."

"Good call."

"Next time take her to the hospital."

"I know, I know," he shook his head. "She's stubborn."

"She's hill folk is what she is," Johnny said, not entirely unkindly. "But you're the man of the house. And if there's an emergency, you've got to take charge."

"It all turned out fine," he said, hoping to change the subject.

"You and your granny-woman wife," Johnny said, elbowing his brother. "I have to say, though, she looks great after one damn day."

"Two," Jess said. "And keep your damn eyes off my granny-woman wife."

"Hill women are the best cooks," Johnny said. "Toss me that bag she packed."

Jess pulled Lillian's bag from his sack and tossed it to Johnny, who grabbed it with his good hand.

"I'm going to take the big one," Johnny said, rooting around inside of the crumpled bag. "I'm hurt. I need energy."

Sam and Kurt reappeared on the shoreline of the south in a noisy rustle. Jess stood. Sam was limping, and Kurt was helping him along.

"Any luck?" Jess hollered across the creek.

The men paused on the sand, where Jess could see a tendril of thorny vine coiled halfway up Sam's thigh. It left cuts in his pants showing slits of pale skin. The vine was bright purple. To Jess, it almost seemed to be moving against Sam's leg as he worked his way into the creek, the current having picked up in the last half hour or so.

"What the hell is that?" Johnny asked, mouth full of biscuit.

"Got cut up by some vine," Sam said.

"Looks like sawbriar," Jess said, squinting across the Lick. "Kurt, can y'all get across okay? Water's movin.'"

"Gimme a hand here," Kurt said as he helped Sam into the creek. Jess met them halfway and Sam threw his other arm over his shoulder. The water soaked the men to their waists as they crossed to the north, seeming to rage between them. Sam sat down on the north end and took a stick to the vine on his leg. Jess tried to reach for it himself, but Sam pushed his hand away.

"Don't touch it with your bare hands. It'll sting you," Sam said.

Jess used the nose of his gun to loosen one of the briars from his leg. They were really set in, especially around the ankle, appearing to almost constrict as the men moved to pull it off.

"What in the hell even is that?" Kurt asked.

Jess got the nose of the gun under a bit of vine, but it only tightened against Sam's leg.

Sam cried out, reaching down instinctually, only to cut up his fingers again from the purple thorns. "Agh, fuck," Sam yelled, as he worked the tendril off his leg. He moved his punctured thumb to his mouth.

"No idea. Probably some local ivy. Any sign of BJ?" Jess looked between him and Kurt.

Sam shook his head firmly, his lips pressed together into a firm line.

"He'll be back," Kurt reassured as he sat down heavily on a rotted stump and dug around in his sack. "Gotta be over there somewhere." He pulled on a heavy pair of welding gloves. "Now sit still, for fuck's sake."

"I don't understand it," Sam said. "He never did anything wrong before," he added, putting his two fingers in his mouth and whistling loudly, echoing in the trees.

"No sign of a trail neither?" Jess asked.

Kurt lit a match below the vine. It seemed to relax its grip on Sam. He unspooled it gingerly from Sam's leg and held it up. It constricted, as though moving on its own. Kurt instinctively tossed it in the creek. The men watched silently as the current dragged it downstream.

Sam grabbed his canteen and poured water on his stings. "No trail," Sam finally said. "We followed for a few hundred feet till something in the thicket got me. I thought I was bit until I looked down to see the vines all moving like. Scared the shit outta me." He pulled off his boot to show thick briars stuck to his sock, which was red with his blood.

"Crazy shit, those vines looked like they were moving on your leg," Johnny asked.

Kurt pulled off the gloves and lit a cigarette, his hands shaking. "I can't believe BJ got through all that," Kurt said.

"Did you see anyone?" Jess asked.

Kurt started but Sam interrupted him. "Nothing."

"Sam—" Kurt said.

"Kurt, God dammit," Sam said, stomping his uninjured foot.

"What?" Jess asked, looking between them.

"Well, I heard something," Kurt said, ignoring Sam's stare.

"Heard what?" Jess asked.

Sam rubbed his face. "It don't make no damn sense."

Kurt took a long drag of the cigarette and stifled a deep cough.

"Well, spit it out," Jess said.

"I thought I heard someone laughing," Kurt said. "In the clearing beyond the timber."

"Laughing? Who?"

"Didn't see who. Just heard a voice. Started when Sam got cut up."

Jess surveyed the area. Last thing he wanted to deal with was some old timer with a pistol and an ax to grind.

"I even asked, 'who's there,'" Sam said.

"And there was some sort of dust in the air. It got all over us." Kurt took off his hat and shook it off in the sand.

"Some black shit," Sam said.

"Right about then we turned right around."

"Cause Kurt got spooked," Sam said.

"Cause you got cut to shit," Kurt said.

"Shit," Sam said, considering the damage to his leg.

"Good Lord, Sammy," Jess said, leaning in closer to Sam's ankles, where big welts were starting to swell under where the briars had lodged.

"It's gotta be some sort of allergic reaction," Sam said. His face was covered in a sheen of sweat, the flies buzzing between him and Johnny. Jess immediately thought that Lillian would know, and another cold spot swept through him. She'd also likely know they had crossed over and he'd get an earful.

"Well, you aren't the only one cut up," Johnny said, holding up his wrapped hand.

"What the hell happened to you?" Kurt said.

"Fell on his ass," Jess said. Johnny pulled the flannel back to inspect the cut.

"Great. Two of youse," Kurt said.

"Driftwood went right through my damn hand."

"Alright. Let's get back to camp," Jess said with the first authority of the day. "We need to head into town and find a doctor."

"Might as well wrap up," Kurt said.

Sam remained seated, defeated.

"Now I see why everyone says this creek sucks," Johnny said, picking up his net and tarp with his good hand.

"I got Sam," Jess said, pulling Sam back up with his right arm. "Can you get along alright?" Jess asked Johnny. He thought Johnny was looking pale in color too.

"Hurts like a bitch," Sam winced and slung his arm around Jess' shoulder.

They moved slowly, making their way back toward camp, Sam's eyes combing the landscape for BJ all the while. Johnny followed quickly behind, and Kurt picked up the rest of the potato sacks, last in line.

"What about BJ?" Sam asked Jess. He was feeling something awful with his leg swelling up tight against his pants leg.

"He'll make his way back," Jess said.

"Couldn't have gone far," Kurt said from behind them.

They walked the rest of the way in silence, each of them turning over some sort of misery in their minds. For Jess, it was his wife's warning. For Johnny, it was the deductible of the urgent care. For Kurt, it was the irritation he'd gotten so few frogs. For Sam, the sinking sickly fear that someone had up and stolen his dog. They reached camp in poor spirits. Kurt and Jess began packing up. Johnny and Sam inspected each other's injuries off to the side.

"We look like hell," Johnny said, his sweat-stained shirt sticking to his torso.

Sam ducked behind a cedar tree, brought his finger to his mouth. He stared straight back across to the south, his forehead sweating something fierce.

"Is it BJ?" Johnny whispered hoarsely.

He shook his head. "Saw something."

"Then what?" Johnny asked.

Sam was out of breath. "We're being watched."

Johnny squinted in the direction of Sam's gaze.

"Listen. There," Sam said, pointing into a line of trees. "You see them bushes rustling?"

Johnny strained through the timber's darkness. He took a step forward, but Sam put his hand out and stopped him. He pointed slowly with his free arm.

Sam followed his arm to a cluster of maples, and just beyond it, a shadowy form. It was the unmistakable shape of an animal, moving with calculated slowness, as though it were tracking something. As though it were tracking them.

"What the hell is that?" Johnny whispered slowly.

"Is what?" Jess said, coming up behind them.

"I don't know, but it's been tracking us for the last ten minutes or so," Sam said. Jess swallowed hard, following their gazes until he saw it. He felt his heart stop. "Black bear?"

"Not likely in these parts," Sam said.

"It looks like a goddamn puma or something," Johnny said. The men watched the shape until it darted forward to the next tree, so quick it was almost like a blur.

"It's long-haired," Jess said. "Ain't never seen a puma like that."

"What are youse looking at?" Kurt asked, coming up behind them.

"Some sort of big cat," Sam said. "On our trail."

"Mountain lion?" Kurt asked, squinting into the forest.

Sam shifted uncomfortably, adjusting his pant legs.

"Let's get the hell out of here," Johnny said nervously. "I'm not getting eaten by a lion next to this shit hole creek." He grabbed his gear and moved past them toward the truck. Jess stood frozen, watching the black blur move in calculated steps between the trees where the four of them had stood not a half an hour earlier.

Jess pulled up his rifle. "I'm going to hold a bead on it. Y'all start the truck." He quickly scoped for the blurry shape in the crosshairs.

"I'll wait with you," Sam said.

"We've got two men hurt, Sam," Jess said. "Just pack up camp. Ain't no way I'm turning my back on this thing until we are ready to move out." He clicked off the safety, held the rifle firmly in his hand and pulled back the slide, bringing a round into the chamber. The animal advanced forward from the trees and into the thorny vines where Sam had been standing. He wondered if maybe it could smell them.

"It's not even slowing down from those thorns," Sam said, awestruck. "Can you tell what it is now?"

"I'm not waiting around to find out," Kurt said. "Come on."

Jess pulled his keys from his pocket and fumbled them into the dirt. Kurt picked them up and followed Johnny and Sam to the truck. Jess followed the figure in the crosshairs. In his line of vision, he more closely examined the target. If it were an animal, it was nothing he had ever seen before. It had heavy shoulders covered with thick, shaggy hair. It was bigger, thicker than any cat he'd ever seen in these parts. It darted forward again. He followed it until he found it again, about ten feet to the northwest. Closer to them. And then, as if it knew Jess was on him, it turned its head to look straight at him. It had a feline-looking face with massive jaws. He thought he could have been wrong, but its eyes looked red-colored. A chill moved across his chest, from the inside out, something he never usually felt when he was the one holding the gun.

"Ready, Jess," Sam yelled from the idling truck, but Jess was frozen where he stood, watching the massive body creep closer toward the southern end of the shores of the Lick. It watched him where he stood watching it, only a hundred and fifty yards away. For a brief moment he wondered how fast this thing could move, and if he'd even be able to take it down before it crossed the space between them. It continued slowly to the edge of the treeline, right before the bank, then paused. Then it stepped right into the sunlight onto the sand. Jess took in the size of it. It was far bigger than a Missouri black bear, and thicker. Including the tail, it had to be ten feet in length.

"What in the hell—" he whispered, then righted his gun.

"Jess, let's get the hell out of here," Sam yelled over the engine. From where Jess stood, it was now only about seventy-five feet away. He felt the line of sweat stretch from his neck to his tailbone and could almost hear his heartbeat in his chest. He swallowed hard, and without thinking any further, he pulled the trigger. The shot echoed in the space between the trees, and a chorus of birds sang out as they flew off, the shot ricocheting—somehow—behind them. The men's heads all whipped around toward the direction of the shot.

Jess looked up—the animal was gone. He couldn't see an ounce of movement on either side of the creek.

"Jess, come on, man," Johnny yelled.

Jess jogged toward the truck and jumped in as Kurt moved over, the men scrambling to see out their windows.

"Did you get it?" Johnny asked.

Jess threw the truck into gear and pulled onto the gravel road, quickly looking behind him where the gunfire had landed before checking back across the creek. Whatever animal it was had disappeared.

"I heard it behind us," Kurt said. "Was that your shot?"

"I don't see no one else," Jess said, looking around frantically. That was nobody else's gun. That was the sound of his own gun. And where the hell had that animal gone? If it was tracking them, it was surely closer than it had been before.

"Well, how the hell did your shot end up behind us?" Sam asked, the dust kicking up beside them.

"It's like your rifle was witched," Kurt said.

"Don't talk like one of the women," Sam said. "Must have been an echo."

Jess' heart was about to bust out of his chest. He told himself that one of the southerners was shooting at them for trespassing, but his gut told him something else entirely. That was nobody else's gun. That was the crack of his own shell.

"Yeah, probably an echo," he said, adjusting the rearview mirror just in time to see a blurry black shape pass not twenty feet behind the truck, just beside where they had made camp that day, precisely where he had just been standing.

9

Lillian had first set eyes on Jess Cedars at church on Palm Sunday morning, two years prior. He was sitting two rows in front of where she and Celeste sat, squeezed in beside his father and two brothers, his dark hair stiffly combed and his white shirt tight against his generous shoulders. He wore cleaner clothes than the boys who had come up beside her in town and stood nearly a half-head taller than everyone else in the congregation. She watched the back of him for the first twenty minutes of service, her mind wondering and her heart stirring something fierce. Were they new to town? Were they one of the neighbor's kin? She slipped off her flats and spread her bare toes in the earth, trying to ground herself against the new sensations that coursed through her.

He had turned around at the sign of peace and froze when he saw her, looking like he'd spied a wild bird in his yard. She saw his face soften, watched his eyes cross her body before they settled back onto her face. Lillian felt a low belly stirring, her whole body going warm. She could feel the outline of her cotton bra against the curve of her breasts, the hard oak beneath her backside. For the first time in her life, she could sense earth's gravity between them, the force of her body against the earth, the force of Jess to her body. He turned around two more times that service, pretending to fidget with his seat. The last time Lillian held his gaze with a smile until he blushed.

Lillian sent out then and there and read his heart. It raced in his broad chest. Jess had been sitting still, hell bent on not turning around a third time to look at the woman behind him. As he tried to focus on the sermon, he felt what he'd later tell Lillian was like arms reaching around him. When he spoke of it, Lillian realized that when her sending out touched upon something, that's what they felt. He was drawn to her long-limbed, otherworldly beauty. She looked different than the girls he'd seen in town. Unafraid, unmarked. The pastor's words became muffled. Jess thought of his mouth on her thighs. Thought of her tapered waist, his seed finding purchase inside of her. Lillian thought of wolves, of buzzards, of termites. All creatures that mate for life.

After service, Jess' father moved his boys through the cluster of people in their small congregation, introducing his three sons to each member until they got to Lillian and Celeste. When Jess moved to shake Lillian's hand, he moved his donut from his right hand to his left and pressed his hand firmly into hers, embarrassed that he left a line of icing on her fingertip. He began a series of apologies until Lillian smiled and licked the icing, right off her finger, his face turning bright red. She knew then that this would be the man who would give her children. She could smell it on him.

Pastor Dory later told Celeste and Lillian that Jess' mother had been a member of the congregation before she had passed. Celeste looked sympathetically at the pastor as he described her mild manner and deep devotion. Celeste had known the woman peripherally but wouldn't speak of her publicly. She always avoided speaking of the dead. Later Celeste told Lillian the woman had chosen to have her babies at the government hospital, and there had been some problems. She said it was a blood pressure issue. The pastor had added that Jess and his brothers went to Camdenton High School, and Jess was their star lineman, but that his ambitions of being a great football player were taken from him when a concussion knocked him out cold and left him with headaches that caused an aura so strong that even the town's best government doctors couldn't treat him.

At the next week's service, Jess and his family were back at church for Easter Sunday, Jess in the same starched shirt. During service, Celeste reached into her pocket and passed a small vial of peppermint oil to Mr. Cedars, Jess' father, during the sign of peace, whispering to him the brief instructions, advising Jess to add droplets mixed with olive oil to his temples. He was also to chew on pumpkin seeds, she added as the man pulled away, nodding earnestly, looking bewildered at the vial in his thick palm. That next week, Jess' father would stop Celeste at the

True Value and thank her for her medicines in front of all the old timers in town. The men leaned on the glass cases and nodded at Celeste. She had treated most of their wives and children. Celeste told Mr. Cedars she was happy to help, and then he announced to the shop that this granny-woman had worked miracles on his boy. Big John behind the counter told the whole group of them that Celeste had treated each one of them through their chickenpox in childhood and she was the utmost authority on all things pain management. Mr. Cedars pressed a hundred-dollar bill into her hand, which she rejected twice until the man sent a handwritten thank you card to the cabin, the crisp bill folded inside.

After service on Easter Octave, Jess walked with Lillian to the refreshments set up in the back of the pastor's truck. Until that point, Lillian had never walked alone with a boy, let alone a suitor. Hers was the world of women, and the menfolk around her were either too old or shuttled into town for government school. Jess was easy energy and all questions. He told her about her work in carpentry in town since graduating. Said that his headaches had gone away since taking Celeste's medicine. He asked about tinctures and how Celeste knew about making them. They leaned against the bed of the pastor's truck for coffee, and Lillian timidly explained about granny medicine, watching his expression closely. Outsiders always considered the women of J Road with a mixture of awe and humor, and she didn't want to be the butt of any boy's joke.

"What was in the medicine she gave me?" he had asked.

"I believe it was a peppermint tincture. Some fractionated coconut oil too, most likely," Lillian had told him, marveling that the townspeople didn't learn basic native medicines in their schools. Nothing much useful in all those glossy textbooks compared to what she had been taught, she reckoned.

"How does that work on a headache?" he followed, not a sign of joking in his voice.

"Well, mint has menthol in it. That helps relax your muscles. It's anti-inflammatory."

"Do you know all this stuff too?" Jess asked, looking all over her face then. "Like all the things your grandmother knows?"

"I'm learning right now. I've been studying from her my whole life."

"Is there like a proper school for it?"

"I learned at her knee. She keeps notebooks. After I watch her treat, I'm to write it all down myself. If we ever run out of firewood, there's so many notebooks, I'll just use that as kindling."

"I like that," he said, moving closer to her side.

"That there's a lot of notebooks?"

"That you're smart," he said, looking down at her mouth. Lillian wondered if he was planning to kiss her, but he was merely thinking her lips were so red in her pale face they looked like a wound. Lillian looked up at him, then around to see Mr. Cedars, Celeste, and the pastor standing and staring directly at them.

Walking home from services later that day, Celeste warned Lillian that Jess' mother being gone would be a hurt that would never heal up right for him.

"We practically just met, gran," Lillian said, creating a tone of mock surprise at Celeste's supposition. Lillian could tell what Celeste was thinking.

"I can read between the lines," Celeste had answered, patting Lillian's hand.

And she had. Lillian was halfway in love, and she knew Jess stirred for her as well. She had felt out for his heart over and over and found it strong if just a bit skittish. It raced when he saw her. She watched the way he took her in, the way she began to live inside of him, a current of new feeling for an otherwise simple sort of man. His pulse too. She knew he had headaches, but she knew he was bound to be good. He was a good woodsman too, and an even better hunter. His place was in the timber, like hers.

Later that summer, when the heat was thick in the trees, Jess asked Lillian for a private walk with him after services. She thought he might ask for a date, but instead he talked. He started by telling her about his mother, how she had attended services at the country church before she returned to the Lord. Lillian had thought immediately of Celeste's advice. *Watch him good so he don't slip into the dark place.* So Lillian kept him talking, bringing him to her like the tide against the shore. She asked questions, drawing him out. He unfurled like a frond. And after he had opened for her, she offered herself. Her own sad story about her own mother, lost to her, the unknown father. Both of them unspooled their sadnesses like a line from a reel. Jess held onto her hand the whole time she spoke, not letting go, even after their palms had started sweating. Hours passed, the older folk having moved their ways home while Jess and Lillian sat on two stumps talking about the space left when mothers die. Jess said it felt like a tooth pulled, the space never closing over. Lillian said it felt like something hanging on a person like an ornament out of season, all wrong.

Jess' mother had been named Gloria. He had only good things to say. He missed her, he told her. He told her about the quiet in the house without her little humming. Lillian ran the outside of her fingers against his cheek to catch a singular tear. She told him it was a good thing, longing for the good that had passed.

A shadow passed across his face. "I feel all broken up about it still."

"She must have been good then. Or else you wouldn't be broken up about it."

He nodded. "Sorry about your folks."

She spread her toes on the forest floor. "It was all blown apart long before I was toddlin." Then quickly, as to reassure him, "Folks feel that I might have been hurting on account of them. My parents. But I never reckoned I was. I was well loved."

He looked her over with something that to her looked like hunger. "I can tell."

Jess didn't push about her being raised up by a granny, and she was grateful for it. Saying it all out loud made her feel even more like an orphan. As they sat in their common grief, Jess asked if he could see her back. He walked her home without trying anything at all. They talked about their favorite birds. For Lillian, it had to be the crow. Always the crow. For Jess, it was the waterbirds. He'd bought a scratch of land at the water's edge and had his own little cabin. He liked to stand at the window and watch for mallards, cormorants, and the elusive Blue Heron.

It was then Lillian was sure she loved him. He was strong without cruelty. He asked her questions. He didn't seem to mind her shapeless dress or hand-me-down shoes, unlike the boys in town who would look her over as they snickered. He walked her to her door, greeting Marjorie, Celeste, and Mr. Cedars respectfully on Lillian's sagging porch. They all had cups of Marjorie's apple cider before saying their goodbyes until the next Sunday.

Lillian and Jess' courtship culminated on the Autumn Equinox with a bout of fervent lovemaking in the cab of his pickup. He had run his hands over her shoulders so softly that she could feel the callouses from his work, and with the windows cracked, the songs of the bullfrogs alongside the touching, the strength of him beneath her as he told her he had fallen in love with her and wished to marry her. When she pulled away from his kiss, the stars all lit up in the night sky shone in on the side of his face like God was giving His blessing. She could feel the stubble from his shave that morning, could taste his tobacco on his lips. Atop him in the driver's seat, she did not think of this common spot to spend her first night with a man. His heart moved beneath her; there was nothing more true. As his hands pulled her waist against his, she knew what he had wanted from her then, so she had asked him to pray with her first, which he had done, breathlessly. It was a curious thing, lovemaking. A brief bright pain, his breath hot against her neck, his pleasure, her body's opening for him, the warm intimacy of their spirits stitched. After, breathless, his hands gripped her. He pulled his mother's wedding ring from his pocket and promptly asked her to marry him.

Celeste gave her consent after Jess came over in his church shoes to ask for her hand. He waited on the porch swatting mosquitoes, holding a handful of wilting Aster from behind his father's wrapped in a newspaper. When he handed it to Celeste, a honeybee crawled from the paper, which Celeste announced was good luck. After supper, Jess returned to his father, and Celeste lit her pipe on the porch, patting the rocker beside hers.

"You sure this is the man for you?" she asked Lillian, her match illuminating the deep wrinkles around her mouth.

"Yes, ma'am," Lillian said.

Celeste blew on her pipe in the twilight, watching the mayflies bounce into the screen. "You're both motherless, you know." And then a pause, as if to herself. "There will be a common pain in that," she said, dropping the match into the coffee tin at her feet. "He ain't as healed up as you, Lily-B."

Lillian felt a little shudder. "How so?"

"That boy's got a hole in his heart big enough to toss a coin purse through," she said, staring out into the darkness. "Gloria dying on him was the great wound of his childhood, and that wound will never fully close. It brought the sadness onto his family. You'll need to know this if you choose a life with him."

"Is that a bad thing? Missing a mother?" Lillian felt a stab of guilt then. She never knew hers long enough to even miss her.

"A chile' needs a mother. A woman to stand strong behind you as you move yourself into the world. A chile' needs someone to look back to in a sort of abandoning thanks."

"What does that mean? Abandoning thanks?"

"It means that the child must leave the parent. Go off on her own. That's what's natural. If the parent leaves, well, it's unnatural. What is unnatural leaves the wound."

"What about me?" Lillian asked quickly.

"You had women about you," Celeste countered. "Plenty."

"So you'll give your blessing?"

Celeste nodded at the potted bushel of rosemary beside the front door. "See that?"

Lillian followed her gaze. "*Rosmarinus officinalis.*"

"Good girl. You've been studying. Now look closer."

Lillian did. The rosemary had sprung a single white flower on its side. "It flowered! After all this time?"

"I grew that particular Rosmarinus from seed over fifty years ago. I was a married woman then. It has never bloomed."

Lillian fingered a delicate cream-colored flower at the end of a fragrant stem. "What's it mean, gran?"

"You must always keep a plant by your door. Watch it when folk come and go. If it blooms, well then, that's a sign from our Lord." Her voice lowered then. "But if it wilts—"

Lillian met her eyes then.

"A wilt means evil beckons. You must always trust what grows from God's green earth, Lillian."

"Does the flower mean I'm ready?"

Celeste took another puff off her pipe. "It's time you make your own family, girl."

Lillian placed her hand on top of Celeste's. "You're my family, gran."

"There will be more," Celeste said then, smiling at Lillian, the smoke collecting above their heads.

Lillian felt her head swimming with the smoke, with love for Jess, with dreams of everything that had not yet come to pass. Would she have his children? Would they grow into old age? "There will?"

"Chil'ren. Several." Celeste said, looking beyond the dark treeline as though seeing it for herself.

"Several?" Lillian repeated, wistfully.

Celeste waited a few moments, as though considering whether or not to share a secret.

"The first will usher in the swarm."

10

In the thin silence of the truck's cab, Jess and the men were rattled. Each thought of what had passed and what might come to be. For Sam, there were only thoughts of BJ, the fear about the cuts on his leg sidelined by his worry for the dog. He chewed on his knuckle, wondering if he should call the police or go to the hospital. The last time he had the stomach to look at his ankle, there were ugly blisters erupting around where he had been pricked. Johnny, meanwhile, felt like an ass for falling, for he hadn't had an injury all year, and his insurance deductible was high so as to keep his monthly payment low. He knew his wife would bitch about his spending money on new tires and then have to go and get his hand sewn-up. For Kurt, it was only the burning thirst for whiskey, a longing that had become just as much a part of his day as breathing. His ex-wife didn't ask for much aside from the $220 monthly child support payment, and the Grey Fox needed his labor as much as he needed their paycheck, so he could drink to his heart's content as far as he was concerned. Jess, however, was the most troubled. The oddness of his gun's fire, the possibility it could have been spooked, the audacity of him even considering being spooked clouding his mind. But the real fear came from whatever kind of cat he had a bead on that day. It had crossed the creek with a speed he had never seen before. What the hell kind of animal could move like that anyway? And those red eyes. He exhaled audibly and checked the rearview mirror again.

"Feel like stopping in for one at Lorna's?" Kurt asked, breaking the silence. His thirst was about to burst through his throat.

"For damn sure," Johnny said, relieved for another hour before breaking the news of his injury to Shae.

"I'm down," Sam added, if a bit sluggishly.

Jess looked at Sam through the rearview mirror. "You boys sure you can hold off seeing the doctor?"

No one protested, so Jess drove past the exit to his cabin and continued two miles east, the men's spirits instantly lifted.

They arrived along with the late afternoon rush. Jess pulled in as the sky's darkening indicated coming weather. Jess and Kurt locked up the truck bed while Sam and Johnny lit cigarettes in silence, the red tips illuminating their faces in the odd light. The gravel lot was already nearly full, and Sam eyed a pair of girls as they made their way in, winking at one as she smiled back at him.

"Cut to shit and still running game," Johnny said, patting him on the shoulder.

As they walked, a buzzing sound seemed to pick up around them. First just an edge within the wind, but then the sound increased.

Kurt cocked his head at Jess. "You hear that?"

"What is—" and at that moment, Jess saw it, or rather, he ducked from it. A cloud of rustling above them, then at them, a massive movement, moving north. A swarm of something.

"What the hell?" Sam said, and the men swatted at the swarm and picked up their pace. The insects barreled into them, bouncing off their shoulders, latching onto their hats.

"Cicadas?" Jess shouted.

"I don't reckon cicadas swarm like that," Sam said, ducking, picking one off his shirt collar and inspecting it. "Them's locusts, man."

"Not in Missouri," Kurt said, huffing to catch up with Sam.

"Least they don't bite," Johnny chuffed, holding the door open as the men crowded inside.

All the tables were taken, so they resorted to leaning against the back wall by the poster of the St. Pauli girl with her bosom and steins. Johnny went to wash up, Sam limping behind him in the muted lights. Kurt held their spot while Jess ordered a bucket of Budweiser and four chasers of Wild Turkey.

"We need to get those two into a doctor," Jess said nervously above the jukebox. He scanned the room, seeing Lorna, the owner, at the other end of the bar, wiping glasses. She and Lillian had come up together. She was always there whenever he came in, it seemed. Always made him feel a bit guilty, as though he should be home with his wife and not drinking in her tavern.

"Not going to happen tonight." Kurt said. He pushed his fist into his front pocket and pulled out a wad of coins for the jukebox. "I bet my balls Sam's driving back out to look for that dog."

"I reckon he'll find some trouble if he does that," Jess said, shooting his whiskey. A 45 of "Pancho & Lefty" flipped onto the jukebox turntable, the record popping along with the music.

"You mean that big cat?" Kurt drained his shot and gulped down about half his beer in one swig.

"Or that goddamn devil creek," Jess said.

Kurt looked right and left, then leaned in closer to Jess. "I think that land is goddamn haunted," he said. "Over on that south side? Something over there just ain't right."

Jess felt his stomach tense up into a knot. "Not right how?" Jess asked, knowing right well what he meant.

Sank into your dreams.

"I mean that creeping vine. It goddamn moved on its own." Kurt took a long swig of his beer. "And that laughter? Christ, almighty." He shook his head and issued a low burp.

Johnny made his way past the bar back to the corner where they stood, Lorna's eyes following him all the way.

"How's the hand?" Jess asked Johnny as he reached for his beer.

"Fuckin hurts," Johnny said. "I need to use the phone. Shae is going to be pissed. I was supposed to power wash the deck tomorrow."

Sam passed Johnny as he made his way to the bar for the phone, Sam's sallow color illuminated under the bar's dim lighting. He looked swollen, as though something was filling him up from the inside. Lorna passed Johnny the phone from under the bar, looking Sam over with an abrupt double-take as he passed. She looked over at Jess then, then back at Sam before pulling a rag from her jeans back pocket, wiping her hands, and making her way over to where the men stood. Sam took a long swig of his beer, then coughed to his side.

"How you boys doin' tonight," Lorna said brightly, her face in all seriousness.

"Not bad, Lorna," said Kurt, his eyes dragging across her body.

"You look like you caught a bug," she said sternly to Sam, pressing her wrist to his forehead as though he were a child in her care. Sam nodded as he swayed.

"Dog ran off on the hunt today," he said, his words slurred.

She pressed her lips together. "Sorry to hear it. Where 'bouts was that?" she asked quickly after.

"Over by J Road," Jess said, his eyes in a stare at her face.

She met his eyes. "Oh yeah?"

"Just bounded away," Sam added. "Didn't come back neither."

"How long did y'all trail him?" she said, her eyes dropping to Sam's leg.

"Few hundred yards. Got cut up something fierce and had to turn back."

"I can see that. You're bleeding all over my floor," Lorna said. "And you've gone cold, by the feel of it. You get bit by something in that forest?"

Sam shook his head. "Naw, but Johnny here fell on his ass and got himself impaled, didn't you, man?" Sam said sluggishly, patting Johnny firmly on the shoulder as he returned.

"You too?" she said, looking over Johnny's crudely wrapped hand. Kurt reached over for an unclaimed whiskey and shot it down.

"Tried to call my wife, but the phone's acting crazy," Johnny said.

"Another round of Turkey, Lorna," Kurt said, but Lorna ignored him, leaning in to look at Sam's eyes.

"Y'all didn't happen to cross the Lick today, did you?" she asked the men, picking up the empties.

"Yes, ma'am," Johnny said. "Bagged about fifty frogs before we called it a day."

"Not much of a catch, yeah?" she said, looking over Sam, her face looking all pinched.

"Not the best," said Johnny. "But we've got them on ice. Anyway, we are toasting to Jess' baby girl," he added, holding up his whiskey.

Lorna ignored Johnny, staring straight at Sam. Into Sam. "I think you should let Gideon know about your hunting dog. Want to use my phone to call over?

"Mighty kind of you, Lorna," Sam said.

"Can you show him for me, Johnny?" Lorna said.

The two men moved to the bar, and Lorna turned on Jess.

"What the hell are you doing bringing two injured men to my bar. Sam bled all over the floor on the john," she spat.

Jess looked behind Lorna with a worried stare.

She took a step closer to Jess and lowered her voice, her face darkening. "Your man needs a granny, Jess Cedars. What if what they have is catchin?"

"We are on our way to the doctor. Just wanted to stop off for one—"

"Might want to reconsider that second round. I just felt his temperature. 94 degrees at best. Something stung him up good."

"How can you tell his temperature just by looking?" Kurt asked.

"Nothing stung us up, Lorna," Jess said, heart pounding.

Lorna picked up the third whiskey glass that Kurt had finished. "Out on the Lick, folk liable to get stung up. You of all boys should have known better. Didn't Lily-B warn you?"

"She did. Yeah, she did, but—" Jess quipped.

"No one saw us, Lorna," Kurt scoffed.

"You may use that tone on your own woman, but not with me, Kurtis." She looked from Kurt to Jess. "Get that man to a granny. I reckon he has about an hour. Couple at the most."

"We'll head down to the urgent care down the way," Jess said, shuffling nervously.

"Just needed to collect our thoughts, is all," Kurt added, softer this time.

Lorna looked at Jess with a thick line between her brows. "Lily-B would tell you the same thing." She picked up the empties and turned from the men.

"Don't forget those whiskeys, babe," Kurt said after her.

"I'll bring the round *and* the check. One hour," she said to Jess in a lowered voice before passing Johnny on her way back to the bar. Kurt watched her walk off, eyebrows raised to his friend.

"Maybe we can catch the end of the game," Johnny said, switching channels on the television above them. Cardinals' outfielder Tommy Edman was sprinting to catch a line drive before lobbing it back to the infield. Jess nervously tapped his foot, wondering if he should call Lillian from the bar telephone.

Sam hobbled back to the table. "No answer at the station," he said.

"What the hell?" Kurt asked. "How can nobody answer at the police station?"

"Well, boys, are we going to talk about what the fuck today was?" Johnny asked.

"What was today?" Kurt asked.

"Two of us fucked up. Big cat. Jess' rifle all jacked—"

"Backfire, is all," Kurt stammered. "Jess don't fuck with the wrong ammo. Right, bud?"

"Man's right," Jess added, sipping his sweating beer.

"Let's finish these and get the hell out of here," Sam said. "My dog knows these hills. I want to be home in case he makes his way home tonight."

"That's over twenty miles, Sam," Kurt said.

"Well, a man can goddamn hope, can't he?"

11

Jess and Lillian had wed on an unseasonably warm Sunday morning the week before Halloween in the country church where they first met. The summer's heat lingered between them as they said their vows, autumn's versicolored leaves changing in the canopy above them. Folks next property over had a controlled burn going, and embers flecked in the distance.

Jess wore one of his father's bolo ties and his Sunday boots. He had his vows handwritten on a piece of paper, the back of which contained a hardware store list. Lillian had smoothed it after their ceremony, preserving it in her cedar chest so that years later, she could read over his thoughts whenever she was feeling sentimental.

Lillian's wedding dress had been hand-sewn by Marjorie. She'd taken a bolt of imitation satin and covered it with Guipure lace. She and Celeste had filled Lillian's hair with Russian sage from behind the doublewide. She had committed her vows to memory.

The reception was at the Climax Springs Elementary School cafeteria. Jess' father brought in homemade fried catfish and a cask of bourbon from a distillery down by the Little Niangua. Celeste had baked a paw paw spice cake and brewed a sassafras tea for the womenfolk.

After the wedding, the men loaded Lillian's trunk from her granny's cabin into the back of Jess' pickup. Lillian stood with her arm around Celeste, who leaned on her cane, and Marjorie, who wiped tears from her wrinkled face.

"You use that head of yours," Celeste said. Lillian thought she could hear the edge of worry in her tone.

"I'm just down the road, gran."

"You call when you need us," Marjorie said, looking intently at Lillian.

"Keep clear-headed, like I taught you." Celeste's face was serious.

"You'll visit, won't you?" Lillian asked.

"Of course, dear," the grannies promised.

Lillian kissed both of them and held onto them until Jess came to stand behind her.

"I'll take good care of your girl," he said to Celeste.

Jess drove Lillian the bumpy road from the cabin, his hand on her left knee, warm through her wedding dress. She turned around to steal one last glimpse at her old home, Celeste's tall form leaning against the porch door, the timbers framing her willowy body, her wave growing smaller and smaller as Jess took her away from the only world she'd ever known.

Lillian hadn't brought much along with her from the hills. A chest full of mostly heirlooms, two pairs of boots, her church shoes, and a .30-06 that had been a gift from the men in the village when she turned ten. She'd use it to shoot at coyotes that came too close to their goats, though everyone knew the rifles on the north were for protection against the south, in case they crossed the boundary. Jess, in contrast, had a whole grown-up home to himself, complete with patchwork furniture, a handmade table and chairs he and his brothers had built, and photographs of each member of his family hanging on the wall beside their framed marriage certificate. His mother's portrait was first beside it. When she opened the door to her new home, Lillian could sense a quiet male loneliness that she immediately committed to filling. They made love at high noon, before he'd even carried in her trunk, and ate leftover corn on the cob, listening to gospel on the AM radio until the sun set.

As a couple, Jess and Lillian were all easiness. He brought home an income, she swept the porch, sold what she canned, and coaxed fresh eggs from the chickens. He hunted; she cooked it up. He provided the cold cabin, and she made it into a warm home. Lillian was happy to be married off. Having left J Road, her granny, and her first life behind, there was the occasional pang of fear. But she reminded herself she was doing what Celeste had said was only natural for womenfolk. It was her duty to be a wife, after all. Why fear what the Lord had set up for her?

Celeste had been right about Jess' wounded heart, though. Since their wedding, when talk of mothers came up, Jess often became quiet. When Lillian would leave for a delivery, he became downright cold as a lakestone. She could often bring him back with a smooth touch on his temple or by pressing her body against his, but she knew there was a dark bolt of fear living inside the man. All twined up alongside his soul. After they were married, lovemaking flowered into pleasure for her. She had trusted her body's longings and steered Jess toward the touch that she'd discovered felt good, though he often tried to avoid the final parts of intimacy. When she asked him why he didn't want her pregnant, he changed the subject. But nature had its own agenda despite man's best plans, and Lillian was late for her monthly by Christmas.

"I don't understand how that could happen," Jess told her, pacing, when she told him.

"Pregnancy can happen if there is any deposit," she added softly.

"But there wasn't a—"

"Deposit?"

"So how could you be?"

"You know, honey, some of your part is left behind. Even before it's over."

Jess looked at her, his brow clouded. "Well, I most certainly did not know that, babe. Not exactly something we learn in school."

"Not in your textbook neither, huh?" she joked, drying her hands after starting the kettle, trying not to giggle at her husband. She locked her eyes onto him. Felt his heart picking up.

Jess stiffened. Lillian put her arms around his waist, looking up into his face. "You sure are handsome, you know that?"

He pulled her into his lap and buried his face in her shoulder. She could feel the stubble of his beard through her dress. "I don't want nothing hurting you," he said.

"Having babies hurts, but it's how we all get here," she soothed, her hand on his neck.

"What if something happens to you?" he looked up at her then, nearly talked out of his mood.

"Granny-women know how to handle an emergency."

"Granny-women?" he sat back suddenly, turning her shoulders to face him.

"The midwife?"

"Awh, Lillian, can't you do this right? At a hospital? They have all the machines you'll need, the medicines—"

She stiffened in his lap. "Hospitals are dirty places, Jess. Ain't no way I'm going to bring a baby into this world in one of those. Not unless my life depends on it."

"Well, what if your life depends on it?"

"God is good. He has equipped womankind for this." She reached for him then, feeling his fear through his skin. She sent him cool patience. "If something comes up, the granny can always call for an ambulance."

"Those machines save lives, Lillian."

"You don't need machines for birthing babies. I've delivered quite a few, and we ain't ever needed a machine."

"What do you do if problems come up?"

"I've only seen one problem." She bit her lip.

"What happened?"

"It was a breech. The baby was upside down. She needed a cesarean, and so they took her to Mercy."

"And was she alright?"

"She was. And, get this—" she added brightly. "It was surprise twins."

"Surprise twins?" Jess repeated slowly.

"Yep—two boys for the price of one. Can you believe it?"

Jess leaned back with a heavy sigh. He took off his hat, rubbed his forehead, and hastily put it back on.

When the time came, Lillian loved him enough to comfort him as she suffered childbirth. She was a midwife after all. Then, after the baby was born and she was sure both baby and Jess were okay, she suggested he give the baby a name. Lillian had to chuckle though, after his necessary deposit nine months before, the Wednesday her water broke, he stood there useless as she begged him to fetch the granny. It's why menfolk weren't often invited into the laboring. Lillian told herself her own labor could be somehow quieter, somehow less vulnerable, unaware of how it would feel on the other end of things after tending to women in labor so many times. Jess was all nerves watching her writhe, something those without children think they can hold in but then can't. It was otherworldly pain. It was the future reaching all the way, all the way inside of her body, and that reaching is no place for menfolk. He paced out front with his crumpled hat in his hands, mumbling to himself in the cold kitchen, nearly frantic, holding the old sepia-colored portrait of his mother that hung in their entryway as a sort of prayer.

Lillian had to admit, Gloria had been something. In the faded portrait, she stood slight-boned but firm with a row of perfectly straight white teeth and the brightest eyes Lillian had ever seen. She had been a schoolteacher in Barry for a school of only eighteen children, one of whom was twenty-two, her own age when she married. Jess had told Lillian that Gloria was wicked smart, that she could do sums in her head, no matter the problem, and she was planning on more college in Kansas City. But she was plucked from the prospect of independence by Jess' father, whose height, confidence, and four hundred acres of strong timber in Fawn Valley lured her away from city life and into three pregnancies, one after another, like the Trinity, until she was called home. Lillian wished she could have met her, for she dearly loved her son.

Hard to tell what kind of child Glory Be would turn into, if she'd have Lillian's pale features or Jess' dark ones. She had Jess' black hair and a tiny birthmark on her left thumb, which meant, Lillian told Jess, she could be left-handed as Lillian was. It was too soon to tell her eye color as she had barely opened her eyes beyond a little slit after nursing. What Lillian did know is that her baby had a clear cry and a belly of hunger that left Lillian's nipples so chapped she turned to the lanolin.

12

Lillian heard the truck's cracked exhaust shortly after dusk. The dogs sprinted around their house, their vibrant bays circling in the air as Jess cut the engine. The baby's eyes fluttered with the sudden disturbance. Next, a muted chorus of men's voices spoke from the driveway. Lillian's heart skipped, and she sat up, bolt straight.

You've got to stop always going from zero to emergency.

Lillian looked down at the baby, latched at her breast, making small sounds of contentment, a bubble at the corner of her mouth. She sent out, feeling her husband's heart beating out front and was filled with relief until the first sense of trouble.

Three soft coos from a hoot owl, out by where the truck had parked.

Not two. Three.

Something moved through her chest, right below the heart. Then a silence. Next, it was just the trees rustling in the evening wind.

Again. Three more hoots.

She sent out—she could sense the men. Four of them, one with a real adrenaline inside of him. She scanned the trees. There were lots of birds, their little flutterings. And then the owls.

Four of them.

All of it, unlucky. She pulled Glory Be off her breast with a sleepy suck, her eyes glazed through a small burp and laid her in the crib. She pulled a sweater over her head, then peeked out of the window to get a glimpse at the hickory. Kurt and Sam stood below the treeline, Kurt opening a beer in the late afternoon heat. Johnny holding a bloodied hand in the other. Sam's face all dark and his heart heavy, standing with one boot off. Her husband, then, moving from the truck toward the house, his heartrate elevated. Lillian stood motionless, closed her eyes, and sent out further and further—nothing—until there was something. A sort of cloud hovering above their place. A thin sort of masculine film. Large animal bodies like a storm that moved, a decreased atmospheric pressure, something warm rising.

Lillian heard the key move in the lock, the floor creak from the movement of heavy boots above her, her heart unclenching at the sound of Jess' voice above her.

The hooting continued, in clumps of three. It wasn't even dark. And that was no Great Horned. This bad omen didn't even wait until midnight.

13

The men had been to J Road, to the creek adjacent to the small hamlet where Lillian had been raised up. Those parts made for good hunting, but certain footings around J had parts that were known to have soured men. Settled them into stiffness like. And though the Lick had been home to her, parts of it were dark.

Lillian had never crossed the Lick to the south, but she heard the hillfolk whisper of it all her life. The grannies spoke of it as a place of shadows. Their people once were like the north, but there had been a schism. Some said it was a fight between the men over the land. Some said it was bad water. Some said it was the Devil himself. The government stepped in. Words turned into fists, and the rest was settled by generations of silence.

In Lillian's time, as far as she knew, the south had no medicine, no assemblies to speak of, no crops that thrived. Celeste had said around the time of the Second World War, southerners would call the northern grannies for help, standing across the creek and hollering over, but after a while, that stopped too. They had no schools, no fueling stations, no trading posts. Their folk lived isolated, and in that absence of form, stories circulated among the hill folk. Some talked of inbreeding. Some talked about how their children grew funny around the time the plant's waste runoff had contaminated the Lick after wartime. It was the grannies who first noticed the oily sheen, advising the farmers to grow further north and avoid fishing in the Lick. The families would take their wagons to the Spencer or the Wet Glaize to fish for nearly a decade until the government came in to clean things up. But the grannies said the damage had been done. There was no contact with any southerner for nearly thirty years. So, the stories turned into superstitions, and by the time the next generation came, talk of them was only a whisper.

In the north, though, the boundary was firm. The Lick was not meant to be crossed.

When Jess had told her they planned to hunt down at the Lick that Saturday, Lillian's response shocked him.

"Why not the St. Francis?" she had asked, sharpness in the edges of her voice.

"Closed," he said quickly as he looked at her.

"Jess, there has to be another place."

He tried to soothe her, telling her it wasn't that far, that he'd be back in no time. She had started pacing, the granny picking up linens and averting her eyes. Lillian shook her head and countered that the Lick was close to private property and dangerous to boot. He bristled at that, adding the four of them with their guns would be just fine, and, anyway, they were smart enough not to cross over where the land was private. Hadn't she known he was raised up in these parts as well? When she got quiet at that, he softened again, reassuring her not to worry, putting his heavy arm around her. But as he spoke, he sensed the coldness that came over his wife. Too tired, she said, to protest post-delivery, she had made one stern issue as she returned to their bed: They were not to cross to the south end. There would be plenty of frogs on the north.

"Honey, don't you worry about it. Ain't nobody been seen on that side of the creek in years."

"I mean it, Jess," she said, urgency in her voice.

He caught the eye of the granny then. "You think I don't know my way around this county?"

"It's just—" she hesitated. "I worry about youse," Lillian added quietly, her big eyes locked onto him.

"I hear you, babe," Jess said, sitting down beside her. He wanted her then. Wanted her soft hands around his neck, wanted her sweetness in his ear as they lay together.

"So you won't cross the stream?"

"We will not cross over." He petted her soft face. She looked so pale to him.

"You promise?"

He nodded, and leaned in to kiss her.

"Say the words," she said. He looked over her features and marveled at her odd ways, the way she broke apart all of his worry, his hardness.

"I promise, babe." He rubbed her arm.

To Lillian, the news of the hunt was certain danger. Most times Jess went out to hunt, it was close to their cabin. If it was a weekend away, they'd head north of the Missouri River, considered the best part of the state for big deer, and even the strangeness of those roads would be a comfort compared to the Lick. Some part of her thought this was leftover worry about his generation's suffering. Women left battered by their worlds, their men turned to drink or sin. It follows the children, she believed, as all grannies knew. She imagined him falling out of a deer stand or catching a drunk man's bullet, and he'd be snatched away from her the way his mother had been snatched from him, the way all the people she's come from had been snatched from her. Jess looked just like the photographs of his mother she'd seen—long in the limbs with deep-set eyes and blackish hair. Striking. She ached to think on it. He was the first man she had met who carried strength without yielding to hardness. He entered her without any desire to cause pain. He was not coarse in spirit, and she loved him for that, believing while close, her love could carry him safely through this part of the world. That she could somehow protect him. Even she knew that was foolish thinking.

She was not alone in this adoration. Since meeting her, Lillian had become the center of Jess' universe. When she'd tie up her hair to light the stove, he stared at the line of her neck. When she walked among the cabbage, her eyes expertly darting between each plant, he wanted to scoop her up and sit her on his lap beside the fire. When she sat cross-legged to fish, silent like the dawn, he longed to make love to her, right there on the dock in the dewy morning. Sometimes when she slept, he placed his hand on her back to feel for her beating heart, like she were in his charge to protect. He wasn't sure about her having his babies, and once even suggested she take the monthly pill that Johnny's wife was on, but she had looked at him with such shock that he never spoke of it again. And so pregnant she became, bringing Jess' worst fears to life.

She went into labor mid-week, her water breaking while she swept cobwebs on the porch. He had been unloading the Chevy, talking of taking some of the firewood down to market to sell, when he heard her moan behind him. When he saw her, he first thought she had kicked over the watering can, but her cries, low and otherworldly, echoed across the gravel drive. He dropped his saw into the red dirt and ran to her. She panted, bent in half.

"What do I do?" he asked, his arm around her back.

"My water's broke," she moaned, the clear fluid collecting in a puddle at her feet. "Call up Marjorie."

Alice, hearing the racket, ran across the yard to join them. "Oh, Lord, I'm sorry," Alice cried, as the paw paws bundled in her apron spilled on the ground.

"No, they're good luck," Lillian groaned as Jess rushed inside to make the call, the dogs on his heels. As he waited for Marjorie to pick up, he paced before the back window, spotting Alice's odd son perched high in the mulberry out back.

Jess sat crumpled outside the birthing room, their bedroom, waiting for updates. Mostly, he listened to the women talk, unless Lillian was having a contraction, which meant she was breathing all heavy or counting in between her moans. This is when he paced the cabin, praying snatches, nearly in tears. Lillian spent some time walking the property line, even wading in the cove a bit, holding onto Wendy with one arm, the other curled around her belly as he or Marjorie flanked her. If he wasn't close by and if the granny would allow it, he'd sit beside her, watching her heavy breathing, asking too many questions, until Marjorie told him to go on and git, he was making her nervous.

When half a day with little dilation passed, Marjorie opened the bedroom door and called for Jess, who sat whittling in his old rocking chair.

"Could you fetch me your ax, son?" she had asked him.

"My ax?" he asked. "Marjorie—for what—"

"Honey, it's to speed the labor," she said, impatiently. And after him as he moved toward the shed, "Make sure it's razor sharp, Mr. Jess. A dull ax might do more harm than good!" Her voice was shrill behind him as he rounded the property line, sweating through his shirt.

Later, he told Lillian, he nearly lost the last of his nerves. He came back with the ax and stole one last worried look at Lillian's heaving belly bent over the end of the bed before the granny pushed him out the door. Lillian watched from up on her elbows, the pain a deep, sickly ache in her spine as the granny inspected the edge with a coarse, arthritic finger, nodding at its sharp end.

"Does he think you were fixin to split me open with my own ax?" Lillian asked between fast breaths.

Marjorie laughed, her toothless mouth dark in the low light. "Some laboring women even ask me that," she said. "Some even beg to die rather than raise another youngin."

Marjorie had been the granny Lillian had known her whole life. She was Celeste's first apprentice in the north. She was born outside of Kansas City and ran away from home at twelve, when her mother married her step-father, a man who was prone to fits of anger when he drank and who, Marjorie had said, shaking her arthritic finger in the air, had roughed up her mother and come after her and her sister in the evil nighttime ways on more than one occasion. When her sister turned sixteen, she forged the Army papers to enlist early, scribbling their mother's signature and using the money to buy Marjorie a train ticket. Marjorie had left a note that she was headed to Chicago, then rode the train southeast instead, cutting off her hair in the rattling bathroom and changing into boy's clothes, so she wouldn't be spotted before getting off in Camden County. She bragged she was never found but secretly admitted years later that she knew no one likely worked too hard to find her.

Celeste had attended the wedding of one of her patients at the civic center that winter and caught sight of Marjorie, very clearly a girl in a pair of ill-fitting boy's pants clearing tables and washing dishes. Celeste had packed her pipe and later approached her in the alley out back as Marjorie pocketed stale bread rolls as she dragged a pail to the dumpster. Marjorie admitted she was a runaway who'd been squatting in a rental outside Onondaga State Park. Celeste took her in, gave her a cot in their cabin, and trained her up in granny medicine. Marjorie took to the warmth like a moth to flame, something she'd never felt before in her short life. She stayed, becoming a familiar fixture on the porch of Celeste's property on the north of J Road. Celeste's specialty was general medicine, while Marjorie's focus was birthing babies. Marjorie knew more about herbs to heal women than the forest itself. She was the first to teach Lillian about berry teas when she started her monthlies, the first to teach her how to avoid plants of the deadly nightshade family. She was the first to teach her to dig autumn roots and store them for the market. She taught her how to listen to a baby in utero, how to coax a baby from its mother. She was also the woman who stood beside Lillian, her arm around her, when they lowered Celeste into the cold ground. She told her loneliness ain't for real, since the spirits of womenfolk never truly leave. They become the earth around us. They become guardian angels, Marjorie assured her.

 Lillian would have had no one else at her baby's delivery. Marjorie did what Lillian had been waiting for her to do, what all granny-women did with the man's ax during a difficult delivery: she stored it under the bed to speed the birth. Bad luck to make a woman linger into day two, and they were down to the evening hours. Marjorie pulled open the bureau, took out one of Jess' clean white shirts, wrapped the ax in it, and kneeled with a grunt to slide it below where Lillian pushed, and with that hill magic, Glory Be was born within the hour into Majorie's knobbed fingers, a perfect little child of God, pink and howling at the full moon under which her mother had labored.

 After the granny-woman had walked off with her canvas briefcase, Jess said that she had given him all sorts of odd talk that day.

 "Like what?" Lillian asked hoarsely into the space between their faces on the bed. Her loins pulsed. She tasted the metallic edge of blood in her mouth.

 "You know, hill talk," he said, tracing the line of his wife's face with his index finger. Lillian lay very still, marveling at how something like intercourse could cause such pain.

 "Like I was to burn a corncob at the front door."

 "That's to ward off evil."

 "Then she insisted I show her any presents for the baby. I gave her the box we had collected, then she said no, they had to be things given to us. I mean to tell you she took what Mary Sue knitted the baby—that little rainbow cap? I liked that."

"I know," Lillian said, wondering how to explain the superstition to Jess. Mary Sue was Jess' great aunt who lived in Springfield. "But no caps or bonnets at all are allowed, Jess." The granny had done good.

"Why no bonnets?"

She sighed from her side on the bed. "It's just tradition."

"The worst was that I had to hang this hornet's nest she brought along."

"Outside the bedroom?"

He always looked a little surprised Lillian knew about these things.

"That's standard. It protects the birthing." Lillian felt the fatigue of the day settling in her low back and longed to sleep. Jess looked down on her then, wringing his hands in the lamplight.

"Come here," she said to him, reaching out her hand, tiredly. He slumped beside her.

"We can get the baby a new hat, babe," she told him.

Jess looked at her as though he was afraid to speak.

"You can tell me," she told him.

"She told me," he said so quietly it was nearly a whisper, "if I followed her instructions, you'd live. And the baby too," he finished, bending to touch Glory Be's tiny fingers. They curled around his finger.

"You did everything right."

"Honey, there was so much blood."

"It's normal. I promise," she said, then asked to distract him, "Did you pray?" Lillian felt sleep pulling her. "It always helps."

"Never stopped. Alice saw me pacing. Probably thought I was crazy."

"Makes sense," she told him.

"You think?"

"On account of Gloria, well, sure."

"I wasn't taking any chances," he told her, stroking the side of her. "I am so damn grateful." He felt his heart swell with love. He never knew he had so much room for feeling inside of him.

She pulled him close, kissing him firmly on his lips, tasting his tobacco, loving that he was somehow still a good man in a cruel world.

"But there was one other thing—" he said, thinking of Eugene the neighbor boy, the odd-looking one Lillian had taken care of this past year.

"Hmm," Lillian said, slipping off to sleep, her hand warm on his chest.

But he didn't tell her. How the boy had watched, for hours from the tree on the property line, rocking in silence, the crows about him. Jess had kept his distance, wishing the boy would go back home, but not having the heart to shoo him off. But then Eugene appeared not ten feet away, his thumb in his mouth, his eyes on Jess but somehow far away. And how he'd told the boy he couldn't visit that day, that they were having a baby, but would he like some of Lillian's cornbread—

"Lily-B's baby?"

"That's right," Jess said, sitting down on the old stump and running his hands through his hair. The boy had called her by her hill name.

"She'll be alright," Eugene had muttered.

"Yes, she'll be alright, son," Jess had said, his mind far away.

"Calling her after your mama?" he asked, his thumb blocking his words.

Jess perked up then. "Miss Lillian tell you that?" Jess considered the boy's soft, round face. His nearly feminine hands. But Eugene just turned and walked back from where he came, leaving Jess to his pacing on the porch.

14

The smell hit Lillian as soon as she opened the bedroom door. Like oil in a fire. Or sulfur maybe, she couldn't place it.

The men had brought something home. Something that didn't belong.

It was stuck to the air that followed them. The smell of something wrong, like hunting out of season. She steeled herself before walking upstairs, her mind racing, full of questions. She thought of Celeste's steady thinking and imagined her beside her, within her.

She took each step quietly, turning the corner to see the men before they could see her. They hovered beside the stove, something different between them, the same faces but with their spirits diluted somehow.

"You boys are back early," Lillian said, greeting them with a pleasant face. She breathed in. The smell was strongest with Sam. Next Kurt. Jess stood strong and quiet. She kissed his temple, breathing in strong. He was clear. She snuck a look at Johnny, his baby brother. He was foggy. Sam's eyes were downcast, but that's how he looked most times she saw him. He was angry red at his core.

"Had to cut it short this time, Lillian," Johnny said.

She smelled blood and saw that Johnny had his hand wrapped in part of Jess' shirt. Jess began to load the last of the firewood into the stove. The four of them stood with small snatches of talk replacing their usual chatter, bodies heavy in their boots, one shuffling between the stove and the cooler, the others looking up at the silence.

"Should I try the sheriff again?" Sam asked.

"Not much they can do in the dark," Johnny said. Lillian looked back and forth between the men for a moment without speaking. There was palpable tension. Kurt smelled of whiskey.

"We can go back in the morning, first thing," Kurt offered.

"I can't leave him all night," Sam protested, rubbing his right eye.

"What's happened?" Lillian asked.

"Sam's dog ran off," Jess said.

"It's my own fault," Sam said, looking up at no one in particular.

"I'm sorry, Sam," Lillian said. "Whereabouts did you last see him?"

Sam shot Jess a look and looked down.

"That's her land, Sam," Johnny said. "She might know something."

"Johnny—" Jess said, his eyes rimmed with fear.

"What is it, boys?" Lillian asked Sam, stepping closer to Jess.

"Down by the Lick, honey," Jess said firmly, swallowing hard.

"We were gigging on the north side, and BJ crossed over," Sam said. "To the south."

Lillian's arm instinctively crossed over where the baby slept at her breast.

"We know you warned us not to cross, but I had to try to fetch BJ."

"And no sign of him?" she asked, her voice quiet.

Sam saw her odd eyes grow almost bigger as she watched him. "I looked around but didn't see anything. Had to turn back cause I got cut to shit over there."

To Lillian, things began to move in slow motion. She heard herself offering to take a look at the cut, felt the start of dread pinprick in her belly.

"He'll turn up, Sammy," Kurt said, taking a long drink of his Budweiser.

"These dogs always do," Johnny said.

As Sam pulled up his pants leg, Lillian took a sharp breath in.

The Lick started down by the Arkansas line as a tiny spring. A tinkle, Celeste used to call it. She used to say you could cross it in a few hearty steps. It gained width and speed as it twisted north into Missouri, its pace growing as it neared its widest point. It was a silent body, peaceful on the top but deadly below. It was unpredictable to boot, flooding in the spring, drying up in summer, and the wind whipped up sharp and cold around its banks, even in high July, despite the heavy forest around it. It had dragged away many a child over the years. A day on the Lick could leave a man sunsick in December or cold to his bones in late summer.

A nice congregation of quiet hill folk on the north kept a steady eye on it, mostly watching the banks for erosion and making sure no animal got stuck, but on the other side, the south side of the Lick, terrain changed. Pockets of sandy-bottomed banks could sink a man to his thigh. A patchwork of thorny vines containing sharp briars grew under the timber, cutting up anyone who trespassed. A heavy canopy of shortleaf pine and oak obscured all sunfall. Legend in those parts was that those vines were planted by the Devil to prick and sting you, thickening up your blood within the hour. Northerners didn't venture south. And those from the south, Celeste had said, they kept to themselves. Unless you crossed into their territory.

"Sammy," Lillian said, looking up with a tenderness that reminded him of his long-dead mother. "You should let me clean this up for you." She took in the swollen red skin and the blackening clots beneath it, saw the inflammation growing in his cheeks and swollen fingers. Her eyes darted to Jess. He stood stiffly and looked over Johnny's hand.

"No, ma'am," Sam said. "I thank you. Don't want to be no trouble. I'll head on over to the doc here in a minute. Just had to have Jess bring me back to my truck."

"Okay," Lillian said, taking in his odd tone. "You let us know what the doc says, alright? Johnny, let me see that hand," Lillian said, moving next to Jess' brother, who was eager for some attention.

"I suppose I'll go along with Sammy here in a minute," he said, unwrapping the hand for Lillian to see. His palm had been punctured, exposing beyond the muscle to the cool bone of his palm. The skin around the wound looked clean, but it was swollen and pink. In the middle though, she saw some unusual discoloration. Perhaps blood coagulating.

"You need to wash that," she said. "Creek water is pretty clean, but still. Soap and water in the bathroom." Johnny moved toward the bathroom, examining his exposed hand with a wince.

"I'll warm youse some supper to go," she said quickly to the men. "Can't have Jess' men go hungry. Please have a seat."

"Awful kind of you, Lillian," Kurt said more to Jess than to Lillian, no one moving to sit down.

She moved behind the kitchen island and reached into her apron for the spell bag. She pinched a bit of wormwood from the dry mixture and sprinkled it behind her, then lit the stove under the cast iron. Glory Be was still against her chest as Lillian pulled the last of the ham from the spring roast from the refrigerator, slicing into the hide, then dropping each thin piece into the pan, the hiss blocking the men's silence. She held the knife steady, cutting meat away from bone, holding the smoky rind intact, as that was Jess' favorite. As she stood, she felt her sinews pull, blood pooling. Childbirth had been exhausting, and her body was tired. Two days since the baby had come and she was still feeling too shadowy for much of anything. Whatever tonight brought up would certainly be taking from her rest.

Jess' back was to Lillian, but she could see the others' faces and the creeping darkness that hung on them. She pulled a cube of snow water from the freezer into the pan, watching the cold spread into heat, and wondered how much time she had. Something was amiss beyond the lost dog. Trackers usually turned up after a day or so. Even if they were wild from a trail, they always made their way home.

Through the back window, one small light was visible in Alice's kitchen window. The last two nights Lillian had seen her up in the witching hour while she was nursing and thought of calling. She'd know what to do about postpartum. Lillian was feeling mighty lonely with Celeste gone and the granny gone back home, but she didn't end up reaching out. Hillfolk turn in early if they've worked the fields that day. And Lillian knew country matters keep a woman from sleep sometimes.

Alice's people had come from Lake Mykee Town, not far from the Lick, and though they didn't speak much of that, they kept each other close. Alice had been keeping an eye on Lillian alongside Jess since the baby had come. First day she dropped off a rabbit casserole. The day before she brought over a basket of cherries and a cup of buckeyes for Lillian's pockets. When Lillian tried to get up to fetch something, Alice would redirect her to her baby, and she or Eugene would take over the chore, bumping into Jess, who looked bewildered by all the fuss.

According to Celeste's notebook, forty days is what a woman needed after labor. Same time the Israelites wandered, same time Christ was tempted in the desert. Lillian was to fast from sugar, fast from lovemaking, fast from lifting and toiling. She was to keep her spirit clear, to pray, the Psalms if possible. Marjorie had left the following on her nightstand to use as needed: white willow bark to chew and a small wooden crucifix.

Unlike Jess, Lillian never questioned the medicine. But what about witching? The men had unearthed something that day, and with Celeste dead and buried, what other grannies on the north could she call with her questions? Lillian watched the pink of the pigmeat between the shapes of her fingers, wondering if she should tell Jess that Sam's dog was likely a goner, wondering how she should subtly suggest to Sam that since he crossed over too, he needed a talisman for his door. She knew the men spoke of her wildness. She was used to it. But this was Jess' best friend, and by the looks of it, something had got him.

Lillian pulled four unmatching plates from their cupboard and placed them on the table beside the plate of pork, hearing a snatch of the men's talk. She lingered as she spread lard on the cold cornbread. Glory cooed from her sling.

"He didn't believe them stories anyway."

Kurt reached out with his fingers, taking a cube of meat and popping it into his mouth. Both looked discolored to her. Kurt swollen with the drink and the pigmeat like a wound. She shuddered and turned away. She had never tasted pork, as it was unclean to her people, but Jess and his company loved it. Jess was not from the deep country, so talk of crops failing and storms brewing was about all he could stomach. When it came to forest medicine or grannies, he was silent with his big arms crossed at his heart. She left that chatter till she was alone with Alice. Thinking of her, Lillian looked up again just as Alice's light flicked off.

When menfolk come back stinking of fear, it's good to know where the other women are.

15

The dogs scratched at the door, Wendy at the center, the skittish males beside her. Their barks were agitated, the same tone as when they were after a squirrel holed up. Jess let the dogs in, and their nervous whines filled the air between the men's voices. The two males circled the table, but Wendy crept close to Lillian, stationing herself between Glory Be and the others. Lillian reached down to scratch behind her ear, wondering which of them she was shielding her from.

"It's okay, girl," she told her.

Jess untied a cord of firewood for the fire, and the men sat to their plates, his brother looking up at Glory Be's pink fist reaching out of her wrap.

"You have Brody cut this, honey?" Jess asked her.

"Sure did," Lillian answered, eyeing the men as they watched Jess feed the fire. "Just this morning."

"How's my little goddaughter?" Johnny asked, breaking the biscuit in half with his healthy hand. The day's stubble stood out on his pale face.

"Sleeping at all hours for now," Lillian said, lowering Glory so Johnny could look at her sleeping face. He peered inside her wrap as she closely looked over his face.

It's in him too.

"Going to use your john, Jess," Sam said, heading to the guest bath off the kitchen with a pronounced limp. Lillian watched him move, something sharp about his smell. Whatever it was they had brought back was spreading.

"Thanks for dinner, honey," Jess said, walking up beside his wife. He gave her a dry kiss on her forehead and turned his face sternly toward her. Wendy lay with a pant above her twin paws and growled lowly.

"I need you and Glory to wait for me in the bedroom," he said into her ear.

Lillian looked up at his face. "You okay?"

"Babe," he said a bit more sternly, his hand firm on her low back. Sam limped back to the stove to join the others, coughing into the crook of his elbow. As he passed, Lillian could see his eyes were cloudy.

"Keep Wendy beside you. I'll be down soon enough." Then his voice louder, for display only. "I know you're tired. I'll finish washing up." Jess looked down wearily at his daughter.

Lillian excused herself with all politeness. The men muttered their tired goodbyes as she made her way past the dogs, back downstairs, the female following her.

Lillian opened the bedroom door, moving in the darkness toward the bed when she heard rustling outside the window. She peeked through the curtains just as the motion light kicked on, and in the orange glow, a husky figure crossed their plot. At first, she thought it might be a fawn. No—the legs were too thick. Too heavy-bodied. She squinted into the darkness, where the animal stood sniffing. It was far larger than any animal she'd ever seen in their parts. It was hulking with dirty black fur covering its hooves. The creature hesitated at the treeline, its front left foot poised in the air, almost as though it was waiting to be seen, before creeping off into the thick underbrush, just out of view. She felt a pinprick across her skin, as though this animal was somehow familiar to her and she had the urge to crawl out after it, but she was no longer one body on this earth—she was also Glory Be, and she recoiled back. Wendy was on it then, just a moment behind Lillian, her barks echoing in the small room, her strong body at the window. Jess was downstairs in an instant, Glory Be howling in the air between them. Lillian closed her eyes and sent her mind out for the heart. She focused narrowly, listening in the quietest of ways, picking up Alice next door, her boys, the fish in the cove, even the birds above them—but there was no other heartbeat immediately around them. Nothing else living, at least.

"What is it?" Jess panted, bursting into the room, his hands in red fists. Lillian's eyes shot open as he switched on the light.

"Company, by the looks of it," she said, soothing the baby and crossing them both as her heart raced. Whatever that was, it was not from these parts. She moved away from the window and quickly scanned the room—rifle in the corner, loaded, cob pipe perched on its shelf. She whispered the unknown spell below her breath as Jess checked the window.

"Coyote?"

She shook her head quickly. "Too big. Plus, I saw hooves," she said. Wendy whined nervously, her nose lifted into the air toward Jess.

Jess looked out the window. "Don't see nothing. Why were you standing in the dark?"

Lillian coaxed Wendy back from the window. "Suppose I could see better that way."

She cast her mind out again, further this time. She could feel the pinprick of the squirrels and one coyote at the property end, and then she found it. Few hundred yards away. How had it gotten so far so fast? She listened—fifty, fifty-two beats per minute. That would be a very large animal. Wendy's barks subsided into a low growl.

"Wendy," he hollered at the dog, moving to the second window to look.

"Don't—" Lillian interrupted. "She got nose of whatever it was." Lillian placed her hand on his shoulder, felt his arm stifling a tremble. "I want her with us tonight."

He stepped back away from the window, pulling the curtains closer together. He looked at her in heavy silence, all he had seen in the day leaving him dumb.

"Lillian—"

"I already know," she said, the baby's cries finally lowering to a whimper.

"Know what?" Jess said, fear lining the edge of his question.

"Y'all brought something home with you tonight," Lillian said to her husband, her voice so low it was nearly a whisper. He met her eyes, and she tried to keep her gaze even, but her heart was racing, and her body ached. Her breasts felt heavy with milk. His eyes darted away from hers to the window as though avoiding her.

"We need to talk," Jess said, shoving his big hands into his front pockets as he looked down.

"Babe, look at me," she said.

Jess strained his face and then met her eyes after a minute.

"Sam's caught something," Lillian said quickly. "Johnny too."

Jess stepped closer to her, lowering his voice before he spoke. "What do you mean, caught something?"

"They're infected," she said. He thought he could hear a hint of something in her voice. Was it fear?

"Infected with what, Lillian?" Her eyes looked strange to him in the low light.

"Can't tell yet." She rocked the baby in her arms, her face nearly trancelike.

"What cut them up?"

"Some sort of vine."

"Like a creeper?"

"Looked like sawbriar to me."

"Cow Vine?"

"No. This was under the trees."

Lillian sat down on the end of the bench and ran her hand across her face. "Well, it's inside of him now."

"Inside of him?" Jess asked. Lillian could feel his heart start to race. "What about Johnny?"

"The center of his wound is unclean. They both need a granny, Jess."

Jess looked at her as though he were about to burst. He exhaled, looking right and left before nodding emphatically. "They're on their way to urgent care. Right after they leave here. I'm sure they'll fix them right up."

Lillian felt herself bristling. All this looked like something she'd only read about in Celeste's journals. It was common knowledge that stepping onto southern land meant bad things were coming. Whatever landed on these men was something the city doctors wouldn't know how to treat. She wasn't sure, but to her, in her gut, the men looked proper witched. She lowered her voice before continuing. "Maybe Johnny, but Sam—" she lowered her voice, as though something was listening to them speak. "He's got something unholy going on, Jess. No city doctor will be able to save him."

Jess looked down at that.

"Did you see his eyes? He needs the button. He needs—" she looked behind him and tried to steady her voice. "He needs the button on his eye, Jess."

"The button? Lillian, this ain't the time for—"

"Hill medicine. He needs hill medicine, Jess. It looks to me like he's been witched."

Jess kept his eyes on her, as though she'd finally gotten his attention.

"Whatever vine cut him up, it's toxic. If it broke the skin, it's inside of him. Those things can spread inside your body, Jess. Celeste's journals talk all about it. And the sickness? It's catching. And, right now, Jess, that something is in our kitchen."

Jess paced between the bed and the door, his face pinched with worry. "Now I want you to stop this crazy talk, Lillian," he said gently. "Before it upsets you. Or the baby."

She felt a bubble of anger behind her ribcage. She could tell he was keeping something from her and moved unthinkingly closer to him. "You saw his eyes."

"Well, he's pretty tore up about the dog, I think."

Lillian stood her ground. "It's more than that. Sam is sick, and he needs help. There's a Yarb doctor over by his Dos Hombres."

Jess shook his head as he looked down. "Sam don't believe in all that."

"Don't matter if he believes or not. Take him there. You can convince him," Lillian said quickly, nearly interrupting him. "His name is Morris. He'll listen to you. It's the apartment directly behind the restaurant. Knock and he'll answer; he sleeps upstairs. Tell him I sent youse. Government doctors are all closed up this time of night anyway."

"Alright," he said, looking stone cold. "I'll try. Let me finish up with them."

"Tell him, Jess," Lillian urged. "Call up the Yarb. He takes walk-ups. Remember, ask for Doc Morris. Sam'll need the button. Or the madstone," she added, fingers tingling, her body filling up with a sort of siren sound.

Jess looked at his wife as though he was seeing her straight on for the first time. She was so vulnerable. Swollen from his baby. But beneath the softness was something he couldn't quite place. Something he saw in the fawns as they were startled drinking from the cove. An extra sense. Something in her couldn't be coaxed from him, he knew, no matter how much he loved her. She'd always run back to where she came from. He started to speak but then stopped himself. He glanced at the window again, looked nervously between Lillian and Glory Be, who whimpered from her swaddle. He felt a line of sweat along his spine.

"Okay. Boys are getting ready to head out," he said flatly as the baby's cries returned. He pulled her in close and kissed her forehead. "I'll be right back. Keep away from that window, you hear?"

"What happened tonight, Jess?"

"Let me get rid of them." He turned and disappeared back upstairs.

Lillian rushed to the door to whisper behind him, urgently, one last time, "The Yarb. Tell him, Jess."

Lillian whistled Wendy back and closed the door, leaning her head against it as though trying to push back against what was coming for them. Wendy was restless, pacing in the small space. Lillian held Glory Be close as she cried her small cries, then felt the need to send out again. She pressed her ear against the walnut panel, listening for any breathing, for that pulpy beat of the heart, but aside from the night birds' fluttering and the small game, there was nothing. Whatever had been lingering had stepped out of range. She moved to the bureau where she fished out a Cremora jar, then sprinkled the ash of the spell papers in each corner. She pulled out her breast for Glory Be to nurse, sitting in the rocker in the dark silence, feeling Wendy's fur with her open hand, tracing the sounds of the men upstairs until she heard Jess' boots walk to the porch. In her mind's eye, she could see him standing with his Mossberg, the two other dogs nosing around the line of the property.

16

Jess watched the boys' trucks pull off, lifting his hand in a final wave. He stood for a moment in the night's silence, scanning the property line, trying to get control over the fear that had been creeping since they had left the Lick that afternoon. First, BJ's disappearance. That dog never disobeyed Sam, and he'd just taken off. Next, their crossing into the south. Then Sam cut to shit, and Johnny hurt too. But what was most unsettling was that *thing* he had seen across the Lick. Its big shoulders and its darting about. He'd spent enough time in deer stands and creek beds to know what it was doing. It was tracking him. Tracking all of them. That thing had moved faster than any other animal he'd ever had a bead on.

As the last of the red taillights disappeared into the darkness, he heard the sounds of a hoot owl and looked up to see a cluster of them in the big oak, looking down on him, shaking their feathers in the night wind. He shuddered as he locked eyes with one of them, as icy fingers of dread spread behind his ribcage. He called for the dogs and locked up.

As he switched off the lights, Jess dreaded he'd have to tell his wife the full extent of what had happened that night. The southern cross, the animal tracking him. He sat down heavily on the bench by the door, pulled off his boots before stripping off his day clothes, leaving them in a pile outside the bathroom. His limbs felt heavy, as though he had lead in his blood. He started the hot water in the bath and leaned with exhaustion on the sink before looking up in the mirror. Aside from some tired looking eyes, he looked alright, though somehow, he didn't feel himself. It was the way you felt before a cold, a sort of cloggy slowness in the back of the throat. A twinge of panic gripped his chest, but he shoved the thought away before stepping into the bathtub to sponge off what was left of the creek from his body.

Lillian lay in bed, looking across the steely dark at her baby's small frame rising and falling in her crib. She closed her eyes, feeling the sinews of her postpartum body move back together in cramping waves. She could hear Jess washing up and was grateful for his safe return. But despite her man's strength, he always seemed to be walking head-on into some sort of disaster. Before her, it was the football injuries. Game after game, ain't nobody ever noticing the nosebleeds and headaches. Then as men, the group of them making choices without thinking on them. She pushed aside the day's worry and focused on what she knew to be good: Jess, a good man who loved her. A healthy baby. A manageable labor. Lillian had presided over some complicated deliveries, most resolved in the old ways but one recent requiring an ambulance. Her cousin Ella, who was forty-two, something the old timers considered a little "later in life surprise." She had pushed for two days until her blood pressure dropped. It ended with a cesarean in the government hospital that left the woman laid up for two weeks with infected sutures. Most women in their parts didn't trust the city doctors, felt a stranger presiding was indecent at best. They said they didn't want their babies in the hands of those who didn't know them. Lillian didn't have the stomach to tell them that some of their own were capable of that as well.

As Jess turned the water off, Lillian breathed the prayers of protection three times, keeping whatever spirits were about from penetrating the sanctity of their cabin. There were all sorts of precautions that were needed in the mountains. There were animals, there was man, but the most menacing was dark magic, and without spells and tinctures, those darknesses could creep inside a man like fog creeps across the cove. Lillian herself wore her own gran's Mozarkite necklace, but she always kept the iron close. Glory Be was a healthy baby, but she was too young for the bag of camphor, so Lillian whispered the prayers extra hard as Jess had been to the hill country, where restless spirits walked and danger lay in every corner, and she didn't want anything touching upon the baby's wellness. Jess thought her superstitious, but he didn't know what she'd seen. His ways were more modern. She did not mention these prayers to her husband. She kept this to herself as she kept most things pertaining to hill country.

Jess stepped heavily into the cold bedroom, a frayed towel around his waist, quietly closing the door behind him. His eyes adjusted to the blackness as he latched the door heavily from the inside, something she'd never seen him do before. He squinted at the baby, asleep on her back in the empty crib, a small dime looped around one corner of the frame on its red twine. Some sort of protection spell, Lillian had told him. He placed his hand on his daughter's back, feeling for her breath, then sat gently on the edge of the bed and sneezed violently three times.

Lillian's eyes shot open. "Bless you, honey." Wendy looked up from the foot of the bed where she lay.

"Hey, babe," Jess whispered, reaching his hand for her shoulder. "Did I wake you?"

"No," she said, reaching for him. "Been waiting on you."

Jess felt a surge of desire for her. Her sweet voice, her long legs, warm beneath his touch, her ample bosom. But he also felt something else underneath the lust—was it fear? Dread? What was all her talk about buttons on the eye? At times, her talk seemed too otherworldly to him, nearly suspicious, as though she were hiding her true self from him. He coughed into his elbow and slid into bed next to her.

"You feeling alright?" She could smell the mossy musk of the forest on his breath.

He shifted beneath the quilt. Then silence. She put her hand on his. "Jess?"

"I don't know. Today," he stammered, "we got proper spooked."

She thought again of the hooves outside the window.

He reached for her waist, pulling her close against his chest. She felt a pain in her low belly. She breathed him in, traced her fingers across his back.

"Sam's a mess. Johnny's cut bad. And Kurt, well, he drank himself stupid like he always does."

"Did you tell Sam about the Yarb?"

"We all tried convincing him to get looked at, but I'm afraid he's going back out there to look for his dog."

"To the Lick?"

Jess stared up at the ceiling.

"Not a good idea after dark," she said.

"No. It ain't."

She lay there, waiting for the next part.

"My rifle, Lillian," he stammered. "It was witched."

"It was what?" she asked, trying to slow her responses to a believable momentum. Her mind scanned the length of J Road. Where had he been off to? Who had spoken to him of witching rifles? These men were too land-proud for such talk.

"Four of us took J Road north until the bend crossed over the Lick. We passed by your old place. I showed the boys."

She blinked into the darkness. She could see in her mind's eye his truck stopping, the dead branches dipping down to touch the rooftop. She knew the Lick like she knew her own body.

"You go inside?"

"Just drove past. Looks mighty run down."

Lillian lay very still in the darkness, thinking of the home of her childhood, Celeste at the stove cooking tinctures. Jess lay staring intently at the ceiling as though waiting to be asked the right question. Wendy snored at their feet. Lillian felt the spell paper ash holding them in with safety. But she could feel something coming. A subtle sort of coming. Like a fog or a front of bad weather. If Jess was to speak in the darkness about what he had seen, the shape of it would then live in their little room. Ash can only do so much. The men had brought something home. Something dark from Lick Creek. There was plenty of darkness huddling in that part of the world, waiting for an excuse to spread out.

"We set up camp about a mile out. Were down on the creek about three hours. Got started on the frogs. But then BJ ran off. Crossed the Lick in a few leaps, Sam said. Sam crossed over to follow, but the dog never came back."

"So, Sam crossed?" Lillian said, the cold feeling spreading out alongside her words.

"Kurt too. But we didn't see no one."

"Then what happened?" she followed quickly.

"Johnny crossed over to check on them, and he fell. Cut his hand up as you saw. And Lillian, I say this not to disrespect you—"

"Say it, and quickly," she said, leaning up on one elbow.

"I waded in. To fetch Johnny."

Lillian felt her chest tighten.

"I couldn't leave my brother," he added firmly. "The branch went nearly clear through his hand—like a knife through butter. Swear I've never seen anything like it. He was sinking down, like into the sand. Shore was, I dunno, different over on that side."

"That's when you crossed?"

"Yeah. He was bleeding something fierce."

"On the sand or in the water?"

"What do you mean?"

"Where did Johnny's blood fall, Jess?"

"On the sand."

"You saw it fall? Think carefully. On what side of the Lick?"

Jess looked awkwardly into the space between them. "South side."

She exhaled audibly, trying to force out the small prick of rising panic. "And where were you standing?"

"Shallow end of the south."

"You touched ground on the southern side then?" she repeated.

"Yeah. To get Johnny," he said. "But we didn't shoot or even gig there. The dog—"

"Don't matter, Jess," she interrupted. "If you crossed, you crossed," Lillian said so quietly he could hardly hear her. For a moment, the silence hung heavily in the space between them.

"I'm telling you," Jess said, his tone more reassuring then, "nobody saw us."

"That's not what I'm worried about."

17

"How far inland did Kurt and Sam go?" Lillian asked.

Jess lay beside her, his forearm crossed over his eyes. "I reckon a hundred yards or so," he said, clearing his throat in between words. "I don't think they even knew where they were, now that I'm thinking on it. Don't think he realized till those vines caught him."

Lillian thought of the coin-shaped drops of blood he left on the kitchen floor. "Anyone else step into the vines?"

"Just Sam. And Lillian when he showed us? It was like they had embedded into him. We tried to help peel it all off, but I'm telling you, those vines looked like they was creeping on their own. Like it was a part of him. Merged with him. With his skin, Lillian. That's when we gave up on finding BJ."

The baby stirred in her sleep, and they were both quiet for a moment, listening to the wind blow outside.

"The vine, Lillian," Jess said, lying stiff as a corpse. "Took us nearly a half hour to get it off him." His eyes were white in the darkness.

"Did you touch it?"

"With my rifle."

"That's good."

"And his eyes. When he crossed back over, they were full of gunk or something."

"What kind of gunk?"

"Looked like some sort of dusty pollen," Jess said. "Chalky, like gunpowder."

"Past time for pollen," Lillian said, thinking she'd have to consult Celeste's notebooks.

"He washed them out in the creek."

"That's when you headed back?"

"We did. I was getting worried maybe some old codger was eyeing us from his tree stand. But that's when things felt off."

"I'm listening," she said, concealing the urgency from her voice.

"I feel crazy saying this, but it's like I could feel eyes on us. I couldn't see anything, but I could feel it."

"Like a coldness?"

"Yeah," he said, "you've felt it?"

"I felt it every time I've looked across that creek," she told him. She thought then of herself at twelve. The tug. The key and the lock.

He turned toward her and changed his voice to a whisper. "Sam was limping, holding one end of the cooler. Then all of a sudden, he put it down, all quiet like. He's the kind of man who understands the hunt. Knows how to listen deeply in the quiet, you know?"

"I know," Lillian said. She knew Sam was a hell of a tracker.

"He said we were being followed."

"How'd he know?"

"At first, I thought someone might be bringing back the dog. Called out a few times. But there was nothing from over there. Nothing but silence. I had the boys go clean up while I kept scoping the creek. No sign of BJ. But," he said, and paused.

"I—," Jess stopped.

"What?"

"I saw something out there, Lillian."

"A person?" she asked quickly.

"No. Some sort of cat. We couldn't be sure since it kept moving on us."

"You said your shot got spooked. Is that the same gun you used on the vines?"

He cleared his throat. "Yes. And I don't want you to think this is some kind of crazy talk. I am a sensible man. I wouldn't have believed it if I didn't see it with my own damn eyes."

Lillian stayed silent, rubbing his arm in a gesture of comfort, but she already knew what was coming.

"The shot, Lillian. It—" he stammered. "I shot it straight, but it—" he broke off.

"It what, Jess?"

"Saying it out loud makes it not seem possible."

She waited in silence.

"It hit the timber behind us."

"Behind you?"

"It hit the bark of the hickory not twenty yards behind where I stood."

Lillian leaned forward. "And no one else was shooting?"

"I know, sounds crazy, don't it?"

Lillian combed her mind for anything on bullets. It was not a topic she knew. Hers was medicine. Bullets were for killing, and that wasn't her discipline. "Where were y'all at this point?"

"By the truck. Sam called out for BJ a few more times, but there was nothing. We got the hell out of there, fast as we could."

"And you never saw anyone?"

Jess hesitated and cleared his throat. "In my rearview mirror, I am pretty sure I saw that big cat that I shot at."

"Pretty sure?"

"It moved so fast. It was like a blur. Blink and it's gone, you know? But I saw it. It had gained on us. Only a handful of feet behind us as I pulled back onto J Road."

Lillian wondered at the men's logic. "How come Johnny didn't go straight to the doctor?"

"Johnny was still bleeding, but it had tapered off. Kurt was thirsty, so we stopped off for one at Lorna's. I think we just wanted to chill the fuck out for a moment. To be sure we were the same men who had walked down into the creek that morning."

"Whiskey won't do nothing for you when you're cut up."

"But then something else happened when we pulled up to Lorna's. Even before we got inside. We were locking up the bed, and we heard this rush. Looked up, and it was like a storm cloud was coming our way. It was moving fast, and by the time we could like register what the hell was going on, it was on us."

"What, Jess?"

"Locusts. Came straight from across the highway, right at us. Flying all heavy, like a cloud of them, right at us. I thought they might just be summer cicadas. But these weren't your run-of-the-mill scissor grinders. These were different-looking. No color on them. They flew like they were after us."

"But we don't have locusts here, Jess."

"That's what Sam said. They got in our hair, under our collars. We just ran to the door, brushing them off. They didn't bite or sting or anything. Just showed up."

The first will bring in the swarm.

"Y'all see Lorna?"

"Yeah," Jess said, sitting up and rubbing his face with both hands. "She seemed to freeze in her tracks when she saw us, started talking crazy as soon as she put eyes on Sam."

"What did she say?" Lillian asked too quickly.

"Said to get him out of there. Said he looked sick."

Lillian knew Lorna must have sensed it too. "She wasn't wrong, Jess."

"Said he needed a granny. Just like you. Asked where we'd been, but Kurt lied. It was like he knew he had stepped in shit."

The silence sat thickly between them for several minutes.

"You reckon Sam's in trouble?" he asked her, his voice thick.

Lillian looked over her husband. She didn't think she could bear it if something bad happened to him, but at the same time, she knew something was coming. "I think all you boys are in some sort of trouble, Jess."

Jess sat very still in the dark.

"I think maybe we kicked up something over there, Lillian." He paused before continuing. "Something bad."

Lillian wondered if it was too late to call up the granny.

"I need to ask you something," he said after a minute. "It—it sounds crazy enough thinking it, and I worry saying it out loud will sound even worse."

"Go on, babe," Lillian coaxed.

"Those are your family's parts. Is there anything you know about them?"

Lillian stiffened. "There's plenty I know about them. What exactly are you looking to know?"

Jess paused, stared at the ceiling in the darkness. She thought then of how little he knew about the women of J Road. Of the superstitions that many had feared were actually real. Buried truths that no one wanted to unearth. Even her. *Don't ask*, she thought selfishly, like a child. But Lillian knew that if she spoke of all the mysteries of the Lick, it would somehow give power to what lay across that creek. She'd be bound to answer as well as bound to protect them to the best of her ability. Her eyes shot over to Glory Be. And who would protect her, Lillian thought, on this craggy mountainside, if something were to happen to Jess? What if what followed Jess home was stronger than a woman waiting on her bleeding to stop? She sighed into the space between them.

Jess continued. "Anything like—supernatural?"

She wondered how much this man could handle hearing. She thought on all that Celeste had told her, all the stories about the Devil, and was silent.

"That thing across the Lick," he admitted finally. "It wasn't normal. It moved faster than anything I've ever seen, Lillian. And I want to know what the hell it was." He turned and stared right at her. "Because whatever it was, I think it witched my rifle and took Sam's hound."

Lillian thought immediately of what had passed by their bedroom window that night.

"You ever see anything like that?" he added.

"There've been stories," she said. "But what I think is that you boys got spellt. And if you been spellt, we are going to need help," Lillian told him, her voice so low he pulled away a bit. If he was rattled by whatever they saw that night, he would be wrecked by the answer to what he asked. She felt the air in the room drop and wondered if the powder was failing. With her eyes closed, she pressed back against whatever pushed in toward them. She felt out again, this time scanning the woods for the bigger game.

"What do you mean spellt?"

"Jess, if you ask these questions, then you'll need to steel yourself to know the answers," she said with a sigh.

"Steel myself to know what?" he said, the edge of frustration breaking through.

Lillian scanned out, out past the main road to the edge of the timber. Nothing. She shot her mind back the other way, scanning the lake's edge—got it.

It was across the water on DeJohn's property, about a quarter mile down.

"Lillian, tell me what you know about J Road."

She sat up in the bed and turned to face him, her breath a line of steel between her breasts, swelling.

"Babe, do you know what granny-women say about bedrooms?"

"What?" Jess said, his skin black metallic in the moonlight.

"They ain't for talk of the Devil," she said as she stood, moving for her sweater.

"The Devil?"

"We need to move this to the kitchen." Lillian turned away from him, slipping her feet into mudders, then picked up the sleeping baby and tied her back to her breast. No way she was leaving her alone for a second with hooves on their property and a properly hexed man beside her. Jess dressed in a hurry behind her. She froze as she picked up a heartbeat directly across the cove. It had moved closer to them. And fast.

"Jess—" she said, standing still.

"What is it, babe?"

"It's whatever was outside our window earlier."

"What about it?"

"It's back. I need to pinch us a powder."

His eyes went still as pools of water. She knew he was wary of hill talk, but it was high time he heard some after what the men had done. If Jess had stepped foot onto the south end, he would have been spied at best, but it was more likely he had picked something up and dragged it home. Sam had gone in deeper. He and Kurt were in real trouble. She pulled open the bedroom door and hurried out, Wendy following close behind her. Jess pulled on his jeans, grabbed his gun, and followed his wife up the steps.

"What do you mean, it's back? What did you see?"

"I didn't see anything," Lillian said. The upstairs was pitch black, with only the sound of the clock ticking above the bullfrogs by the water's edge.

"Did you hear something?"

"No," she said, thinking of how to explain this to Jess.

"Well, how do you know it's back?" he asked, his tone like that of a frustrated boy.

She reached the top of the steps and turned to face him. "I felt it."

Jess' face was inches from hers, but he was covered in shadows. She closed her eyes, sending over to DeJohn's.

"Two of them. Water's edge at DeJohn's."

"What?" he said, moving quickly in the dark to the window, pulling the binoculars off the nail beside the sink. "I don't understand how you could—Jesus Christ, Lillian," he said, stumbling backward. "That's what I saw over the Lick. That's what I shot at before my rifle was witched." He pointed forward in the darkness, his hand shaking.

"Let me see," she said, taking the binoculars from Jess. She took in the hulking shoulders, the hooves moving so quickly they were more darting than galloping. "They're making their way over. You locked up the chickens, right?"

"I did," Jess said, his voice shaking. "Now there are two? What the hell are those things?"

Lillian took a long, slow breath in as she looked him over. "That there is an Ozark howler."

He took the binoculars back. "Jesus Christ. That ain't myth?"

"If it is, that myth is making its way back to our timber."

18

Tyresius sat reading the day-old paper, the last of a cup of tea gone cold in front of her. It was an hour till dawn, and she had given up trying to sleep, the uneasy dreams continuing to shock her awake. She lit her lamp and made her way to the kitchen, even before her dogs were up. For the past three days, the dreams had been about the coming swarm of locusts, whose untimely arrival had kept her phone ringing until the power went out. But last night, her dreams changed shape. Now they were about the south. And their peculiar hill folk. Images of their people, huddled on the shoreline of Lick Creek, their bodies crowding the rocky sand, croaking in their odd language, goat eyes blazing in the moonlight. And just before she woke for good that morning, she saw in her dream the face of their leader, sneering into the coming daylight, lifting her filthy skirts as if planning to cross over. They were coming, she saw, to collect one of their own that had gotten away. Tyresius had sat up in bed, sweating, pulling on her glasses, oscillating between thinking of dreams as a construct of her imagination and dreams as a foreshadowing to reality. She did not have long to consider between the two, for as she finished with her morning cup of tea, she looked down at the arrangement of leaves in the bottom of her cup.

If those leaves had anything to say about things, there was a storm brewing. And it was going to be a big one.

Tyresius was one of the last grannies left off the J Road. An old woman by today's standards, she still practiced medicine on the far north end of Lick since returning one year before from Livonia, where she had seen patients out of the back of a small apothecary shop on Lydon Place, down the street from an ice cream shop, a guitar repair store, and a deli with an old TomBoy canopy. In the alley behind the shop, she and the owner of a Pho restaurant shared a hanging garden that provided their herbs for cooking and the majority of her needs for tinctures.

When Tyresius got the call from Marjorie LeftHand that Celeste had gone to the shadows, she had packed up her S-10 and driven overnight the nine hours from Detroit to Camdenton, her pack of dogs kenneled in the bed beside her trunks and trays of seedlings, her body stiff the whole way. Her hip had been hurting since Champaign, but by St. Louis, she felt she had been mule-kicked both in body and spirit. Bodies and their illnesses never much touched Tyresius, but the thought of Celeste leaving this world did. It rocked her to her bones. Celeste had been the great love of her life.

Tyresius and Celeste first met in 1942 in Columbia, Missouri at a botany conference at Browden Center back when Tyresius was still known as Tammy. They were the only two women in attendance. Tammy listened to Celeste's talk on polyploid phylogenetics, taking in the speaker's waist-length, white-blonde hair and nearly translucent skin, and was halfway in love before Celeste had gotten to Homology. Celeste had noticed her during the presentation as well, feeling Tammy's eyes all over her as she spoke. Careful to look equally at each attendee, she'd scan the room uniformly until her eyes landed on Tammy, who'd display a sly smile, sending bolts of desire all through Tammy's body. A lady stood out at a science conference attended by nearly four hundred men, but a woman as beautiful as Celeste? Tammy hovered in the doorway, picturing Celeste's pale body below her own, hip to hip. Every man in the room lined up to speak to her after, and Tammy had to wait by the refreshment table in between seminars in order to secure a moment with her, offering her hand in introduction. By fall, they were inseparable.

Both were women who had pursued careers in science, though it was fairly unheard of in the Midwest at that time; both had difficult fathers who had turned to drink or silence; both had mothers who did not protect them, though Celeste was from the country and Tammy from St. Louis, and both were lesbians— Tyresius, aware of her inclinations since childhood and a figure in the Gaslight Square district where the gay nightclub Crystal Palace operated, and Celeste, fully closeted and actively tormented by her desires until liberated by Tyresius in 1942. Celeste had left home for school, initially to study in the Department of Education at the University of Missouri with the goal of running the schoolhouse back in her hometown in Camden County, but quickly changed her major to Biology after walking past an open door as students were completing a lab on antibiotic resistance. Tammy was a doctoral student in St. Louis and had traveled to the conference to collect samples for her doctoral advisor, Dr. Teddy Hawthorne. She originally signed up for the chemistry speaker, but the session was full, and so she wandered into Celeste's seminar. Years later, both women would often wonder how one change in registration or traffic could have so profoundly changed the course of their lives.

By 1945, after a years-long, romantic written correspondence and twice yearly clandestine meetings in Columbia, Celeste graduated with her degree in nursing and moved to St. Louis to be with Tammy. She found work at one of the city hospitals making $140 per month tending to patients, carrying in scuttles of coal, cleaning the ward and patient rooms, and taking notes for the attending physician. Since she was church-going, she was given two evenings off per week. The women rented a room on the riverfront, which they furnished with old steamer trunks, their books and notebooks, and their most valuable possession: a Victor Victrola gramophone. They spent their evenings talking over records, growing in understanding of the other, as neither had ever shared a bedroom before, let alone lived with a romantic partner. Tammy was the activist. She secured her dark hair back, donned men's trousers, and could talk to anyone, even about politics, even if it gave her the reputation of being a rabble-rouser. In contrast, Celeste was introspective and mannered, a burden-bearer with a rich inner life who struggled with bad dreams. She'd wake sometimes in a sweat, talking of predatory cats, even a buffalo. Started when she was a child, she said. Tammy would lift her spirits while Celeste kept Tammy grounded. It was a near-perfect match.

Women in love in any capacity was expressly forbidden in 1945, and though St. Louis was bustling, there was no language for what they were and no safe place to express it. They lived as "cousins," so as to avoid the term "degenerates" to their neighbors and especially their employers. Tammy had been promoted to research assistant for a Professor Don Dottie. Their specialty was the Geomorphology of the Mississippi River. Dr. Dottie's wife, Lucy, managed his four rental rooms on the back of their large home off Broadway, one of which housed the lovers. Tammy and Celeste's small one-bedroom had thin walls but a view of the river, which fascinated Tammy as it contained nearly five hundred species of fish, amphibians, and mammals. Lucy provided their dinners, though she wasn't the most thoughtful cook, and Tammy and Celeste would often opt for takeout or cook noodles on their hotplate.

Tall and lean, Tammy was boyish in features and dress, preferring slacks and saddle oxfords to Celeste's tailored tweed dresses and pumps. Tammy would take the bus to pick up Celeste at St. Louis University Hospital after her night shift ended, and they'd walk from the stop the few blocks home in the predawn light. If no one was around, Celeste would slip her fingers into Tammy's or her arm around her waist, resting her fingers where it tapered in, her favorite place on her body. On weekends, they'd take the bus to the Fabulous Fox for a show or walk around the Jewel Box in Forest Park, one of Celeste's favorite places in the city. At night, they'd return to their shared room, the record player on as loud as it was allowed to disguise any sound of their lovemaking. Looking back, Tammy would always think of loving Celeste as something corseted, never fully able to speak as she desired, never able to show as she desired.

But their time in St. Louis was not to be. One cool autumn morning, Tammy and Celeste rounded the corner to their room, Lucy Dottie was sweeping the porch, surprising the young lovers. Spotting her on the steps, they dropped their hands, but it was too late. Lucy promptly turned around and walked back inside, face pinched. Things started changing after that. Lucy would come by for rent, lingering a bit long in the doorway. Sometimes she'd drop things like, "Hate to put it like this, Tammy, but you sure don't dress at all like a lady."

Tammy brushed it off, but Celeste was rattled.

"That's no way to talk to someone," Celeste snapped back at Lucy a week or so later, after Lucy slipped in a sly remark.

"Just saying, your *cousin* looks a little queer to me, Celeste," Lucy said, and she'd stand there, her tongue pressing into her bottom lip. Between the women was a growing feeling of being unsettled, as though waiting on the aftershocks after a big earthquake.

Then, that summer, Celeste and Tammy took the train to Fairground Park to swim. It was around that time that Celeste's father passed, leaving the family plot to her, his only living heir, provided that she continue to care for her ailing mother. The women were thrilled by the prospect but unwilling to discuss leaving the comforts of the city. Celeste's home was rocky and mountainous, surrounded by space, and ten times more conservative than the city. Plus, where would they work? The nearest hospital was one hundred miles away.

The Dotties were in Springfield for the weekend, so Celeste and Tammy enjoyed the anonymity of the city without inquiring eyes. Both of them stripped down to their skivvies, Ty in a tank top that showed her long torso and firm chest beneath it as it clung to her wet skin. Celeste swam in a proper swimsuit. After a half day in the water, the women sat on Dottie's back deck smoking cigarettes on one of Celeste's old quilts, feeling the sun's heat restore their warmth. They talked more about the cabin. Could they sell it? Could they rent it? Could they live on it? A little plot of land, their own cow, a cabin without anyone's eyes on them? They must have lost track of time, kissing in the warm sunlight, only to stir hearing footsteps off in the distance.

They turned to see no other than Dr. and Mrs. Dottie standing there before them, Mrs. Lucy Dottie's mouth wide open with shock. The women pulled apart as Lucy took a step toward them.

"Is this what I think it is?" she asked, bloated with audacity.

Tammy stood up to try to explain when Celeste interrupted.

"Well, what exactly do you think it is, Mrs. Dottie?" Celeste said, looking up from her seat, stretching her long bare legs before her in the sun.

Lucy kept at it. "Are you two *together?*"

"Well, ma'am, we are standing here together," Tammy answered, jumping in.

Lucy scoffed, looking Tammy up and down. "I mean, in the way a man and a woman are together."

"And what way is that?" Celeste asked, anger in the corners of her voice.

Tammy touched her arm, whispering *don't*.

"Because if you are, you can go on and git," Lucy spit.

"Don't you talk to her like an animal, Lucy," Tammy said, stepping in front of Celeste, her face still gentle.

"Unnatural. And ungodly," Lucy said harshly, her face turning red. Her husband stepped forward, looking more uncomfortable than anything.

"Alright—let's just take a minute here," Dr. Dottie said, taking his wife's elbow.

"How dare you deceive us," Lucy said, and then turned to her husband. "They lied to us, honey. We cannot stand for this. It's indecent." She stamped her foot as she spoke. "What will the other boarders think?"

"Enough, Lucy," he said firmly. "Tammy," he said gently, "we can discuss this at the office on Monday."

Lucy continued as she walked up the steps to her home. "I've told you, Don, I knew something was off about these two," her voice shrill in the air behind her.

"There's nothing off about us, Lucy," Celeste said to her back. "And since you're claiming to be so godly, let me remind you of Matthew 7."

"And what exactly is that?" Lucy asked as she turned, her voice filled with vitriol. "I find it amusing how a liar like you and a masquerader like your 'cousin,' can dare bring up the Bible at a time like this."

"Judge not, that ye be not judged," Celeste responded stonily, looking ahead at the Mississippi channeling by.

"You two can pack your bags," she said, pointing one well-lacquered fingernail at them before turning back to her ascent. "I want you out by the weekend." Lucy shot Don a withering stare before slamming the back door of their house. He raised his eyebrows at the women, placed his hat back on his head, and followed his wife inside. And with that, the move to J Road was finalized.

19

"What do you know about these howlers?" Jess asked Lillian. He was trying to hide it, but his hands had started shaking. It had started in the woods. He felt maybe it was residual from his gun going all strange, but the shaking had gotten worse. It seemed to be coming from his core, or somewhere inside his chest. He shoved his hands into his pockets and stared straight ahead, as though his posture could ward off whatever was inside of him.

"I ain't never seen one till tonight, but some of the grannies have."

"Where?"

"Marjorie spotted one by Green's Mill. Sometime 'round when I was born, Celeste said." Lillian lit the stove in darkness, prepping the kettle with dried pine needles. It was the strongest thing she had for fighting illness, a sort of blanket anti-inflammatory for whatever might be churning around in a sick person's system. "It was hunkered down in a thicket of black henbane."

"What's henbane?"

"Poisonous plant. Part of the nightshade family. Invasive." her voice trailed.

"Does the Department of Conservation know about this? I mean, I've never heard a damn thing about any howlers. Surely there's someone—"

"And you wouldn't," Lillian said. "Most people don't even believe in them. Think it's an old granny tale," she scoffed. "Anyway, they have odd ways of hunting."

"What odd ways?"

"They mimic sounds. Sounds that might draw a particular person out. For instance, when Marjorie heard one, it was around when my mother was in labor. And the howler was crying like a baby. Like a human baby. It was luring her in."

"How can an animal mimic a baby?"

"Myna Birds, Mockingbirds, even crows. It's not the only one."

"Hell of a lot meaner looking than a crow."

"Sometimes it cries, sometimes it laughs. Celeste said howlers mimic babies since they have a taste for mother's milk."

"Now that's just woman talk, Lillian."

Lillian sat back and crossed her arms. "Says the man who claims his gun was spooked."

Jess was on edge. He alternated between warily watching his wife, pacing the length of the room, and checking the property with the binoculars. They kept their voices low, the lights off, and the dogs inside.

"I need to call up Alice," Lillian said, adding honey to the tea and stirring it around with a spoon. The sound was grating to Jess. Too loud. Too sharp. He wished he could cover his ears.

"It's midnight," he said. She could see his eyes were rimmed with red. "Won't you be waking her?"

"Probably," she said. Lillian took him in as she handed him his tea, resting her hand on his slumped shoulders. He looked like he was catching a cold. She knew she'd need to be gentle with what she had to tell him. Marrying backwoods would come with certain changes in his life, but in their time together, there had been no need as of yet to talk about tinctures, howlers, powders, or the haunted J Road Lillian had fled to find a life more ordinary. Now he had brought the out-of-the-ordinary straight back to their doorstep.

Jess winced into his cup. "This tastes awful."

"Best to drink it fast," she said, taking a long sip herself. Glory Be's small toes fanned into a curl outside of her wrap. Lillian moved to the phone and dialed Alice's number, looking through the wide window at the side of their cabin, all the windows darkened. It rang three times, four. "Come on, pick up. Pick up," she said, watching through the window until the light turned on.

"Hello?" Brody answered, sleepily.

"Brody, it's Lillian next door. Please put your mama on for me. It's urgent."

Another light turned on at Alice's. Some mumbled talk before Alice came on.

"Lily-B, what's going on?"

"Alice, we've got two howlers at the water line. They just crossed over from DeJohn's."

"Howlers?" she said, her voice more alert. Lillian could hear footsteps. Jess watched her from his seat. "Are you sure?"

"Just caught them in the binoculars. Jess saw one over at the Lick yesterday when they were on the hunt. I reckon about 120 pounds each. One a little bigger than the other. I saw the hooves myself."

Lillian could hear the click of a lighter, and Alice drew in a deep breath. "You reckon it followed him back?"

"It's possible," Lillian said sadly, looking over at Jess, who fiddled with his pocketknife.

"Jess going outside to check it out?"

"Ain't no one going outside till dawn."

"I'm looking now. Can't see anything outside. What brought them out, you think?"

"I'm working on finding that out. Your goats in the barn?"

"Yes. Where are they now?"

Lillian closed her eyes and exhaled slowly. "Cove's edge. By the canoe."

Alice drew in a sharp inhale. "God damn," she said. "You weren't joking."

"Mhm." Lillian bit her lip and considered what to do next.

"Ugly as hell. Haven't ever laid eyes on one myself before right now."

Lillian could hear Alice's boys in the background making a ruckus around her.

"What do we do?" Alice whispered.

"Let me think on it," she said, squinting outside into the darkness, a feeling of doom settling in the room between her and her husband. "Suppose I'll call up the granny."

"That's a good idea. Should we call Gideon?"

Lillian felt the pulpy adrenaline of their hearts surrounding their property. "Figure he'll think us a couple of crazies," she said. She could hear Alice's breath through the receiver.

"Don't feel good looking on them, does it?"

"No, ma'am. Like something not meant to be seen. You keep Brody and Eugene close?"

"Will do. Those boys aren't even to get near the windows," Alice said sharply. "Keep me posted, okay? We've got plenty of ammo over here."

"Sure thing."

"Thanks, Lily-B," Alice said before hanging up.

Lillian turned to see Jess standing right behind her, his face shining with perspiration in the moonlight.

"Okay, now we aren't in the bedroom anymore, Lillian," his voice gritty. "I'm ready for some answers."

She watched him steadily, tempering her store of information. He would only need to know what would keep them safe. She looked past him through the uncovered windows, their reflections illuminated to the darkness outside, where a blurry figure darted off from where it stood. It was watching them. She pushed her mind outside. Sent out for their bodies for a moment. These heartbeats were slower. No adrenaline.

No fear.

Her eyes darted to the left. Alice's lights were back off.

"We need to close these blinds," she said urgently, moving to close the wood slats. Jess followed, squinting outside, trying to see what she knew he wouldn't be able to see even in daylight.

"What did Alice say?" Jess asked, following her to the window.

"Jess, if you want to be alive through the end of this weekend, I suggest you listen first and ask questions later," she said. Lillian hadn't intended on that level of sharpness, but they didn't have much time. If his feet had touched southern soil, he was in trouble, and that trouble could have very well followed him back. They had howlers on their property, hoot owls talking over the men's shoulders, and pressure from the outside she hadn't felt since she moved across Highway 7. Now there were a handful of men cut up after crossing old boundary lines. She and Jess closed the last of the slats, and he turned to face her.

"Alright," he said, his arms across his chest. "I'm listening."

Lillian walked back to her cup of tea and patted the spot beside her on the couch.

"Like I told you, I suspect you've been hexed."

"Is that why the howlers are out there?"

"I reckon they followed you home."

"Why would that be a hex?"

"Howlers are spies. They do the dirty work."

"Spies for who?"

Lillian swallowed hard and looked at Jess. "The Devil."

20

"Where y'all went tonight, well," she swallowed, hating to say it out loud. "It belongs to the other side."

"The other side?" he said, his brows knitted together. "You mean the people over there?"

Lillian paused, nodding. "And others."

"Come on. Ain't that just superstition?"

"It's just the rules around J Road, Jess. We didn't ever cross the Lick. Plenty of fishing and gigging, but from the north side. It's why I made you promise."

He exhaled loudly and looked down at his hands, pretending to fidget with his cuff.

"Besides, south of Lick Creek is rough country," she said into the darkness between them. The clock in the kitchen chimed 3:00 am. Witching hour.

"And you ain't never been?"

"Never beyond waist-deep in the creek," she answered. "I disobeyed Celeste plenty, but not ever that," she admitted, shaking her head.

"I wonder what's over that ridge anyway," he said more to himself than to Lillian. "Sam went in but didn't say much about it."

She studied his shadowed face, wondering what else he hadn't told her. "Dark nights that are reluctant to dawn," she said as his eyes met hers. "Predators without fear. Brambles in the crops. I think that's what got Sam. Thorns that branch across the walking path. They'll cut you, as you saw. Northern granny-women even talk of things—supernatural things."

"Like them howlers?"

"Other things."

"Like?"

"Witchcraft."

"How do you know for sure if you ain't ever been?" he asked.

"Celeste treated a child on the South once. Other grannies visited too. They had hushed conversations about it. There were ungodly things."

"Ungodly things?" His tone changed from defensive to fearful.

"Children born without eyes. No socket, no brow, nothing. Just smooth above the nose, all the way until the hairline."

"Christ," Jess said.

"Pigs born all wrong like. With forked tongues. Not even fit for slaughter. They just let them run free."

"You say the grannies saw all this?"

"Marjorie knows. She's seen 'em."

"And no one ever reported it?"

"Reported it? To whom?"

"The law?"

"Jess, you know our people ain't never had much to do with the law."

"Well, what about the church? They should be able to do something."

"Tried that. According to Celeste's notebooks, the Baptists cast them out. Only the Catholics got involved. Some ritual for an exorcism, I think."

"Did it work?"

"Marjorie said they needed to examine the person who was suspected of having the Devil in them. The southerners wouldn't let anyone near them. And when they did a search, they didn't find nothing but a few tore-up buildings. No people, no livestock, nothing."

"Where do you think they went?"

"Hill country is pretty vast," she said, thinking on all the crannies in their parts. Fiery Fork, Goose Creek. "I'm sure they found someplace to hide out. But some of the grannies said it was something else. They said anytime out-of-towners got close, the Devil would cast a mist over the eyes of those searching."

"Why would the Devil want anything to do with goddamn middle Missouri?" Jess asked with a scoff. "We ain't got no money, barely any resources."

"We got souls," Lillian said. "We got strong-backed men who know the land. And the womenfolk—" Lillian paused, missing Celeste then. "They manage the homestead. Their love is boundless. Devil ain't got that. I reckon that's the sort of thing he was after."

She pushed herself up with a wince and walked downstairs to the old cedar chest, pulling one of the thick notebooks from inside and bringing it back upstairs to the table. She lit a candle, her face illuminated across the table. Jess looked at her face, all lit up from below, and through her clean beauty, he thought, for just a split second, that her features looked different—nearly evil, if that was even possible.

"According to Celeste's notes," she said, "'the Devil first appeared in those parts in the 1800s. Plenty of pastors tried their hand at conversion,' she writes here, 'but it was vastly unsuccessful.'"

Jess took another sip of his tea. It had gone cold.

"In one of her notebooks dated—when was the first World War?"

"1914 or so."

"That's the entry here. 1919. Story is that two women met him walking along a dirt path. That path eventually became Highway 7. Said he, 'stepped right out of the brush and tipped his hat at them. Both reported they felt a chill move through them.'"

"Where on Highway 7?"

Lillian held her finger on the page to keep her place and looked at him straight on. "6100 North State Highway 7. South of Roach."

"And that's—"

"J Road."

"Jesus Christ, Lillian. That's a damn story."

She continued. "'Some said he took the shape of a goat, some said a crow. But he eventually made his way into the community. Did odd jobs. Real good with the ladies. Gained the trust of some of them. Probably by doing them favors. After some time, he even got some of the grannies to do his bidding. The dark grannies, likely.'"

"But did any of your people ever actually see anything?"

Lillian closed the journal and sat back. She retied her hair back up on her head before answering. "The hills are full of different kinds of, well, people, as you know. But the south—well, they're even more different. If you want to call them that. They have different ways. Some of them, the rumors say, are witches. Dark grannies. And the granny-women I grew up with say they saw some of them."

"Witches, like with broomsticks?"

"More like putting the hurt on others, without even touching them. And they move different too, she wrote."

"Like how?" he asked quickly, thinking of the blur he had seen that day.

"They move fast, almost like double time. I never seen one up close, but I've felt them. Like blurs of energy, just the black of their hair in the air behind them."

He waited a few moments before asking the next question. "What is a dark granny?"

Lillian considered his face. "They know what the grannies know. About hearth and home. The pleasures of loving this life, loving our Lord. But the dark granny, they use their knowledge for other purposes."

"Like harming?"

"Remember why Satan was cast out?"

"Pride, right?"

"Kicked out of heaven for it. Like a petulant child. And the only way he can get to God, to punish him for that rejection, is to get us to sin. Our sin hurts the Lord."

Jess felt his stomach lurch from the tea. He felt off.

"The dark grannies did his work to tempt us. Lured men into bed. Lured women into the drink. Or these days, crank. To sloth, envy. We don't know if they even know the evil they do. Celeste said many folk have logic behind their reasons. They want their little scratch, is all. But that don't make it right. They believe they are pleasing the Devil, so to them, what they do is just fine." Lillian leaned toward her husband, taking in his cold features. "But it ain't fine, Jess. They were all but chased off some time ago. Many crossed the Lick for unsettled lands."

"I don't see how you can see the Devil and want to do evil. Evil feels wrong."

"But to most, sin feels good. It's why we do it," she said. She thought of the tug she'd felt so long ago. The beckoning of its warm embrace. If only she were to offer herself to Him. She looked over her husband. He'd caught whatever it was Sam had. It hovered around their little cabin. She shivered to think of her man, all brightness and heart, stung up with whatever that presence had inside of it.

"Do you think one of these 'dark grannies' took Sam's hound?"

"Not sure. What I do believe is that you and the boys had a curse thrown your way."

Sam quickly asked, "How do you know if you've been cursed?"

She looked down at her tea. "Sudden illness. Livestock dying off."

"Why would anyone curse a man for looking for his hound that run off?"

"Some do it for revenge, I suppose. Or if you've taken something of theirs."

He sat up straight up then. "We didn't take one damn thing from the south side of the Lick. Hell, not one firearm was discharged."

"The taking doesn't always have to be a *thing*, Jess. It could be something thematic. Like going back on your word or touching sacred ground."

"So the south of the Lick is sacred now?" He stood up with an angry pace.

"To them, it is. Northerners swore to not trespass years ago. To leave them to their own devices. And if you boys did, then I'm just saying, they might have seen that as a sort of invitation to come after you."

"How exactly does someone turn dark?" Jess asked, rubbing on his neck. "Are they bit or something?"

"Grannies say the Devil taught them his ways. Started small. Like stirring up trouble with a pox, messing with a marriage, causing anxiety, mostly. Cure is in the Bible. Every cure for a man's soul. Reading and writing, it disarms the beast. But somewhere, somehow those people realized they had more power doing harm than doing good, I suppose."

"What did the good grannies do when others turned, well, bad?"

"Way Celeste saw it, it was best to keep their space. She said that darkness might have more power in the short term, but everyone knows it's bad. Truly, everything longs for the light."

Everything was finally making sense in Jess' mind. He stared at his hands as though they held the answers to something he was pondering before breaking into a croupy series of coughs. He reckoned it was time to start talking himself. "I don't want to alarm you, honey, but ever since I came to bed tonight, I feel like I've got something coming on."

Lillian felt her stomach bottom out a bit. "I thought you might be feeling poorly," she said, forcing her voice to be calm. She moved to examine his face in the moonlight. "You don't feel warm, though."

"I know," Jess said despondently. "I feel cold, don't I?"

Lillian loved him hard then. She put her arm around him.

"I should maybe check in with the urgent care?"

"I don't reckon the urgent care has anything for getting spellt. What hurts?"

"My throat feels all swollen. Like there's something stuck in it."

She felt around his throat with her fingers.

"Are those things still out there?"

Lillian fingered the stone around her neck which lay between the warmth of her and Glory Be, eyeing the telephone. She felt the heartbeats move around to the side of the cabin, but the powders held. Wendy growled at her feet. "Due west. I need to call up Marjorie."

"What do they want from me?" Jess looked like a child that had been caught in a bold-faced lie.

Pound of flesh, Lillian thought. "Revenge," Lillian said, and Jess heard the edge of anger in her voice. "It wants revenge."

"This is too much."

"Celeste used to treat southerners back before I was born. She said you can know one by their eyes. They're all wrong. Pupils were changed somehow. Sideways."

"Like a goat's?"

"She said their eyes had cowls that never quite sloughed off. Sometimes the babies were born still in their sacs."

"How do they see—with that cowl on their eyes?"

"Something about it made them see better at night, I think," she said, feeling the bitter tea warm her belly. The motion-detecting light around the back of the cabin turned on. Jess jumped in his seat, and Lillian tracked the pulp of the heartbeat. Jess started to stand slowly, and she put out her hand, directing him back to his seat.

"It's alright. They can't get in."

"How do you know?"

"I've got a spell on the cabin."

"Lillian, you're starting to scare me."

"Don't be—"

"I'm getting my gun."

"No time for that, Jess. They're too fast for bullets." She moved to the window, peeking out. "Did anything else out of the ordinary happen? You hear anything? See anyone?"

Jess made his way down the steps to his bedroom closet, grabbing his rifle. No time to dig out the shotgun, he thought.

"Didn't see," he said from the bedroom, his voice booming. "Heard."

Lillian held her breath as he came back to stand before her, leaning the gun against the corner.

"There was laughter. Like a child's."

"Did you see a child?"

"Kurt did. Just heard. Right when Sam got cut up. Sun was up, shining right through that thicket, and I looked everywhere through my scope. There was no one. Sounded like they were right there, but there was no one."

"What'd y'all do?"

"We weren't close to any of the shacks down there. I thought maybe it was a screech owl."

"Could have been," she said, knowing full well it wasn't. "Did you hear anything from the dog—a bark, a yelp?"

"Nothing. We called and called, but not even the twigs underfoot were snapping. He must have covered some ground."

"That dog ain't making his way home, Jess."

"Don't say that, Lillian."

She moved past him quickly then, grabbing a pair of rubber gloves from beneath the kitchen sink and pressing them into Jess' hands.

"Put these on," she said quickly, then opened her cabinet as she rustled around with her free hand, the other holding the baby in her sling. She pulled out a small vial of lemon balm before steering him ahead toward the bathroom beside the kitchen, the one Sam had used that evening.

"This is lemon balm. Celeste used to call it Sweet Melissa. It's antiviral when mixed into teas. It's also used to detect infection."

"What do I do with it?" he asked, holding the gloves in his thumb and forefinger.

"I want you to sprinkle some into the basin," she told him, standing back. "If something was hanging on Sam, it'll show us."

Jess pulled on the gloves. "How will a hex show from just lemon balm?"

"You'll see." Lillian made a circle around the basin with her finger. "Right here," she pointed. "And don't touch anything else, you hear?"

Jess took the lemon balm and sprinkled the yellow liquid into the sink basin. He moved back next to Lillian, who kept both arms around the baby. The two of them stood silently before the old dripping faucet, the clock in the kitchen making slow clicks, the two of them looking at the sink as if it were about to communicate. After about twenty seconds, the drops of water in the sink basin started changing. First, a sort of slow vibration or movement, as though they were trying to merge back together.

Jess' eyes widened. "What the hell?"

The droplets then began to bubble, first just little iridescent pops before changing color from clear to a sort of pink and then into blood red, right there in the sink where Sam had washed up. Jess jumped back into Lillian, his arms out as though to shield her.

"Now the towel," she nudged.

He stared, his mouth open.

"Quick, Jess."

Jess shook the balm on the towel, his other hand out as though to hold his wife back.

Two red spots appeared slowly in the center of the towel, impressions from Sam's eyes. Lillian and Jess looked at each other, frozen in their places.

"What the hell, Lillian?"

"It's the hex," she told him steadily, watching the balm bubble around the bloody smudges.

They backed into the kitchen with calculated steps, as if walking in a minefield. A cold dread hovered in the silence.

"I don't want any bastard howler or witch after my wife and child," Jess said, a new anger in his tone. "And what if I brought something home to you? What if it's catching?" he said as his eyes darted between the mirror and his wife.

Lillian stepped closer to him, gently taking his chin in her hand. "I know that people have crossed before and been okay, Jess." She said this as much to herself as to her husband. She turned his head to the side, examining his lymph nodes. "Anything other than your throat bothering you? Your eyes?" she asked, running her fingers across his temple. As she moved her hands around his throat, she could not feel exactly what was off. But there was something. It was his smell. He looked the same, talked the same, and whatever this was, she thought, was hiding from her. She wished at that moment she had been learned up in generals like Celeste instead of just midwifery. Whatever Jess and his men had stumbled upon, it had latched somewhere secret onto Sam, working its way into their world to spread discord. It was now coiled inside of him in his own home, where he, a single man, thankfully, would have to tend to his punishment without a healer within fifty miles.

"I don't even know anymore," he said in between panicky breaths.

Suddenly, there was a scratch at the back door. One long stroke, like thick nails against a board. Both of them jumped, and the dogs were at the door then, their barks piercing the silence. In her mind's eye, Lillian checked the clusters of selenite at each level of the cabin. It would bend inward if one were trying to get inside. She sent out for the hearts.

Two. Same size as the ones from earlier. And just outside. With just a few feet of space and eight inches of oak between them and her family. Jess stood in front of his wife and child, watching a shadow cross the porch.

"Is what cursed us waiting just past that door?"

She turned slowly toward him. "That one is just the messenger."

"How do you know?"

"Can you hear any of the night sounds? Katydids? Crickets?"

Jess stood, his face pale, and listened. Silence.

21

Celeste and Tammy packed their trunks as the bell of the Delta Queen rang, cutting over the album spinning on their gramophone. Celeste folded her dresses, still reeling from the eviction, while Tammy was running over their options in her head.

"She can't just turn us out like this," Celeste said, shaking her head.

"Obviously she can," Tammy said, dragging one of the steamers from the closet to the center of the room with a thump. "It's her room anyway."

"I can't believe her husband didn't speak up. What a chicken."

"He has to live with her," Tammy said, raising her eyebrows. "Anyway, honey, I've been thinking about it, and I think this is a good thing for us. Get us out of the city. And we won't have to pay rent."

"I suppose that's something."

"That something is fantastic."

Celeste sighed. "What if we have the same problems in the country as we do here?"

"Like bigoted landlords?"

"Or worse."

"Won't be an issue if we're the new landlords." She looked out the window at the river raging by. "Plus, despite our view, it's crowded here. The river is crowded with boats, polluted with sewage. Factory runoff, even. I, for one, would love some fresh air."

"But I don't know a single queer person in Camden County. I mean, not one. We will be losing our little Gaslight community here. Off J Road, it will be just us."

Tammy walked over and sat beside her on the bed. She pushed a strand of white-blonde hair behind her ear. "It'll be a gas, babe. All that open land? We will have privacy. That's something we've never had before. Maybe we can even get dogs."

"We should go even farther, Tammy. New York. Paris. I know we wouldn't have to hide there. We could walk around for the whole world to see. I mean, could you even imagine?"

Tammy looked Celeste's hopeful face over before responding. "I don't know if any city is all the way safe for us, babe." Tammy slipped one of her arms around Celeste's warm waist. "Think of all the money we'd be saving up."

"You don't know the rural parts like I do, Tammy. If we are discovered, it would mean trouble. Big trouble."

"So, we won't be discovered," Tammy insisted.

"How can you be sure?" Celeste asked. "Two unmarried women living together. We would never be able to touch. If someone caught us touching or kissing, we'd be doomed. Plus, with no man around, there would always be eyes on us," Celeste said, kicking at a bunched-up corner of the rug.

Tammy lit a cigarette and paced back and forth a bit. She thought over being direct with Celeste about something she'd only read about in the medical journals. The chuff-chuff of a steamboat interrupted the silence.

"Okay, hear me out. I've got two words for you: Joan of Arc, Deborah Samson."

"That's technically five words," Celeste said, stuffing stockings in her steamer.

"Five pertinent words," Tammy said and waited, watching her face.

"Okay, I'll bite. What about Joan of Arc, and who is Deborah Samson?" Celeste asked.

Tammy squatted in front of Celeste on the bed, an edge of excitement in her tone. "Think about it. Joan of Arc cut her hair short, wore trousers. Deborah Samson, another 'masquerader,' was an American soldier. These women dressed as men. After years of service, Samson was eventually discovered. They weren't even mad when they found out who she was. I read she was actually medaled."

"What are you talking about?"

"I'm talking about a new identity, babe."

Celeste shook her head. "Tammy, we can't turn you into a boy."

Tammy inched closer, took Celeste by the arms. "Yes, we can. Think about it. I dress like a man anyway. I'm handsome like a fella. And in a new town, no one would have any idea. Plus, if I'm your husband, no man will bother us. I'd be the man of the house. There'll be no talk at all. We could live freely."

Celeste scanned Tammy's face, realized she was actually considering this. "But you'd have to change so much. Everything."

Tammy touched the side of Celeste's pale face, loving her even more for that. "You changed your home for me. I can change some for you too."

"Are you really serious about this?" Celeste asked. She took the cigarette from Tammy and took a long drag.

Tammy examined herself in the mirror with an exaggerated pose. "Already have the trousers. I just need a proper haircut.

Celeste fanned her face with a newspaper as she watched Tammy. She considered her long legs and reached for her then.

"Oh," Tammy said, moving into her embrace. "And a new name."

Celeste kissed her shoulder.

"Something tough," Tammy said, shoving her hands in her pockets and walking with a swagger. "Like Cary Grant. Gary Cooper?"

Celeste giggled. "That's a little much."

Tammy took back the cigarette and leaned against the open window.

Celeste pulled up her legs beneath her and watched her lovingly. "What about something benign? James or Charles?"

"I want something with a T, so I don't have to get used to it," Tammy said.

"Tommy?"

"No, that's my cousin's name. He's a real dimwit. We need something unique."

"Maybe from a book?" Celeste asked.

"Wait—who is the one from Homer, who gives the advice?"

"Hermes?" Celeste said.

"No—it's—T. T . . . Tyresius!"

"That's a mouthful," Celeste said.

"You don't like it?"

"Well, it's a T name for sure. And you're kind of dark and swarthy, like a Greek."

"That's it," Tammy paced excitedly. "Tyresius lives as both man and woman. This is also my plan," she said, looking earnestly at Celeste.

"If it keeps us safe, then I'm happy," Celeste said, standing to meet Tammy.

"So, you like it then?"

Celeste pulled her back into an embrace in front of the open window. The hazy steel-truss bridge shimmered in the summer's distant heat. Voices of children and their stickball rang up from the street below. If someone had been walking along Main Street just then, with the Mississippi to their left and they'd looked up, they would see two figures in a window. One's arm fanning her face, her white-blonde hair pulled back, a sheen of sweat on her breast as she faced her lover, just inches from her, his hand on the small of her back. If that person were to pause their journey, they would have thought these two so in love, that nothing would have the power to bust it up.

Celeste longed to be alongside Tammy, to be loved by her. "God, I love you," she said, pressing herself against Tammy's long, taut body. She traced her fingers along her waist.

"How are you going to cover these?" she asked, her hands framing Tammy's curves.

"I'll find a tailor," Tammy said, moving in to kiss her, the summer heat between their bodies.

"Tammy—" Celeste started before Tammy interrupted her.

"No—call me Tyresius," she said, pressing her forehead against hers. "I want to be newly baptized."

"Okay, Tyresius," Celeste giggled, her lips moving to her neck, her shoulder as her fingers cupped her breasts.

"Tell me you love me," Tammy said. She started to unzip her skirt. "Say my new name."

"I love you," Celeste said, crawling slowly atop her lover as the steamboat's mellow whistle sounded on the river.

◉◉◉

The next parts happened fast: a wire to Celeste's family, two train tickets, the key to their rented room taped to a blank postcard on their stripped bed.

They left no forwarding address.

The next day, an arrival in exhaustion half the state over waiting until dusk for the forty-mile trip over poorly marked roads to the property. That first day they traveled to the family plot. It was so covered in brush they had to borrow the neighbor's tribe of goats to get it cleaned up. Celeste's hands were so blistered after that first day Tammy had to feed her bites of their canned beef stew.

Celeste introduced Tammy as her husband, Tyresius St. James, from St. Louis, but said they could call him "Ty," as everyone at the university did. Celeste's mother, legally blind from cataracts and exhausted from life, held out a limp hand, nodding at the space between the two women. Celeste and Tyresius pulled their two chests and gramophone into the little cabin, which they swept, furnished with colorful items from local shops, and hung-up fly strips. That first month, Ty used local Eastern Red cedar to build two slatted Adirondacks so they could spend evenings on the screened porch and watch the creek rush by.

By the start of the next year they had met most, if not all, of their neighbors, established a vegetable garden, planted a small orchard in the rocky steep at the edge of the property, and set up their own medical office out of the back trailer off J Road from two card tables covered in homespun Wether's wool Afghans from the Brady's homestead off Highway 5. They had only female patients and their children that first winter. No one suspected a thing.

With her new identity, Tyresius was able to walk in a new lane of power she had never before experienced. Assumed male, she received invites to FFA meetings to discuss local Camden County agriculture, learning about Ozark medicine and the best perennials for their growing zone. She was invited to four different Protestant men's groups; hell, she was even offered a spot on the local school Board of Education without even having applied. The generous bounty of power held by men, restricted to only men, filled her with an unbelieving awe. She took every medical leadership opportunity offered to her, bringing back snippets of information to Celeste, who, not having received the same warm political welcome, ingested the data to tend to her busy stream of patients. But mostly, Tyresius spent time working in their small clinic as Yarb doctor alongside his wife, the young granny-woman. They treated all sorts of ailments, even practiced some dentistry. By 1951, there were nearly two dozen Ozark granny-women spread out across the mountains, but only three in Camden County. There was Celeste, a young apprentice named Marjorie LeftHand who came down from Kansas City, and Lottie Smith, a native woman of advanced age who was an invaluable source of information for the other grannies and Tyresius. Celeste's mother, Mammy, lived in the main house, Celeste and Tyresius in the trailer out back. And happiness born of safety snuck up to them before they even realized what it was they were feeling.

22

My name is Lillian Black. I am the granddaughter of Celeste Black, an Ozark granny-woman whose people settled in these parts even before we were free from the English. If you are not from these parts, then you should know that granny-women are medicine women who assist in all sorts of healing in Ozark land. You may have heard about how granny-women are sometimes feared by city folk, that they dabble in dark magic, but Celeste was no practitioner of witchcraft. She was a woman of the light. Celeste was the Lick's common granny until her death one year ago. I, her only surviving kin, am her sole apprentice. My studies are in midwifery.

Our people's homestead has always been the land north of Lick Creek in Camden County, Missouri. Our hamlet can be found in the central hills of the Ozarks, near Niangua off Highway J, commonly known as J Road by the locals. Our ancestors were Scotch-Irish Jesuit yeoman farmers from the west of Europe known for their horses and hunting dogs. They traveled through rough weather to the middle west after landing in this country, first settling in Ste. Genevieve for the Jesuits in the group to find schools. But two brothers within that party found the city too modern, their ways too European, so they took off farther west, settling in the quiet hills of central Missouri almost fifty years before Missouri was even made a proper state. In their village, they first made camp and provided it with their name, *Sealbhadair cù dubh*. According to Celeste's library, translated from the Scottish, their name means "keeper of the black dog." Besides the camp, they opened a church, carved an altar, planted seeds from trade, found wives, and then produced children—one each. Their children continued their traditions, and then their grandchildren. However, no offspring of the brothers ever produced more than one child. Some called that a gift, some a curse. But it's been hundreds of years, and nothing has changed.

Celeste kept a series of journals, mostly medical. I learned at her knee most of my life but have had to consult these repeatedly since she passed. After she was buried, I sold off most everything but the timber, a few household items, like her old gramophone and hope chest, and these journals. They are the most valuable. They contain nearly eight years of medical notes. However, the cabin where I grew up still stands, empty on our land.

After Jess and I married, he moved me and Celeste's hope chest into our cabin, and I've been going through them slowly, I must admit, as her tight script isn't quite what I am used to. The obstetrics chapters, though, have been my focus, and in one section, she noted the prevalence of the RH-negative constitution as the cause of the one-child syndrome in the family. Celeste wrote there was no tincture for this condition. She herself only had the one child, my mother. And my mother only had me. So, the family line of those two brothers is now settled with me. Or with Glory, I suppose. Celeste once told me I would have several children of my own, but I can't imagine how.

Celeste presided over six thousand healings before her death at the unnaturally old age of 109. Many people didn't believe her age, but I had seen her birth certificate, dated to 1915 and containing the embossed seal of Camden County. The day I arrived at her cabin to collect her personals, I found it in the box below her bed, stored with some old photographs. There was some jewelry, some notes in another's longhand, a coil of yellowish hair tied in a faded ribbon, and a black and white photograph of Celeste and the man who had once been her husband. Celeste had been tall and willow-thin with a bolt of white-blonde hair behind her. The man stood just around her height, was slight-boned and dark-featured. He had a serious face. Feline looking. They had matching Mozarkite. The man wore his on his ring finger. Celeste on a necklace which I now wear in her memory.

Celeste had been married just that one time, but the marriage did not last, and he moved north. She never spoke of him to me. Lots of people had theories about all that, but they were just that.

Stories.

Women on their own have always had it hardest.

Celeste was first known in these parts as Celeste "Keeper of the Black Dog," though that surname was shortened to "Black" some time before my mother's birth on account of it being too long to fit on the deed's paperwork. She was known around the north side of the Lick as just Celeste or C. Black. She called me Lily-B. It's the name the women of J Road have always called me. Jess always uses my full name, and I prefer that.

The granny-women in the Ozarks during Celeste's time helped with all things the land-loyal government distrusters needed help with: birthing, dying, tuberculosis, tick bites, rabies, food poisoning, suicide attempts, gunshots, blood diseases, and, of course, witching. Granny-women could run circles around those Yarb doctors who came by after all the action, but who asked for paper money. And Celeste was the first choice of the north of Lick Creek grannies. There were other services performed. Mostly services protecting women who were taken against their will, but there were also love charms and fertility charms. The grannies didn't bother much with those. They took an oath similar to what the government doctors took: Don't ever put the hurt on anyone. And Celeste never did. Marjorie said that many a woman came by looking for spells to put on a local boy to make him love her, but Celeste would often recommend the same things she herself practiced: reading the Bible and using her words. If the boy didn't see her gifts, he wasn't fit to be her husband.

There are a few reasons why I left the cabin off J Road. The simplest reason is my man, Jess Carlton Cedars. It is less dangerous for a woman to bed down with a good man and have a proper church with a roof than for her to live alone, as Celeste would attest to, had she still been living. Another is the property was in structural decline, worth nothing aside from the acreage it stood on. A few menfolk offered to buy it off me once Celeste passed, but the price wasn't right, and I didn't appreciate them trying to take advantage of a local woman. I am no simpleton. A woman deserves honest neighbors, but money makes the best of men twist about. See Matthew 6:24. I left Celeste and Marjorie, who promised they'd take the last spring's earnings for a new roof, but that never did come to pass. Celeste passed soon after, and Marjorie, elderly herself, moved her things into a room with a handicap ramp behind Mimosa Beach. My husband will do what he sees fit with the premises once the time is right.

The other reason I left J Road involves something I haven't yet told anyone. Putting it simply, I had eyes on me. I don't mean curious neighbors, neither. This was something bigger. Something from across the Lick. It came from the trees, or maybe it was part of the land itself. I've been churchgoing since before I could remember, and this didn't feel like Grace, for it took none of my sending out to pick up on this. Whatever it was, it found me.

And though I couldn't quite put a finger on what this watching was or what it wanted, the older I got, the stronger the feeling grew. Like a pinprick of intuition when I was little. More curious than menacing. The year I turned twelve, and discovered my gift, the pinprick grew into a flush of feeling. I'd follow a rabbit after she disappeared into the thicket or one of Marjorie's crows after I lost sight of it and feel it as an invitation. Just a little fluttering of movement in my chest, just a little lift under the heart.

When I'd first cast out, I'd sometimes pick up on my watcher across the creek. Always silent, always just out of sight. I assumed this is what all northerners felt, part of why they were wary of the south. But that year, the year I started my menses, Celeste read to me of Eve's seduction, opened the book to the photograph with the glossy image of Eve taking the fruit from the Devil, his serpent body coiled around a tree, the muscles rippling with anticipation.

"You keep your wits, child," Celeste had said, as though she had known what lingered in the dark timber. "The Devil hath power to assume a pleasing shape."

She had been right. Whatever watched was a dark sort of beckoning. Its slow, pulpy heart had me in its crosshairs. It was as though I had been chosen by an older power, as though my watcher was the forest itself. But when I tried to catch its gaze, the water muddied.

Once that summer, and only once, I tried to speak to it. Learned my lesson, and fast enough. Celeste had been off with a patient, so I walked across the brush to the banks of the Lick, felt the cold sand beneath my toes, the creek's tiny white caps breathing as it rippled beside the active banks. I sent out, my pulse inching within the massive, slow beat of the forest. And without missing my cast, the watcher caught me, like a key in a lock. I froze, held by it. And then I felt a cold tug. Right at the base of my throat. I remember gasping. Another tug. The second one jerked me forward. I imagined eyes opening in the south's dark timber. Eyes without a face, suspended in the treeline's coldness. Another. Like a parent might use on a child not budging. I would not say I was being pulled over but rather extended a trenchant welcome. But even at twelve, I remembered Celeste's warning. There was no crossing the Lick. I opened my eyes, closing the cast, released so fast that I fell back into the dirt. I sat there panting beside the Lick's gurgle.

I never reached out again. Never felt so big a presence. Until whatever had been outside our cabin the night the boys trespassed. The howler was big game. It was doing the watcher's bidding.

Time passed, and I grew. So did the feeling. Wherever I walked, I carried one of our guns, a handful of shells in my pockets. If I wore shoes, I carried a Bowie in my boot. I kept the boundary, and the presence lingered from just out of range. It felt, for lack of any other way to describe it, like a calling over. Like a beckoning. I had never known a man, but this had felt like what the books in the cabin called courtship. I was being silently courted.

When I turned nineteen and met Jess, I nearly forgot about its shadow. Until my wedding day, the day I felt it most strongly. The day Jess drove me off that property forever. I turned around to see Celeste and Marjorie standing in their skirts, waving at the bed of the truck as their forms got smaller, and just beyond them, the great pulse of the forest. While Celeste shooed me off to my future, this presence seemed to pull me back.

Folks on either side of Lick Creek do not mix. Celeste told me she did not travel to the south of Lick Creek but once in her long life. First, it was strongly discouraged by our people. Even our Jesuit forefathers wrote that their attempts to converse with the southerners never did go well, though the men made several attempts. Celeste's notes mention they were "cursed by the Babel." Secondly, it was a hazardous trek. There was no path, no roads paved, no electricity. As a result, there was no communication, so there were plenty of stories in its place. All of those stories dissuaded us. The grannies whispered that the menfolk walked around unclothed like animals, that they committed the sin of rage. Their women were rumored to be feral, never washing, menstruating without coverage. They had their own church, a sort of country gathering space, with no altar and no sacraments. The Jesuits suspected that inbreeding was the cause of their wildness. Some suggested their ways may have been attributed to bad water, but we pulled water from the same source. They kept no assemblies, nor did they keep livestock. It was speculated, though not confirmed, that one of their black practices was cannibalism.

In the two hundred years or so since our people settled the Lick, the rift between the northerners and southerners only increased. By the time I was born, things had settled into a sort of ancient understanding. We stayed away from one another. They wanted no part of our cities, and we wanted no part of their black magic. There was chatter about powerful people in those parts. People who would turn on you if you looked at them wrong. Then your babies could be born hexed, or your livestock would drop dead, or your crops could fail. The old timers talked of plants that could sting and infect you. Animals that could swap shapes with one another. So, no one traveled to the south of Lick Creek. Celeste said she once treated a northerner woman who lost her way, accidentally crossing over before realizing her error. The woman had stepped on some sort of thorn. It led to infection of her whole leg. When Celeste's tinctures couldn't heal her, she called the Yarb doctor. When he couldn't heal her, they sent her to the city doctor. He cut her foot off at the ankle and gave her a cane and a false foot that fit into a sneaker she hobbled around on until the day she died. The woman refused to speak of it and crossed herself whenever anyone inquired as to the cause of her injuries. It seems that those who ventured south came back with a sort of hurt on them they never recovered from. If they came back at all.

Celeste said she reckoned the southerners had their own granny-women. When I asked where they were learned up, she told me she didn't know, but the word had been that they learned their gifts from the Devil himself. That was high talk. Some said they lay with one another, saying it kept their bloodlines pure. The southerners all had the same sort of slanted pupil you don't see in the north. Helped them see in the dark since there ain't no electricity running on the south side. Everyone on the north could feel that dark magic from across that wide creek. It was a sort of bad electricity from their side, making you dizzy when you got too close.

Celeste had my mother under unusual circumstances. No one attended the birth; Celeste presided over it herself. On her own. It sounds country, I know, but many a granny-woman took care of birthing their own babies, especially if the weather were bad or if they didn't trust the neighbors to help with much aside from fetching clean towels. The father was a city man by the name of Tyresius who came up along the Missouri River where his family made their money in flour-milling. Weak-hearted, I'd gamble to say, since he left my granny alone to raise up the child. Celeste met him when working in the city as a nurse. He was a researcher for St. Louis University. Sometime after the child was born, the relationship ran its course. Celeste did not speak of him to me. Anything I heard came from gossip from the neighbors, few of whom even remembered him since it had been nearly half a century since their marriage ended. In the photograph of the two of them, he stood tallish with neat, dark hair and in a physician's coat. He had deeply set, dark eyes and was slight in build. They stood two feet apart at least, a table of laboratory materials between them. On the ring finger of his left hand was a large ring with a clay-colored stone. Celeste had the same stone on a thin leather strap she wore around her neck. Before she died, I asked her if she had loved that man in the photograph, and she just looked me over before answering that she had. I did not bury her with her necklace. I now wear it around my own neck. I wanted a piece of her to walk with me, though she is with our Lord in the next life.

Raising my mother alone, Celeste assumed incorrectly the girl would grow into her gifts as Celeste herself had. My mother, however, was very stubborn-minded. I know that in adolescence, she developed a taste for grain whiskey, or Brown Bear Hooch as the tavern owners called what hillfolk cooked up themselves in their unlit sheds. My grandmother was a teetotaler and claims my mother's taste for the poison came while in the government school off Highway 5, where she met those doomed to despair by the country and so would dull their light with liquor. My mother had balked at my grandmother's rules, painting her fingernails and face, and refusing church when she first started her menses. She eventually ran away from home around the age of fifteen. She washed back up some ten or so years later, her body bruised in ways even Celeste, accustomed to country injury, could not speak of to me. Celeste took her in again and soon realized she was already pregnant with me. She stayed with Celeste through her seventh month or so, unhappy with the discomfort of pregnancy, which can be hard on some women. After an unusually fast birth in her childhood bedroom at Celeste's cabin, presided over by Marjorie—the notes in Celeste's notebooks say I was born quick and in a rush of gray-colored liquid, small for my age, refusing the breast and crying nonstop for nearly a week—my mother once again ran off, this time with Celeste's coin purse, thinking it was a savings, when in reality, it was little more than a handful of change and some prayer cards. My grandmother, in her late seventies by then, did not chase her daughter but instead invested in a wet nurse whose own child had just been weaned, gave me a name (she chose the name Lillian, after her own mother), and raised me up, learning me to walk by holding tight to her apron strings.

My mother's body was found three days after, mangled beyond repair when her automobile went off the road and into the ravine off Route 1. According to the coroner, due to the time in the ravine or the amphetamines in her blood, she looked older than Celeste did in her own advanced age. So, Celeste became my mother. I was to call her Celeste, though. She said the word "mother," well, that was special, and our relationship was a different sort of sacred.

There are no photographs of my mother. I do not even know her name.

Her face could be anyone's in the crowd.

Though it sounds like the birth of sadness, my life did not register my mother's absence. My main toil was isolation, never loneliness. There is a difference. My childhood was white clover and trefoil perfuming the air. It was the vetch spread under my toes. It was errands to collect arnica, streamside, for Celeste's tinctures. That was the closest I ever got to the south. I'd part the branches of the willow and look across the creek to where the land was forbidden and where everything was shadow. Occasionally, a blurred body or two would pass across the way. I never saw more than that flicker of movement, but I always felt us sensing each other. Me, their hearts; them, well, whatever they sensed. When I told Celeste about spotting one of them, she said they were as suspicious of us as we were of them. I protested that their darkness was too much, and she explained the canopy was too thick to allow sunlight to touch the earth beneath the trees, and though the soil was fertile, nothing grew. It wasn't born to be bad. It was made that way. Hurt people hurt, the Christians say, and hurt people had made their land sour. They toiled it, their men turning to the drink, their fists between them, their hate settling into the crops, turning the corn to dust, the dogs turning against their masters, their womenfolk producing stillborn in more frequency than any other county in the state.

The south of Lick wasn't always held by the Devil. The grannies claimed that, according to hill people, it had once been a steep country populated by orchards and surrounded by woody shrubs and living mulches. Then the settlers moved in. Time passed, the first and second World War took many of the boys, and the people stopped tending. Once an Army truck dropped off two southside soldiers who had fought the Germans and survived. According to some neighbors, the boys took one look at the old country and got back into the truck, eventually hitching a ride to St. Louis.

Time passed. The southerners moved farther inland. Their orchards grew gnarled, the fruit rotted on the ground. Two years later, when I had just started reading, Celeste said, the Codling moths and ground beetles came like something out of Revelation. That first morning, the women looked into the forest, mistaking the full-grown larvae in their coarse, silken cocoons having settled into the scales of bark for a late spring blooming. Once they spotted the pestilence, they backed away, pulling the children from the forest floor more deeply inland north. Then the women moved to neem the whole of the north end to prevent the infestation from moving over. I remember that spring, though I was not yet writing my full name. The beekeeper two plots over boarded up his hives and moved them across the highway then filled his smoker with the neem, moving slowly creekside, combing the whole creek bed with the insecticide. It was that day I peeked from behind Celeste's clover across the Lick to see the body of a southern child, not much older than me, swatting the moths from the trees like it was some kind of game.

When Celeste spoke of her one trip across the Lick to the south, she said she had been wholly unprepared for what she saw. She had been called over once, years before my mother's birth, to assist in some dentistry, and said there were children who lived clustered together on the land, eyes wild in their faces, moving about like grazing animals. They dug holes to sleep in, foraged for berries. Unable to tolerate the cruelty of their fathers or the inability of their mothers to protect them, they ran to the hills where the wind shaped them. Celeste worked on a girl nearly woman-aged who could not speak. Her father held her mouth open for the extraction. As Celeste was wrapping up, the woman bit down, cutting her hand nearly halfway to the bone. It left a scar I'd trace with my fingers when I was young and eye-level with her hand. Celeste had pried herself free, and the man just laughed. She wrapped her hand and hurried back toward the shallow end of the creek. She told us she had the peculiar feeling of being followed, but every time she turned around on the bumpy road, there was no one there. The laughter continued, though no one appeared. On the third time, instead of turning, she pulled a pocket mirror out, lifting it before her eyes to see behind her. Not twenty yards behind was a woman in a white dress, squatting in the dusty road, urinating. Without turning again, Celeste walked steadily home and refused all work on the south side from that day on. She treated her wound with potato poultice and hung talismans in every doorframe.

Celeste wasn't the only one with stories about the south of Lick. When the other grannies would gather for prayer, I'd press my ear to the door and hear them talk of what they had seen:

Some say it all started with a Quapaw woman fleeing robbers at the creek's south side. She had been on foot, followed by men on horseback. They found her dead from a bite wound on the back. She had been the last good woman left on the south. Even Indian magic couldn't save her from the Devil.

One woman who kept trying to escape the south would send messages with pigeons across the creek. She was found dead in a pile of her birds' feathers. Postmaster said back when his route still extended south, whenever he was on her old property, he'd hear the birds' cooing, but there were never any to be seen.

Another woman who'd drowned in the Lick was sometimes seen walking the southern banks in a white robe. The granny-women said she had fish netting for hair and webs between her fingers.

A southern child had been spotted at the treeline with clear blue eyes like the creek, and instead of teeth, fangs like an adder, though those don't nest in Ozark country.

A girl had been nearly cut in half by her father's Farmall. When the law went to inspect the crime scene, they claimed they found the girl standing beside the barn. She walked toward them, split in half to let the men pass through, just to have both halves reunite once she passed.

Man at the filling station at 7 and J-Road said the old woman who once lived at the end of his property was buried with her jewels. Grave robbers kept after the plot, but they were always guarded by the goats she kept. Once he was walking past her old shack, and her goats were on him. Said they bit anyone who got near the grave.

One granny-woman's mother was dying from a fever. At the end, she told her family that they could trust the crows, but the buzzards were one with the southern spirit. If you needed information on the Devil, you'd have to catch a buzzard when the sun was low in the west. But to get it to talk, you'd have to pay in carrion. Or, you could seek him out yourself. To see the Devil in his true form, just look square between your horse's ears.

But most say the Devil got into the Lick through the murder of the Boyd baby. A woman, a girl rather, given over in marriage to settle her father's gambling debt, was crazed from the birth. Granny women treat this malady with healers, but there was no such medicine on the south. The girl killed her baby and fed it to her husband. He never knew the difference. When he found out, he killed her with the ax that had been stowed under the bed in the delivery. He buried the ax with the dead girl and then shot himself with his rifle on the fresh grave. And the flowers on her grave, they say, never wither.

These snatches of stories hung in my mind like unworn suits in the back of the closet.

23

By the time Sam pulled onto the gravel outside of his apartment, he could barely see straight. His legs were pulsing with pain, which spread up into his torso. He felt cold all over, and his vision was blurry. His plan was to get inside, check out the damage, and drive over to Mercy to get his cuts checked out, but what he really wanted to do first is scope the property to see if BJ had made his way back. His heart was stinging something fierce, worse even than when his mama had died.

His place was dark inside, and he bumped hard into the table, right onto the part of his leg that had been cut up. "God dammit," he shouted out, grabbing his leg with one hand while reaching for the light switch with the other. When the lights came on, he saw that his hand had blood on it. He was bleeding through the denim, and heavily. He limped to his telephone and tried to dial up Jess since Brutus didn't have a phone, but his vision was so blurry, he kept dialing the number wrong. He felt like vomiting, so he sat down on the step to get his head straight.

You alright, Sammy?

Sam's head jerked up. He looked around the room hastily. A woman's voice. It was no more than just a whisper, but he was quite certain it was—he must be hallucinating.

Sammy?

It was hers. It was his mother's voice. He felt a sudden cramp in his side and leaned against the wall with a groan.

Might want to get that looked at, darlin'.

"Mama?" Sam asked, looking around. He held onto the wall as he stood with a limp, his fingers leaving blood stains against the white walls. He peeked through his one street-view window but couldn't see anyone within earshot. He suddenly felt ridiculous, and shook his head as though to cast off his thoughts. His mother had been dead for over fourteen years. He was sure he had heard her voice, though. Could be this fever he'd caught.

Sammy, are you hungry?

He whipped his head around again. Nothing. It felt almost as though the voice were coming from within him. This time he was sure he had heard her. He stumbled toward his front door, opened it to a hot rush of air and the humming of locusts in the night air. He squinted into the darkness, hearing voices to his right where a group of people stood smoking outside the Watering Hole, the embers a blurry orange at the end of their faces. He looked at them through stinging eyes.

"Did y'all just say something?" he managed to ask, holding onto his rusted banister with both hands.

They stood where they were, their faces a blur. One said something he could not understand, as though his voice were being played backward on a record player. *Close the door, Sammy. You're letting all the bugs inside.*

"Rosie?" Sam said into the night's darkness, thinking his voice sounded like it did when he was a boy, and one of the faces turned his way. It took a step forward to him, then another, in a sort of jerking motion. Its face was all twisted like. Sam stepped back, nearly slipped on his front step as the figures moved toward him, then hastily made his way back inside his room, latching the door behind him. The throbbing in his legs was nearly unbearable. He limped to the bathroom, each step piercing, an agony, and stood before the toilet where he unbuttoned his jeans, dropping them down as he winced. As he pissed, the angry red cuts throbbed just below his thighs. He lowered his jeans even farther to see a white puslike substance oozing out of the cuts. Red lines streaked up toward his groin, one reaching into his midsection. He lifted his shirt, following the line, and froze when he saw a slight movement beneath his skin. He blinked then squinted more closely at his belly where he swore he thought he could see something slithering inside of him, as though the red tendril moved within him.

"Jesus fucking Christ," Sam grunted, losing his balance and falling back, his body slamming against the wall, his head leaving a dent the size of a small basketball in the drywall above the towel rack. He slid to the floor, boots squeaking against the tile. He reached back and touched his head, feeling a warm wetness. When he brought his hand to his face, he squinted to see the blood between his fingers and felt dizzy again. He lay his face against the cool floor, his body burning as his breathing grew more rapid. Between blinks, he could see old track marks on the linoleum from the bottom of his boots. He reminded himself to finally clean up the place once he was feeling better. He wondered for a second how serious this sickness was when another wave of nausea moved back over him. He turned to his side, tried to vomit, but nothing came up. The room spun around him as he heaved. He pulled his knees closer to his chest and whimpered. He could still hear the muted voices from the bar next door. The air conditioner hummed. Cars rushed by outside.

"Help me," Sam whispered to the empty space around him, suddenly aware of how alone he was with no one there to hear his cries. "Somebody please," he cried.

Nothing. Alone like he'd always been. The lonely had always followed him.

"Please," he whimpered.

As he lay dying, Sam saw his body from above. It was as though he had two selves. The body on the ground and the spirit looking from above. Was it his spirit looking down on his body? Had he already died? No—there was still the pain. The two parts of him had been severed but were in some capacity still connected. His body lay in a puddle of his own blood and pus, muddy pants around his knees, legs ruined, and from his hovering view, he looked very small, helpless even, his legs swollen to an unbelievable size. A bloody smear interrupted the blue and white wallpaper on the drywall behind him.

"Get up," he told his body below, but his other self did not move. He could see his body's skin rippling with pain. It was coming from the tendril beneath his skin, twisting between organs and bones. The Sam above covered his mouth with his hand. Then he saw movement from the corners of the room, something dark, first like a shadow, then like fingers, making its way up from the corners.

"Get the fuck up," he screamed at himself, but his body did not move. And then, from behind the tub, from the windowsill, even the drain in the sink, from behind the toilet, came spiders. First slowly, their spindly legs reaching tentatively from their space as he lay motionless, then suddenly very fast, moving as though running from something or to something. A few inched their way up the wall to where he hovered above, a few lingered in the tub, most of them moved their way toward his body, which lay motionless on the ground. As they inched closer, Sam felt the breath knocked out of him. He tried to scream but could utter no sound. Just then, one of the larger spiders crawled onto his back, looking like a shadow against his undershirt.

"What the fuck?" Sam tried to say as looked down, feeling his body shake from the inside out.

Sammy, it's time for school, honey.

Rosie stood in the doorway of the bathroom, her hands on her hips. She wore her pink bathrobe, the one she'd keep on while cooking breakfast. Her head was tilted to the side as she looked down at him, as though his body lying there was the most normal thing. She was the same as he remembered her, a curler in the front of her hair, the smell of his father's tobacco hanging on her clothes under her drugstore perfume.

"My God—Mom? Am I dreaming?"

Rosie leaned over his motionless body, one hand reaching out to shake his shoulder. The spider on his back scurried down to his left leg. He could see hair on its back.

Are you not feeling well, honey?

"Mom," Sam screamed at his mother below him, hearing his voice reverberate in the small room. "Mom, I'm here," he said, the panic filling his whole body. She did not hear him from where he hovered above, but talked to his body below, kneeling beside him. His insides still twisted, the room spinning as though he was on a carnival ride. He was unable to move any part of his body, yet every part of him burned.

You need to get up now, Sammy. Your father needs to use the restroom. You know how particular your father is.

"This isn't real," he said to himself, his wounds burning—no, freezing, he thought.

Sammy—

Honey—

Her voice slowed as she spoke, like a record player put into the wrong speed.

"Mom, I'm here," he croaked. She paused then, as though finally hearing him, and turned to twist her head up to where he hovered, her face gaunt.

"Can you hear me?" he asked. "Mom, please," he cried.

Weren't your mama's only boy,
But her favorite one it seems,
She began to cry when you said goodbye,
And sank into your dreams.

It was then she opened her mouth, ever so slowly as though to finally speak to him. A spider crawled from between her teeth.

Sam screamed then, feeling the sensation of falling freely, his guts lunging. He tasted something metallic and realized he was bleeding from his mouth. He looked down at his crumpled form, with spiders on his body, some disappearing under his clothes. His mother's eyes were blank, and there were more on her then, one on her neck, her eyes having changed to black orbs. He looked back at his body, thought he saw one enter one of the larger wounds on his leg before the shaking started. First as a tremble, then more violent. Convulsions as he screamed, before it turned into a pink, foamy gurgle.

"Oh, God, please help," he heaved. "It hurts." His whole form was a tremor gaining like a storm, hands clenched, teeth grinding as his head whipped back and forth before Sam lost consciousness, his face slapping with a thud against the cold floor.

Nobody heard his dying words,
Ah, but that's the way it goes.

24

The telephone rang, startling both Jess and Lillian. Jess sat unmoving, staring over at it. Neither moved until Glory cried out on the fifth ring.

"You gonna pick up?" she asked softly.

"Who could be calling so late?"

"It's nearly dawn."

"That means bad news."

"Good news always sleeps till noon."

Jess stood, started, then stopped, then moved quickly to answer. "Hello," he said in a low voice, his back to her.

"Yeah," he said, rubbing his eyes with his index finger. Then a pause. "Yeah. Okay. He what now?" His shoulders stiffened. Lillian could hear a man's voice on the other end of the line. She felt something then—the same pushing in she had sensed when she saw the cloven hoofs. Trying out the corners. Sniffing for vulnerability. Lillian stood, whistled for Wendy, and turned slowly around in the darkened room. She closed her eyes, sending out even further. She sent out again, but there was nothing like she had felt before. She scanned back across the cover where the howlers had been earlier. Nothing. Just the flutterings of small game in the area. The clearest hearts she could pick up were the ones inside the cabin. The three of them, the three dogs. Something, though, felt almost present there with them. Something much vaster than a heart. It was almost like an atmosphere, pressing in against their space from the air around them.

"Well how do they know—" he said. Jess turned to her, his eyes wide, horror spreading across his face as his hand gripped the phone. She could feel the pushing in getting stronger. The sulfur smell. Wendy stood alert at her hip, watching Jess along with her.

"Mhm. Yeah." Jess said despondently as the dog whined. He rubbed his free hand through his hair. "That's what Gideon told you?"

Lillian watched his expression, waiting. She already knew what he was about to tell her. She held the baby more closely to her breast.

"Okay. I'll head over now," Jess said before hanging up. He sat in a crumple on the couch.

"What happened?" she asked.

"Sam's dead," he said, staring right through her, his voice flat.

Lillian covered her mouth with her hand.

"That was Kurt. He just got the call from the sheriff."

"Oh, my Lord," she said, feeling the pressure pushing in even more.

It's here for your man next.

"What?" she said, her head whipping around the room, the pressure making her dizzy all of a sudden.

"I've got to go over there," Jess said, moving quickly. Lillian checked the corners—there was nothing. Wendy hadn't picked up on anything either. Where had that voice come from?

She followed Jess downstairs, knowing already what had taken Sam. It was whatever latched onto him at the Lick. It was also whatever was outside their cabin, pushing in. She wondered with a heavy dread if it was there for Jess next.

For all of you.

"Do you hear that?" Lillian asked, pausing frozen on the steps, her eyes far away. Jess flipped on the light inside their bedroom. She listened again, but there was nothing. She wondered if she had imagined it. She found Jess in the closet as he pulled a tee-shirt over his undershirt.

"Where are you going? Sun's not even up."

"Sam's. Police are there now. Kurt is on his way too. Nobody answered at Johnny's." He buttoned a flannel over his tee-shirt and brushed past her.

"Are they sure he's gone?" she asked, her eyes following him.

"Kurt said one of the bartenders next door called the police. Folks saw him, and he looked bad. I don't know. Said the guy knocked on his door a bunch, but Sam didn't answer." Jess was frantically pulling on his jeans. "When they found him, he was already dead."

She sat down on the end of the hope chest. Poor Sam. She thought of his tired smile that morning when she was petting his dog.

Jess sighed with heaviness. "Police had to knock down the door to get in."

"Jess, before you go," Lillian said, moving closer to him, her voice in a whisper. "We don't know what's outside."

"The law's waiting on me. Kurt said they want a statement." He moved for his gun.

Whatever had taken Sam would surely be after Jess now too. No strong-backed man drops dead like that. There was something else. And whatever that something else was had followed the men out of the south, across Highway 7, and was here with them now.

Just waiting.

She whipped her head around again. Wendy watched her with a low growl. Jess pocketed a handful of bullets, then his wallet. She stepped into the hallway, staring at her reflection before the forest's blackness. She pressed her palm against the cedar jamb and sent out.

You are not to enter here—

There was no answer aside from a slow chill collecting at her toes. She returned to Jess, her heart wild inside of her. If he left the cabin, there was no way she could protect him.

"I just can't believe it," Jess said. "He was just here."

She knew then that this would all come to a head. There was no dodging whatever was after them. She had to think clearly about what to do next.

"I won't be long," Jess said, peeking out their window. "Dawn's coming." He tucked in his shirt. "You said you can feel them howlers, right? You said you sense them?"

"I can sense them," she said, stifling her tears.

"Well, will you check the coast is clear? I'll run for the truck when you tell me the coast is clear."

"Okay, but there's something I need to tell you before you go." Jess thought she looked all willowy on the edge of the chest. "What got Sam–" she said slowly, then cleared her throat, feeling what was on the outside, its mounting pressure, like opening your eyes under lake water and trying to still see.

"What?"

"It's here," she said quietly, her eyes on the floor between them.

"What do you mean?" Jess said, coming to kneel before her, feeling sick to his stomach. "Outside? Is it them howlers?" he asked, studying her face, holding her arms in his big hands. "It's ten feet to the truck. I have my gun—"

"It's something else. Something bigger. I can feel it," she said, bringing her hands to her chest.

He looked at her without speaking.

"I can't protect you if you go," she said, feeling tears welling up in her eyes as she looked up at him, her lips pressed together. He pulled his Springfield Armory .45 from his top drawer and set it down next to her on the pillow.

"Now you listen to me, Lillian. I am going to be alright," Jess told her, hoping to believe his own words. "I'm going to go talk to Gideon and find out what happened to Sam. And then I'm coming straight back here."

You didn't warn him good enough.

Lillian squeezed her eyes shut hard, talking back to whatever it was speaking to her, only her.

You don't know me.

He's already sick with it.

"You are to stay right here," Jess insisted. She could see beads of sweat on his upper lip. "You hear me? Do not leave this house. The door stays locked. You see anything untoward, you shoot it. You're just as good of a shot as I am." He pushed the gun across the white sheet, so it touched her thigh, and then he stood back up.

"Jess, you don't understand."

"Thing is," Jess said, "This was always his fear."

"Whose fear?"

"Sam's. Dying alone," Jess said, his Adam's apple dropping. "Used to say he was gonna die alone in that room and a stranger would find him."

She thought of Sam's nervous face. His dog, eager to please. The horror dipped into her belly. He died in the way he had feared. She knew Jess' fear was her dying on him in childbirth, but that hadn't happened. And hers? Everything before the baby seemed like a dream that she was slowly forgetting. Her primary concern was for Glory Be's safety. Aside from that and Jess, she could think of nothing else.

"Kurt was coughing on the phone just now," Jess said. "Like Sam had been on the way back."

She followed him back up to the kitchen, the baby in her right arm, the gun in her left. He stood in the over-bright lights, his face looking tired. The dread inched across her body like ice numbing out feeling.

"Now, babe, I need you to check for those things. I just need to get to the truck. Are they close?"

She breathed in deeply, sending out beyond him into the start of the dawn. She felt the forest floor, felt in the cove's scummy water, pushed all the way to the lake road. There were the morning sounds, the morning hearts. But no howlers. All clear. "They're gone," she said. "It's almost dawn. I don't think they hang out much in daylight off their own land."

He leaned in and gave her a dry kiss on her forehead and ran his hand across the outline of Glory Be's head. "Say a prayer for us boys, will you? I know your prayers work double."

"You be careful, okay?" she said, as Jess slipped out into the day's first light, scoping the property line and hurrying to the truck. She watched him through the window. She did not know what her husband was walking into or how she would be able to fight what was pressing in on them or what was growing inside of him. He jumped into the cab without incident, and the truck started on the second try.

Jess rode east into the sunrise as the day's first light rose over their property, streaking its rays into their cabin. She called to her ancestors then. To Celeste. To the women before Celeste, unnamed in the cosmos.

Please. Watch over us.

She watched the dust till even that disappeared.

25

Lillian set the .45 on the end table, staring at its coldness. The house felt profoundly silent without Jess. She sat down, her heartbeat wild in her chest. Wendy lay with her face on her paws, watching her.

Whose voice had spoken to her? It was as though the voice had come from within, directly to her, but from a dark place inside herself. She had been raised up by a granny and knew that infection, that illness could start with such things. And ever since the boys went on the hunt, things in their home had changed. Like they'd been knocked off axis. She straightened up as Wendy circled the room, felt the twist of worry but remembered the hand-carved wooden plaque Celeste hung above the mantle:

"Screw Your Courage To The Sticking Place"

Lillian began with a smudge. She first lit a match to the tip of a Palo Santo branch, watching the flame take up, blackening the sides as it grew to fingernail length. She walked through the small cabin, lifting the smoke to the corners of each room, whispering the prayers of protection. She left the burning stick in the bathroom sink where Sam had washed up, watching the smoke curl before the mirror, doubling its size. She pushed back against what pushed into their space, her prayer a ribcage of protection around each of them. After she blessed each room, she pinched out the flame. The room seemed to lighten. She pushed again, but this time, it was inward as opposed to out. She closed her eyes, scanning her mind for what spoke to her, through her.

First, just the image of the timber. Miles of it, lush with buckeye butterfly and bellflowers. Lillian combed her mind. What caused Sam's injury? What would cure this fever growing in Jess? Eyes closed, she took herself further in her mind's eye to the cottage where she had been raised on the north end of the Lick. She recalled

Celeste's tincture table. What ailments had she watched Celeste treat? She felt her feet carrying her across the dirty path to the water's edge. She peered across the creek into the darkness of the south, which hummed with some sort of nervous energy. Looking into the dark brush, she understood. The hurt had to be part of the healing. Whatever antidote was needed would be where the injury was caused. *You do not cross.*

Her eyes snapped open. The voice was louder then. Morning's rosy light crept in through the east windows. She stayed the course. Closing her eyes once again, she saw her body take a step forward into the Lick in her mind, scanning the line of trees. Bur Oak. Hickory. Willow. Then a low rustling. A blur of movement.

And then she spotted it. Low to the ground, but unmistakable. It was the form of a woman, crouching in the dirt. Her spine was badly bent with age or injury, she could not tell, her face cast down. She had ropes of stone-colored hair that hung across her shoulders, nearly touching the dirt below her bare feet. On one leg, there was a badly healed scar. Lillian took in another slow breath. The woman's face lifted. Her eyes opened. They were the eyes of the goat.

If you cross to us, you will never cross back.

A southern woman. So, they were real. Somehow, this woman's voice spoke from inside of Lillian's mind. How she had gained access to her, Lillian did not know. She stood frozen in place, fingering her grandmother's necklace around her neck. She spoke back from within.

I will decide that. Not you.

Then laughter. A shrill, menacing laughter, pulling all the warmth from Lillian's body. Her heart leapt in her chest. Had Jess passed something onto her? *I'll be waitin, Lily-B.*

Lillian was pulled from her thoughts by Glory's crying. Returning her arms around her baby, she looked up, suddenly uncertain. She was just days post-delivery. This was no time to fight a southern demon.

If she were to return for the antidote, she would need the granny's help. Lillian's options were limited. She could stay with the baby, but Jess could possibly fare the same as Sam. She could go to the Lick, bringing Glory along to retrieve the antidote. That was out of the question. Or she could leave the baby in the care of Marjorie while she went for the antidote. It had to be the last option. It was the least dangerous.

"Hello," Marjorie answered, no sign of sleep in her voice.

"It's Lillian."

"I was wondering when you'd ring. You heard then?"

"About Sam?"

"I don't know about any Sam."

"What are you talking about then?"

"Look outside."

Lillian opened a wooden slat with two fingers. She heard it first—a furious buzzing, movement in the trees. Then she saw it. Locusts. Just a few, flopping about clumsily as they landed.

"Are these native insects?" Lillian asked.

"No," Marjorie said dimly. "Haven't been here since the Rocky Mountain Plague. That was over a century ago. I've already had three calls this morning, and it's barely dawn. People are talking."

"That's odd," Lillian said, her eyes scanning the property. "Not many here."

"Will be soon. You best have your man cover your garden before they send it to ruin."

"He's already gone."

"Gone where?"

"Marjorie, I need your help."

"You feeling okay, girl?"

"Baby is good, but the blood is still coming."

"That's to be expected."

"There's something else."

"Well, get to it, girl."

"When Jess and his men went gigging yesterday—," Lillian said. She could hear Marjorie sucking her teeth.

"Over on the Lick?"

"Mhm. Well, there was an accident."

"What kind of accident?" Marjorie asked, her voice lowered.

"Sam Ebbons' dog ran off. Crossed the Lick to the south."

"I knew it was no good when Jess said what he planned to do."

"I know."

"Did they follow the dog?"

"Two did. One was cut up by some briars."

"On the south?"

"Yes. That was Sam."

"That boy will need help, Lillian. That's the false vine. It's poison."

Lillian cleared her throat. "He's dead."

Marjorie took her breath in sharply. "Already?"

"Jess just left to give a statement to the law."

"Lillian?" she asked, her voice lower. "Did all the men touch southern soil?"

Lillian gripped the phone, her eyes shut tightly. "Yes."

"Jess?"

"He told me when they got back last night."

"But what of your warning? I was there, I heard you clear as the day—"

"One of the men fell, and he crossed to help. Damn fool."

Marjorie was silent for a moment. "You saw them after?"

"I did."

"Any sickness on Jess yet?"

Lillian hesitated, knowing what she was going to say next. "The start of something."

"You know it will be coming after your man now, don't youse?"

"I know," Lillian nearly whispered into the phone. "Marjorie, we had two howlers last night."

"Good Lord, child. Where?"

"Water's edge. I think the powders kept them out."

"That won't hold them forever."

"I don't know what to do."

"It's daylight. You're safe for now. But you're going to need the antidote. Something stronger than what you've got in the cabin."

Lillian stood in silence, feeling her belly ache, her breasts swollen with milk. *Better not cross.*

Her head whipped around again.

"Do you understand, girl?" Marjorie repeated.

"I figured I'd need to work something up."

"No," she added urgently. "It's more than that. You're going to need to go south for the antidote. The remedy must be center to the injury. It's just how it's done."

"What will I need to get?"

"Depends on each boy. They have a spell over those banks. It causes the senses to dumb. Lets the dark ones inside."

"How does it dumb the senses?"

"Vision impaired. Throat starts to swell."

"Jess' throat is hurtin, he said. And he talked about pollen. All dusty like."

"That ain't no pollen. That there's a protection spell."

"You mean by the southerners?"

"Alright. Let me think," Marjorie said. Lillian could hear her shuffling footsteps and some pages turning. "For the physical cuts, *Vitis vinifera* is what you'll need," she said quickly. "Not hard to find. Grows everywhere on those banks."

"Grape vine?"

"Not just any grape vine, girl. You need the genus that grows southern."

"Grows southern," she repeated.

"For the protection spell, I'm afraid I'll have to consult my books. Sure do wish your grandmother was here. She'd know what we need."

"And Marjorie," she said, before pausing. "There's something else."

"I'm listening."

"I'm hearing things."

"What kind of things?"

"A voice. Talking to me. But here's the thing—"

"It's from within you," Marjorie finished. "Is that how it feels?"

"Marjorie, I'm scared."

"I know," she said quickly. "But there ain't no time for that. You're going to need to head south. And fast. I'm sorry I can't go in your place. It has to be kin who retrieves it."

"I know this."

"I'll stay with the baby."

"I'm going to need to ask Alice for her truck. Jess has ours."

"Hurry, girl. You don't have—" she was saying, and then the phone went dead.

26

Lillian gingerly pulled a pair of jeans up over her hips, wincing as she buttoned them. She heard the first pings of the locusts on the bedroom windows, and when she pulled back the drapes of the bedroom, she could see pockets of them landing on trees and the underbrush below them. Then the light beside the bed kicked off with a slow grinding noise.

Electricity was out. No way she could dig out the generator without Jess.

She rushed through her list of what she'd need: gun, shells, pocketknife. She felt heavy in her skin, as though she were still in the haze of labor. How had all of this happened so quickly?

She strapped Glory Be into her carrier and paused, looking at the baby's sleepy face. This would be the first time the baby left the house. Just a few days old. She looked so small, asleep in the car seat. The clock chimed in the living room. 6:16 am. She locked the dogs indoors before leaving. There was no time to cover the garden. On her way across the driveway, she saw dozens more locusts, their sturdy olive-patterned bodies and membranous wings clouding in the early morning sunlight. They buzzed as they bumped clumsily into one another, their clicking mating calls blocking out the other forest sounds.

Alice was already at the door lighting a cigarette when Lillian stepped onto her porch.

"Howlers clear out?"

"Around 5 am," Lillian said.

"Brody heard what happened," Alice said, stepping past the screen to scan the timber around her property line. "That Sam Ebbons is dead," she said, staring into Lillian's face. "You know anything about that?"

"Just that I've got to get to town, and fast."

"Jess got your truck?"

"He does."

"Take mine," Alice said, fishing the keys out of her pocket.

"Thank you, Alice," Lillian said, the baby heavy in her arm. "I'll put gas in it for you," she said, taking the keys.

"So you don't know how Sam died?"

"Jess went to meet the sheriff. I suppose I'll know more when he gets back. You lose power?"

"About ten minutes ago," she said, scanning the property line as she stepped out beside her on the porch. "Lily-B," she said, hesitating. "What the hell is going on?" she asked, her voice lowered. "First howlers, then a swarm. Now a boy is dead?"

"I know," Lillian said, feeling her knees almost give out from under her. "I'm hoping I can find some answers for us today."

"Whole town's about. No power. Radio is full of stories about people out of doors in the city, fights breaking out." A locust flew between them. Alice looked around, her eyes wide.

"Don't worry, Alice. We'll know more soon. Have Brody pull out our generator if you want to save your deep freeze. It's up in the garage."

"You need me to stay with the baby?"

"I'm picking up the granny, but I'll let you know if I need you."

⚜

Lillian drove the speed limit all the way into town, the baby strapped in beside her in the truck. The two major stop lights were out. Some people were coming to the stops, waiting their turns, but many were driving through. The big lights on the marquee were dark. There was a huge line at the General Store, and Earl, the general manager, was out front, trying to direct traffic, his arms wide. There was a handwritten sign taped to the front door that read "cash only."

The locusts had started to fill the air between the buildings, landing on the hot asphalt, on children's backs as they walked, on the sides of trucks. Somehow, the light looked all wrong in the sky, as though a storm was coming. Lillian made a careful, complete stop at Highway 5, right at the J Road intersection, before heading to Marjorie's rented room, a big old storm cloud moving in low from the east. She knew that whatever had been unearthed on the south side had now spread beyond the north of the Lick into Camden County. Her mind moved to the form of the southern woman, and she felt a wave of nausea move over her body.

Granny Marjorie stood out front of her faded double-wide, a bulging sack in her liver-spotted hand. She swatted at locusts as she made her way to the truck and plopped in wordlessly beside Lillian, casting a worried look around.

"These end of times, I say."

"Don't be dramatic," Lillian said, forcing a tired smile.

"Any word from Jess?" Marjorie asked, looking back alongside Lillian as she reversed the truck. Flocks of black birds collected in the sky, flying in haphazard patterns.

"Nothing yet."

"I'll stay as long as you need me," she said, patting her hand on the shift.

"I'll head out as soon as I drop you off," Lillian said, her hands gripping the wheel of the truck. "I can't waste any more time."

"You know what to look for?"

Lillian turned back onto the highway, passing two cars that had pulled over, the two drivers in some sort of argument. One man had the other by his shirt.

She shook her head. "Have you ever seen anything like this?"

Marjorie lifted her eyebrows, tilting her head a bit to the right with a "told you so" look on her face.

"What is going on out there, Marjorie?"

"Not sure yet, my dear. But what I am sure about is what you need to do. You focus on yourself and getting what you need off that southern soil, girl. Leave these crazy city folk to figure out their own business. Now, what do you look for? Say it to me."

"Okay. Long stalks, coarse margins, bristled underbellies."

"Right. The flowers will be just falling off. You'll see some grapes ripening on them. Don't bother none with those. You just need the leaves."

"Just the leaves, right."

They rode in silence for a moment, alone on the two-lane highway until a police car sped by them, sirens blaring.

"You know what got into the boy who died?" Marjorie asked.

"Some sort of briar. And Jess' brother fell on a piece of driftwood."

Marjorie chewed on the inside of her lip and scanned the highway. "I'll cook up something with the lemon balm to see if it works on the brother."

"What will we do with the grape leaf?"

"We can start with the tea. And the tea leaves, we'll bury 'em after he drinks it all down. You have to bury them on y'all's property."

Marjorie looked under the blanket at the baby, her thick black lashes wet against the pale cheeks. She reached out a finger to stroke the side of her face.

"Growing already," she said, the edge of mirth returning to her voice.

"You think? In just two days?"

"She doing much aside from sleeping?" Marjorie asked.

"She's doing the sleeping for the both of us."

"She opened her eyes for you yet?" Marjorie peered closer at the baby and cast a sidelong glance at Lillian.

"Just little slits as of yet. Probably dark like Jess', I reckon. She got his black hair and all."

"Give it time," Marjorie said, and rolled down her window before thinking better of it and rolled it back up. "Lock your doors now, Lillian. I'm already hearing stories about the menfolk catching crazy," she said.

Lillian did as she was told, and the two of them rode the rest of the way in silence, their guts filled with the dread of what was to come.

27

Marjorie's instructions were clear. Lillian was to retrieve the grape vine to counter the protection spell. Grape, a symbol of welcome in the ancient world, could be used to undo anything that cast someone or something out. It had to be procured from the source, however, which meant Lillian would have to, for the first time in her life, cross to the south end of the Lick.

Marjorie hoped that since the errand would be in the early morning, there would be fewer threats about. She knew full well what waited for Lillian on the south end. Lillian did not ask for more details on this. Marjorie would remain at home with Glory Be until Lillian returned, and then the women would tend to Jess. Marjorie planned to work up a tincture for Johnny's hand and keep watch for howlers. She had no intention of leaving the baby with Jess. Lillian dared not address this in any capacity.

Lillian rummaged through Jess' dresser, stuffing bullets into her two front pockets.

"You need to nurse before going," the granny ordered. "Both breasts."

"But she's asleep."

"Wake her, girl. If you get cut up, your milk won't be no good."

Lillian felt a flash of fear and looked at the granny, who motioned her to the rocker. Marjorie lifted Glory from her crib as Lillian unbuttoned her shirt, lifting her bra. Glory turned instinctively toward the breast and latched immediately.

"Try to relax. You'll pass your worry to her."

Lillian rested her head against the back of the rocker and closed her eyes. She thought of the sound of Celeste's rocker creaking on the porch, the feel of Jess' right hand on her left knee as they drove. She pictured the mayflies bouncing against their orange porch light, thought of Wendy's soft fur against her calf. Her heartbeat slowed a bit, and then Glory's body settled into a sort of calm against hers.

"You have any of that milk froze up?"

"I don't," she said, thinking of how the look of the breast pumps reminded her of the dairy farm down by Barry that had frightened her as a child.

"I brought along some of the powders from the supermarket."

"Marjorie, Glory can't drink that."

"Just in case," Marjorie said, pulling up the footstool and sitting with a sigh in front of mother and child. "Now, Lily-B, I need to talk to you about some things. And I need to be sure you're really listening."

Glory Be curled her finger around Lillian's Mozarkite necklace.

"I'm listening," Lillian told the granny, looking over the age on her face. Marjorie would know what to do, Lillian was sure of it.

Marjorie took Lillian's free hand in both of hers. "I need you to be strong for me, Lily-B. Can you do that?"

"Of course."

"You're going somewhere ain't none of us have been in some time," she said, a painful smile on her face. "Celeste was the last to cross, and she was bit up. You know this."

"I know," Lillian said, feeling her stomach drop.

"I can't quite get a read on things over there. I've been trying. That ain't my gift anyway. Sure do wish Celeste was still here to ask on things. Don't know what they've been up to. There ain't been no word in so long. But what I do know is something's crossed back over. To our side. And whatever that is? It's brought some dark magic along with it."

Lillian held her breath. Jess.

"A boy dead. The sickness on the men. Howlers about. And these locusts? Things ain't right, girl." She shook her head, her eyes on Glory Be.

Lillian worked to keep her heart steady as the baby nursed. She felt her suckling pause and switched her to the other breast. Marjorie looked at her a moment before continuing, as though weighing what information would be best to share.

"I saw the southerners once," she said quietly, without looking up from the baby.

"You did? When?"

"Around when your mother was born," she said, flashing a look up into Lillian's eyes before quickly looking down again. "Feral bunch. Almost like they ain't human no more."

"How do you mean?"

"Don't wash up. Speak in a dark tongue. And they used tricks to get their way."

"Is that the dark magic you're talking about?"

"It is, Lily-B."

"There's some about that in Celeste's journals," Lillian said.

"All I'm saying, girl, is you're likely to encounter it today." Her chin quivered a bit. "Celeste and I kept you away from all that for most of your life. Didn't want you to have to see any more darkness than necessary. But you're a woman now. A mother in her own right. And today you might see what was between you and that timber all those years."

Lillian swallowed slowly. "What's in that timber?" A dread surrounded her insides.

"The Devil," Marjorie said.

"Marjorie," Lillian said. "In what form?"

"I never looked on Him. But I sure did feel it. Stronger in them woods than what I ran from when I was a chile so long ago. Heavily concentrated like. Like all of what went sour in a man settled right beyond that creek."

"What did it feel like?"

"Like cold mostly. Like unfeeling. And guarded by things that warn you of what's comin'. Current that'll drag you off. Water moccasins. But if you get past that, the cold is what's got *inside* folks over there, Lily-B." Marjorie's face was steely, looking right at her, though her grip on Lillian's hand intensified.

Lillian remembered that cold feeling of being watched. Of not being snatched or stung up, but more like being courted. Like the Devil courted Eve. She rocked her baby and steeled herself.

"And now it's turned its eye on your man. Which means it has its eye on you too. Those boys made a mess when they crossed that creek, and now you have to go and clean up. And that's honorable. You are a good wife to Jess Cedars. He and his boys have been stuck. Stuck with the Devil's poison. Ain't no fair that it's kin that has to be the one to fetch the remedy. I just hate that it has to be you."

"I just want Jess to be okay."

"Course you do." She inched the stool closer. "Now listen, Lily-B," she said sternly. She paused for a moment, her eyes starting to go far away. Her grip on Lillian's hand slackened. It looked to Lillian as though she was in a sort of trance. And then her voice. The voice she heard cooing to Glory Be as Lillian pushed on all fours. The voice she sometimes heard when Marjorie and Celeste would brew their tinctures in the doublewide in the dusk. She was hearing it again at that moment, clear as day. Marjorie was speaking to her from somewhere else, her voice hollowed, slower.

"What causes the injury must be included in the recovery." Her voice echoed. "The injury was southern-born, so the antidote must be southern procured."

Lillian watched with cold awe. Marjorie's eyes were blank. Far off.

"First, beware the false vine. The vine that crawls below," Marjorie murmured. "Grape vine is dark in color. It grows above us, heavenward. Reach for it, and it will pull apart thinly, like the web of a spider. Store it away from the light. A granny satchel. About the waist. Say it out loud: 'Away from the light.'"

"Away from the light," Lillian repeated.

"Nice vine shall climb, false vine will blind. What got the boy was false vine. The false vine will beckon, like the Devil in the garden."

"How does it beckon?"

"It will seem to move along with you. It will curl between your ankles like a cat. It will try to get you to look. But if you do," Marjorie's eyes snapped up then, her grip intensifying, "if you look upon it, it will sting like the rattler. It cannot sting you if you do not look. Do not look down at the false vine."

"How do I see where to step?"

"You must trust your step. Say it out loud to me: Do not look down at the false vine."

Lillian's voice trembled. "Do not look down at the false vine."

"There was a gentleman's agreement between north and south, some seventy years ago. We were never to cross, you hear? Never. If we did, they could lay claim."

"Lay claim to what?"

Her voice started coming more rapidly. Double time. "If you are seen, you may be approached. If you are, you are not to speak to anything that speaks to you."

"Marjorie, I think they already speak to me. I hear them. In my mind."

Her eyes were still far away. "This is one of their tricks."

"How did they get inside of me?"

"Ignore the voices," she murmured. "They do not speak the truth."

"But how did they get inside of my mind?"

"Dark magic."

"Where did they learn such things?"

"The Devil. He has given them power. It has changed them. They are the Changed Ones."

Lillian listened with a thumping heart. She pulled the baby from her breast and moved her to her shoulder to burp.

"You must not look at the Changed Ones. You must not look—but—if you must look, use a mirror, with them behind you. A woman's mirror, perhaps, from your pocket. They cannot approach you unless you first gaze directly upon them."

"What happens if I look?"

"You are not to answer their questions. No matter what they ask, no matter what they tell you. Do not speak in their tongues."

Lillian's heart felt frozen in her chest. It felt like an ice cold chest. "What happens if they do?"

Marjorie shook her head as she spoke. "It may ensnare you. They desire to return you to Him. You are to steel your ears against what would speak to you."

Lillian felt her baby's heartbeat against her chest—a bird's wing.

"They are liars. Brokers. They will try to be familiar. They are known to use a voice that is both foreign and friend."

"I don't understand."

"They look to trick. They delight in this. The closer you are, the shorter the strike."

The baby hiccupped as Lillian patted her back.

"Like the Devil, they delight in harm, for they are his kin," Marjorie continued, her voice echoing in the room.

"How did I not learn of this before?"

"You are learning now," she said firmly, her lips pressed together. "Say it out loud: Do not speak to the Changed Ones."

"Do not speak to the Changed Ones."

"Keep three feet from all of them, but especially the women. The men cannot, by their creed, touch a female who is not kin. The men can only lay hands of harm on other men. The women can only lay hands of harm on other women."

"What do they want from me?"

"You do not know your worth. Do not, I repeat, do not get near the women. Say it."

"Do not get near the women."

"And one more thing. Beware their beasts. They do their bidding. They are their trackers. They are their spies."

"The howler?"

"They will follow. Unafraid even of the daylight. Its fangs have the poison of the adder. It has the shape of a cat but is hooved."

Lillian gripped the baby against her body, suddenly doubting herself, doubting this whole trip. What if one of these howlers got her? Who would care for Glory? But then, suddenly, a darker fear presented itself: What if Jess got taken by what took Sam? What if those howlers kept coming?

Marjorie's voice picked up tempo again, her eyes glassy and dazed, shocking her out of her thoughts. "The howler may cry for you. To lure you. Do not follow."

Like a baby.

"They will smell your milk on you. They may beckon to you, child. If you hear them—"

"Marjorie, why did Celeste not warn me of this?"

"Celeste may have seen this for you. We all must stand against what we fear."

"How will I know the right thing to do?"

"You will know. When the time is right."

"Is there no other way?"

Her eyes snapped up to Lillian's. "If Jess Cedars is to be saved, you must be the one to make this crossing."

"What do I do if I encounter one of them? If I can't talk, if I can't look?"

"There is only one thing to do."

"What, Marjorie?"

Marjorie looked into Lillian's yellowish eyes. "Run."

"I am afraid."

"It's time to go now," said Marjorie. "For Glory."

Lillian placed her hand on Glory Be's back as she slept, feeling her little breaths, and said a prayer over her. She placed her in her crib, then took the granny's hands in hers and kissed them too before stepping out to the porch, a small bag on her back. She sat to pull on her shoes, swatting a series of locusts from her line of vision before seeing a set of muddied boots stand before her.

"You going over there?" Eugene asked. He held a giant sycamore leaf in his hand.

"Mhm," Lillian said softly. "I won't be long." She tied her boot in a strong knot.

"That howler is still about, I reckon." He took a step toward her. His lips were chapped.

"It's possible," she said. "Best to stay inside, darlin," she said above the buzzing. A locust landed on his shoulder. She felt for his heart, which thumped steadily. A healthy boy. "Eugene, baby," she said, flicking off the insect from his arm and resting her hand there. "You okay?"

Eugene turned to face her then, his mouth slack. "They're waiting for you," he said in a voice that was not his. His head shook back and forth for a moment, then centered, his eyes rolling back in his head.

"Eugene," she said, reaching for his arms. "Eugene. What did you say?"

Eugene pulled back, a sheen of sweat covering his body before recovering himself. He pressed his thumb back into his mouth.

Lillian had to stay seated to catch her breath. "Eugene, you stay by your mama, and indoors, you hear?"

Eugene seemed to look both at and beyond her. His dark lashes were clumped with sweat. He made heavy breathing sounds. He pulled something from his pocket, Alice's small salt cellar gripped in his dirty hand.

"For your pocket," he whispered, his voice back to normal.

"Okay," Lillian said nervously, pulling her bag from her back and opening the tie.

"No," he said again in the strange voice. "For your pocket."

Lillian hesitated but then took it and stuffed it down into her front jeans pocket. She squeezed him into a quick hug.

The drive to J Road was a series of sickeningly familiar turns. The old petrol station at the corner, the owner out front fanning himself. The failed fencing. The homes dotting the landscape, their tired machinery out front, the waist-high, knee-high weeds masking flaking paint, tattered flags in the wind. An old hound dog lay on a sagging porch in the morning sun. The Mountain Church stood as it always had up on Grey Hill, its sharp edges softened by time. Crossing under the overpass, Lillian saw a man standing, unmoving on the bridge, his face twisted, as though being pulled down by an invisible hand. And between all of these, the locusts, suddenly everywhere, descending as much in sound as they did in body, as though the timber had always belonged to them. Lillian took the turns unthinkingly, wondering how something as simple as a drive to these parts reminded her she could not leave who she had always been, the displaced orphan, no matter if she moved, married, or produced a child. She had hoped that returning to J Road as a mother, as a wife with a purpose, would make her feel she had been launched from her meager river origins, but as she searched inside for the confidence she'd need to cross over that damned creek, there seemed to be none waiting for her. And as she turned onto J Road, that narrow two-lane road that led to Lick Creek, she found she was still the castaway she had always been.

A half mile down, Lillian turned onto the rocky shoulder beside Celeste's unpaved turnoff. She was expecting the gate that kept trespassers out, a cut padlock lay on the dust beside a set of fresh tracks. She took the turn slowly, noticing the potholes had grown deeper since she left a year before, the overgrown branches scratching the top of the truck. Anyone passing this turn on J Road would think it all abandoned. She wondered for a moment if this part of the world should just stay that way, for everyone's safety.

She took the small turns familiarly, and the balm of routine settled inside of her. On her old drive, she was able to see what she had loved about J Road. The shimmer of the Lick to her left, flanked by wild switchgrass. Pawpaws and muscadines, coiled against the bark of the timbers that bordered the water, wild rye along the roadside. Fox squirrels sat in clusters in the timber. A doe darted across her path not fifty yards ahead.

As Lillian pulled up beside the old cabin, a murder of crows lifted off a nearby tree branch only to settle back down heavily onto the cabin's sagging roof. Marjorie's birds. When Lillian was little, Marjorie would always leave out peanuts or boiled eggs. The crows would deposit singular earrings, lost keys, bones even. The bones would scare Lillian, but Marjorie hushed her at that. She'd tell Lillian to make friends with the crows. Said they'd always help a woman in her time of need.

Lillian shut off the motor, feeling the heat between her breasts and shoulder blades. She knew she should be in bed beside her baby. A woman needs her rest after labor.

Looking across the dirt yard, she was shocked by how small the plot was. She wondered for a moment how she could have lived in such a tiny place for nearly twenty years, with the whole world just out there on the other side of the highway.

She rested her forearms on the steering wheel, remembering walking barefoot on the irregular path between the shoddy cabins, collecting samples for her grandmother, thinking this parcel would be her life forever. Just church and her gran and those tinctures. She had never known a man, never known motherhood, never known life across J Road. And now she was back, more alive than ever, but filled with a terror she had never known she was capable of feeling. All that was ahead of her that day sat more ominous than anything she could have possibly conceived of.

She left the keys under the seat, bringing only the burlap bag and gun with her. Under her clothes was a small granny purse to store the vine. As she walked under the canopy, she glanced down the path that led to the Lick, hearing the rushing water in the distance, and she felt a chill. The old feeling of being watched came back. Just as she remembered it, it did not feel like a particular person. It was the tug of a vast, dark suitor. To her, it felt like the whole fragrant forest was waiting on her next move. She sunk to her knees, grabbing a fistful of the clay dirt in her fingers and rubbing her hands together. She sent out, asking to be remembered by the timber. She was still, waiting for a reply. But there was nothing. She moved quickly to the old porch, lingering for a moment to collect her strength. With a small push on the unlocked front door, she was back inside.

The cabin was unchanged. Most of the furniture had gone with her to Jess' after Celeste passed; the rest she had given away to neighbors or left out in the dirt yard for pickers. The small wood-burning stove still stood in the corner, and the bedframe, naked save the metal, sat on its side in the corner. Aside from the spiderwebs and mouse droppings, which would never have been allowed in Celeste's time, the cabin had been left untouched. She leaned against the wooden counter.

"How am I going to survive this?" she asked out loud as she looked around, missing her grandmother so badly, her bones felt it.

Celeste may have very well once been a beautiful woman, but her professional focus was so intently on things so wholly unconnected to such standards that

Lillian never even wondered such things about her. The lines in her face were deep from years lived. She worked while there was daylight and prayed when the sun was down. She believed that little good came after the sun set for the night and so spent that time preparing for the next day. Her daughter, Lillian's mother, she had told Lillian, did not agree with these restrictions. Their neighbors, the Tories, had the plot four acres to the west. They were decent people, good to their animals, and they had a daughter around Lillian's mother's age named Sarah. Sarah told Lillian once she would hear her mother's voice raised to Celeste, carried across the catfish pond on clear nights. Then she'd be gone for stretches at a time, and Celeste would be left with her silence, her hands in the pockets of her apron. The respect of rules and boundaries had apparently skipped a generation.

Celeste had not been a quietish woman, but she was a woman of few words unless speech was warranted. She listened more than she spoke, even when tending to patients. She'd sit and let them speak of their ailments, tonguing the clove buds she kept in the pouch of her cheek, considering the symptoms before reaching in her bag for the correct tincture. The Yarb docs would confuse her silence for incompetence. The two are nowhere near the same, but some just preferred the granny-women to be as they thought they should be.

Their world north of the Lick was the penumbra of women. Occasionally, the neighbors would visit, but the men often stayed on the porch, their rifles always close, as though watching for something. Or waiting. Often, the kitchen or the porch would fill with neighbor women and their children, just out of the line of the world's attention, obscured, the world dozing around them. They would talk of tea, their bodies, the land they worked. For Lillian, joining these gatherings felt like parting a curtain into an inherited world of mystery and power city folk would never understand.

One curious thing about Celeste's life was that she kept away from menfolk. Alice had said many men tried to get her hand, especially after her husband ran off, but she never allowed one inside. They'd leave firewood or chestnuts on her porch, sometimes even writing her verse. Alice had asked, "who wouldn't want to tie their horse to such a woman?" Celeste had been healthy and self-sufficient, so there was no need for a man to add to her work. Her one daughter and one granddaughter were enough for her, Alice supposed.

Celeste died one week after treating her last patient. It was a woman who had stepped on a nail and waited six days to call. Lillian had accompanied her to the appointment, as she had for all of her patients in the last nine years of her life, and by the time they arrived, she was in the middle of seizing. Celeste sent Lillian down to the corner store to call for an ambulance, saying the shots at the hospital were this woman's only hope. While she was gone, Celeste fashioned a potato poultice and warned her to keep hearty laughter in the home for the next three days during treatment. Celeste waited on the woman's porch until the ambulance arrived forty-five minutes later, Celeste's left hand shaking around the handle of the cane the whole time. When the hospital men arrived, Celeste was downright mute. Later Lillian asked how come she didn't speak to them, and Celeste had told her when words don't come, you are not to speak. It is the Lord's way of keeping you safe from sharing something not meant to be shared.

Women got the hurt on them in all sorts of ways off J Road. Some ran off to the city and picked up city sickness. Some were kilt by animals or machinery. Some by cruelty. The grannies knew there were contagions that eat a woman up from the inside, turning the bile black. Things like not speaking their minds. Too much sweetness can rot you like sugar on the tooth. Too much patience never helped anyone but those who were waiting to take take take. Celeste used to say these things, most deadly to womenfolk could rot out her guts by the turn of the season.

It wasn't the black bile that got Celeste. It was just her day. She told Lillian so.

On Celeste's last day, Lillian returned home from fueling to find her grandmother in bed, her faded but unfrayed quilt around her body. It was the quilt that Lillian kept on her own wedding bed.

She had some last words for her granddaughter that Lillian could not make sense of. As she sat beside her bed, the old woman spoke of an old song she had heard from a native woman who had traveled east. The woman, named Louise, was one of the last from a local Osage tribe and had been born with a curve in her spine that had caused her great pain.

"Louise paid her way onto the boat east with lavender," Celeste had whispered from her bed, the quilt pulled around her cheeks, almost in second childishness. "She was away so long, we thought she had died. There had been no word. But the next winter she was back, thinner, and with a spine that was no longer twisted. She told us she spent half a year in a place called the Dibang. Have you read of that, Lillian?"

Lillian stirred her tea and told her she had not.

"It's in the east. Where there are many healers," she said, a dreamlike tone in her voice. Next, she took Lillian's hand.

"Lily-B," she said, stuttering. "There is something you must know before I go."

"Okay, gran," Lillian said, sitting beside her on the bed, looking over the ingredient list on one of the tinctures she had beside her. Celeste gripped her hand with what was left of her strength when she said the next part.

"Louise, the native woman, she had visions. She would speak of these to other grannies. But never for mere stories. She only spoke of the visions to prevent harm."

"And why was that?" Lillian asked.

"Because there is delight in God's plan. But sometimes we must work to thwart the Devil," Celeste said, her eyes dark in her sunken face. "What Louise told me pertains to you, child."

Lillian furrowed her brow. "How so?"

Celeste took many breaths before speaking again. "She told us of a woman she heard of in the east. Also an orphan. Young, like you. She had a journey. To face the darkness." Celeste was interrupted by a series of watery coughs.

Lillian paged through a notebook, looking for Celeste's notes on suppressing the cough. "Gran, maybe you should try to sleep now—"

"Louise had a dream that you, too, would also face the darkness. Like the orphan girl." She coughed once more into her fist and lay her head back onto the pillow.

Lillian thought her grandmother might be hallucinating, but she stayed still, continuing to listen.

"What kind of darkness?"

"He takes many disguises, my girl," she whispered. "This is where you must listen carefully. To the Osage, the buffalo is sacred. Did you know that the south of the Lick was once Osage land?"

Lillian shook her head.

"Louise said that the demon would slip into sacred spaces. It would lie and trick."

"So it moved into the buffalo?" Lillian asked.

Celeste nodded. "But the buffalo is a proud creature. He would not have this demon take his shape without some sort of mark."

"How is he marked, then?"

"He is blanched of color," she said, her voice fading.

"What do you mean, blanched?"

"He was pale in color."

Lillian softly closed the book. "Do you want to try to drink some tea now?"

Her grandmother grabbed her wrist with more strength. "If you see it, you cannot run," she whispered.

"Who, gran?"

"The white buffalo."

"Okay," Lillian said, feeling Celeste's forehead.

"If there is to be great healing, there must also be a great journey," Celeste said weakly. "When you see it, it is your time to fight."

"There are no buffalo in our parts, though," Lillian told her, helping her up to sip her tea. Celeste managed a small sip before lying back again and exhaling in exhaustion.

"When you meet him, he will be in the umbra," she said, closing her eyes. "The darkest inner part." She coughed, a spittle of blood landing on her chin. Lillian moved to wipe it from her face, and Celeste looked up at her weakly. "If you see it, you must fight. Louise told us. It is the only way. Do you understand?"

"I do, gran. Now take a sip for me."

Looking back, Lillian thought she barely knew a thing about her grandmother. How would all of those secrets lie not one hundred yards from their property, yet Celeste maintained her silence about them? Celeste's life seemed suddenly mysterious. What else had she kept from Lillian? How little we know people, Lillian thought. For twenty years, she knew her grandmother's habits, how she ground her coffee to nearly a dust, the sound of her slight snore, which grew more pronounced later in her age. But the woman she was? Her longings and fears beyond the tea leaves and the tinctures? No idea. Lillian took one last look around the empty cabin, supposing that nobody really knows anybody.

28

Jess sped down Highway 7, his heart racing. Sam dead? How could that be possible? He had just seen him. Was it those vines that cut him up? Had he done it to himself? Sam was tore up about the dog, but that was to be expected. It couldn't have been any sort of sickness. He was healthy as a horse the day before. It couldn't have been suicide, Jess thought, holding the wheel with his left hand, so he could roll down the window on the passenger side. He was in last night's clothes and feeling sickly, his eyes stinging from lack of sleep, his throat burning.

He turned on the radio to drown out his thoughts, but there was only dead air on the local station. He flipped around to the AM, finding two holy rollers preaching like their hair was on fire. Plenty of static between the three other stations. As he pulled up to Highway 5, he saw people outdoors looking up, insects swarming everywhere in the sky, clinging to people's clothing.

By the time Jess pulled into the gravel lot of Sam's rented room, there was a small crowd assembled: two police cars, one with its lights on, and an ambulance parked beside Sam's truck, Kurt's pickup, and a crowd of people, including two servers from Dos Hombres and Judy, the daytime bartender from the Watering Hole hovering just beyond them. Judy was holding her arms across her chest as though hugging herself. Kurt sat off on the fire escape steps, slouching and looking down. Jess pulled in a ways off and quickly walked to Sam's door, where a cop in plainclothes blocked his entry with a meaty hand.

"I'm Jess Cedars—y'all asked for me?" he said to the cop, who nodded back to where Jess had come from without looking at him. Jess followed his gaze to where Gideon Underwood stood leaning against his vehicle, a cigar smashed in the corner of his mouth. Jess was feeling winded as he took in the scene, as though he could not get a deep breath, no matter how much air he took in. He lumbered to Gideon, wondering if this all had been some sort of mistake.

"Thanks for coming, Jess," Gideon said, pulling off his smudged aviators and looking Jess over with a sort of detached curiosity Jess did not like one bit.

"Sheriff. What's this all about?"

Gideon extended his hand. "Sorry, we can't let you inside. Detectives are collecting evidence." Jess gave him a quick handshake as he looked back behind. The police were moving around inside of Sam's, tea-length vinyl gloves on their hands. One of them was assembling police tape around his small front entryway.

"Jesus Christ," Jess said.

"This here's a crime scene, Jess," Gideon said.

"Where's Sam?" Jess asked, watching Kurt talk soundlessly to a medic beside the ambulance. The medic placed a blood pressure cuff on Kurt's left arm and looked over at Jess.

"Sam's in the back of that ambulance, son," Gideon said, watching Jess' face.

"Jesus Christ," Jess said again, beginning a short pace beside Gideon's patrol car. "I was just with him. What the hell happened?"

"We thought you might be able to help us with that," Gideon said, noticing the sheen of sweat covering Jess' face and neck.

"We went out gigging yesterday. Seemed fine. Got cut up by some vines by the creek, though. Dog ran off, and he was tore up about that."

Gideon pulled a small notebook out from his front pocket and thumbed through a few pages. "Your man Kurt said you had to cut the trip short. Was that on account of the injury?" Gideon looked to where Kurt sat, the medic typing notes into a computer. Jess felt like vomiting right there on the ground. His throat felt thick, and despite the sweat, he was shivering. He felt afraid of himself.

Your fault.

"What?" Jess said, looking up.

"You alright, son?" Gideon asked, putting his hand on the boy's shoulder. "You look a little—unwell."

Left your friend to die.

"I'm going to—" Jess said, feeling his insides twisting, as though something had him from within. He ran behind Gideon's car and vomited onto the gravel.

Gideon returned his glasses to his face and made a note on his pad. Jess retched twice more, managing to stand despite the sickness, then wiped his mouth with the back of his hand, and heard Gideon's boots behind him as he passed a warm bottle of water over Jess' shoulder. Jess opened it and drank it almost all down before standing again. He tried focusing on Gideon, but he was seeing double.

"Good Lord, son. What did you boys get into last night?" Gideon asked, adjusting his belt as he peered more closely at Jess.

"A few beers after a day out on the water's all," he said, eyeing Kurt again. He looked about tore up as Jess did.

"It would be a lot easier on us if you boys would come down to the station to give us a statement," Gideon said. Jess felt a wave of anger move through him.

"Are we under arrest?"

"God, no," Gideon said, stifling a false sort of laugh. "Just want to know what happened last night, is all."

"Has anyone told Brutus?" Jess asked.

"I have an officer on his way to his place right now. No phone on file."

Jess leaned against the side of the patrol car, took off his hat, and ran his hand across his scalp, feeling the chills radiate through his body. His skin felt cold to the touch.

Gideon stepped a few inches closer to Jess. Jess could see the deep pockets under his eyes, as though all the shit he saw was hanging right there under his gaze.

"Where'd youse go yesterday, Jess?" Gideon looked down at his notebook, but it was just for show. Jess thought he could see his pulse in his neck.

"Spent the day giggin. Back by 10 pm. The boys were on their way shortly after."

"Get many frogs?" Gideon asked, swatting at a bug between them.

"I need to sit down."

"Right here, son," Gideon said, nodding him into the front seat of his car.

"Didn't get many. Day was a bust. Sammy's dog ran off, and then it all went to hell."

"Sorry to hear it," he said. "How'd it go to hell, exactly?"

"Like I said. Dog didn't come back, is all. And Johnny got cut up on some driftwood." Jess leaned his head back against the rest, his vision swirling before him.

"Where'd he lose the dog?"

"Down by the Lick."

"'Cross J Road?" Gideon asked, looking around the scene again, this time just for show, one thick eyebrow raised.

"Yeah," Jess squinted his shut.

"How did Sam get all cut up?"

"Some kind of vine got him."

"A vine, you say?"

"Like I told youse."

"Whereabouts on the Lick?"

"The southern end. My wife," Jess said, opening the door again to spit into the dusty gravel. "She—she said not to cross over to the south—"

"South of the Lick?"

"Yeah. On account of the private property."

Gideon's eye twitched, and he waited.

"But Sam ran off." He cleared his throat and took another drink from the warm bottle of water. "After his dog. Kurt too. But we didn't see no one."

"How long do you suppose they were over on the South?"

"'Bout twenty minutes, is all. That's when Sam got all tangled up. Is that what got him in the end?"

"We're looking into that. Now, why do you reckon Sam would step into a bramble like that?" Gideon asked, interrupted by the sound of a light thump on his windshield where two locusts crawled toward the roof.

"I told you," Jess said, feeling irritation in his chest. "His dog bounded off. He said he ran off like someone had called him off us, Sam said. Wait—Sammy didn't do this—didn't kill himself, did he?"

Gideon took his time inhaling and exhaling before answering Jess. "No, he did not. Sam aspirated, Jess," Gideon said, squinting across the lot to the detectives moving in and out of Sam's place.

"Aspirated—what is that?" Jess asked.

"Breathed in fluid. Into the lungs."

"What kind of fluid?" Jess asked, pulling at his collar with his index finger.

"Organic matter," Gideon said. "Vomit. We will know more when the examiner takes a look at him."

"I've got to talk to Kurt," Jess said, starting to open the door.

"Few more quick questions, son," Gideon said, putting his hand out on Jess' arm. "Kurt told us you boys spotted some kind of wild animal. A big cat of some kind?"

Jess shuddered, remembering the big shoulders on the howler. "Something like that. Don't reckon it was a bobcat. It seemed to be tracking us." He briefly considered mentioning his own cabin, but thought better of it. A bolt of worry moved through him. He had to get back home.

"You see anyone over on the south side?"

"No, sir," Jess said. "We did stop by Lorna's for one. On our way home. That's about it. Johnny and Sam said they were going to head to the urgent care."

"Johnny is over at Mercy Southwest."

"Johnny?" Jess said, looking over at Gideon's sagging face. He tried to remember if he already knew that, or if he had only suggested it to his brother.

"Admitted him last night. Rattler bite, apparently."

"Rattler? Johnny wasn't bit by no rattler, Gideon."

"He told us that too. Strange, don't you think?"

Jess wiped his eyes, trying to narrow his focus through the windshield.

"Doc at Mercy has him stable. His arm is swole up twice the normal size. His wife said he's double, sweating something fierce."

"No one saw no snake."

"The docs did a blood test."

"I need to get over there," Jess said, swallowing hard as he stood unsteadily, making his way back around the front of the vehicle, grateful to be out in the fresh air.

"Might be a good idea to get checked out while you're there, Jess," Gideon added, closing the heavy door.

"What's that supposed to mean?" Jess said sharply.

Gideon turned at his tone, thought he could see something cruel shimmering in the outline of Jess' features. He took a step toward Jess, his tongue in the pocket of his front lip. "It means you look like hell, son."

29

The sun was high in the sky when Lillian walked into the timber toward Lick Creek. She wore a small canvas bag on her back, in which she stored a small mirror, a knife, and a bottle of water. She carried her husband's shotgun in her left hand. Eugene's salt cellar lay stuffed in her pocket. She had left everything else behind. Around her was the crepitating song of the locusts. As she moved, she felt a sort of electrical pull forward. It was almost as Eugene said, almost as though they were waiting for her.

Lily-B, she heard called to her from somewhere deep inside of her own mind.

She ignored the voice. When she reached the end of the treeline, she surveyed the Lick. The water was high, white capped where it crossed over rock as it rushed downstream, too high for her to wade in where she was. She had no choice but to travel a half mile upstream to cross.

Don't cross the border.

She shook her head firmly, ignoring all sounds but what the forest held. There was no trail beside the treeline, and she trudged through the grasses, slowed by the rocky ground. She paused briefly to retie her hair and slipped, nearly falling into the creek, but she righted herself at the last minute, feeling that she had been somehow pulled toward the water. Her heart rushed. She closed her eyes, sent out, and felt the myriad presences around her, their pulsing lifeblood, too many sizes to count.

As soon as the water was thigh-high, Lillian stood prepared to cross the Lick for the first time in her life. In her mind was a kind of exhilaration that only comes from the courage to face a thing for the first time. As she stepped in, she felt her foot crunch on something. Looking down was an old game call crushed into the clay. The kind used to mimic rabbits in distress. She pushed forward, feeling the water's clean coldness against the skin beneath her jeans, then pushed again, knee-high, the current a soft sucking around her before wading waist-high in the water, her mind on her only task: the grape leaves for her husband, then a hasty retreat. As she pushed ahead, she felt the old feeling of being watched by something curious. She kept her gaze forward.

Heed the border.

As she approached the forbidden south side, she took one quick look behind her before turning her gaze on the new shore. The ecosystem had changed. Thicker trees past the shore, a blanket of creeping vines below them, darkness between the two. Few streaks of sunlight broke through the canopy, and she couldn't see any of the regular signs of life from her land. No squirrels, no birds, no sound save for the locusts that swirled about. Lillian took in a slow inhale, cupped the stone around her neck for luck, and made her way toward the forest ahead.

The trees on the south were thicker in the trunk than across the Lick, likely a result of the absence of controlled burns. They'd have them every five years in the north, but the south was always just darkness and silence, while the north was lit with fire. Lillian took one last look around before steeling her eyes up as she stepped under the canopy. Immediately, she felt the coarse edges of the brush below her. As soon as she stepped within, the false vine seemed to move along with her. She pushed ahead, trusting her steps as Marjorie advised, keeping her gaze up for the simple *Vitis*, which would be carrying fruit by this time of year. Moving forward while not looking at the path felt unnatural, but the ground held her, and some of the panic quieted. As she drew more deeply into the canopy layer, the air changed. Became cooler, the wind picked up, and she felt the movement increase at her feet. She noticed it first like a fingernail against her ankle, and then, as though spindly hands curled around her, the vine seeming to switch around, the enemy everywhere. It felt like stepping on daggers that moved about on their own, and a chill ran across her bones as she thought of them, moving beneath her jeans cuff and across her skin as she moved, a sort of dance between them. The more she stepped forward, the more the vines moved about, ready to clutch, making her movement increasingly unsteady, the worry in the center of her chest spreading to terror. She paused for a moment, leaning against a thick tree for support, her eyes squeezed shut. She heard Marjorie's voice, low and calm in her memory: *I'm sorry I can't go in your place. It has to be kin who retrieves it.*

Then the voice changed into something sinister. Sharp.

Trespasser.

Exhaling slowly, she looked up and readied herself to keep going, but just then, her step muddied by the vines, Lillian stumbled onto her side, dropping the shotgun as her palm caught the spill, but scratching up her hip bone something awful on the thorns. The vines were around her wrist then, one coiling around her waist, between her fingers then, and she squeezed her eyes shut, moving to her knees, reaching about for the gun she had dropped, and feeling the end of it, she tried to lift it to no avail. The vines curled around it, and she felt it pulling away from her. She scrambled forward, panting audibly, feeling about the sharp edges, but the vines had swallowed it. It was gone.

If Jess Cedars is to be saved, you must be the one to make this crossing.

Lillian stood. She had bitten the inside of her cheek and tasted blood. However, growing all around her, nearly eighty feet in woody length, was the *Vitis* grape she had come for.

Trespasser.

She slid off the backpack, a slight rumbling of thunder from the east, and felt a change in the atmosphere, as though the air was almost electric. She pulled her knife from the bag and made a series of cuttings, careful to cut the stem before its main stalk so as not to injure the plant. She could feel the false vine continuing around her feet, one curling completely around her left foot, giving her the feeling of being held by a spiky hand. She continued to gather the *Vitis* leaves, wrapping them carefully before putting them in her granny purse. Then, thinking of slowing the infection from the new cut on her side, she carefully pulled a few more leaves off the stalk and pressed the veiny layers against her skin, tucking them under her clothes before rebuttoning her pants.

Suddenly, something happened that was new for her. Without the sending out, she felt heartbeats around her. She did not have to close her eyes or cast her attention around her. It was a sensation that was second nature, like an additional sense that arrived without the calling. She merely understood bodies were moving toward her, and quickly, as though closing in. And alongside it, a faint sound. Not animal, but child. It was the sound of Glory Be. The sound of her crying.

It was as Marjorie warned. The spies.

Mama.

Sending out had always been a deliberate search, like pushing out a long, slow breath before pulling it back in slowly. It was work. Here, though, the sensation had been automatic. And this reading, she felt moved more strongly through her, alerting her to many bodies, many large bodies around her, but one especially large, pulpy heart very close, a hundred yards or so. As she maneuvered the backpack onto her back, the salt cellar fell from her pocket, and, turning on its side, emptied nearly all its contents on the forest floor.

"Christ, no!" she said, sinking down to feel about the ground again, her eyes squinted shut. She moved her hands through the sharper vines, feeling the thick cords of the false ivy's leaves until her fingers found Eugene's cellar. The top had broken off.

Lillian scooped handfuls of salt into her pocket, feeling the hearts nearly inside of her own body then, the beating alongside of her own. The sounds of Glory's cries continued, closer then. Could they feel her heart? she wondered. She turned slowly, trying to find the bodies in the trees, but the darkness blanketed everything. She stood, quickly backing up the way she came, her side cramping up as she moved. The feeling of the hearts only intensified as she neared the banks of the Lick, but she pushed on. As the trees gave way to the clearing, she spotted a blurred figure just beyond the umbra. She paused, hearing it disrupting the water, and squinted against the darkness as the thunder boomed again, this time louder, closer, the lightning flashing soundlessly.

Then it was before her, in the flash of light from the sky. The buffalo. Standing cooling in the Lick, its tail swishing around its heavy cowlike body. It was paler in color than the pictures of buffalo she'd seen, very nearly white and nearly motionless, standing gently against the rush of the current. Two giant brown horns curving to the side hung above its batlike ears.

Do not run from the white buffalo. When you see it, it means it is your time to fight.

Lillian felt a cold chill move through her chest. But then, the other hearts arrived. Five—no, six of them. Circling her. Slow and pulpy, along the shore of the Lick, blocking her return. She knew these hearts. Howlers. She felt the pulling of both grannies' commands. Celeste had told her she could not run from the buffalo, but Marjorie told her to flee the howlers. What was she to do? She quickly moved along the treeline, the buffalo in her line of vision, toward the clearing inland, once again through the vines that clutched at her ankles. Feeling the hearts closer, she increased her pace until she could hear their footsteps, sounding like horses moving across the forest floor, hearing their breath even, closer and closer still.

She felt it before she knew what was happening. As though she was hit from behind, suddenly. Knocked onto her belly on the forest floor, she squinted her eyes and tried to get up, something grabbing her sack and yanking her back with tremendous strength, so much so she was picked up off of her feet. She quickly pulled her arms free from the bag's ties and threw herself forward, making it to the brightness of the clearing just as something bit down on her calf. Lillian screamed out, falling onto her knees in the tall grass in the clearing. Twisting to see what it was, she saw a huge black animal with matted fur and dark eyes, red-rimmed, with several more in the distance behind it. She kicked out as hard as she could with her uninjured leg, catching whatever had bit her in the snout, and with a deep yelp, it cowered back. She crawled backward, the sting of its saliva running through her leg. In the meadow clearing stood a neglected-looking building with a deeply faded wooden cross at the top, two stories with faded paint and boarded-up stained glass windows on the east side, as though to block the morning sun. She made a run for it through the piercing stings of her bite, landing with a fall on the sagging porch as the crack of thunder boomed low in the sky, the howler that bit her just behind her. Beyond that one, were several more, all with the same hulking shoulders and oversized fangs, long legs with hooves at the end and demonic red eyes. She lay frozen, waiting for it to pounce again, its muzzle dripping saliva as it stood. The wind moved through its terrible, thick fur, the clouds moving quickly above them as though an extension of them, and the others gathered beyond the one waiting for her in a sort of V formation. She scooted her body back against the building, knowing there was no way to fight these animals. All their eyes watched her like prey, but unlike the animals she had seen, these eyes lacked indifference. They seemed almost humanly intelligent. And in their gaze was a sort of hate as they circled, panting. Lillian lifted herself to the door, attempted to pull it open, but immediately jerked her hand away. The handle was ice cold. In the middle of summer. A red burn line appeared in her palm.

Pushing against the door with her shoulder, she shoved inside, kicking the door shut behind her. Shadows of the beast crossed in the line of light under the door, and she felt a coldness move through her. She turned, adjusting to the darkness of the room, whimpering as she looked down at her leg where she had been bitten, blood soaking into the denim around the wound. She limped forward in the darkness.

The stinking heat of the room was immediate, and her eyes had to adjust to the low light. She moved a few steps ahead quietly, the thunder continuing outside, candlelight flickering to the sides of the pews. The space was mostly empty save for a few bodies bent in prayer, dusty rays of light streaked between them. The church had been sorely neglected. There were missing windows on the top level, and what windows were in place were coarsely boarded up. The vestibule contained a spray of papers, littering the floor around it. A cluster of pigeons huddled in exposed rafters. She leaned against the entrance's withered arch, reaching for her wound. There was no altar, no preacher, just a dozen or so pews with a handful of silent parishioners.

Lillian peeked between two of the boards on the windows. The animals' thick bodies moved back and forth like wolves waiting to pounce. The one closest to the church panted low beside the treeline, its red eyes peering back at her, its smoky breath coiling in the dirt at its feet. They were just as Celeste had described them when she was a child, asking about the cries that to her, did not sound like coyotes. She wondered if they could smell the blood and looked back outside to try to count if more had come. They were hulking, slow-moving, otherworldly hunger in their jowls. Whatever they were, they kept away from the old church.

She breathed in slowly, feeling the ache in her calf, her palm raw with pain. She felt cold spreading under her skin at the wound, her leg tingling, and she knew she'd need to see a granny soon. If only Marjorie were closer. There had to be someone here, perhaps in a back room or a secretary with a phone, and she made her way down the side aisle to a closed door. Locked. She took in the room, its once clean lines around the area where an altar must have once stood.

The sound of her footsteps, though, roused the parishioners, and she heard a grunting sound behind her. As she turned, one whipped up his head, his face twisted with anger. She froze before slowly backing away. It was an older man, his hair in long strings. His face was filthy around bright eyes that looked goatlike. And there was redness dripping from his mouth, thicker than blood, it seemed. Suddenly, he stood, very quickly, moaning into the quiet space of the church, alerting the others. Lillian felt a fist of horror in her belly and limped quickly back toward the door as they all turned to look toward her, their mouths red with moaning intensity, several raising their arms to point at her. She moved as quickly as possible toward the door. It was these men or the howlers. But at least outside, she was not trapped, and as she pushed back outside, the men's voices rose from moaning into a shrill, screaming cry. She looked around, looking back toward the treeline, where the howlers lay crouched in wait. Beyond them, just past the line of trees, was her escape. A clearing to Lick Creek just a few hundred meters from her. This was her only chance. No more time for thinking. She took off running, the howlers moving to follow her as she raced, slowed by the injury, the men's cries behind her as lightning cracked between them. She pushed ahead, looking back only once to see the church men in pursuit as well, moving faster than any human person should be able to move, almost like darting shadows in the rain. She tried to increase her pace but felt her energy draining from her wounds, her literal lifeblood leaving a live trail behind her. The more the blood drained from her, the more her mind moved in sadness and hope to Glory, small and helpless in the care of Marjorie. She pushed forward, pumping her arms as she ran, looking heavenward, the rain sudden, soaking her. If she could make it to the water, she had a chance.

Please, God—

30

Jess threw his truck into reverse and pulled out of the gravel lot, kicking up a cloud of dust behind him. He felt like shit. His head was pounding and his throat felt scratched up. Sam dead. Now Johnny at Mercy for a snake bite that he didn't even know had happened. And Kurt looked worse than hungover. He had tried calling Johnny from two different phones, but all the lines were down across Camden County. He wanted to get home and crawl into bed to sleep off whatever was ailing him. Maybe Lillian could make him one of her peppermint tinctures to help with his head. Then he could call up his brother. This was worse than any migraine he'd ever had before. It pierced down into his neck. This time, his vision was blurry, something he hadn't felt before, and he felt like vomiting again.

Sam. Aspirated. He had just seen him, upright, walking from his porch to his truck. How could someone be here one minute, then gone the next? What kind of grown ass man dies from choking on his own vomit?

He barely finished his second beer, so it couldn't have been that. Was it the cuts that did it? Had he picked something up? Was it catching?

First his mother, then Sam. Jess suddenly felt an anger bubble up inside of him, obscuring even the pain in his head. Anger at Gideon's goddamn tone, anger at Kurt's sullen face, anger at his truck, beat to hell. Anger at Sam's dog that got them into all this, anger at Sam for chasing him, anger at the damn town, their odd shit, anger even at his wife—he tried to stop himself there. Anger at the locusts all over everything he planted that spring. Anger at all the blood he'd seen. Anger at the baby who cried constantly, keeping his wife from him—*Jess, enough*, he thought. Anger that Lillian had been right about the south, its danger, anger that he crossed anyway, anger at fucking Johnny for never listening to him, and anger at his swelling throat. What if something happened to him? Who would help Lillian with the damn baby? *Jesus*, he thought to himself. *Calm down.*

He rolled down his window, letting the wind blow steadily inside the cab. He turned up the radio, hoping to hear something angry, but all he heard was static. He took the turns too fast, feeling thick in his throat.

You're next.

Then she'll just bed down with some other man in no time.

"What in the goddamn hell is that?" Jess screamed. He shook off the thoughts that darted around inside of his head, took a deep breath in as he drove, feeling the hot wind across his face, before erupting in a fit of phlegmy coughing, his chest tight. His eyes stung so bad he pulled over at the old Shell station on 7-13, sweaty hands limp on the wheel, his head splitting with pain, tasting blood. He leaned his head back against the seat and closed his eyes, distracted by a pair of locusts thumping through the open window to buzz in the space beside him. They were clumsy, falling more than they flew. He picked them up and threw them out of the cab, cleared his throat, and spit on the gravel beside the truck before killing the engine.

He sat there a moment, his thoughts moving away from why and into the now what. He was going to find Kurt and find out what the hell happened. He was going to call up Gideon and ask for some help with whatever the hell those things were on his land. He pushed open the door, it feeling awfully heavy to him, wiping his eyes with the back of his hands. In these sorts of situations, he would always have called up Sam, who'd be there with his gun and enough rounds to take out those damn cats from the south of the Lick, but Sam was gone, snatched away, and he felt the hole inside of him stretch even wider.

Tony Ruth, the seventeen-year-old boy manning the Shell was the youngest son of George and Rikki Ruth, soybean farmers who had sixty acres on the forty-fourth mile marker. His big brother Craig had played ball with Jess at the high school until a combine had ripped off his arm at the shoulder. Jess and his father had even visited the hospital and sat sadly alongside his parents. Tony had been stocking cigarettes behind the bulletproof glass before Jess' stumbling pulled him from his task. He lumbered toward the station with difficulty, sicker looking than drunk, the corners of his mouth bloody, his skin all pale and shiny looking. Tony briefly considered calling the manager but then thought better of it. Too early to be shaking up trouble, and he had already been late twice that week. A bell chimed Jess' arrival. Jess walked up to the glass.

"Bathroom?" Jess mumbled.

"You're Jess Cedars, right?" Tony asked, looking him up and down with concern. "My brother is Craig. Y'all played ball together way back when."

"What's that?" Jess mumbled. The anger foamed inside of him again. What the hell was wrong with these kids?

"Are you feeling alright?"

"I said 'bathroom,' you prick," Jess said loudly, slamming his hand down on the counter. "You not paying attention to customers anymore?" He felt the heat of his breath as he spoke, felt his eyes stinging.

The boy backed away from the glass and picked up the phone, trying numbers, before realizing the line was dead.

"BATHROOM," Jess said, pointing to the side of the building.

Tony lifted a key from the wall and pushed it under the glass to Jess.

"Fucking prick," Jess said under his breath as he moved back outside. His legs felt heavy as he moved, and he dropped the key twice in the dust before managing to unlock the bathroom door. He vomited twice in the filthy toilet, the first time bile, the second time—blood.

Tony pulled out the two-way radio from under the cash register. Charlie, the owner, left it on for emergencies whenever he stepped away from the station. It lay next to an unloaded snub-nosed pistol, a book of matches, an envelope full of receipts, and three rolls of pennies.

"Y'ello," Charlie Warren answered on his radio, frustrated at further communication from his least reliable employee.

"Mr. Warren, we, ugh, have a problem. Over here at the station," Tony said into the radio.

"This radio is for emergencies only. You can't leave early today; I don't have anyone else coming in until—"

"There's a guy here, Mr. Warren. Real sick, looks like—"

"What's he doing?" Charlie said, looking out his window. There had been chaos afoot in town all that day, and he was already on edge that it would somehow catch up to one of his businesses.

"He's in the bathroom now. He could barely walk and was mumbling something. Sounded like he was speaking in another language or something."

"Goddamn immigrants stealing from me—"

"This ain't an immigrant, Mr. Warren. It's Jess Cedars."

"Cedars? What the hell is he doing drunk at this hour?" Charlie said into the radio.

"I couldn't understand him. And his mouth's all bloody. Like foamy."

"Probably out hunting all night," Charlie said despondently. "Alright. I'm on my way."

31

Lillian made it to the treeline and into the coarse brush, breath heaving inside of her chest. Thorny vines cut into her ankles as she ran, but she did not look down, and as she pushed through the tearing, the growling of the howlers behind her was joined by something even more menacing, a sort of shrieking, and all of it growing closer, so close that she could hear the breath of one of them, of something, behind her. It was at this moment that a sort of sinking dread crept inside of her. Thoughts of Glory Be. Who would take care of her if something happened to her? Next, a dread about Jess. The voices somehow implanted into her own thoughts.

Already too late.
You've left them.
Both to rot, as your mother left you.
Too late.

The thoughts cut into her heart. How could she think such a thing? Yet some part of her knew this voice was not from her, just within her. She darted between trees, trying not to let the words touch her.

An orphan. Leaving your child.
Like mother, like daughter.

You run or you fight, but are never trapped.

Lillian nearly cried out as she ran, from the obscenity of the thoughts, from the deep throb of what had cut her, what had bitten her. She didn't dare consider the extent of her injuries, but pushed, pushed, thinking only of one step ahead.

And then suddenly, twin lights appeared ahead, like eyes from the otherworld. The dark brush around her was suddenly illuminated, the vines nearly shrinking from it. Lillian was nearly blinded herself but pushed forward, moving again to the right and the left to try and shake the howlers. Through the lights, she saw the glimmering reflection of the water just before her. She was nearly at the creek's edge. A few more feet and she would reach it.

It's too late.

No—there's still hope.

She pushed ahead toward the water, the lights just beyond it, hearing the snapping teeth before something bit down into her, deeper than before, and there was another terrible piercing pain, this one meeting the bone of her ankle, and she fell hard against the ground, feeling the vines coil against her legs, her torso, moving as though they were living things. The tall bank was just feet before her, and without thinking, she turned to face what had attacked her, this time, fury replacing fear. As she did, she met the red gaze of one of the howlers, from the shadows, fully visible in the lights. It poised hulking above her as some sort of otherworldly guard, its jaws wide with sleek black lips like a cat's, poised to bite down on her. Using her hands as claws, her foot having disappeared inside the heavy jaws of the howler, she found herself filled not with fear but a rage that felt utterly foreign, yet someplace she had been before, maybe lifetimes before. The animal's teeth sank deeper into the flesh of her left leg, shaking it back and forth, like a dog tearing meat from a bone, the white teeth sinking into pooling blood around her knee. And as she watched its teeth clamp down, she saw its nostrils widen, taking in her leaking breast milk, its hellish eyes raking over her. Its jaws slackening, it raised its thick head and emitted a hellish bugle, a scream deeper than the elk's, followed by panting grunts as though to call its brothers or claim its prey. Its sandpaper tongue moved toward her chest, and she screamed out, then reached for it, pushed her thumbs deep into its red eyes, pushing past lids and into the red gaze, the wet jelly of the eyeball making way for her thumbs. She could feel the hate and desire to cause hurt pulsing beside her own blood in her body like twin flames. And if anyone had been close enough to see her beside the blinded beast, who was then releasing its grip as it howled itself, they would have seen something curious. Lillian's own eyes shifted into something even more unusual, the yellow receding as the pupil stretched horizontally before a thin cowl moved to cover it. Lillian, of course, could not see herself, but to anyone else, it would have been bestial, an inhuman reaction to a blind rage that, unbeknownst to Lillian, had lain silently coiled within her since her conception, against the brick wall behind a bar in Climax Springs, Missouri, between her feral southern mother and an anonymous trucker from Dixon, not knowing this brief coupling would produce a half-wild child whose grandmother's steering would save her life.

The howler, effectively blinded by Lillian's thumbnails, pulled away as she kept on it, screaming, scrambling to her feet, standing on her one good leg, forgetting her pain for a moment as hate propelled her, pushing her thumbs past the wet sclera until she felt bone, and as the animal cried out again, releasing her in a mangled mess of blood, other figures collecting in speed beyond it. Feeling their hearts approaching, she did not stall. Temporarily free, she turned and looked toward the twin lights again—so close. And getting her balance, she pushed herself forward and jumped—no, leapt—thinking of herself flying enough to feel the crash of the shallow end of Lick Creek hard against her hip and hitting her head on the ground beneath the water.

They were on her then. Hands, claws, talons, it felt like, digging into the flesh of her legs just below the water's surface. Something dragged her body backward by the belt loops on her jeans, her chin bumping on the rocks below the water's surface, back to the south as she clawed forward fruitlessly, tasting blood, her eyes on the north ahead, kicking at whatever was behind her, crying out chants of spells, prayers. She was pulled from the water, rolled onto rocky sand, coughing out water, nearly blind from it. And then they were tearing at her hair, her shirt. She felt a nail hook on Celeste's leather necklace, pulling her neck to the side before she grabbed it back. She recognized a human form, a woman, grizzled with age but strong, her eyes horizontal like the goat's, her body moving in a way that seemed too quick for human ability. She felt the skin on her legs tearing, felt the warm blood stinging. The pain was otherworldly, immediate. She looked down to see one woman biting into her where the howlers had been at her, her teeth having disappeared below the skin of her ankle, her eyes frantic with the taste. Lillian thought then with a horrible sinking feeling that there would be no out. That she would die there, and she'd never again see Glory's sweet face or feel Jess' warm hands again.

You left them, didn't you?

Like you were left.

"No—" she screamed, hearing the word come out slowly. She felt herself slowing, the heavy pain holding her back as her kicking slowed. Funny thing happens when you're facing destruction, when you've been beaten, she thought. Really, it's not adrenaline she felt but sadness. Longing too—for even to live one more day broken and in pain, even the horrible days, one more of those is better than the darkness of nothingness. Looking up into the clear sky, she felt Death's primal beckoning in the air around her, smelled it even. A sort of stinking release as she heard herself crying out beside the growls of the women and the sounds of insects beyond that. With each puncture of her skin, she sank deeper into the belly of the beast.

A woman crawled over her then, holding her arms down, kneeling on her belly with a cruel grimace, her lips pulled back into a primeval snarl to show rows of teeth not human at all, silky red with her blood, and Lillian screamed into the small space between them. The woman's knees pressed into her tender belly as she moved onto her, and the pain spread out to her chest, down her legs. She rocked back and forth, but her arms and legs were pinned, and as she leaned forward toward her neck, she screamed out one last plea, her eyes changing again with her fury as another beside the witch, an ancient-looking one with tendrils of gray tangles in an arc, pressed a black fire poker into the witch's shoulder. Her mouth moved too, speaking something Lillian could not understand. The howlers backed up. The ancient one spoke again, some sort of broken English that sounded familiar in some way, something she remembered maybe hearing as a child from across the Lick while hiding in Celeste's skirts but could not quite comprehend, as though her words stood right out of reach. The woman on top of Lillian hissed something back, responding in the same tongue before leaning back on her haunches as she tensed, cloudy spittle dripping from her rows of uneven, sharp teeth, still digging her weight into her body. Lillian coughed, tasting blood.

Things swirled before Lillian's vision. There were grannies and the yarns they broke from, there was the image of a woman who resembled Lillian, dancing in a bar in low light, a tight skirt, her long ropes of hair hiding her face with her otherworldly eyes, men circling her. Then, that same figure pregnant, deep with child beside Celeste's hearth, singing a song in an odd language, and then, suddenly, looking up as though at Lillian, with the eye of the goat. Her eyes far away, Lillian remembered Marjorie's rules: *You are not to look.* But it was too late. She had no mirror to use to look behind her. She had gazed on all of them.

"I said no—," the Changed One ordered in a flat voice before she returned to the language Lillian could not understand. Her command, whatever it was, echoed around in the trees, where a few turkey vultures, disturbed by their movement, lifted away in flight. She felt her eyes lose focus from the weight of the woman on her body.

I can understand them.

Do not speak to them.

The ancient one leaned closer to her with a quick hobble, filth in the lines of her face, her eyes rimmed red and black in the odd pupils. She looked as though she were rotting as she stood. Lillian panted and waited, her heart wild in her chest. She was waiting, she felt, to die.

You should die, you left them to die.

Her blood had pooled through her clothes on the ground beneath her, her head swimming from the falls. The howlers stood around as though in some sort of ceremony, their breath in the air between them, their eyes the color of blood as though waiting for her command to tear the rest of her apart. The one she had blinded stood among them, panting, undeterred by its injury.

As the ancient one leaned close, she sniffed at Lillian several times like an animal, making sounds like a record playing voices backward. She lifted a lock of her hair, smelled again. She opened Lillian's mouth with her gnarled hand, looked inside, turned to the other and smiled, showing her rows of small, sharp teeth in a black maw. Lillian shook with horror, squinting her eyes shut against what was before her.

She spoke directly to Lillian then, the words beginning to clear between them. Lillian began to recognize sounds, then a moment later, words—daughter, or was it mother? Lillian shook her head, struggling to get free from the other woman's weight.

"Off," the Changed One ordered to the other, poking her in the ass to move her aside, and Lillian breathed in with relief, rolling to her side, dry heaving until she caught her breath. The Changed One moved the end of the poker against Lillian's chest. Against her heart.

"Didn't you see her eyes?" she said to the other witch, nudging her roughly as Lillian looked between them with horror.

"What tribe, child?" the ancient one asked, urgency in her dark, grizzled voice.

Lillian lifted her weight to her elbows, her vision beginning to clear, but her fear as sharp as before.

Left them to rot.

Stop.

The witch repeated her question, this time with agitation in her odd voice. Beneath her ratted dress Lillian could see a red twine on her neck and a weight at the end of it. It was iron.

Protection.

This was a granny. A southern granny. She looked too long gone for this world, but she was a granny.

"Which is your tribe?" she hissed in a low voice, her eyes that same horizontal.

Lillian thought at that moment that her eyes were somehow the same color as this woman's, a yellowish green. She remembered then that Marjorie had told her not to let them hear her voice.

Lillian broke Marjorie's rule then. She communicated. "Are you a granny?"

"Answer me," the Changed One said, pushing the poker more firmly against her body.

"Black," Lillian managed to get out, her heartbeat in her throat. She scanned the landscape, longed for the water—if she could just get to the water. The menfolk from the church appeared about ten yards behind the howlers, their massive haunches amid the vines. She remembered what Marjorie had told her. The men could not touch her. She sent her mind out, feeling for how many surrounded her. She felt eleven hearts around her. Five human. Farther, across the creek, there were more. Many more. She stopped counting at fifteen, sixteen.

You will never make it.

Already gone.

The dogs shall tear your man's flesh.

Lillian shook off the voice, swallowing hard, watching the faces of the Changed Ones. She didn't have much time. She could hear the creek's course from where she lay bleeding, the sounds of the water's collision against the rock. This sound she had heard so many times growing up, never knowing that only a few hundred feet beyond where she stood, hiding in Celeste's skirts, there was this danger. These creatures.

"Black? The healer?" the dark granny said to Lillian, her dirty tendrils dangling closer to Lillian. Her skin was empty of color, the eyes blacker than charcoal. Lillian saw a nictitating membrane, or a third eye quickly opening and closing across her gaze. Lillian swallowed. She had seen them in animals but never in people. Lillian thought she saw eagerness in her ragged expression and could smell her as the wind lifted the heavy clumps of hair from her face. To Lillian, she looked like the Beast.

"Yes. Celeste Black," she whispered, her body shivering.

The Changed One registered her weight on the end of her poker, looking down on Lillian as though she had some sort of new understanding. She smoothed her filthy skirts and ran a gnarled finger along the line of blood that had collected at Lillian's ankle before placing the bloody finger in her mouth. Lillian dragged her legs under her, trying to inch away. She couldn't bear to look at her wounds. Who could help her at this point? How could she manage to drive back to Marjorie's tinctures when she couldn't use her legs?

The Changed One widened her eyes. "You're Sugar's."

"Sugar's?" Lillian managed to speak, feeling as though she were suffocating. The granny blinked again, the same strange membrane quickly moving across her eyes. A locust landed on her cheek, but she did not seem to notice.

"You Lily-B," she scoffed, saying Lillian's private name. Her voice still felt like an echo.

"How do you know my name?" Lillian asked.

Do not speak to them.

"You got Sugar's blood in you."

"How do you know my name?"

"Lily-B. Black Dog's ward," the Changed One said to the other, ignoring Lillian.

"Ward?" Lillian said, confused.

"Black Dog never bred," the dark granny snarled, her face floating close to Lillian's at the outer edge of the circle. The other woman moved behind her.

"This here Sugar's bastard," the Changed One said to the menfolk behind her, amusement on her sagging face. "Little granny-woman in training." She toed her injured leg with the end of her foot. "He has been waiting for her."

Lillian was frozen, her mind racing. Who was Sugar? And Lillian, her bastard? Who has been waiting for her? Lillian looked between the two Changed Ones, her mind racing. She felt panic rising in her chest, her fingers tingling. Was she somehow related to this Sugar? Did that make her southern? If she was, how could Celeste have been her grandmother? Had Celeste adopted her? What had Celeste not told her before her death? Her breath felt heavy all of a sudden, and her vision swam before her. The bodies of the Changed Ones were blurry to her. She had seen this before in new mothers who had lost too much blood. She lay her head back, thinking she could collect her strength for just a moment, some part of her knowing that if she failed, then Jess would fall, and there would be no one to raise up Glory, for just a second.

"Guess Lily-B ain't cut out for the south," she heard one of the Changed Ones snicker.

He's already gone. You know that.
You let him go, let him get infected.

Lillian looked up, the sky, just as blue here on the south as it was outside her cabin. She felt so tired—the pulsing pain louder than anything else. She felt helpless against the fatigue.

Don't lie there—get up. Get up.

"We must deliver her to Him."

No, she thought. She couldn't die there in the south. Where the babies and snakes coil together, where the howlers drink mother's milk. Where the Changed Ones taste blood. Lillian coughed, lay back where she had collapsed on the bank on the south of the Lick before passing out again.

Images swirled in her half-conscious mind. First, she was beside the cabin with Jess. It was high noon, but the sky was nearly black. She sent out. And felt them. There were predators moving in. Howlers, she thought, circling them at the start of the treeline. She turned to Jess, tried to speak to him, but he could not hear her, his eyes vacant as though looking miles away. She turned his face toward hers, even pounded on his chest, but he moved past her and into the timber without reacting to her. She screamed out, her heart pounding, but he walked into the darkness as it enveloped him. The animals circled her then, the one she had blinded closest to her, its heart huge and pulpy, the heartbeat slow. When she looked more closely at it, she saw it was not the beast but a child. A girl child. She was naked, wearing nothing, and filth covered its small, pale body, its yellow goat eyes following her from where it stood beside the scummy cove, cuts across its leg, horned beetles crawling across her toes. The child turned to her and spoke in a phantom voice.

"Hello, Lily-B," she said, the same slow heartbeat as the howler.

"Who are you?" Lillian heard herself asking, sounding in slow motion.

"Don't you recognize me?" the child asked, her head cocked to the side.

"No," Lillian said, shaking her head.

"I am your mother," she said, with a small laugh.

Lillian looked into her goat eyes, fear rising in her belly before backing up, still shaking her head before the child moved from the scummy cove toward her, rushing, growing larger and faster, her laughter growing louder, more piercing until it shrieked into the air, the birds lifting from the timber around them into the sky.

A memory next. In it, Lillian stood at Celeste's hip, a short breeze reaching in between the timbers. Her line of vision was heavy skirts, veined hands, village dogs. They stood at the north bank of the Lick, watching a figure move across the creek. The body darted from one tree to another before freezing and looking over at where she and her grandmother stood. Lillian narrowed her eyes to try to get a better look, sent out for a heartbeat. There was a small face, caked in dirt, through which two goat eyes peered back at her.

"Why can't we talk to her?" she heard her own voice from decades before, looking up at Celeste's face, which was far away. Celeste shook her head slowly, as though in half time.

"We do not mix with the south," she answered, her mouth still moving through the words that had been spoken.

"But why?"

"Across the Lick there," Celeste said, leaning low with a wince, pointing across, her breath smelling of those cloves she kept in her cheek, "babies and snakes, they sleep together, share the same bread."

"Did you see?"

Celeste nodded.

"Are snakes their pets?"

"No. Snakes cannot be trained up like dogs."

"Do they keep dogs?"

The creek was raging, the current visible then, rising in her memory, the white caps roaring. She had lost sight of the child across the way.

"What happened to their dogs?"

"They change them over."

"Into what, granny?"

"Into night creatures."

"What are night creatures?"

"We call them howlers."

"What's that?" Lillian could see herself slipping behind Celeste's skirts so as to hide herself.

"An animal who does their bidding," her grandmother answered, her voice sounding further and further away. "They track. And hunt."

"Who do they hunt?"

Celeste gripped Lillian's hand firmly, her eyes firmly across the Lick. "Us, darlin'."

Lillian looked at her grandmother, as though she were standing there with her then, as though there had been no time.

"What do they want from us?"

"The old stories say they follow the children. They'll hunt anyone, but they like the chillun best. Once you're bitten by a howler, you turn into the darkness, like them, and then, they can take your shape."

"And that's dark magic?"

"It is. They have a taste for the mother's milk," she said, lighting her pipe.

"Did I ever taste mother's milk?"

Celeste shook her head. "No. Your mother was lost to us."

"Who is my mother?" Lillian asked.

"Someone who conceived you under the redbud," Celeste said, looking sternly down at her, the pouches of her face sagging with age.

"What is a redbud?"

"It is the tree where Judas hanged himself."

Lillian felt a ripple of fear current through her. "Am I bad like Judas?" she asked.

"Doing bad is all choice," Celeste said, circling clockwise around her granddaughter's body as she spoke.

"But what if the Devil is inside of me?" she asked, her panic-filled eyes following Celeste's cycling body.

Celeste took a long pull from her pipe, squatting down to eye level with Lillian. Lillian could smell the tobacco on her breath. "He knocks on everyone's door, child," she said, tapping out the pipe on the rock next to her. "It's up to each of us to know how to best lock the door against him."

32

Marjorie had been sitting on Lillian and Jess' porch watching the locusts bump into the screen when she heard the pickup. She looked at her pocket watch. Four hours since Lillian had gone. She put out her cigarette and hobbled in, hoping to see Lillian pull up, but when she looked outside, she saw Jess swerving in the driveway before parking with a jerk. She peered through the curtain at him where he sat in the truck, but the truck window was too dirty for her to see much. After a while, she saw him push the door open with effort before nearly falling into the gravel. His face was pale with deeply red-rimmed eyes. His mouth was open, crusted over with what looked like bile or vomit. She stepped back and crossed herself. He had been changed, she knew immediately. She had never seen one in person, though. Only read about them. She quickly made her way downstairs to watch over the baby, her spell bag close by as she listened carefully for his approach. She heard him struggling with the key in the lock before he roughly pushed open the door.

"Hello, Jess," she said, rubbing her hip from the bottom of the step. He came in, pausing to look down on her, the smell of him overwhelming.

"Why the hell are you back?" Jess asked, his voice slurred.

She swallowed slowly, trying to keep her voice even. "Just watching the baby for youse," she answered, taking in his greasy skin, the red-rimmed eyes.

"Where's Lillian?" he asked dully.

"She had to run a quick errand. For some feminines," Marjorie lied. "I'm with the baby until she gets back."

He stood there, taking her in at the bottom of the steps. His weight moved from the left leg to the right then back to the left again. "Awful irresponsible of her to leave the baby like this," he slurred. "What if she gets hungry?"

Marjorie could hear the buzz of the insects around the cabin, stronger than before, as though the locusts were somehow drawn to the cabin. "I reckon she'll be right back." Marjorie could hear sirens in the distance.

He coughed a series of times. "I'm going to lie down," he muttered. "Think I'm coming down with something."

"That would be fine, Jess. I'll be downstairs with the baby if you need me." She hurried off, holding onto the banister as she rounded the corner and met the eyes of the dog, Wendy, who growled softly from outside of the bedroom door.

33

Jess parked roughly, his vision swimming. He wanted sleep, needed it. And if he didn't make it in the damn cabin, he'd sleep in his truck if need be. He limped his way to the front door, his hands in front of him as if he were blindfolded, trying with his last strength to push out the hateful thoughts that had been crowding his mind, thoughts that were wholly unlike him, thoughts that made him afraid.

She's out there. Bleeding heavy.

Your fault. Giggin with a new baby at home.

Jess pushed against the door, but it was locked. He fell to his knees for the spare behind the loose board, reaching into the dark space, feeling crawlers on his wrist, finding the key and struggling to stand. He brushed off the insects, the dogs suddenly upon him, circling.

"Git," he said, as they barked into the afternoon heat. Jess shivered as he opened the front door, his shirt soaked against his chest.

"Lillian?" he croaked.

He heard the sound of a woman's voice from the bottom of the steps. It sounded like the old granny Lillian was close to, but she was different somehow. Her face was all twisted up, as though her expression had been drawn on by a child. He felt his chest fill up with a coldness as she stood, rubbing her hip, a smirk on her broken face.

"Why the hell are you back?" Jess asked, feeling uneasy looking at her as her features moved about between menacing and cold.

"Just watching the baby for youse," she answered, a slow smile spreading across her dead-looking face. Her expression shifted around as if pixelated.

"Where's Lillian?" he asked as he took a step back.

"She had to run a quick errand," the granny said, her voice slowing. Her mouth was moving, but the words became slurred. He turned his head but could not understand her. As she stood, her face twisted into the shadows. He rubbed his eyes, disbelieving his wife would leave the baby with whatever witchy woman this was.

"Awful irresponsible of her to leave the baby like this," he said. "What if she gets hungry?"

He could hear the buzz of the insects around the house, stronger than before, their rubbing adding to his pounding headache. The woman said something else, but he couldn't hear her. He spit out a series of coughs, thinking he was about to be sick again.

"I'm going to lie down," he muttered, making his way past her shadowed form. "Think I'm coming down with something." He moved past the unlit stove, using his hands to steer him to the sink. He felt cold to the bone.

Damn women can't even keep a fire, even with the timber chopped.

He turned on the sink to wash his face and heard a sound from behind him. He turned around quickly to see Lillian's dog, Wendy, by the stairwell. Her shape was blurry in his vision, as though she were shaking or shimmering in the shadows. Through his stinging eyes, he could see her eyeing him. It was almost as though she were looking at him with suspicion. She took a step forward, her head lowered, as though she were cornering. He had seen her doing that with coyotes before.

That's your own dog. Don't be foolish.

He drank down two glasses of water from the tap, ignoring the stabbing feeling in his throat before a series of coughs left him bent over the sink, retching. After he was finished, he slunk to the floor, his heart beating all haphazardly.

Wendy crept forward, her head low and muscles rigid. He wiped the back of his hand across his mouth, leaving a blood-streaked line of spittle across his chin.

"Go on, git," he said to her, kicking out one leg at her nearly helpless.

Wendy took another step forward, a deep growl coming from her throat. He looked her over and hated her.

"I said git," he hollered as he stumbled toward her.

She inched backward, baring her teeth. With the room spinning around him,

Jess made his way to his feet, his gut twisted with stabbing pains and inched to the couch, his temples throbbing. He collapsed, splayed out on his belly, passing out with his shoes on.

In his dream, Jess felt faceless, light. He was walking alongside his father's property line, his chest clear as though untethered by the sadness that had always hung on him. He breathed in, felt his spine lengthen within him. The light was clearer than it seemed to be when walking through the real world, vivid colors of the cabin, the timber enhanced by its rays. His mind felt clear, his senses somehow less opaque. Even the sounds were sharper. As he lay with the southern hex raging inside of him, the rippling anger subsided for just a moment, and he dreamed. First, his childhood, before he had lost his mother. Next, Lillian, her long legs and wide eyes looking him over beside the Lick. He ached for her then, wondering where she had gone, for he knew she could help him feel better, he was sure of it. He watched her move through the brush, her feet in the sand, those strands of hair that always got loose from her bun on her neck, curled from the sweat of her day. He felt a moment of hope then, for in his dreams, as those with true illnesses know, he could feel that something was very off, had gone very wrong. He knew that just beyond this moment of bliss in his dream, that there was something else. The inverse of the clarity, waiting to show itself. As he lay unconscious, dying, he knew then that something was beside him in his body, and that he, like Sam, may very well be close to death himself. For a moment, he felt a surge of happiness—he would get to see his mother again—before the dreamlike reality of his child flashed before him.

Not yet—

What if the baby longs for me? Like I longed for Gloria?

Jess dreamed next of Sam, feeling in his body the way Jess was feeling, a moment of brotherly sadness hanging in his heart before his dreams were taken over by the voice from earlier, the one that had said the dark things. It seemed to be one with his own then.

Left your friend to die.

Yes, I know it. You don't have to remind me.

Then he was back on his land with his father, the cusp of winter on them, the last of the leaves teetering on the hickory and the wind picking up, just the edge of sharpness on it. They were still bringing in the harvest, the apples and potatoes to last them through spring. Trevor, the middle boy, standing, teething against the rubber sides of the pack and play, a puddle of drool collecting under his chin, and Johnny, not even born yet. Gloria was full with pregnancy, her ankles swelled up. Jess, not even ten yet, stood beside her shelling beans at the table.

"You'll be a good boy for me when I go to have this baby?" She reached over, smoothing Jess' hair from his face. Her fingernails were painted pink. One was chipped.

"Yes, ma'am," Jess said, irritated he'd have to once again lose her to yet another child. There was no fear in his mind. He saw himself then, before knowing the touch of emptiness.

"Do you think it's going to be a girl or a boy this time?" Gloria asked him, a little smile on her face. He could see, even in his dreams, that she was tired in late pregnancy, the way his wife had been.

"Boy, I reckon," Jess said, seeing his own fingers squeezing the stems before dropping the pods to the side for the chickens.

"How come you reckon?"

Young Jess shrugged. "Cause that's what you had so far. It's just science."

In the dream, Gloria laughed and pulled him alongside her. Jess could feel the warmth from her side against his shoulder. He could smell her skin, and as he lay there dreaming, face down on the couch, the fireplace cold beside him, the baby crying downstairs, and Wendy lying at the top of the steps, watching his chest as it rose and fell, he wondered if anything had ever happened for real. Had it all been a dream for him? Dreamed his mother, dreamed his child, dreamed every moment of his life? But soon after, as though the Lick had caught up with his dreams, this memory of Gloria turned on him too.

"Sweet boy," she said to him, in their old kitchen, the kitchen his father still cooked in with the same stained linoleum and pots and pans she once used. "You know what's science?" she said, straining to squat before him, his wrists in her soft hands. He could see sweat along her upper lip. Even as he slept, he could not remember if this was a memory or if this was the new part of him that had started speaking from within. "The likelihood of me split in half on that birthing table, Jess Cedars." She burst into menacing laughter then, her head spilling back with it.

Jess felt his insides seize up.

Not a memory.

Her hands gripped him more firmly. Her face hardened then.

This isn't real, not even real.

"And there's nothing you can do about it, is there?" She clapped her hands together, her fingers stretching longer somehow. "Aside from, of course, burying this all inside, staying small," she snickered, as though it were a joke.

Jess tried to pull away, but she held him firmly. He shook his head, squinting his eyes closed.

"Weak little man," she shrieked. "Keep it inside till you're FULL OF IT and it ROTS THERE. Growing like a tumor to ruin your SHIT LITTLE LIFE until your wife runs out on you and you're alone alone alone like your brute of a father."

"Mama," Jess said, his voice adult then.

"Till you rot from the fear," Gloria said, her voice a pinpoint of shrillness.

Not real.

She inched closer then, her face sharpened at the edges, swelling, turning. "Till your whore wife turns you out."

"Mama—"

"For you to grow into the kind of man who'd let his best friend die." Her voice rose like a bell out of tune, pounding into his head.

"Lillian told me not to cross—I told them."

"You know how he died, don't you?" Gloria said, her face straining into something Jess no longer recognized. Stretched and purpled, her teeth growing smaller and more numerous. "Choked on his own vomit. ALONE. Died as he always feared. Do you know what that means, Jess? It's a big word for a dumb country boy like you, I know—"

Jess pulled back, but she towered over him then, her body massive, her teeth blackening. "Look how you treat those who love you."

"No, I'd—"

Wake up.

Her face was no longer the face he remembered. This was no longer a dream, some part of him realized. There was something inside of him, steering his thoughts, as though reading his fears.

"You'll carry me like a disease in your core till the day you die," she said, a deep voice replacing his mother's. "Until the day you die."

"Stop now," his child's voice said.

"Is that how you speak to your mother?"

"Stop—"

"Kind of boy who would disrespect his own mother?"

Stop.

"Would you let me die, Jess?"

No.

Gloria reached for his neck then, her long spindly fingers around his throat, first softly but then very quickly. Jess was frozen there, in fear, in longing for his mother, in regret for all he hadn't done, hadn't said, when her grip tightened there, the thumbs pressing against his airways. He tried to breathe in but couldn't. He pulled away but was frozen, his chest burning, eyes wide on her face, which had grown, swelled into the space of his mind. He reached his hands up to touch hers, ice cold, stronger than anything he'd ever felt.

I'm so sorry.

In his sleep, Jess moaned before vomiting. The granny ran to his side, moving to clear his airway, her hand firm on his back.

34

Lillian felt cold water splash hard against her face, knocking her back into the present moment. It came again, the sudden coldness, as she choked in breath. When she opened her eyes, all she could see was the gray sky, a storm coming in low from the west, before the pain of her bites brought her back to where she had been, and she scrambled to her elbows, wildly taking in her surroundings. The two Changed Ones hovered above her, one with her arms crossed, the other leaning in toward her with eager interest, their ratted hair hanging in tendrils around their dirty faces.

Lillian blinked at the first drops of rain that fell between them, the sky electric above the women. Behind them, the howlers waited in a collective pant, resting their weight on their haunches, as though waiting for a signal. From where she sat, Lillian could see the dark red intelligence of their eyes. These were the same ones that had been on her property. The same ones that had tracked Jess. She felt another pulse of pain and looked down at her legs. Deep gashes tore through her skin beneath her blood-soaked jeans. Her heart filled with fear at the realization that she was bleeding out, sitting in a pool of her own blood, and that the day was coming to an end, bringing darkness on top of all the other terror on the south of the Lick. Without light, her return was hopeless. This was not her land. She felt dizzy, her vision swirling.

I'm afraid.

If Jess Cedars is to be saved, you must be the one to make this crossing.

"Answer me," the dark granny said.

Lillian turned to the side and vomited. The woman firmly nudged her shoulder with her filthy boot.

"Where's the Black woman?"

Lillian coughed into the space between them before answering. "Dead," she said looking at the old woman's boot inches from her face.

"Who is your healer then?" the Changed One hissed.

"Me."

The dark grannies laughed in a shrill chorus, the elder leaning in closer. "A southerner. As a north granny?"

Lillian took in the whole of the crowd, bent on killing her, thinking she may be sick again. She took in a slow breath and inched herself back, looking between the two women. Haggard, otherworldly. She suddenly realized the purpose of their conversation, for them ceasing their attack. They first considered her a trespasser. But then they realized she was one of theirs.

Blessed is the one
whose delight is in the law of the Lord.
That person is like a tree planted by streams of water,
whose leaf does not wither—

"If I'm truly of the south, then I'm one of yours," Lillian said, dragging herself to her elbow. She saw the teeth of the howlers in the distance. "And if I'm one of yours, why are you hurting me?"

The witch's sneer disappeared as her eyes narrowed.

"Your howlers have torn me open. That witch—"

Lillian recoiled as the dark granny hobbled forward, pointing a twisted finger at her face. "You crossed the boundary."

"I just needed the antidote. I just want to make my way home."

"There's no back across," the dark granny said. "Whatever crosses, He claims."

Lillian felt suddenly cold again. If they weren't going to kill her, what did they want with her? "I'm just here for a tincture. We have someone very sick, and he needs—"

"You've crossed. It's the agreement."

"You killed a man. Took his dog. Where's that in the agreement?"

"That dog ran to us freely."

Lillian felt the anger rising up inside of her again, like a brother to the fear. "You put the hurt on my man."

"He trespassed," she hissed again.

Lillian felt a strange sort of hate rising inside of her. She got to her knees, and then to her feet, feeling suddenly as equals to these Changed Ones, even as the howlers crept forward. As she breathed in, she felt something alongside of her breath. It was the opposite of sending out—something was pushing into her. Like that time so many years ago, she'd reached across to the south and felt the hand in the glove.

The dark suitor. He was with them. She cast her eyes around, cast out her net, touching upon the pulse of the south. Whatever it was felt sickly familiar, like the smell of an old blanket. Like an old home, even surrounded by evil. It was then Celeste's face came back to her.

If you see it, you must fight. It is the only way.

She would not be taken in by evil. These people had put a curse on her man and had taken Sam's sight hound. And for what? To honor an agreement she had no part of?

"Those rules were made up decades ago by those who are long dead," Lillian said, blocking out what pressed inside of her.

"That's not how it works, Lily-B," the dark granny said, pointing her cane toward Lillian. Behind her, in the tempest, she felt it again, what she had felt at twelve. Eyes, red-rimmed, faceless, tugging her toward a dark timber. She had not felt before what she felt now. That the tug was not curious. It was sinister. Darker than dark, as though all hate in the world swirled into its void above where she lay shivering in the rain on the south.

Lillian evaluated what she had left. No talk would work on these people. Her gun had been taken. There was a spiritual darkness here that felt to her heart like a downed live wire. What weapons could she use against these people and their dark magic? No gun, no knife was left. Then one last idea presented itself. There was one weapon.

Eugene.

Thank the Lord for that boy, Lillian thought. And, screwing up her strength inside of her, Lillian took one last look around. A murder of crows landed on the tops of the pines. She calculated her run to the Lick would be about seventy-five yards at most. They were faster than her, even if her legs weren't injured. But Eugene would buy her some time. Lillian took her chance. She got to her knees, wincing.

The Changed Ones crouched, inching forward. Lillian saw even more of the crows, their inky wings poised in the periphery. A few had started circling, one swooping down, pecking at one of the men in the distance. The Changed One turned at the caws. The howlers moved closer to her. Next, more birds. They were suddenly everywhere. In the trees, in the air. Lillian steadied her weight. The fury that had been bubbling inside grew to a loudness inside of her head. How dare this woman turn on one of her own. She was a granny too. A new one, still learning, but she deserved care. The Changed One took a hobbling step forward. Reaching up, Lillian snatched a lock of the witch's hair, ripping it from her rotting head. As the woman shrieked, Lillian spat into the dust between them.

The dark granny laughed, the blackened nubs of her teeth spreading across her face.

"Southern magic isn't good on one of your own, Lily-B," the Changed One said, her membrane crossing her gaze. She looked Lillian straight in the eye without any sign of fear. "You will meet the Devil tonight. He has been waiting a long time for you."

Lillian felt the heat rise from the base of her spine to the top of her head, feeling herself almost growing taller with it. She hadn't planned to do harm, but this southern bitch had messed with the wrong woman. She would not be dragged to any lair of darkness. Slowly, she slid her left hand into her pocket for what was left of the salt from Eugene. In her heart, there was a sort of lifting.

"I will do no such thing. And this here's northern magic," Lillian said, spraying the salt in an arc around her. Onto the Changed Ones, onto the space between them, and onto the ground in an arc around her as she turned to flee, dragging one leg along. Behind her, a howl seemed to reach up from the earth. The Changed Ones screamed into the air between them, the birds descending then, squawking as they dove in mobs, a black curtain between the howlers as Lillian moved with as much speed as she could muster back into the trees.

"Bring her back," the elder Changed One ordered, her pursuit blocked by the arc of salt. The other woman attempted to reach across the circle to grab for Lillian but recoiled back as though shocked. The howlers sprang toward her, some with crows pecking at their haunches, blocked temporarily by the barrier. Lillian pressed ahead, guessing she'd have twenty, maybe thirty seconds before they found a way around the barrier. But she moved, as fast as she'd ever moved, past the pain, willing her muscles forward on her one usable leg, her voice crying out.

With the lock of rotted hair clutched in her right hand, Lillian pushed into the false vine, the rush of the Lick just before her. She focused only on one step ahead, the image of her newborn in her mind's eye. She ran from the horror of the moment, from the witch talk, from the bites that had met bone with what was left in her legs, making one more break for her life, for her baby, as a chorus of black hissing roared behind her.

"You can't run from who you are!" the dark granny shrieked, her voice getting smaller behind Lillian.

Eugene's salt had obscured her trail, the crows had bought her time, and unlike last time, Lillian did not look back. She was too afraid to see their dead faces, their rows of rotted teeth, their sallow skin. She was too afraid to even consider what they had told her. About this Sugar, about southern blood. About the Devil. Was she to turn into a witch like those women? Would she need saving like Jess? What if she couldn't get home in time to give her husband the serum?

"You can't run from us forever," echoed from somewhere around her. They were through the salt barrier.

Lillian could see it then, the white caps of the Lick. The wind across the water. She passed out of the timber and into the clearing, the rain heavier then. The buffalo was long gone. She forced the thought of her pain from her mind, thinking only of Glory, who would need her milk, for her husband, sick with whatever had crawled inside of him. There was only this hope. Not her mother or her bad blood or Celeste or the Devil. Just the feathers of hope.

As she cleared the bank, she knew that this moment was her last chance. With the panting of the howlers behind her, this time her leap was clearer. She moved in the air without thinking, feeling the space below her feet, the turn in her belly in the space between earth and water, almost feeling like time had slowed before she crashed into the sudden coldness of the Lick. It buoyed her body, and she scrambled halfway across, whipping her head around to check if they had followed. The women stood tall on the south bank, not twenty feet behind her, their wind tangling their hair in terrible arcs, their mouths maws of black, pressing against the air as though they had met an invisible fence.

They could not cross.

The howlers, however, did not face the same restrictions, and they pushed off the ground behind the women with otherworldly strength, leaping into the water after her. Lillian turned again, the cold everywhere, moving half above and half below water toward the north, feeling the current drag her as she swam against it, their webbed growls only feet behind her.

Suddenly, a shot rang out into the air on the north side. A rifle. Then its cracking echoed in the trees, and birds flew from their nesting to the skies. From just past the banks stood the shadow of a man pointing a gun. Beyond him, a place with lights.

35

The howlers continued undeterred behind Lillian. She could hear the weight of their hooves against the forest floor, the branches breaking beneath their steps. She whipped her head back, briefly considered them, terrible in size and completely otherworldly, before she pushed her body forward toward the sound of the gun. She swam under, surfaced waist-high, then shoulder-high, her movement slow, fighting the current, feeling its subtle pull, seeing her blood carried under the clear water down the river to disappear forever. She felt this part of her being pulled away, felt the pull of the current, and longed for the strength to simply survive, to not disappear forever as her mother had. The dizziness increased as she pushed ahead, ignoring what pierced her mind and swimming with all the strength in her arms, reaching the north side with a cry of relief or pain, she could not tell. She used her fingers and elbows to pull herself forward in the rocky sand, thinking only of one step ahead, one step closer to where the lights were. As she reached the ledge, she threw her body over the bank to the mossy forest ground, the beasts in the current just moments behind her.

Over the bank was an idling pickup, its light beaming ahead against the southern howlers. Behind it were a few more trucks, all with their brights cutting into the coming darkness on the south. Next to the pickup stood the shadow of a man, obscured by the lights. He held a rifle pointed at the south. Beside him was a large wooden box that seemed to hum with life. A hive. Around him flew a cluster of bees in a sort of hesitation, the pheromones stinking of fruit in the air between them. Lillian clawed her way toward them, getting to her feet before falling again, panting, blood ribboning from her ankles, from her womanhood. She could hear the Changed Ones hissing from across the bank into the air and winced, even the sound of them chasing her, their arms about them like wings on wild creatures.

"You're one of us, Lily-B," one screeched in her dark language as Lillian cried out, limping forward. "We will follow—"

"They can't cross, can they?" Lillian screamed at the man as she scrambled toward the lights, his engine overpowering the silence. He did not look at her but held his rifle steady, the howlers in his crosshairs. She limped toward him just as the howlers scratched across the ledge to the north bank, their massive claws lifting their bodies toward where they stood.

"Get in the truck," he shouted without turning from his aim.

Lillian obeyed, her legs limp beneath her. She pulled open the creaking door and lifted her torn body inside, pushing the door lock down, leaving bloody prints behind her on the bland-colored door. She collapsed inside the idling vehicle, too tired to reach across to roll the window up. In her right fist, clenched tight, was the torn tendril of the witch's hair. She shoved it deep into the pocket where the salt had been and closed her eyes, her body shaking uncontrollably. She felt around for the grape leaves, first her granny purse, which was gone from her body, next her pocket, which was empty, then against her wounds from the forest. Gone. All of it. From the creek or her falling, even the ones against her body had wilted away.

Gone. I lost it. Oh, my God.

All for nothing.

"Proverbs 28:1," the man stated loudly as the howlers cleared the bank with a slow stalking, their red eyes scanning, wholly unafraid. In the bright lights of the truck, she could see the outline of their jaws, rimmed red with blood dripping against their massive chests, their hooves. The rain pelted against their matted fur.

"The wicked flee when no man pursueth," the man said as he pulled the trigger, hitting the first howler in its chest. Its weight dropped heavily back down the ledge with a cry. The second moved nimbly away, so quickly it was as though he moved within time. The man kept his gun aimed, following the beast through the low bushes in the fragrant treeline.

"Mister, get in," Lillian said hoarsely through the window as she spotted more crossing the Lick. "More are coming!"

The man did not look at her but calmly worked the top of his wooden box with his other hand as the howler's shadow reappeared about twenty feet away, crouching, preparing to pounce.

"But the righteous are bold as a lion," he continued as he aimed up his rifle.

The howler jumped toward him, landing not ten feet before the truck with a thump. In the lights of the truck, Lillian could see its heaving chest, otherworldly, its shoulders massive, its eyes filled with blazing evil. Beyond it, several more advanced over the bank, only a few feet away from the truck. Lillian could hear gunshots from behind them, from the trucks that idled in the distance.

"Those who trust in themselves are fools," he said, shooting again at the beast, who dodged to the left as his slim body recoiled back against the kick. Suddenly, a sound filled the air—bees, hundreds—no, thousands of them—moving forward and onto the first howler's shoulder and back, onto its head too. It froze, then twisted, screeching into the air. The rest flew toward the Lick, seemingly in pursuit of whatever else had followed. The howler paused before a bullet grazed its left side. Then it turned to run, disappearing across the creek to the south with two great strides, the others following back into the southern darkness.

The man lowered his gun, quickly joining her inside the truck, laying his gun in the space between them. He shoved in the clutch and moved the truck into reverse.

"But those who walk in wisdom are kept safe," he said as he turned off the road. Lillian stared at him before closing her eyes with a profound sense of relief, resting her head against the back of the seat.

"Christ, you are cut up, miss," he said as the truck shook on the road. He glanced over nervously, taking in her bleeding body. Lillian felt a deep cramping in her belly as she slunk against the door. She tried to focus on the sound of the engine, the call of the locusts roaring in through the windows, anything but the pain.

"What about the bees?" Lillian whispered, feeling her strength ebb even further away as the truck picked up speed on the gravel road. She watched the yellow center line, her hands gripping her waist. She had never felt so sick. It was as though something had infected her and was spreading.

"They'll find their way back," he said, wiping his brow with a dark handkerchief. "Always do."

He drove until the nearest clearing showed light from the moon, and he pulled over, roughly pulling on the brake and turning toward her with a flashlight pointed at her face.

"Let me see your eyes," he said, leaning back suddenly against the door and pointing the gun toward Lillian. She felt her stomach turn, she didn't know from nerves or from the bites. He held a flashlight up to her face, which she recoiled from.

The witch had said you were southern blood.

Her mind moved again to Glory. Did he know? Would it show in her eyes? Would he shoot her if he knew? Lillian panted heavily as his eyes scanned her. He took in her filthy clothes, the mud covering the wet clothes that clung to her body. She sat frozen, clothes torn on her body, the pain ribboning through her, her breasts leaking milk, her abdomen still swollen from Glory. Her ankles and feet were starting to cramp, swelling from the bites. She felt the poison from the bite crawling up to her hips, her waist. Was she contaminated? She needed to get to Glory. Was she even safe to go to Glory?

She turned her body slowly toward the man, holding a hand up to block the light. "Please," she begged, as she recoiled back against the truck's door.

"Did you understand them?" he asked her.

"Understand what?" she lied, considering pushing open the door and making her way back to Alice's truck, but at this point, she could barely move her hand to the handle, let alone move about the forest on mangled legs.

"Look at me," he hollered suddenly, his voice booming. Lillian reluctantly obeyed. He moved a lock of her wet hair with the barrel of the gun, looking over her odd-colored eyes. He reached out with his trigger hand, roughly steadying her face. She watched him watching her, her heart wild, his eyes frantic. His eyes were pointed but not hateful. He had soft, brown eyes in an old face that was covered with a thick gray beard. He did not look like he had held this gun on many people, let alone women. She swallowed hard and was silent.

"Answer me," he said more sternly, his face pinched. "Did you understand the witch?"

Lillian stammered, covering her fear. "I don't understand what you're asking me."

"What did the witch say to you?" He pushed the barrel into her shoulder.

"I'm not sure," Lillian lied. "Some sort of gibberish."

"I saw you speaking to her."

"Please, sir. My pickup is just up the road. I left it about a mile from where J Road meets Highway 7."

"I know. By Celeste Black's old place."

"How did you know that?"

"Because we've been following you."

"I need to get home to my daughter. She's only two days old."

"Well, what in the hell are you doing out this way?"

"I'm Celeste Black's granddaughter. I came back to visit her grave."

The man lowered the gun. "She was northern. Why did you need to cross the Lick?"

"You knew my grandmother?"

"The south is off limits. You should know better than that," he said sternly. "Just yesterday, a boy crossed over looking for a lost dog. He was dead before this morning."

Lillian bit her tongue, sent out a prayer for Jess, for her baby.

"You were inches from death, you fool." He stared at her, unblinkingly.

"I know that. I appreciate—" Lillian felt her body starting to shake.

"And seeing as you've been bit," he said, looking at the blood on the floor, "we don't have much time." He looked over his shoulder quickly before pulling back onto the road.

"Where are we going?"

"To Tyresius. She will know what to do." He tensed his jaw as he shifted gears.

"Christ, they got you good. Surprised you made it out."

Lillian closed her eyes again, suddenly feeling very tired.

He reached across, jostling her awake. "Listen, girl. Even a scratch means trouble. You need to stay awake."

Lillian blinked open her eyes and swallowed, the taste of blood in her mouth.

"Who is Tyresius?" She felt as though she were floating above her body in the truck, hearing herself speak.

"Granny-woman."

"She have tinctures?"

"How else could we manage out here for all those years?"

"What happens if you don't get the tincture?"

"You become one with the goat," he said flatly, picking up speed as he flicked on his brights. Lillian felt dizzy as he said it, watching the light fade indifferently toward the west.

But if she had southern blood, she thought, wasn't she already one with the goat?

36

Jess felt himself in the space right before waking, choking in breath, the monster of his mother still hanging in his line of vision, the feel of her spidery hands around his neck echoing.

That was not Gloria, he told himself. That was the demon from the Lick Lillian had warned him about. It had taken shape according to his fears. A demon that, like Lillian said, delighted in tormenting.

He sucked in air, opening his eyes to find himself back in his cabin, the room spinning, the light all wrong, curtains billowing, the monster standing beside not one, but three of those things he saw through his crosshairs on the Lick. In his blurred vision, he could make out their shaggy fur, the red-rimmed eyes, even the thick hooves, heavy against the hardwood.

"You followed me," Jess muttered, his insides twisting.

The witch mumbled something, her face a blur of horror, the animals circling her as he stumbled backward.

"Leave me alone!" he half shouted, half crying, grabbing the poker from the stove and swinging it around. The monster backed up. Jess stumbled to his feet.

"That's right. You ain't my mother." One of the howlers lunged at him, and he swung, striking it in its hindquarters. It yelped as it darted to the side. Would Lillian come home to this? He was infected, sure as hell as Sam had been. The monster's face was a twisted blur.

"Get out of my house," he hollered, swinging desperately in the blurry space before him as he limped heavily to the door. If he could just get to his truck, get to the main road, call for help. A hand then, a claw on his shoulder, pulling him backward, and he threw his weight forward, swinging wildly as he moved. That time his swing landed, thumping hard against the body of the witch. She stumbled but righted herself, bringing her mangled hand to the side of her head and pulling it away to see a spot of blood. She laughed then, showing her rows of rotten teeth growing wider and wider.

She'll get Glory Be. Get the baby.

The monster woman turned, a beast on her heels, and scurried down the steps. Jess took a step, stumbled, coughed, then followed, the poker under his arm, nearly slipping on the steps down to his bedroom. He heard her then, speaking in some foreign tongue, saw her arm reach out and felt a spray of dust on his skin. It got in his eyes, his nose, burning him. He fell to his knees, her hands on him again, and he reached for her then, her twig neck in his hands. The howlers were on him then, one sinking its teeth into his leg. He dropped the woman and swung the poker, hearing the whining cries before it ran off. Another beast hovered close to the witch, its eyes somehow familiar, its teeth bared. The witch moved again for him then, pressing something hot to his forehead and chanting snatches of something.

"You stay away from Glory!" he hollered, his voice thick in his throat. His forehead burned—seared, and he reached out frantically, shoving her frame away and then mounting her, striking her blackened face before finding her neck once again as the red-eyed howler circled, howling, and he clamped down, seeing her blurred face shake and swell under his hands until she stopped moving. He coughed into the space, sweat covering him, throat burning.

Get Glory Be. Get the baby.

Jess stumbled off the witch's body, leaning weakly against the wall until he got to the door of the bedroom, and, pushing it open, he looked to the crib to where Glory lay, shaking through her sobs, and as he limped toward her, he saw it—the rows of black teeth, the blurred, blackened face, in his baby—oh, God, no, she got Glory Be—and as he moved closer, the last beast came for him from behind, tackling his body, its teeth tearing into his hands, toward his face and so Jess, unarmed, did the only thing he could think of and bit down on the beast's shoulder, tearing through flesh so that the two of them fell apart, the beast chasing Jess from his ruined daughter's room, their changed faces twisted in his mind, his heart beating thickly, his breath catching in his chest with each raspy exhale.

He stumbled outside the door, pulling it shut behind him before tripping over the body of the witch again on his way up the steps.

Oh, God, the baby, she's gone, she's turned.

They'll take Lillian too, will we all be turned?

37

Lillian lay shivering on a bare Formica table, bleeding onto an old afghan that had been wrapped around her. She was barely conscious. A moment before, the man who had saved her, a Mr. Pete Forrert from Walkers Corner, had carried her from the truck into this woman's cabin, dripping a line of blood all the way from his pickup into Tyresius' kitchen. He spoke quickly as he rushed her inside, promising that Tyresius could help her, telling her coldly to hang on, giving her body little shakes, imploring her to think of her baby. He burst through the screen door in the last of the day's light, seeing the inky black spreading below her skin, looking as though her veins had filled with darkness itself.

"Ty," Lillian heard him holler from deep in his chest, and there was a commotion as the table was cleared and she was wrapped as she lay limply under the light, the fan's blades moving in a slow blur above her.

"Name?" A woman's voice said more than asked. She was quite elderly with deeply set dark eyes in a web of heavy wrinkles.

"Lillian," she whispered as the woman bent to light the gas stove, illuminating the deep creases in her brow. Though her vision was blurry, Lillian thought she looked familiar. She was long-limbed, built like a man almost, and wore a woodworking apron over trousers. She moved quickly to examine Lillian, pulling on latex gloves that smacked against her skin.

"My name is Ty. I'm going to take a look at your wounds now—"

"Please, help—it hurts," Lillian whimpered.

"I found her at the bank, just like Marjorie's crow said."

Lillian tried to speak but found she didn't have the strength. Ty lifted each of Lillian's arms, examining the black color that ran through her veins. She slowly unbuttoned Lillian's shirt, pushing her thick glasses back up the bridge of her nose to examine Lillian's torso, and her eyes locked in on Lillian's leather necklace—Celeste's necklace. She stared at it for a quick second before her eyes met Lillian's. The woman was some sort of healer. She had a kitchen that resembled what Celeste's once looked like, though with government instruments beside the vials.

Lillian looked down, seeing the blackened veins crisscross her abdomen. "Is it their venom?" Lillian asked hoarsely. To Lillian, it looked as though a child had drawn all over her skin with a marker.

"It is," the woman said, feeling her lymph nodes. "Phospholipases toxin."

"It b-burns."

She moved over a milking stool. "Normal to feel some pain as it moves through you."

When first bitten, Lillian could only feel a slight burning. The primary pain was the wound itself. But by the time she and the man were on the road, her whole body ached from the venom that inched through her body. Her muscles cramped so severely her fingers bent into claws, her head pounded, and her eyes stung from what felt like a fever. The black pain reached around her neck to the top of her spine. Her tongue felt thick and slow. She felt for her own pulse, beyond worry. Was this what Sam had felt? What Jess was feeling? She lay back on the table, pulling the afghan closer around her shoulders, thinking she was surely closer to the next world than this one. She squinted her eyes shut and prayed with what hope was left inside of her.

Ty shone her light into Lillian's face, checking each pupil. She looked in her eyes and her nose, took her pulse. She took in a sharp breath as she moved to examine the wounds on her legs, only her close-cropped gray hair visible to Lillian.

"How long ago was the attack?"

"About a half hour," Pete said. "Maybe more. She was pretty cut up by the time I found her."

"We're lucky you found her when you did," Ty said calmly, as though she saw this sort of thing every day. She used her elbow to start a stream of water and washed an instrument in the sink behind her. Lillian listened to the clamor, whimpering from the table, her eyes closed.

"We're going to remove your jeans to get a better look at the wounds, alright?"

Lillian could barely manage a small whimper from the table. The woman gingerly pulled off the jeans, soaked with creek water and blood, and covered Lillian to her knees. Lillian lay still, her eyes shut, focusing on her breathing. The pain felt like needles dragging through her skin.

"I am going to apply an antiseptic called goldenseal. It will burn a little, but it's best for cleaning deep wounds. Try to lie still for me, now."

Lillian felt the cold sting of the antiseptic and held her breath. She thought only of Glory's little fingers, her little shock of black hair, and she held her mind there, her lips pressed together so tightly, they turned from pink to white. Pete watched from the corner, his gun in his hand.

Tyresius used a dropper to apply a milky substance into Lillian's wounds. The pain was nauseating, radiating through her skin, channeled all through her. She clenched her jaw. It was worse than childbirth.

"Fetch me a cluster of cedarwood," Ty told Pete.

"Are you a granny?" Lillian sputtered through chattering teeth.

"I am. Here's rosemary for the pain," she said. "Open your mouth now."

Lillian obeyed and felt the woman press a quarter-size bulb in her mouth.

"Chew, do not swallow."

Lillian mumbled as she began to chew, and the edges of the pain cleared.

"How do I not know of you?"

"I lived away for some time. Recently moved back."

"Did you know my grandmother?" Lillian asked. "Celeste Black? She lived off 11, not far from here."

The man returned with a handful of something green and placed it on the counter behind them. "Carl radioed. Howlers about a mile out."

"I knew her," the woman said as she assessed the cuts on her legs. "Great healer, Celeste was."

Pete looked over the woman's shoulder at Lillian under the kitchen lights, his eyes wide. The man looked at her face, then away quickly as the woman pressed gauze to the deeper cut on her ankle, her other hand bracing it. Lillian cried out, the pain returning suddenly and bright.

"Did the howlers get you, or were you bit by folk?"

"Both," Lillian said, as the woman pulled a wad of something from the corner of her mouth and pressed it into the wounds. Lillian thought of the balm of sleep, wishing for anything to ease her pain until she felt it suddenly cut in half. The woman held still, exhaling slowly through pursed lips. The wounds were still throbbing, but after a moment, she didn't seem to mind the pain so much.

"Dwarf Mallow?" Lillian asked.

The woman pulled a strip of cotton from a bolt on her table, half of her face obscured by the table. "Cohosh. Take a deep breath now. And another. Two more and then it won't sting as much."

Lillian attempted to slow her breath, telling herself she didn't have long to hurt. She kept her mind on her baby, sent out a channel of love for her Jess, lifted a prayer for Marjorie, reaching miles west for a sign. After a minute, the pain's edges continued to blur, and after another, it lessened considerably, enough for her to comfortably open her eyes.

Lillian looked around, thinking this granny's cabin looked similar to the one she grew up in. She imagined all she loved in her little cabin and sent a warm line of love out of her chest, imagining seeing it leave her body and traveling across Highway 7 past Mimosa Beach to their bedroom, landing in a soft glow around the body of her baby, of Jess.

Please—

"How long postpartum?" the woman asked.

"Few days," Lillian added through chattering teeth.

"You shouldn't be out and about yet."

"I know, but—" Lillian said, stopping her thinking short before revealing anything that would leave her vulnerable.

"But what," she said, pausing with a pitcher of water in her hands.

Lillian whispered nearly too quiet to hear. "I had an errand."

"Mr. Pete, please let in my pack and latch the door," the woman said as she secured the gauze on Lillian's right leg with sap.

"They really got you, didn't they?" Ty said, looking more closely at her other leg, as it dangled from the table, dripping blood onto her stone floor.

"Will the Changed Ones come?"

Ty shook her head as she wrung blood from the rag into a bucket between her feet. "Folk can't cross in body form. Just the howlers," she said. The sight of her own blood was making Lillian dizzy.

"Am I going to be alright?" she asked, feeling a wave of nausea move through her and laying her head back on the hard table. There were dogs barking then, circling where she lay on the table.

"I believe you are."

"But the other leg," she murmured almost below her breath. "I could barely walk."

"Those hounds of hell don't have anything on granny medicine."

"Ty?" the man said nervously, "they're outside. I don't know how many."

Lillian weakly sent out, reading three heartbeats. "Three of them," she told the woman.

Ty and Pete looked down curiously at her then. "Keep the radios close," Ty said to Pete. "And your gun. Powders will hold us." Pete's radio crackled, and he moved to the next room and began speaking to whomever was on the other end.

"They were on my property earlier too," Lillian added.

"They seem to be following you."

Lillian thought guiltily of how she had brought trouble to this old healer and her husband. She wondered how much she should share.

"Mr. Pete is not my husband," the woman quickly said.

Lillian looked over at her then.

She continued cleaning Lillian's unbandaged leg. "Your gift is the reading of hearts. Mine is the reading of minds," she said without looking at her.

Lillian's eyes widened. "Can you read everyone's minds?"

"Just other grannies," the woman said. "And talk that way too. Ever try it?"

Lillian shook her head no. There was a stretch of quiet, save the sound of dogs sniffing, water being wrung, and the sudden howls of animals close by. Lillian's heart froze.

"Nice that you took over for Celeste."

Just then, there was a series of cries from outside, just like the ones Lillian had heard from the south earlier. They were the clear sounds of Glory Be's cry, but louder, as though amplified by a speaker. Lillian sat up on her elbows, her wounds burning more intensely. She looked around worriedly.

"My baby," Lillian stammered.

"Did Marjorie tell you they imitate?" Ty asked, undistracted.

"She did—but they sound just like my baby."

"Mhm. Tricksters, those. But not to worry. We have more powders than there are howlers. Now, I am going to lay you on your back for your other leg," she said, her brow creased again, one coarse hand behind Lillian's back as she reclined her onto the table. "This one's going to require some strength from you, Lillian."

"I expected that. I can't even look."

"I'm going to start again with the cleaning antiseptic."

Lillian's head pounded as the wounds were cleaned. The pain was brighter than any light she had ever seen, as though splitting her open. She began to shake again, first subtly, unable to stop it. As the cleaning agent foamed, the shakes became almost violent, rocking the table against the stone floor.

"Mr. Pete?" Ty called calmly.

"I'm going to be sick," Lillian said helplessly as Pete came in and steadied the table.

The woman reached for a milking bucket and placed it beside her. Lillian was promptly sick into it, throwing up nothing but bile before just heaving, as though her body was trying to rid itself of something. She lay back, exhausted, bringing her arms to her belly, feeling her breast milk wet under her clothes. Lillian felt something cool placed on her forehead.

"Thank you," she said, as her eyes squinted shut, and she felt as though she could cry.

"All that you're feeling is normal. You aren't the first to be bit. And I know it stings. This is what we've been using for as long as I can remember. Take heart, dear."

Lillian felt drowsy from the pain, on the edge of a dream. "So, others have been bitten? By the Changed Ones even?"

"Plenty have been bit by the southern women, but you're the first I've seen since before I left. Just moved back last year."

Lillian wondered if Celeste had ever treated any before a line of pain moved from her left leg all the way up through her body.

"The sting you're feeling?" Ty added, "Legend has it that it will burn whenever howlers are near. It will be a good sentinel for you, but it will never fully heal, I'm afraid."

"As long as you can get me healed up, so I can get back to my baby," Lillian said. "I don't care what I look like or what the hurt is they put on me."

"Soon enough. This leg is going to need stitches," Ty said.

Lillian could feel nothing but the searing of the injuries, but she could not bring herself to look down at her torn-up body.

"Was it tooth or nail that cut you this deep?"

"I didn't see," Lillian started. "I was on my belly when the woman got me."

"She bit in deep. Terrible wench."

Lillian counted her breaths as she lay still through the stitches. "Granny Marjorie called them 'Changed Ones.'"

"Fitting," Ty offered, her eyebrows raised. "How did they catch you? All our literature on them has them slow-moving."

"They were darting about. Like shadows in the light," Lillian said, covering her eyes with the palm of her hand. "But the ones I saw were limping."

"Did you save any of the grape leaf you went over for?" Ty asked.

Lillian shook her head. "All gone."

"Not to worry. I'll be sending you on your way with something much stronger," she said. "How'd you end up getting away?"

"I was at the water's edge when one of the Changed Ones got me in the leg. Dragged me out of the Lick. They were so fast. I used salt to finally get away after I saw the lights, but then the current almost got me," Lillian said, exhaling slowly. "I only moved across J Road a year ago, but I don't remember the Lick being that rough."

"You know what they say. Old rivers grow wilder as time goes by," Tyresius said tiredly.

Lillian heard a series of footsteps and, looking ahead, noticed several pairs of eyes from a pack of beagles panting into her face. She reached a hand out to touch the one in front, feeling her lick between her fingers. She closed her eyes, trying to focus on anything but the sting of the stitches. She imagined Glory's face, her little fists balled beneath her chin.

Ty put a small handful of what looked like chive grass into her mouth, then pulled out the wetted herb. "This will feel cold. That's normal," she said evenly.

"What's it from?"

"The cold is from the tincture."

"What did you use?"

"Moly. It's antivenom. Those bites coagulate."

"The bites from the people?"

Pete leaned in from his chair. "We hear they've lain with rattlers," he said, pulling out a pouch of tobacco and repacking his pipe.

"If my man wasn't bit, how did he get the venom in him?" Lillian asked, pulling the afghan more tightly around her.

"He step on the south?"

"He and his men did. He was barely out of the water."

"Stramonium dust," Ty said. "You step foot on the south, the seeds release it. Can spread to twenty, thirty feet even. Too small to even notice you're breathing it in."

Lillian felt another cramp in her abdomen, either from healing up or that witch leaning on her.

"Marjorie with your baby?" Ty asked, only the top of her head visible as she stitched.

"Yes. At my cabin," Lillian answered, looking around for a clock. "I need to get back soon. She's likely to be hungry."

Ty sat up and took off her glasses, wiping them with the end of her shirt, and looked at Lillian. "You aren't to nurse after this," she said sternly.

"How can the baby—"

"The toxin will be secreted in the breast milk." Her expression was severe. "You'll poison your child on the spot. Bind up until you're bone dry." She returned her glasses to her nose before moving back to Lillian's ankle.

"I don't trust the store-bought food."

"Store-bought food is just fine. Lots of people use it."

"How long will the toxin be inside of me?"

Ty put a dab of petroleum jelly on her ankle before closing it with a butterfly closure bandage. "Till at least deer season, but it may take longer," she said.

Lillian lay quietly, scanning the length of the granny's profile. "You look so familiar to me," she said.

"Mhm," Tyresius said, ambling over to a cabinet and pulling bulbs from a low drawer.

"As Celeste's ward—"

"Granddaughter," Lillian corrected, her brow furrowing.

Why did everyone keep calling me a ward?

I thought you already knew.

Lillian bolted up at the sound of the woman's voice inside her head.

"Don't worry. All friendly talk here," Ty said. "I remember when your mother was a young girl."

"You knew my mother too?"

"Just a little. Knew Celeste much better."

"How did y'all meet?"

"Botany conference in Columbia. Three-quarters of a century ago," she chuckled. "Can you believe that? Worked tinctures together for years before I left," she said, starting a stitch on Lillian's calf.

"Why did you leave J Road?"

"I left to run an apothecary up north after your mother moved in with Celeste. Returned shortly after your grandmother passed."

Lillian tried pushing a thought across the table to Ty. *Moved in?*

Moved in. The thought slid right inside of her mind. Just like the thoughts she'd had back at the cabin, but clearer. Fewer shadows.

Lillian lay wondering at Tyresius. How could she have never known of someone who knew Celeste so well, who knew her family? She felt a sudden longing for her grandmother, but also for the family she had grown herself. Her husband. Their baby.

"I remember hearing about you. Marjorie would send me a letter around Christmas every year, keep me up to date," she said, adjusting the light above Lillian and narrowing her giant, magnified eyes. Lillian reached out her hand to pet one red-headed beagle as the woman continued her stitches.

"You've lost a lot of blood, dear," she said, cleaning off her ankles with a warm cloth, "and this one is going to leave quite a scar. Story for your grandchildren one day."

"Don't mind the scar, just as long as I'm okay for my baby."

"You'll need to repeat this treatment on your own in about twelve hours," she said.

Ty helped Lillian to a sitting position, so she could observe the cleaning, the packing of the wound, and the sutures. The skin around the wounds was raw, but everything was clean, and she could already feel the angry swelling going down.

"What did you use on the bites?"

"Sweet gum and garlic, after cleaning the wound. You may consider honey as well. Do you have any from our parts?"

Lillian's mind moved in many directions. "I don't think so."

"We'll send you home with some of Mr. Pete's. I'm going to brew you a tea, and then you'll be on your way," Ty said, standing to remove her apron. Lillian pulled the afghan closer around her. Ty's dogs nosed her again as they sniffed the corners of the room.

"These are gorgeous pups. Have three of my own back home." She reached out weakly, trying to pet one. "Celeste never let us keep pups of our own."

"She always did prefer herbs," Ty said.

38

Tyresius didn't like to think on it. Staring at the face of this girl she was stitching, kin of the child who brought an end to her marriage, well, it made her heart cramp up inside. But she was the healer, and she was determined to help. She guiltily read over the girl's thoughts, amazed at her courage. Her name was Lillian, surely chosen by her wife, as she always admired Lilith. The girl's face was odd like her mother's had been. Oval in shape, and a smallish chin with wide-set yellowish eyes and soft, almost feline features. She was less hardened than Sugar had been, though. The father was surely common-born. She was polite too. Raised up sweet by her grandmother. A stab of longing moved through Ty's chest as she washed up, thinking on her wife.

Tyresius' marriage to Celeste, which had lasted nearly thirty years, long by modern standards, the blink of an eye by Ozark standards, was strained neither by infidelity, nor boredom, nor poverty. None of those regular offenses poisoned the two women in love. It ended because of a child. A child from the south of the Lick.

Tyresius remembered it all with painful reluctance. The whole hurt was an organ of pain that lived within her. She carried it along with her for her whole long life after the split. She couldn't touch another woman without thinking on her wife's long spine, bent over her work, the warmth of the back of her knee, the smell of her hair when she combed it out at night. There is no remedy, no tincture for love lost. Time cannot heal what was never meant to be broken.

The mess with the southerners, as far as Ty could tell, started with Celeste's clandestine trips across the Lick. Northerners were forbidden, as they had been for a hundred years, but a letter or two had arrived over the years, some crudely composed, even one with pleas for help from a cluster of southern womenfolk who worried for their children. The southerners had some turning ceremony on the full moon before the girl hit puberty. The details were so horrifying she was reluctant to dwell on it. The girls were to be bound in loyalty to the clan, so their Achilles' tendons were cut—just on one foot, so they could still work the fields. Then they were bred, and repeatedly, with many men, the old timers wrote, so that no one would show preference to any one child, as the child could be anyone's. Celeste had wept when she first read about it.

On her first trip over, Celeste went to help with a dental emergency but came home with a bite from one of the hill people. They eventually needed to treat it with antivenom. Antivenom. Unlike Celeste, who was not hardened by the violence, Tyresius was furious, adamant Celeste never return. But her wife had protested, claiming it was her ethical responsibility to care for young girls who had no care to speak of. They spoke in low voices about it at night. Tyresius was terrified for Celeste, furious she even considered supporting such people with medical care. Her mind was wild with the crossover between reptile and human. How could a human bite produce such massive coagulation? This would drive her research once leaving Camden County. Most of what terrifies us, puzzles us, is what also compels us. This first bite, this contact, Ty believed, is what bound her wife somehow to these people.

Despite the agreements in place between northerners and southerners, Celeste was adamant, saying there were children in all stages of need. She talked about a very young one that she had noticed, around eighteen months of age, reaching out for Celeste with her filthy arms. How could she possibly turn away from them?

"Because she is in their care, not yours."

"Well, they clearly aren't caring for her," Celeste had said.

"What about taking care of yourself?" Ty had countered. "If you're gravely injured, who will heal the northern folk?"

"It's not up to us to pick and choose who we treat," Celeste protested.

It lasted days, the two of them lying close in their bed, unable to speak through all their feelings. Eventually, Tyresius was able to compel her to promise. Which Celeste did do. She promised she wouldn't return back across.

It was about this time, after a few years living and working among the people, building the tinctures, that the women came into the gifts. Working in granny medicine for long enough allowed each a certain *talent*. For Marjorie, it was birthing. She could read the minds of the babies, coax them in with her own special ways. She, too, could speak to the crows. A crow had a nest outside of her trailer that a raccoon had crawled into. Marjorie spotted its body as it scaled the tree and scared it off with a whistle. The raccoon dropped the fledgling, who Marjorie quickly picked up. She dressed the bird's cut with salt water and then did what is hardest: she set her free. The adult crows were forever in her favor after that. She left them coins; they delivered messages. Marjorie cooked for them, left them small trinkets. For Celeste, her talent was visions of the future. She could see which roads to avoid, which paths to sidestep to avoid the rattler. She had a soft spot for the castaways, the downtrodden. She was a follower of Christ, and this shone through every tincture she made, every patient she cared for. For Tyresius, though, her gift was perception. She could read people's thoughts and even, if the connection was honest, communicate without speaking. And she had been reading Celeste's thoughts since the gifts started manifesting. And what she saw broke her up inside. They were thoughts about lovemaking. Thoughts about what she had missed out on. Thoughts of, and this part was hard for Ty to even think on, lying with a man. Resentment that she chose to live with a woman. Thoughts of longing—for pregnancy, for motherhood.

All things that Ty could never provide for her.

They had grown so close by that point, they could speak without speaking. To each other's minds, Ty would say before Celeste interrupted, to each other's hearts. But each had their tiny secrets, which, though beginning as small as a pinprick, grew into chasms.

A week after Celeste's bite, on a Tuesday evening, Ty was out back whittling, Celeste closing up the trailer for the night. The disruption started with some voices, far off—Celeste first thought it was a coyote's cry—but the noises continued, grew louder, and were very certainly human. Both women went to the porch, Ty with her Benelli, Marjorie cowering a bit behind them, and saw a series of lights. To Ty, they looked like fires in the trees. Worried that there was a brush fire, the three women ran to the Lick, where they saw a handful of southern women, naked, filthy. They cried out, their mouths black. They carried torches and howled across. Ty and Celeste stood frozen. Others from the south collected, and they watched for hours, it felt like. The southerners waved, they gestured, their tongues were foreign to them. And beckoning the grannies, calling them across. Celeste and Marjorie looked between them but did not budge. One woman, younger than the others, a child herself, not twelve, stood crying, carrying a young child, maybe one, two years old in her arms. The men had rushed up behind them, fury in their eyes, howls in their mouths. It was a terrible sight. Ty had never seen such anger, such anguish. It was beyond what she had seen in the slums of the city.

Two days later, though, it happened again. The crying out, coyote-like. This time, just the younger southern woman came with the child. And unable to cross the Lick, she cried out to them. Again, Celeste and Tyresius approached. She spoke to them, but they could not understand their tongue. Celeste walked forward to the water's edge. The woman lifted the child, asleep, crusted in filth, lifted it across as though to hand her to Celeste. Tyresius could read Celeste's longing.

No, she thought. *Not this way.*

But it was too late. The women pushed the child's body, naked, forward. Celeste shook her head, tried to shoo her back before the menfolk would be alerted, before the Devil, if indeed they spoke the truth, would know. Then the sounds of them, the men's deep cries, angry from deep in the forest along with the dark footsteps of the howler from their hills. This southern woman was a desperate mother, longing for a different life for her daughter. Before she turned sour on southern land. One word, echoing—the child's name. "Sugar." And then the woman pushing the child across, her body floating, bobbing, before sinking a little, and then Celeste reaching in, the child clinging to Celeste's breast. And everything then changed.

39

It was 1976, and Tyresius could see that things were changing in the world. Celeste's business was taking off, allowing them enough extra money to repair the roof on their cabin, even purchase more land, the eighty acres south of them. There were three full-time grannies, so Celeste could work on raising up Sugar. But the child was feral. She knew no language, no ritual, no trust. She was small for her age, they believed three or four, the mother had indicated, but she was the size of an eighteen-month-old at best, her eyes yellow-colored, with the pupil of the goat. She had trouble with language, with fine motor coordination. She was temperamental too, screaming into the night like a colicky baby, her cries echoing across the timbers.

Neighbors started talking, one even called the state, but no one ever showed. Most of the government people let the hill folk handle their family matters. But the marriage had become strained. Celeste withdrew more into her study of the south, of the child. It was an extraordinary gift of goodness. She would sacrifice herself to keep this child away from the hurt on the south, even if it meant losing everything else. And so, she taught her. To speak, to write. And Sugar eventually calmed. But something lay beneath her. It was in that wild gaze. The eye of the south. A feral anger, like what lay beneath the fox, the coyote. They had a massive argument the third week the child was with them.

"We need to call the state, Celeste. This girl will be marked as missing."

"They don't register births on the south, Ty, you know that."

"You don't feel like this is kidnapping?"

Celeste wheeled on her then. "Kidnapping? You saw it. That woman practically left Sugar to drown."

"That's not what I—"

"Well, what did you mean?" Celeste spat.

"I mean that this child is, well, *different*."

Celeste had frozen then, crossing her arms. "Not too unlike us, right?"

"That's not what I meant, and you know it."

"I won't cast her out like we were cast out."

Ty read her thoughts. She was angry at her for some reason. Why had she never talked to her? The realization sunk into Ty then with a sinking loneliness that would haunt her for decades. Celeste was frustrated by childlessness.

"Ty, she is in my care."

And then, she said it. The words that cut through everything they had been through. "And it isn't like I have any other chance at mothering, do I?"

Tyresius had known Celeste felt the pull of motherhood, something Ty never herself felt, but she never thought of it that way—that a baby was something she felt she was lacking, that it was something Ty couldn't give to her. She had backed out of the cabin at that, eyes stinging, her wife's lips pressed together in cold anger. Ty grabbed the keys, dropped them twice, then took the truck into town just to walk aimlessly in the aisles at the hardware store. That night, she moved her pillow and one of the quilts to the cot in the kitchen. Celeste moved the baby to the wedding bed. And they never slept beside each other again.

Looking back, Tyresius regretted no fewer than one hundred things. Not things she did, things she did not do. There were four things, however, that haunted her the most after she left town.

#4: She didn't insist on help. They could have asked one of the grannies, a pastor, anyone, to help counsel them with raising up Sugar. They needed help, and she never asked for it.

#3: She didn't tell her how badly her feelings were hurt that Celeste never expressed she wanted to be a mother. If Celeste had told her, Ty was sure they could have worked something out. There were babies needing families all over the south of the state.

#2: She never told Celeste how angry and hurt she felt that she turned away from Ty in her motherhood. They could have done it together, had Celeste wanted it. But some part of her, Ty felt, sensed Celeste wanted to do this herself. Alone.

#1: That she walked away. That she was able to leave her wife, their life together. That she walked away and didn't look back.

So, after Sugar had been in Celeste's care for not even a year, Ty left. She first went back to St. Louis and got her old job back at the university hospital in a different department. She dropped the masculine masquerade, though she kept the name Tyresius, eager to forget Tammy's optimism. She wrote Celeste a letter on the first of every month, often crumbling each a few times, only to start again with a more conciliatory tone. The letters were never returned, but they were also never answered. After thirty-six months, Tyresius stopped writing.

In 1979, she was offered a transfer to Detroit, which she accepted, the landmarks of the old city she had shared with Celeste too heavy on her heart. Up north, she settled in as a member of the senior research team at Detroit Clinical Research Center, got her first tattoo (battle ax, left inner bicep), became an active member of the LGBT community, met an activist named Debra, a talkative arborist who was a native of Michigan and with whom she lived with for thirty-three years. There was no discussion of children. They spent their time either gardening or walking their three beagles. It was a pleasant sort of companionship, but it was different than her dreams. Unstirring. Tyresius grew quiet in middle age. She worked tinctures, committed to the ones she and Celeste were unable to concoct when they lived alongside the Lick. She thought constantly of natural antivenoms and located powerful, natural occurring compounds that could potentially cure the southerners. Potentially, impossibly, returning her wife to her.

In the years that would pass, she would receive snatches of information from the neighbors about Celeste. She had patched the roof. Sugar had grown up, grown wild. She had been arrested at twelve. Then arrested again. Then Sugar's disappearance and return— pregnant. Ty wrote again but heard nothing back. Then the newspaper clipping mailed to her by Marjorie that Sugar had died in an automobile accident, leaving a baby to be raised by Celeste. She'd heard about Celeste's business, her famous tinctures, the city booming with the tourism industry near the big hospital at the fifth mile marker. But in all that time, Tyresius never heard from Celeste herself. Not a word.

It about broke Tyresius' heart.

40

"I thought I knew the stories of all the grannies on the north," Lillian said, sitting very still as Ty put a small stitch in the back of her head from when she'd been dragged from the creek bed. She wondered why Celeste had never spoken to her about Ty. The more she learned about the place of her childhood, the more she wondered at what else she had never known.

"Consider me emergency medicine," she said, finishing the stitch with a paste of oregano.

"Could I come study with you sometime? I mean, if it's not a burden. I'd love to ask you about your chemistry," Lillian said. "Already, I feel so much better. I don't know how to thank you."

"You can thank me by listening carefully, child," she said, handing her a steaming cup of pine needle tea.

"I'm going to give you the antidote now. I'm going to place it on your tongue, and then I want you to swallow it down, without chewing. Do you understand?"

Lillian was out of questions at this point.

"After that, you will sip this tea. It will taste bitter. Do you understand?"

"Yes," Lillian said.

Ty held up a sliver of what looked like garlic in her hand, the long stems still attached. "This is moly," Ty said, nodding at the bag. "You know of it?"

Lillian considered the black root and milky flower. She shook her head.

"*Galanthus nivalis*. You can use it topically, but it's far more effective if it's administered orally. We use it to contradict stramonium poisoning. You ready?"

Lillian opened her mouth, and using her right hand, Ty held her jaw like it was a dog's.

"Swallow. Now, and fast," she said, Pete still sitting in the corner, the rifle still sitting on his lap, his finger on the trigger. Lillian swallowed it down in all its bitterness with a gagging cough, the taste horrific.

"Now the tea," Ty said, nodding to the cup in Lillian's hands. As Lillian sipped, Ty pulled a handful of large bulbs from the counter behind her and cut off several slices, placing them in an old Crown Royal bag and setting it beside Lillian on the table.

"She swallow it?" Pete asked.

"Yes. Now we wait," Ty said.

Pete carried his gun to the windows, using the barrel to move the drapes gently out of the way.

Lillian began sipping the bitter tea. "I've never heard of moly."

"It's newer to us too," Tyresius said, thinking of how useful it would have been to have had this against howler bites some fifty, sixty years before. "That false vine Marjorie warned you about? From the same family as Jimsonweed. Cousin to water hemlock. Moly is its only antidote."

"Where do you grow it?"

"In high sun. Mine are grown on the 60th mile marker. I'll be sending you off with some for use at home. The bulbs are to be planted in the fall."

Lillian stretched her legs, feeling more alert. The pain was still there, but it had diminished to a bright itch at her wounds. Lillian looked down at her heavily wrapped legs, feeling the ache of the wound but none of the nausea. She felt the warmth of the teacup around her hands. Things felt lighter, nearly dreamlike. She looked over Tyresius' arthritic fingers as she worked. Was she dreaming this exchange? What had she just been given? She had never known moly in these parts, nor had she ever heard of it used. She looked around at the old apothecary setup in this cabin, so very grateful for this granny and her use of her medicines. With her spirits somewhat restored, she thought immediately of Glory and sat up again. She worried about Jess and wondered if he had returned yet from Sam's.

"She'll be good now, Ty?" Pete said as he walked in, clearing his throat, interrupting her train of thought.

With her back still turned, she moved to the sink and began to wash her hands with a bar of lye, nodding over her shoulder. She must have been nearing a hundred years old but moved like a woman half her age.

"Did it take?" he asked, a little more urgently.

"I'll know by sunset," she answered tiredly, turning to scan Lillian's face. *You'll be alright, child.*

Lillian's eyes shot up to meet the woman's.

"I'll take you to your truck whenever she says you're ready," he said to Lillian, and left them, the floorboards creaking beneath his weight.

Lillian looked pleadingly into Tyresius' face. If she could see what was rattling around inside Lillian's head, she knew that Lillian had understood the old grannies from the south. She knew what Lillian knew. She held the woman's gaze. Lillian started and then stopped. She could not utter aloud what she had heard before escaping the south.

We can talk this way if you'd like. Just think what you're going to say. I'll do the same.

Lillian hesitated, then, with another burst of worry for Glory and Jess, her thoughts burst to the front of her mind. *So, you know I understood the Changed Ones?*

Tyresius nodded her head.

Is what the witch told me true?

Which part? Tyresius continued washing up at the sink, Lillian staring at her profile, marveling at this silent speech between them.

That I am the child of someone named Sugar?

The woman turned around and pulled up a stool. She looked suddenly very tired, or very sad. Lillian could not tell.

So I'm one of them? Lillian felt the terror ice her chest again before Tyresius stood, putting her hand up against Lillian's shoulder to steady her.

This is correct.

How could that be?

"Your mother," she said before trailing off, *as you now know, was a southern orphan. Celeste raised her as her own.*

So Celeste and I aren't—?

Ty shook her head. *Not related.*

But Celeste's husband? The doctor in the photograph?

Ty tensed before once again shaking her head. Lillian's head swam with this new information.

"And my father?"

We don't know. Your mother took lovers from the north, but we don't know who or when.

She turned a small mirror to Lillian, holding it up so she could look into her face. *Did you see their eyes?*

Their eyes aren't like mine—the shape of the pupil—

It does not always show up in the pupil. It may be the cowl, it may be the color.

Lillian stared closer at her eyes in the mirror. She saw the yellowish iris, something she always thought was an offshoot of green. But considering more closely, she could see a slight slit-shape of the pupil.

This is to allow a broader range of light to be tolerated.

Lillian sat back, the full realization of her wild origins suddenly upon her. Would she pass this to her child? Would she turn out like the witches? How had she not known? Why did no one tell her?

Will I turn into one of them? I can't go home to my baby if I will become like that.

The granny pressed the purple bag into her hand.

You are already one of them.

Lillian shuddered. *Didn't your tincture work?*

You are but half southern. You may see them change in moments of pain. Or anger. Did your granny see anything when you were laboring?

She didn't mention anything.

Tyresius looked down. *Like Celeste, Marjorie always wanted to protect you.*

Tyresius took a light and examined Lillian's eyes.

Do you see anything?

Just the color. You have the southern color.

Oh, God. Why didn't Celeste tell me any of this?

Tyresius cocked her head, looking her over. *To keep you safe, of course.*

So, she adopted me after my mother died?

Celeste took in your mother when she was a baby. She wanted her to have—well, not a southern life.

The vague impression of the woman dancing in low light in the bar, the faces of the men sizing her up once again flashed in Lillian's mind. Lillian shuddered at the echo. So that was Sugar then, she thought.

I heard my mother was too much for Celeste.

Yes.

Why am I not like that? Like her?

How you were nurtured keeps you clear.

But I am still one of them. How is it that I can be like them but not be—all the way like them?

Everyone has the choice.

It is a choice?

It is always a choice.

Lillian sat back, watching her pack of beagles panting beside the back door. The sun was beginning to set in the west.

There's one more thing, she pressed. Lillian felt an icy chill spread down her spine. *You already know.*

"Jess?"

She nodded.

Is he dying?

Yes. He doesn't have much time.

Glory?

She is alive. And safe. "Your home has a guard," Ty said, forcing calmness as she saw the body of Marjorie in the hallway, the blood foaming at the corner of her mouth. *She keeps your child safe.*

"Glory—"

And you are clear to return to attend to what circles your home.

What is circling my home?

Tyresius stood up, helping Lillian to a standing position. *Shadows.*

What kind of shadows?

Did you encounter any males on the south?

Yes. In the church.

That is no church.

It looked as if it might be one. I saw stained glass windows.

One hundred years ago it was their assembly house. They also had services. But those days have been over for some time. What did the menfolk do? Did they approach you?

Yes. They pointed, screeched like the others.

Did they touch you at all?

No—

Then the southern women followed?

"Yes," Lillian said.

Tyresius looked pensively out the window. *It is the menfolk that are at your cabin now.* Lillian took in a sharp breath.

I thought they couldn't cross?

They are in spirit.

How do I fight them?

They are within him.

How do I get them out?

You must use the antidote. She pushed the purple bag into Lillian's hands. *There are all sorts of wounds. This is so he will not turn. Or if he has already turned—*

Into one of them?

She paused then. *You must somehow get it inside of him. Brew it in a tea, anything. But you must get him to ingest the moly.*

Lillian's mind was frantic. Jess turned into one of those monsters. And the baby, so close to all that.

"Keep your mind steady," Ty said then.

"I know we have just met. Why are you helping me?" Lillian asked, as a feeling of dreaded helplessness covered over her. She struggled to hold back tears.

Tyresius stiffened. "Because Celeste would have wanted me to. She knew this day would come."

"What day?"

Tyresius scanned her face, looking suddenly sad. "The reckoning."

41

Marjorie lay motionless on Lillian's floor, her neck bent unnaturally to the left and swollen with the compression of her cervical vertebrae. Her breathing was shallow, her heart rate increased. She was a midwife by trade, but she was sure her neck was broken. She knew she didn't have much time. Her head hurt something awful, but she couldn't feel much else. From where she lay at the bottom of the steps, she could see under Lillian's bedroom door, where the bitch of the litter of dogs Lillian had raised up whined beside the crib where Glory Be was crying up a storm. That dog had saved Glory. She was sure of it.

Marjorie closed her eyes, wincing as the pain pulsed. She had failed against the Devil's strength. She was an old woman after all, but even the sassafras powder had done little aside from make the man cough. Whatever coiled inside of him was something she had not seen nor encountered before. She swallowed, felt blood start to pool in her mouth.

Knowing she had but minutes left, Marjorie closed her eyes and sent out her heart, sending it far and wide, sounding a silent alarm to every ally in the timbers. Every crow, every fawn, every granny—the moth, the cricket, the hare. She sent out a cry for help, imagining a pair of lips blowing the wormwood west, an incantation to lie in their land to protect the child, protect Lily-B, protect the home from whatever evil had been brought back, a prayer for the granny ancestry to link hands and form a veil of safety. She prayed to the timber, to the wind between each rustling tree, to the carp in the cove, to the groundcover. She felt her breathing grow more difficult, and with it, a sort of letting go of her responsibility to this home, this girl. She had passed it along to the wind, to the earth beneath her, which had held her up these last eighty years. Her mind returned to the dusty yard of her childhood, the big silent machines she walked between, the chipped paint, her mother, brittle, the men around her, coarse. The fear, the constant fear of those things and how they cut into the girls, made them hard, made them scared. She remembered running, clandestine, from Kansas City. Away from the horrors of men, their snatching, their pushing, and how she slipped away, like water into the drain after a storm. She felt a dull clang of pride, remembering her thin torso in the train latrine, chopping off her locks of brown hair as the car shook on the tracks, flushing the strands away and considering her face in the dirty mirror. She had survived. Time after time, Marjorie knew. She had survived. Been brave in the face of danger. And done good.

As she lay motionless, she heard the call of the Kildeer outside. The sweetest of the common country bird, it loves the farmland, the water's edge, a golden reflection from the dusty water.

Marjorie knew her life had not been a conventional one. She never married, never had her own children, but in her care, she had birthed over seven hundred babies. This hill town in southern Missouri had been a beautiful home to her. She loved Celeste's sassafras tea and hickory nut bakes. The grove of pawpaws that little Lily-B toddled in, the late frost on the persimmons. And summer in the deep of the coves, the mayflies bouncing between the dogwoods, pregnant with bloom.

In her last moments, Marjorie was not cold. In her life alongside the other women of J Road, they had created a place of safety, a place of healing. So many babies born, so many souls escorted home. And Glory Be. Her last baby. She had stayed even then to protect her. She had done good.

In the pulsing pain, she turned her mind to the simpler things. Things that are eclipsed by the working senses. Evening on a screened-in porch, the southern rain just starting, a strong fire, just starting to take, a mother first holding her baby.

The dog whined again from behind the door.

Please, Lord, let Lily-B make it home. Please let her be okay.

And then Marjorie's breathing stopped.

Wendy lay with her head between her paws beside the baby's crib, watching the old woman from the small space under the door. She was close to the cold place. Her brothers had run off into the night and were circling the den. Wendy could feel her own panting shallow from where the pack lead had bitten her, and she whined into the space before her. She would stay with the small one until the lead woman returned.

Wendy looked again toward the door, outside which the old woman lay. She sniffed in, heard her take her last breath, then nosed in the air before dragging herself under the crib to wait.

Wendy had seen this before. The squirrel's pelt in the road, the carp belly floating in the cove. It was nothing personal. She turned again to her charge. The baby, who lay on her back, crying into the night air.

42

After thirty minutes, Lillian was strong enough to stand. Ty handed her the bag, put her bony hand onto Lillian's shoulder.
It is natural to be afraid.
What if he is stronger than I am? What if Glory—
"Whatever has kept you safe, also keeps your child safe," she said, her face steely. *For you are of the same blood.*
Is there no one who can help me?
Tyresius held her gaze. *Each one's fight is their own.*
The woman leaned back for a moonshine jug, pulled off the cork, and put her nose to the opening. On her hand sat a ring with a large stone. The same clay-colored stone that hung from the leather strap around Lillian's neck. She saw Lillian looking as she took a swig. She wiped her mouth with the back of her hand and offered the jug to Lillian, speaking without words.

Lillian sipped, noticing the stone before grimacing and wiping her burning mouth with the back of her hand. "The stone," she muttered, her eyes moving to Ty's. The woman's eyes fluttered a little at this, and again Lillian tried to place her familiarity. It was then the likeness returned—the tall, willowy stance, the strong shoulders. The man in the photograph. Could it be? But why?
So, you remember now, she said without saying, the words weighing sad in her mind.
That was you, from the photograph? Lillian thought to her. *But how?*
Times were not always as they are now. For the two of us to be together, I had to become someone else.
My God, Lillian thought. *My grandmother. She never spoke at all about this. About anything.*
No one did much of that.

But why?

"Safer this way."

Lillian felt a profound longing for Celeste. To talk to her, but more so, to listen. The courage it would have taken to love like that. To sacrifice safety. For love. *I wish she had told me*, Lillian thought suddenly, wishing she had known Celeste. The woman who saved her mother from a life in the south. With feral eyes and creatures as company. Lillian shuddered to think.

The borders all had to tighten to protect your mother. You know this.

Lillian felt profound longing for Jess and his strong arms around her body.

Lillian passed the jug back, saying nothing. Ty corked it and put it back on her apothecary shelf.

What the Changed One said—

Yes, she said without saying in the silence. *Your mother was passed to Celeste from the north end of the creek. Naked, feral. Barely walking. Bloody. Her own mother loved her, wanted a life free of violence for her. She passed her across the water. Celeste lifted her, the baby clung to her, she took her in.*

Did they look for her?

No one claimed her. They were perhaps afraid of Celeste's strength and wouldn't come forward. Or perhaps the more powerful ones did not know.

"The women of the south, they knew her name. Kept calling her Sugar."

"That's the name her mother gave her. Celeste kept it as she raised her up."

Didn't she worry I would be, you know, like them?

Like how? Tyresius' face seemed puzzled.

Like, all wrong.

She looked down into her hands, turned the ring once on her finger. *Celeste believed the children—could be saved.*

Like me?

Like you.

Pete shuffled back into the room. Ty looked soberly at him, the lines in her face showing deep sadness under the side lamp.

"Tyresius?" Pete asked.

Thank you for telling me about where I'm from.

Ty squared herself again in front of Lillian. *Tie your man to the chair. Use only a Bowline knot. You know this knot?*

The rabbit comes out of its hole?

"She good?" Pete asked.

That's the one. You know it?

I do.

"She's clean," Ty said to Pete.

Thank you for the truth.

Everyone deserves the truth. And girl. One more thing. You need to steel yourself.

Lillian swallowed, knowing what she would say.

The Devil will be inside of him.

What do I do?

He will spit words at you. He knows what you fear. And he will use it against you. But it is not your husband who will be speaking. He will not mean what he says.

What words? Lillian thought.

The worst ones. Now listen carefully.

"Ty?"

You get him to take the moly. It is the only thing you must think of. Do not let his words distract you. The south is what will speak to you, but you must not listen. It is not him speaking. This is the southern menfolk and their devils. Men whose hurt is spread like sulfur. You must not let the words touch you. Get the moly inside of him.

I will.

"She's ready," Tyresius told Pete.

43

Celeste stood beside her husband at her mother's gravesite, his hand steadily around hers. Though Tammy's switch to Tyresius made her outwardly present as a man, she would always be a wife to Celeste. Celeste loved Tammy as a woman, the sacral curve of her spine, her supple lips, the space between her navel and pubic bone. She loved the way their chests felt, pressed together as they kissed, the way her belly curved out, ever so slightly. These parts were still under her trousers, of course, but saying *my husband* felt fraudulent. Ty was no man.

In their years off J Road, they were blessed to be able to explore the pleasure of walking through the world as a couple, the way husbands walked with wives through town or market, the way couples touched unthinkingly, his hand placed low on the back, as if to steer her, brushing away a stray lock of hair across coffee in the diner, walking hand in hand to their pew at church, things they had never been free to do in St. Louis, things lovers who are free to walk the world together take for granted, even in their most ordinary moments. There was a bliss to not being watched, to just being a woman and man, to being overlooked. Celeste had seen her parents move through the world as parallels, never lovingly. Her mother had winced from her father, seeming to tolerate his touch. Growing up, she wondered how the coarse corners of men could ever compare to the supple softness of a woman's body, but growing up, she'd shoved all that away. She had suitors, men from church, neighbors' sons, but she never met their eyes. Their large hands, swollen with veins, their broadness, their roughness unsettled her. She longed for the sweet folds of a woman's form, the soft run of her lips, her eyes parted in pleasure. The thoughts made her blush, made her wonder if she was built all wrong, until she moved away to school. Until she met Tammy. And then, beneath Tammy's touch, she knew that everything she had been feeling, all her longings and fantasies, had been natural. She had been built by the Lord, and in loving Tammy, she was being true to how she'd been constructed by His perfect hand. She knew her lust was pure, as it was linked to the radiant angel of love.

After their move to Camden County, Ty and Celeste's lives became full. The sounds of the paddle steamers were replaced by bullfrogs, and instead of the buses, they took their donkey or walked. Instead of a hospital, they worked to aid a community from the trailer on their property. It was a world of women (mostly), away from the world's judgment. And each year, the grannies' gifts grew, each of them unique, each of them uncurling like a frond in spring, unique in its gestation within each woman. For Ty, a certain communication. She was always so good at knowing what to say and when, knowing what was thought, what was expected. It was most useful in their business dealings. For Marjorie, it was babies. She would speak to them, coax them out. She could make any disastrous birthing situation manageable. She coaxed babies into this world.

But for Celeste, her gift was everything that would be their undoing. It was seeing the future. And it had become a heavy burden.

Because futures are not always good.

But the good thing about futures, is they can be changed. Just takes a little courage, is all.

I know, dear reader, that you've read about me already. Perhaps you've formed an understanding of my coldness in sending Tammy away. My self-imposed isolation. My firmness with Sugar. My boundaries for Lillian. But forgive me this, for it was necessary. In medicine, you take extraordinary measures to keep patients alive. That's all I was doing.

I was called to the Lick three times that last summer before everything changed. Twice I was accompanied by Marjorie and Tammy. On that second trip, as you've read, I was given Sugar. But there was a third trip. A secret one.

It was the last year before my monthly menses ended for good. I arrived home late one night after visiting two influenza-stricken families across Highway 5. One had a newborn who had symptoms, and I was concerned about the baby, how he was sleeping, his cough. Tammy had waited up, kept supper ready, and soon after, retired to bed, leaving me to my notebooks on the porch. I was not tired, so I started the kettle for tea. That was when I felt it. The heavy eyes on me from across the Lick. We often felt them looking across when we sat on the porch, dragging our attention to them, but the agreement was that vast chasms of space would remain respected. We would not cross to them, and they would not cross to us. But that night, I saw something I had not seen before: a signal fire. Two torches, waving in the midst of darkness from across the Lick. Someone was beckoning. I felt the heavy sinking feeling. The Lick was best avoided, especially in spring when the currents were strong, pulling like a man against us, and it was not safe for fishing, let alone crossing. In the darkness. I don't know why I decided to answer the signal. Tammy was asleep, and some part of me felt like I had taxed her enough that day by being off on appointments. So, I turned off the stove and walked along the path, the moonlight reflecting on the stones, the crickets in song. Walking alone at night in the timber is never safe, but it was my timber, and I know its ways. Plus, the fire called for me. I was not afraid.

Across the creek was one of them. A female. In my time in the south, I had never seen this particular one. She was older. Broken in spirit. Most of the women were unkempt, but she was even more so than the others. When she saw me approach, she subdued the fire and called up one from behind her by lifting her right arm up. The other could speak snatches of our language. Later, I learned the communicator had learned from reading our Bible, which she had found in the structure that once stood as a congregation for the southern folk decades before. The older woman gestured toward the water as she herself waded in, hobbling, as though injured. I hesitated before the communicator spoke to me.

The older one spoke, the one behind her watching her before interpreting. She spoke in a dark tongue, a hissing speech, like an insect's rubbing. Her mouth did not close as she spoke. I could see rows of ruined teeth. The communicator stood behind her, listening and then translating in broken sentences with each pause, her head tilted toward the woman.

"We have called you for your help," she muttered, her accent thick.

I could barely hear, so I lifted my skirt above the water, feeling as if I were in a dream, and stepped in up to my calves, the water cold and fast against my legs, nearly pushing me off balance. We met, each of us, ten feet or so into the Lick on our respective sides, our dresses raised to our knees. Where that courage to wade in came from, to this day, I still do not know.

"We need something of you," the communicator said. I glanced behind me. There was only the darkness in the distance.

"Is it medical care?" I asked eagerly, then waited, taking in their filthy clothes, their matted hair.

The broken one spoke more quickly, and the communicator continued. "We have been watching you."

"Do you need food?"

"We called you only when you could no longer create children."

I felt a shiver run through my body and took a step back. "How did you know that?"

She continued but more intensely. "We have been watching."

I stared at them then, their postures, considering their stances. Their hands hung openly, they seemed to ache from within. To me, it seemed they were eager to speak. I felt for the pulse of what would come next but did not see harm. The old woman waded in even farther, her filthy skirt in the current. She gestured her hands wildly as she clicked in her dark speech. I could see dark veins under their pale skin. It was as though ink ran through them. They did not seem to me of this world.

"What do you need?" I asked, my frustration growing. I felt disbelief for my audacity then. These people had not been good to us, had rejected our ways, even inflicting violence on us as we tried to help them. I should have woken Tammy.

"First, you listen," the interpreter said in her hissing accent.

I stood frozen, feeling ready to run back at any sign of violence.

"Witches, your people called us," the communicator said to the other in their dead tongue, both of their limping ending about two feet from where I stood. "We know how you speak of us."

"Some have used that word," I said above the current's roar.

"You know nothing of the goat," she said, smiling as her translator continued. I looked between their filthy faces.

"The goat?"

"You have heard the stories. You know that the Devil is among us?"

I swallowed then, the fear rising in my chest. Both women narrowed their eyes at the question. The older continued her hissing and clicking.

"Black Dog, listen now—" the communicator said quickly. "Here is the life of the girl in our part. When she is born, she is nursed. But when she begins to walk, she is cut." The translator spat out that word—cut—as the older woman lifted one leg to show a crudely healed scar that wrapped around the back of her ankle.

I stepped closer. It was an old wound, but it seemed to be angry with infection. "Who cuts you?"

The old woman hissed. "The Dark One," the translator continued, and I took one step back.

"Who?"

"Who you call the Devil."

"I don't understand. Why do they cut you?"

"She who is cut cannot run. They took the girls, cut them first on the right ankle. Then at the menses, the second ankle. Before given over to him. It is His right, He says."

I felt my heartbeat increase. This couldn't be. "Given over why?"

"And one, every six years, is chosen to be his new concubine."

I had moved my hands to my mouth then.

"The mothers, they are helpless."

I was silent. I could see what lay before them. Some sick tradition they had kept secret all these decades. Secluded. Powerless.

"If the menfolk protest, then more is cut. A tongue, first. An eye put out. Like your stinking book."

I did not have the words to speak to this.

"Was there no one to protect you?"

"Who can fight Him?" the translator spit. "No one has the power. Your God did not stop this," the dark woman hissed.

"Did you try the law? Maybe we can help—"

The women hissed together, quieting me. I felt the wind whipping up between us then, as though a storm was brewing.

"This is now what I have to tell you. He has chosen his next girl. She will be cut at the next full moon."

I stepped in toward her, almost instinctively.

"She is my daughter's child. We do not want Him to take her."

"Of course you—"

"We need her to cross over."

"To cross?"

"To the north. She will soon be offered over to you."

I shook my head then. "I am bound not to cross—"

"As we are bound. He cannot follow, as we cannot."

"I can't just take a child," I told her then, thinking of the questions, the law on us.

"If you do not, she will be next."

"But—"

"You must keep her hidden. He knows what we plan."

I didn't want to ask, but I already knew. It was in our folklore, for as long back as I could remember. The witches, lying with the Devil. This was no metaphor.

"So you know," the translator growled. I realized then, this old one. She could read thoughts. It was her dark gift.

I straightened my spine then. "What would you have me do with her?"

"Raise her as yours. If she has crossed over, He cannot claim her."

I thought then, selfishly, that I was no match for the Devil. Would he pursue this child? Would he pursue me? Tyresius? "How will she assimilate? Her eyes—" I asked.

Then, beyond them, a howling, deeper than the cry of the wolf, and angrier, as though from the source of anger itself. Their heads snapped back, and they began to creep backward, showing their terrible translucent skin, their inky veins. I saw the scars curling around both calves as they hobbled back. And as they retreated, the old woman spoke just once more, her body moving almost in a jerking motion. "The next full moon. The eve of the Solstice. We will signal again. Only once."

"But why—why do you stay? Why don't you take the children, cross here, anywhere?" I asked, desperate then.

"After enough time," she hissed, "the darkness is all you see," she said, her voice fading. They ducked into the overgrowth, their crippling shifting sickening in the moonlight.

I tried to follow them with my eyes, but I was left in the darkness. I walked back with only a sliver of moonlight on the stones to guide me, turmoil in my soul. I had never spoken so long with any of the southerners, and as the Lick was our boundary, I was not to cross to inquire as to their claims. Offering a child to me? This talk of the Devil? And what was this ritual? Would their people follow? Could they even? Could I raise a child at fifty years old, passing her off as my own? What would Tyresius say? I latched the cabin door, checked the lock twice, my heart racing, and lit my pipe on the porch, taking in the cherry tobacco in long, slow breaths to calm my nerves.

It was a long while before I lay down beside my wife, my body still cold from the Lick. I stared up at the wooden boards of the room and prayed.

I will say of the Lord, "He is my refuge and my fortress,
my God, in whom I trust."

I prayed for this to have been a dream, prayed that there was no such thing as witches and that the Devil did not take children, not one hundred yards from my cabin.

He will cover you with his feathers,
and under his wings you will find refuge;
his faithfulness will be your shield and rampart.

I felt my mind pulled in every direction, my breath shallow with panic. I lay watching my wife's face, tried to pull the moon's sweetness over me like a blanket, but sleep did not come.

You will not fear the terror of night,
nor the arrow that flies by day,
nor the pestilence that stalks in the darkness,
nor the plague that destroys at midday.

I gave up on sleep and sat on the porch to knit. My fingers worked furiously by the kerosene lamp. For the first time in my life, the needle tore my skin, the blood dripping down on my apron. I looked into the night, feeling their eyes on me.

"Because he loves me," says the Lord, "I will rescue him;
I will protect him, for he acknowledges my name.

I spoke nothing of what had transpired that night.

A week passed. Alongside the time, the dreams. If you know the old poet Homer, you know his Tyresius could see the future. But my Tyresius? She only read the present. What each person thought, what each feared, blooming in her mind, good and bad, side by side, like sisters. I, however, was the seer. I should have been named Tyresius. What would come, the sweetness and the terrible, awful truth of pain, like sheets of snow down a ledge onto the unsuspecting. And what I saw for my family came to me on a Friday morning as I stood peeling potatoes: The baby, her name already chosen. Sugar. Colicky for years, sullen then after. Next, Sugar at four or so, speaking of her origin, remembering her true parents. Next, her body, quick like the others from which she was born, me too slow, Sugar trying to swim the current of the Lick, trying to cross back home, hissing toward the south. Then my crying out, Tammy following her, their footsteps on the south, my wife lifting her, the howlers on my Tammy then, the brambles, the sickness after. Her cold body.

What would you do if you knew your wife was to die before you? Be torn open by howlers from nave to chops. The soft breast where you'd had brought your mouth, tasting her rose wet sweetness over and over. Her carotid punctured by poisonous fangs. What would you choose if you, in your mind's eye, saw that certain future? My visions had never been wrong. Not once. You might be thinking, well, I'd tell her the truth. The truth always wins. But what if your lover was brave? Brave enough to change for you, to cut her hair and don trousers and live in another body, another identity? Would that type of woman not stare down a howler? That very bravery would have been her undoing. What if you knew she'd refuse, try to change the course of the future? Like her Greek namesake, well, we all know how well that turned out.

No. I dropped the potatoes into the sink and made my choice. Stepped into the cold hole of loneliness where I'd live out the next fifty years of my life. Worth it, if Tammy were to be saved. I would not have my love's blood on my hands. She deserved to live, even if it meant I had to break her heart to ensure it.

The only thing that would get my wife to leave was to lie. To ensure she believed I no longer wanted her love. Let's say the woman you loved, because she loved you and because she presumed that being a mother was something you wanted so badly, would allow herself to be passed over, so you could have that motherhood.

So that is what I did. I made her believe it.

Some people look up at the sky and wonder how they got here. Me? I scan the woods for danger, to see who I can protect. Lord knows there's enough danger in this cold world.

I'll just take you right to it.

What Tyresius' end would have been would have been sickness from the south. From their venom, their protection charms. I do not have the tinctures for such things. It is dark medicine known only to their dark healers. They have not yet been devised by those of us on the north.

So, I imagined what would unravel her love for me. First, a pinprick of longing. I crafted images of it in my mind. I coiled these false hopes as I lay beside her in bed. When she touched me, God forgive me, I imagined a man, tall and broad, his heavy body against mine, his member entering me, his seed finding purchase. As she touched me, she'd read these thoughts and stiffen, at first, in disbelief. I could read her thoughts—*no—this isn't real*—but I pressed back, believing in the false pleasure. I had never known a man, but I watched him take form in my mind, the percussive piano foot of his breath as he moved, and the images worked their way through her mind like droplets of ink into clear water. I forced the obscene images into my heart, breaking the treasure of our union, stifling my tears as her hands moved across me. I let her mind comb over mine, like fingers through hair, the cold shock of her understanding as she thought, her heart sinking, then my heart sinking, that she would never be able to give me what I most deeply longed for. My wife's love unclenched by her feet of clay. And I, most wretched, let her think what she needed to know.

She believed what she read. And moved then, away from me, a subtle shift like the shoreline under the power of the tide. My wife.

Please do not think I am cold. For this was the only thing that would make her go. It is true. I held the false hope in my mind. Please forgive me.

In breaking her heart, I saved her life.

Or else, she would have died for me. For Sugar.

That's no way to tend to the woman you love.

44

Lillian sped down J Road toward Highway 7, her mind pulled back to what she had learned that day, that her origins had become even more mysterious, even more unsettling than she could have possibly imagined. She was feeling physically better from Tyresius' tinctures, but her legs were cut to hell and would take months to fully heal. She couldn't stop thinking about the eyes of the Changed Ones, and how her eye color, the odd color, was the same yellowish hue. A southern-born mother meant she had half of the south inside of her, half of their feral tendencies, half of their rage, even half of the darkness. Yet those things didn't seem to have shown themselves to her thus far. She was a Christian. A mother, a wife, and she loved her people, loved her land, and her animals. She wondered what made the southerners the way they were, what had turned them into the Changed Ones. She also wondered at their supernatural speed, their teeth that could bite straight through skin, tear into it with the appetite of an animal. She shivered, thinking that part of them could also run through her.

After turning onto 7, the low fuel light flicked on in Alice's truck.

"Damnit," she said, knowing this would delay her arrival home by even more time, which was precious. She pulled into the Moto Mart and limped out to the side of the truck, locusts flying around under the bright, fluorescent lights, and quickly began filling the tank, her mind worrying over Glory, over Marjorie.

Your baby has a guard.

Her breasts were full, leaking painfully, but it was useless. She was poisoned and would have to drain and dump the milk, then dry herself up. She rested her forehead against the truck, feeling defeated. From where she stood, she could hear a chorus of male voices coming from inside, where a group of young men pulled beer from the coolers, a sort of bold energy between them. They were about her age, maybe a little younger. Not hill folk. More like the uppity kids who'd come in on weekends for parties at Tan-Tar-A. They pushed through the door with too-loud voices and walked back to their pickup parked on the other side of the pump where she stood. She turned her back to them, keeping her eyes down, but she could feel the heat of their gazes on her. She could see her reflection from the driver's side window, dirt caked around her face, her tee-shirt clinging to her swollen chest.

"You alright there, beautiful?" the largest of the three asked from between the pumps. Through the glass, she could see his large body leaning between them as though for show. His eyes had a dangerous shine to them. She could tell he had been used to chatting up girls. She nodded curtly, keeping her back to them.

"Where you headed? Into town?"

"Home," Lillian said. A slight ripple of anger moved through her chest. "To my husband."

"That's a shame," he said playfully, or perhaps menacingly. Lillian picked up immediately on their heartbeats. Slightly racing, as though excited about something.

"He shouldn't let his wife out to pump the gas," he said with a sort of mock sympathy. Lillian looked up to see him smirking at the other two.

Come on, come on, she thought as she watched the pump, which moved agonizingly slowly. Lillian ignored them, watching their faces from the reflection in her car door. She had been staring at some form of danger in others' eyes for the past day and was done with it.

No more.

She heard the sound of one of the cans of beer opening as the tank filled, and she shoved the nozzle back into the pump, avoiding looking up.

"Looks like you've had a day," the big one started again, stepping over the pump median to where Lillian stood. "Want to stop in for one with us before you head home?" he asked, until seeing her fully, his greasy face taking in the bloody jeans, the blood stain down her filthy legs with wide eyes. His shirt was unbuttoned to the mid-chest, showing off a set of for-show muscles. She could smell the exhaust from their truck, covered in mud from whatever it was they'd been up to that day. When she looked up and met his eyes, he staggered a bit, his eyes bloodshot, forcing a smile, though he'd been startled by her appearance. He looked drunk.

"No, thanks," she said firmly but pleasantly, the exhaust in the air between them. She looked over at their truck. "Might want to check your gaskets," she said, attempting to divert the conversation.

"Christ, what happened to you?" the second man asked, suddenly beside his friend. His eyes combed over her, stopping at her chest, which was soaked wet with leaking breast milk and blood. His mouth was agape with a mixture of disgust and curiosity. Lillian felt small beside them, the gas pump blocking the view of the cashier inside. There was only the vast, empty highway behind them as they stood there in the heat of the evening. The day's intensity had worn on her, but she felt a rage return, the same rage she had felt earlier, the new sort of rage that seemed to bloom darkly inside of her, a rage she had never before listened to. It seemed to fill her up from the inside, pressing against her skin, reaching her face, her neck hot, and she caught a glimpse of her expression in the side mirror, noticing her eyes were—was it cloudy? She leaned forward toward the image of herself, and whatever cloudy cover had been there moved, more like slipped, to the side, clearing away. The membrane. The taller man took another step toward her, sizing her up as he would a rack of candy bars.

"Real ice queen, that one," one mumbled from behind her, and the three of them laughed.

"You need some help, miss?" he said, his tongue in the side of his mouth. "We can take you to a doctor if that's what—"

"No, sir," she said quickly, lifting the handle on her door.

"How the hell did you get all cut up like that?" the second asked, moving his big hand against the door so that she could not open it. She stood for a moment, watching her hand hold the handle limply, seeing the keys dangling from the ignition. In the reflection, she looked very small compared to these men and knew the third was likely also a large man waiting to assist in whatever these boys had in mind next to their dirty truck. There was no way to know what someone intended, where they had come from, what they were capable of. She had seen that her whole life. She had seen it that day when the Changed Ones turned on even one of their own. She turned to look up at him, only inches away from her. This one was used to bossing women around.

"I think you boys need to step away from me and my vehicle," she said before shoving his shoulder back with hers, catching him off balance as he stumbled into the other, and, taking the opportunity, she quickly jumped into the truck, her legs burning, locking the door, just as the big one attempted to open it, rattling it over and over as their faces leaned in to peer at her. The one she had shoved slapped his thick hand against her window as she started it up quickly, leaving a hot print where his hand had been.

"Now, there's no need for you to be rude," the first hollered through the glass in mock sweetness as she threw the truck into gear and pulled off, the other shouting "Bitch!" in protest as she left a cloud of dust like a white halo behind her. She turned back onto the main road, checking her eyes repeatedly in the rearview mirror. The cloudiness was gone, but she was sure she'd seen it. It had come twice in the last few minutes when she had felt her anger. Her focus alternated between the road ahead and her own gaze in the mirror, wondering if it had always been there, or if it was new as a consequence of what she'd been through that night. Would others notice? Would Jess?

Oh, God, Jess. Glory.

She accelerated, hoping for no law on the roads, but after a moment, she spotted the truck from the station a hundred or so yards behind her but closing in, roughly passing a compact car to place itself between it and her with a jerky swerve. It would be just a minute or so until they were on her, and she pressed the gas pedal down, her speed increasing to 65, then 70, then 76. A moment later, they passed her, pausing in the opposite lane for a moment with their taunts. One threw a beer can at her truck, which bounced off the hood before flying off to the shoulder of the highway, their laughter in the air over the sound of the highway, that shrillness feeling more dangerous than anything else in the warm night air. She felt out and could read their hearts, which had grown swollen with a sort of dark adrenaline. Like an animal in pursuit of prey. She felt the fury return, bubbling up under her ribcage, watching them in the rearview mirror, missing the cowl covering her eyes in a split second before it slipped back away. The men accelerated then, pulling in front of her, slowing their truck immediately so that she had to pump the brakes, feeling her ribcage press against the seatbelt. They slowed to nearly fifty, then forty-five miles per hour, the one in the backseat turning to leer at her. Lillian righted her focus. She could see their intentions through their pulse.

She was being hunted. They were hunting her.

And after what she had been through, for the world outside of J Road to turn on her was simply too much.

She took a deep breath and did something new to her. Holding the breath in the center of her chest, she sent it out, pushing it through her chest, through the windshield, through the space between the vehicles, into theirs, a ball of force which burst forward. She slowed her breath, steering it as though she were a puppeteer, then counted to ten. Seconds later, she heard the pop of their back tire, causing their back end to fishtail before they veered too quickly to the side as the driver frantically braked before the truck rolled once, then again into the corn off the side of the highway. She flew past them, seeing the truck righted in the middle of the corn, its front end crumpled.

She drove full speed back toward her home and did not look back.

45

Lillian knew Alice's truck announced her arrival. She hoped Marjorie would run out with Glory Be, but when she pulled up beside Jess' truck, the cabin was dark. She turned off the motor, listening to the locusts' snapping overpowering the forest's silence. She craned her neck to look in the cabin windows and could see no fire on the stove.

She limped cautiously toward the cabin, armed only with Tyresius' moly stuffed deep in her front pockets. As she walked, no barks announced her arrival. The air felt sickly sweet with summer heat. She sent out, but there was little stirring of hearts surrounding her. Small adrenaline hearts like birds, but high in the trees. No fawns, no hares. No bullfrogs. No crickets. Nothing except the locusts. They covered the cabin, the trees beside it, crawling on the blackness of the windows as though looking for a way inside. She froze before Celeste's rosemary bush, transplanted from the Lick after her marriage to Jess. Its crown was visibly wilted.

She pushed open the front door, and the stench was immediate. Sulfur and sweat. The same smell that hung on the men when they got back from the Lick, but much, much stronger. The same smell that was in that rundown church over on the south side.

It was the smell of the menfolk of the Lick. It smelled like rot.

Like death.

Like the Devil.

She felt a bolt of fear and reminded herself of the old needlework above Marjorie's back door:

What should be the fear?

I do not set my life at a pin's fee.

And for my soul, what can it do to that,

Being a thing immortal as itself?

She took a deep breath and moved to light the lamp to her right. It was then that the scene appeared in all its ugly brightness.

Jess, seated in the corner. Hulking. Mouth open. His skin covered in a sort of oily sheen. It was as the grannies had warned. It was the body of her husband, but changed. He sat sagging, heaving in rattled breaths, his eyes pointed and black. But this was not her husband's spirit. It was the thing that had taken hold of Jess. His features were all swollen, his eyes burning in eager stillness. By the looks of it, there was a haze covering his pupils. His soul had been taken over. She dropped the keys on the ground at the sight of him.

"Hey, honey," she said weakly as she stood before him.

It was then an odd sound picked up in the air. Soft at first, as though someone were playing music from across the cove. The song sounded old-timey, something her grandmother would have hummed over the stove. She looked around as the sound continued, out of tune before her eyes settled on where it was coming from: Celeste's gramophone. It was playing by itself from its place in the corner. Jess had brought back evil. Her eyes moved back to him, her mind racing.

"Where you been off to?" Jess asked, his voice bloated with what sounded like darkness. Lillian cast her eyes down as Marjorie had advised. She took in a slow breath and felt out for her borders. North, south—south was gone. The powder had all been blown away. She looked up for the tourmaline sac which hung by the door. Gone. The front door's border had been breached. Where the men had come in from the hunt. With whatever this was hanging on them then. They brought it inside with them. Just walked it right into her world. Her child's home.

"Looking for something, darlin'?" the thing inside of Jess asked.

Lillian turned to see Jess pull the pouch from his pocket and set it on the end table beside his Taurus Judge. She took a step back, sending out for heartbeats in the house. Counted one, two on their level, one, two below. The granny and Glory Be.

"What are you doing with the Judge?" she asked.

He sat in his chair, his eyes pinned to her. "Keeping watch." His eyes combed over her. "You look mighty cut up, miss," he said.

Lillian wondered at his words. Jess didn't speak like that. "Ran into a bit of trouble," she said, swallowing. "Sorry I took so long." She stood frozen, the sound of the record slowing as if a hand were guiding it.

"The old woman said you were running errands."

"Yeah, had some business to attend to." She glanced for the shotgun he kept under the couch. Gone. "When did you get back?" she asked meekly, feeling the courage drain out of her. Her wounds pulsed.

"What kind of business?"

Lillian's mind raced. She wasn't to speak to them, but she didn't know what else to do. "Just some talk with the grannies on the north," she said.

"Now, Lillian," he said. "I'm a man of great patience. But when I ask you a question, I expect an honest answer."

"Jess—"

"You're lying."

She stared at her husband in shock. It was even as though the tone of his voice had changed. This tone, this attitude, it was nothing like she'd ever seen from him. From anyone, except for folks she'd see from time to time on the television, or in books.

He pushed up from his chair, the clothes hanging on him all wrong, as though another person lived inside of his body.

She took a step backward, scanned the perimeter of the property. Next door: four heartbeats. Downstairs. She'd have to move away from him, to get to the baby. She did not mean to engage the creature inside of Jess. She knew better than to talk to it.

Jess made his way to her and took her face with his hand. "Casting out your little net, are you?" He held her roughly as she held his gaze. She had not told Jess about her sending out. Whatever this was, he—it knew. His hand gripped her more tightly, and she winced. She told herself that this was not her man. One eye looked lower than the other, the skin all shiny taut. She steeled herself, cleared her mind.

It laughed then. "Don't you worry, little one. I'm not here to hurt you. Or the baby."

"What are you here for?" she asked, squirming in his grip.

"I've been waiting for you," he told her, his stinking breath filling the air between them.

"For what?"

He cocked his head at her then, his mouth spreading into a slow smile. "Don't you know me?" he asked, the bottom of his voice dropping into darkness. And it was then she did know him. It was her watcher. She felt her heart seize with cold fear and gasped, beside herself. She shoved against his chest, slipping from his grip She slunk back around the table, keeping it centered between the two of them. She could see his right hand was badly torn up. He had wrapped it in a towel from the kitchen, but it had bled through.

"You're one of us," he growled. Lillian mirrored him as he moved.

"Don't think so."

"Glory Be too. Come to me," it said to her, reaching out its mangled hand.

Lillian froze. The whole macabre perversion of the scene felt somehow familiar. She wondered if this was the southern part of her, that it longed to get back to where it came from.

"That's right. You do long for home. I'm here to bring you back."

Lillian dug her fingernails into her palms. She thought of Glory Be and Marjorie waiting below.

Have not I commanded thee? Be strong and of a good courage. The Lord thy God is with thee whithersoever thou goest.

"I don't get near anyone who ain't my husband," she said, a low boil of anger rising beyond the fear in her chest.

"Shut your whore mouth," he growled, his voice unlike Jess', and she swallowed hard, steeling herself against his words.

She felt a buoying courage in her breast. "What happened to your hand?" she asked.

"Your dog got to me," it said. It was hard not to look at whatever Jess was. She agonized over his skin, all wrong, the voice that was not his coming out of his body. *Wendy*, she thought. Lillian swallowed.

"Since you've been waiting on me, why don't you tell me who you are?"

"I believe you think of me as your dark suitor," he mocked, his voice all wrong. It was the beast. The one who had tugged at her since childhood, somehow inside of Jess, speaking from her husband's body.

"Sower of discord" she said as she stood across from him, her wounds throbbing. She stared into him. Jess had to be in there somewhere.

Do not speak to it.

It laughed at her then, moving quickly around the table as she limped to dodge him.

"Tell me your name so I can greet you properly," Lillian said.

"A visitor. Here to bring one of his southern women home." Jess pressed his big hands onto the table between them, the injured one leaking blood onto the wood.

"Visitors shouldn't enter without invitation."

"Your husband invited me in when he crossed over to my land."

Lillian froze, anger flicking across her face. "You're a liar."

"And you're a whore," it said, its mouth black like them, like the women back in the south. A slow, snarling laugh came from Jess' body. Its eyes narrowed on her then.

Her lip trembled before she steeled herself back to who she knew she was. "Well, my Jess don't call people names."

"Ain't wrong, am I, Lily-B?" he said.

Lillian moved to keep the same distance between them. Tyresius' pain medicine was wearing off, and she'd need more soon. She would need to get the moly in him, but how?

"A whore just like Sugar," he growled again.

"You knew my mother?" she asked, trying to keep it talking, horrified at Jess' smooth brow, his sweet face, occupied, consumed by this dark spirit, eyeing the kitchen for a way to administer the drug.

"That's all you got, isn't it," she said angrily, feeling the natural quiver move her hatred to the front of heart. Its face was flat. She pressed aside the anger and made a move for the kitchen when he reached out for her, grabbing her firmly by her wrist and twisting it behind her.

"Let me go," she cried, worrying immediately for the heartbeats below.

"Don't you worry about your granny," the creature inside Jess snickered, knowing her thoughts, his face stinking inches from hers. "She's waiting for you downstairs," an echo of a laugh ending his words. Lillian wiped her mind as she moved quickly for the steps downstairs, Jess pulling her back with a rough jerk and blocking her way, putting his heavy hand on top of hers at the stove. He looked inflamed. The stench on him was terrible. Rotting. He felt across the back of her neck with his free hand, filling her with fear. As she watched his taut face, she worked to keep her mind clear, clear. He pulled her against him, the heat of his skin sticking in the air between them.

Swallowing her disgust, she turned toward his soiled face, leaning into that part of her that she had always pushed off. The part that must have come from the south she now realized. The slow temper she'd kept penned her whole life, like a controlled burn. The cold part. The part she'd chased away with healing and prayer. But those things wouldn't save her now. No prayer would do what she needed to do herself.

So, Lillian set up a curtain between herself and her better nature and leaned into the darkness of this creature, feeling some buried part of her stir, as if the part of her she now knew was southern could somehow speak to him like this. She shuddered as she raised her body to the tiptoes to move her lips to his neck, running her hands across his broad back, feeling what it would have felt like had she crossed the Lick those years ago, had she become one of the witch brides of the beast.

He gripped her arms then, running his hands across her shoulders then down to her backside, his fingers brushing against her bandaged wounds. Her chance had presented itself. She wasn't strong enough to fight him, and she had no borders.

There was just this one way. Meeting darkness with darkness. In the windows to the west, she saw that a crow had landed on the window ledge. It plucked a locust from the glass before stretching its wings. Another joined it a moment after. Another. There was hope.

Two heartbeats, two heartbeats.

She looked back at him sweetly in full falseness, then slowly unbuttoned her jeans, turning around to press her backside against him as she lowered her torn clothes. She saw her reflection in the window, then beyond herself, Eugene in the yard, standing, eyes wide, thumb in his mouth. She blocked her thoughts of him.

Her jeans dipped over her hips. He breathed heavily against her neck, his coarse thumbs pushing into the flesh of her belly. He moved his face to her shoulder, his teeth grazing her warm skin. She winced as she reached in her front pocket for the Moly, flattened against the moist skin of her hip, and taking a pinch, popped it into her mouth and began to chew until it mixed with her saliva. She turned back around, the antidote in her cheeks, the stench reaching up from his skin, sallow in the now roaring fire of his skin, presenting herself to him.

"Is this what you want?" she asked, stepping back so his eyes could comb across her. Looking into the face that was not her husband's, she moved against him, first slowly, to incite arousal, his hands gripping her tightly, the fingernails digging into the skin of her flank. He pulled her to the couch where he lay against her, then she took his mouth to hers and began to kiss him, first softly, then deeply, moving her tongue deeply against his, the sulfur nearly overpowering her, her tongue tracing his, wrapping her legs around him to hold him to her as she pressed the moly more deeply inside of his mouth. Their mouths joined, she felt the moly pass between them and shoved down her nausea, his awful grip on her increasing before he abruptly pushed her off hard, howling into the space between them as her body smashed against the ground.

He reached out for her neck, but roughly, not the way Jess usually touched her. She could see the tint of his saliva on his lips—green. He had ingested it. She scrambled back, but he caught her by the hair.

Then, his grip broken, he howled, bending in half as his cries filled the room. Lillian looked up to see a shadowy figure from the corner.

Jess cowered back, his skin speckled, burned, seared from each dusting of salt.

Eugene stood limply, a leather satchel of salt in his left hand, a rope in the other.

Jess' mouth began to foam, his head shaking back and forth, as a dog shakes of water.

Lillian scrambled to Eugene, blocking him with her body. They stood together, watching Jess, the blood between her legs starting anew as he twisted.

"And when I passed by thee," she whispered, "and saw thee polluted in thine own blood—"

"When thou wast in thy blood," Eugene said.

"Live."

The demon inside Jess moved toward them in fury, stumbling, the cowl from his eyes parting to show the beast, then moved, then straight again, then horizontal, but it could not move beyond the salt. Lillian and Eugene inched back against the wall.

"Can he get us, Lily-B?" Eugene asked, voice trembling.

"No. You did so good, Eugene." She wrapped her arms around the boy, watching the artery in Jess' neck furiously pulsing. "This will hold him for now," she whispered.

Jess crashed to his knees then, his hands on either side of his head as though trying to contain a splitting headache. He howled out, before falling and hitting his head against the side of the stove, hard enough to knock him out cold. She moved fast then, taking the rope from Eugene, ran to tie Jess in the king of knots, as Tyresius had told her, and stepped away. Jess was unconscious, his eyes oozing something like pus, his clothes wet with whatever was inside of him. From his lips, a line of pink foam escaped. She tested the tie before checking his pulse and stepping back.

"What do we do?" Eugene whispered.

Lillian's wounds ached. Her breasts were swollen, soured. "The Bible says to be sober-minded. To be watchful."

"Watchful for what?"

"For the Devil, child," she whispered. "The Devil prowls, seeking someone to devour."

They sat in silence before Jess, tied to the cold stove, his right side close enough to sear his body had the stove been lit. His breath rattled.

She turned toward Eugene. "How did you know?"

He looked without speaking, watching Jess as he lay so very changed on the floor.

"Eugene," she said, shaking him gently.

He looked back at her then, his eyes wide. "The voice was inside of me."

"Thank you, baby. Thank you so much," she said, pulling him against her. "I have to get Glory. You stay put, you hear? Holler if Jess moves?" she asked.

"That ain't Mr. Jess," Eugene said, his eyes never leaving Jess' form.

She stepped backward before limping downstairs. "I know, Eugene. Stay right here. I will be right back."

Two heartbeats, two heartbeats, she told herself as she moved, in what felt like half time, her body in slow motion, but when she reached the bottom step, she nearly tripped over something solid and heavy.

She hit the lights. The slumped form of the granny lay before her. Cold, her head twisted all wrong on her neck, her eyes open and motionless. Lillian screamed before falling on her knees before the body, "Oh, Marjorie—" *Two heartbeats*, she realized, terrified, as she stood, everything moving in half time, her eyes lingering on the form of the dead woman before her.

"Glory."

Lillian pushed the door open to encounter a sudden push back. She hit the wall behind her, a series of growls from behind the door. She pushed forward again, and the door gave, causing her to collide with the front of the hope chest. Then, a terrifying snarl before a whine and a series of licks as Wendy bounded into her.

Two heartbeats.

Wendy was on her then, licking her face as she put her arms around her, lifting her to her knees to check the crib where Glory lay.

The second heartbeat. Glory Be. She was safe. Covered in tears and spit up with a soiled diaper, but she was safe. Wendy had guarded her. She lifted Glory, crying, kissing her small face, waking her to her hunger, her searing cries filling the room.

"I am so sorry, Glory. I am so sorry."

The baby's eyes opened to her mother's fully for the first time; Lillian could see them full on in the overhead light. The odd yellowish color, not unlike her own, but covered by a membrane. And quickly, as soon as she noticed it, the blinking cowl vanished.

She's like me. My God—

Her heart racing, they sat on the floor, the baby in Lillian's arms and Wendy again by her side. She ran her fingers through Wendy's fur as she sobbed. For Marjorie, cold outside. For Jess.

"I guess it was you who bit Jess then," she said, noticing a bloody tuft of her fur in her hand. She leaned closer, feeling along Wendy's side when she noticed the bite mark on her side. Wendy stood still, hovering with a heavy pant, her eyes heavy.

The poison, Lillian realized.

She reached into her pocket, mouthed another slip of the moly, chewing quickly. Then, prying Wendy's mouth open, she shoved the moly in the back behind her tongue, holding it closed as Wendy twisted, rubbing her jowls before she reluctantly swallowed. Lillian leaned against the crib, bleeding onto the floor, Wendy against her on her right side, Glory howling into her neck. She lay watching the form of the granny—and waited.

Please, Lord, she prayed, an incantation, *Please please please.*

46

The moly worked its way through Jess Cedars' temporarily subdued parasympathetic nervous system, the plant steadily counteracting the powerful stramonium poisoning that would change the course of the man's life. Jess would survive, but the pain in his joints, incorrectly diagnosed by the city doctors as arthritis, would bother him until he was an old man, when he would become dependent upon a cane to move between job sites or his many grandchildren.

As he lay tied to the wood-burning stove, the neighbor boy Eugene, whom he had always considered curiously and whom he had always let walk silently beside him as he worked on his lot, watched Jess closely, taking his pulse twice as he lay writhing. And below them, his wife waited out his healing in their bedroom beside her grandmother's notebook, which she had opened to a cutout from the Missouri Department of Conservation, citing Celeste's scrawl from 1978:

Jimsonweed (common) with a sketch beside it. *Sharp smelling, unpleasant.*
Family: nightshade (cousins to pepper, tobacco, tomato, potato, eggplant)
Note: annual with purple stems, note the 5-pointed flowers, can grow up to 6-7 in., funnel shaped, white in color with a "violet throat."
*blooms in May, strong perfume.
Warning: all plant parts toxic, particularly the seeds. Alkaloid compounds present. Signs of poisoning include convulsions, hallucinations, death if ingested; increased CO_2 in the air increases plant toxicity

According to Celeste's notes, when jimsonweed's thorny apple seed pods were crushed, which in the case of Jess and his boys, stepped on, the dust from the seed was released into the air, signaling the warning. The southerners had witched the Jimson, the dust inhaled by anyone who dared trespass on the south side.

As night changed to dawn, Jess' visions changed from ones of terror to ones of his childhood, as though he had returned to the body of the nine-year-old he was before pain became his shadow.

First, his grandfather cracking walnuts from the porch rocker, his heavy, knobbed fingers splitting the shells before dropping them into the wooden bucket, handing Jess the occasional half. Next, Jess' father lacing his boots on the porch. It was Jess' first time accompanying him on a hunt. That day, Jess Sr. would let him use his gun for the shooting.

"You think you'll be strong enough to hold it up?" he asked him from all his height above.

"I can hold the aim," Jess said, eyeing the barrel in his small hands.

Jess Sr. looked far off into the timber. "You'll see a deer before you hear it."

In his memory, he could see his mother through the bay, her belly swollen in late pregnancy with Johnny, Trevor playing jacks on the ground beside her.

Then, his first solo hunt. Arms heavy from five hours in the deer stand at Indian Mound. The cedar was more familiar to him than his own heart. On one side of him, a clearing four hundred yards long, trees lining either side. Behind him, a 250-foot drop to the river flats below. Legend had it, the mound was the resting place of a great Osage chief who lived to one hundred and eight years. Six hours in. Nothing but squirrels and the rustling of leaves in the old sycamore. An unopened tin flask of whiskey beside him. As he waited, he thought of the fire he'd make behind the cabin later, the weight in the bed of a good deer, a nice mount, and coils of sausage to last through summer. A small diversion in the still drew his eyes to where the clearing met the treeline. The snout of a deer emerged from a cautious graze. Through his scope, he saw it feeding, steam rising from its nostrils into the pale air, heard his heart beating in his own ears. Ninety yards out, the deer calculated each step, eyeing the shadows and its numerous dangers. With a round already in the chamber, Jess feathered off the safety, crosshairs centered on the chest. Held his aim still. The deer stepped into the clearing. A mature buck, nine points in all. The setting sun illuminated the trees. Jess breathed in slowly, trying to pair his breaths with his adrenaline heart.

"Squeeze, don't pull," his grandfather said as he handed him another walnut half.

Sixty yards out, the whitetail eased into the clearing, one hoof over the other. Jess adjusted his aim broadside, centering the crosshairs over the heart, his aching back forgotten. Then the squeeze. The buck raised his head as the crack of the shot echoed through the timber, dying off among the treetops acres away as the buck fell to its side. Jess exhaled, looking through his scope.

The gun smoke cleared.

47

"Lillian?" she heard someone call sometime later. She had fallen asleep and was roused by the sound of voices upstairs.

"Jess," Lillian said out loud. Wendy jumped up alongside her. Glory whimpered in her arms.

Lillian stood with a limp and lay Glory back in her soiled crib. She grabbed Jess' old Mossberg, pocketing a handful of shells. Wendy followed her upstairs, nosing the air. Jess' voice was there, having subsided into exhausted moans.

"Lillian," he said tiredly when he saw her, looking between her and Eugene, sitting cross-legged on the floor beside the couch. "What the hell is going on?" He struggled against his ties.

Lillian positioned herself in front of Eugene and aimed the old hunting rifle at Jess. Her legs shook from beneath her. She'd bled through her jeans and Tyresius' dressings. "What's your name?" Lillian asked.

"Why do you have my gun?"

"Tell me your name," she repeated, more sternly.

"Lillian—"

She limped forward, pressed the barrel against his cheek.

"You're going to p-point my own shotgun at me?" he asked.

"Or I'll blow you straight to hell," she added, blinking away the cowl as her husband, watching her, turned pale.

"M-my name is Jess Cedars," he said, swallowing, his eyes wide. "And I woke up tied to my own goddamn stove," he added as he struggled against his restraints.

Looking down at him, she could tell that Jess' eyes were clear. He was soaked with sweat, but he was back. Her husband was back. A sob filled her throat as she dropped the gun and pressed against him, her hands gripping his body.

"Lillian," he muffled into her chest.

She moved to untie his hands, weeping, shaking her head.

He sat up, surveying the scene as he rubbed his wrists, wincing at his mangled hand. Wendy moved to their sides cautiously, licking Jess' wrists.

"Your legs," he said, looking down at her bandaged body. "What—"

"I'll explain later," she said, wiping her tears away with her dirty sleeve. She helped him to the couch. Eugene pushed his thumb back into his mouth.

"Lillian—I don't remember how I got here," he said as he looked around, the worry a stone in his heart.

She reached around for his broad shoulders, and she held him there for a bit.

Tyresius had saved them. Saved all of them.

48

Sheriff Gideon was the first to arrive. He'd been roused from his recliner by his wife, who'd been carrying the Bible around in her front apron pocket since the locusts had arrived. She held out the phone, said it was Jess Cedars. Said he was calling about a body on his property. A dead granny-woman who had broken her neck. Gideon drank day-old coffee on the way to Jess' cabin, the deputy and coroner in the car behind him.

Lillian watched them pull up from the window, Alice behind her, feeding a bottle full of store-bought formula to Glory Be.

Gideon stepped inside, removed his hat, took one look at Lillian, his mouth hanging open, his soggy cigar stuck to his bottom lip, and froze in his place.

"Now, what happened to you, young miss?" he asked.

"Current at the Lick," Lillian said, looking down at her wrapped legs. "Cut me up good."

Gideon looked between her and Jess, his eyes wide. "You doctor yourself up, Miss Lillian?" Wendy nosed his hand as he looked around. The two males had shown back up that morning, covered in burrs and were pacing on the back porch, waiting to be cleaned up.

"Granny-woman over on the north end fixed me up. Tyresius St. James."

"That's it," he said, exasperated, pulling a pen and tiny notebook from his front pocket. "That damn creek is off limits from here on out. Lost one boy already. And what were you doing swimming already?" he asked. "You're supposed to be taking it easy after the baby."

"I know, sheriff. My Jess already gave me a talking to. Just wanted a little relaxation," she said, looking down with the lie. "Suppose I should have stayed closer." Through the window, she could see the deputy and coroner step gingerly past her chicken coop. "Reckon y'all would like some coffee. I'll get it started."

"That would be just fine, Lillian," Gideon said.

Jess led the three men to the basement as Lillian warmed the kettle, her heart aching. Jess couldn't remember anything from the day before. Not leaving Sam's, not Marjorie looking after Glory Be, not the dogs running off. And nothing about her coming home and knocking him out cold. When he had come to, Lillian had filled him in briefly but told him the other details had to wait. They had to tend to Marjorie. She led him down the stairs and pulled back the quilt.

"My Lord," he had said. "That poor woman." He sat at the bottom of the steps, his head in his hands. After a moment, he closed her eyes, covered her back up, and called the sheriff.

The men took photographs, examined the angle at which Marjorie lay, and talked in low voices. After a bit, the coroner came upstairs, pushing his heavy spectacles back onto his nose. He explained the broken neck had likely been caused by the fall down the old stairs. He recommended a safety gate in addition to a handrail. Lillian began to cry and excused herself. Jess looked beside himself. Gideon patted Jess on the shoulder, assured him he wouldn't be fined for his structure not being up to code.

They took Marjorie with them, her body zipped in a black bag. On his paper, the coroner noted the cause of death as "accidental," while Gideon eyed the staircase one last time and Jess signed the report. They had blamed the fall on the old stairs, but Lillian knew the truth. It wasn't the steps. It was the watcher, working from within Jess.

"You may want to consider a runner here, Jess," Gideon said, crouching at the top of the steps.

"Yes, sir," Jess said, looking worn but clear-eyed since Gideon had seen him last. He was slowly starting to feel like himself again, but he was winded. Lillian knew that things would never quite be the same for them. For anyone who had been touched by the events of that weekend.

"Too much craziness this week, Jess," Gideon said, shaking his head as he stood. Jess eyed the stairwell alongside Gideon, kneeling to take a look at the lip of carpet that had caused the fall. For a moment, he wondered—the time when he was out a black hole in his memory—but then Lillian's words echoed in his mind.

Trust in the Lord. Do not lean on your own understanding.

"But you seem to be feeling better at least," Gideon added, shaking Jess from his thoughts.

Lillian handed both of the men cups of coffee.

"Much better," Jess said, wondering what else he had forgotten. "But Marjorie—" Jess' voice caught in his throat, his gut still in knots. "She delivered my Glory."

The men looked at the baby, who slept in a sling hung around Alice's chest. Jess knew then his conscience would itch inside of him for all of time.

"I suppose we will see youse at Sam's funeral," Gideon said.

"Yes, sir," Jess said.

As the men spoke, Lillian stared at the county's body bag with Marjorie inside of it. She remembered her calmness during the delivery, and her heart lunged in her chest. She imagined her bending to place the ax, her singing "Fair Charlotte" through the labor. She remembered her smooth hand on her forehead as she pushed, telling her to think of the water, cool with the evening's wind, the dragonflies' dance on the surface. Lillian nearly choked from the sadness. She could not imagine Jess capable of such violence, but even if it had been his body, it was not his spirit. Marjorie had fought the Devil and died a hero. She'd protected Glory.

She did not speak of Jess' possession to anyone, did not speak of Marjorie's likely cause of death to Jess. This would be something for only her and Tyresius to discuss. Ty would advise her on how to confront the sadness, how to work through it, and eventually how to bury the pain, as it would not be possible to prosecute evil itself. Her best defense would be to live a good life by the Lord's good book.

Lillian buried the Changed One's tendril of hair in the persimmon to the south of their lot, per Ozark custom. This would prevent anyone on the south of the Lick from accessing their land going forward. She did not farm that patch of land the next season. Even her dogs kept a wide berth.

The county released Marjorie's body three days later. Lillian was the only listed next of kin. Gideon closed the case and busied himself with chasing down the boys responsible for the petty theft while the electrical grid had been down.

They buried Marjorie down on J Road in the same plot as Celeste. Celeste had been the one to pluck her out of trouble, so they felt it right she should be beside her instead of digging up long-gone kin. Jess dug the grave himself. Lillian cut a hickory stick the length of her body and buried her with a silver dollar in her mouth. A few of Celeste's neighbors came in their wagons or on tractors to pay their final respects. Tyresius was there, holding Glory Be. Pete waited in the truck down the way. Wendy stood as sentinel. She was as good as new but knew her time would come as would everyone's. Shepherds prefer to die as they live—in protection.

After saying the final prayers, the group moved to Ty's cabin for evening coffee and pudding. Lillian lingered long, scanning the graveyard, thinking of the mysteries of J Road and of the women who walked their part of the world. She did not send out that day, as all the hearts she reckoned she cared for most sat inside of the granny's cabin. She heard the prairie tiger beetles, saw the bumelia borer perched on a tree trunk. The cicadas were already down for the day, but the katydids were out, their chorus alive in the treeline. She turned her head in the direction of the Lick, felt a cold shiver, and crossed herself before taking her husband's hand.

Lillian never did see the white buffalo again, but he did visit her in her dreams, once every harvest moon, two weeks after the equinox.

49

Lillian spent the next two months healing up from the birth and recovering from her injuries. Jess saw a city doctor, just for show, to appease Johnny and his father. Johnny and Jess attended Sam's funeral the following Friday. Kurt was still too sick to get out of bed, but Gideon later told Jess it wasn't the sickness but the liquor that had gotten ahold of him this time.

Brutus stood across from Jess at the graveyard as they lowered Sam down into the ground beside his mother. He leaned on his gun and didn't shed one tear. In fact, Johnny said to Jess after, the man looked angry.

"Can you blame him?" Jess had asked his little brother.

"Suppose not," Johnny said. He later told Jess there'd be no more hunting in his future. He was moving his family to a property on the 14th mile marker—one with better city access and fewer rural complications. Jess told him he understood.

The locusts disappeared after about a week. The crows hung around, though. When Lillian packed up Marjorie's trailer, she left a quarter in the feed bowl in the back window. Sent out a thank you for that day on the south when they'd helped her. Within a week, a family of crows took up residence in the oak beside their cabin. Lillian would continue to speak to them in her small way, to leave them gifts. Small shiny things. Peanuts, shell on. Earrings she'd find in the road. Bits of yarn. In turn, she gained their trust. A good omen, she thought.

As she regained her strength, Lillian spent hours reading through all of the notebooks in Celeste's trunks, finding endless recipes for tinctures, reflections on modern medicine's failings, and even finding the notebook from the date of Sugar's adoption. She marveled at Celeste's patience with the child, remembering the same language from her own childhood. Despite reading about her mother, Lillian did not long for her. She wondered if she would have bonded to her had she had the chance to know her. But Lillian's heart was dry to Sugar. Instead, it was full for Marjorie. For Celeste. Wendy even. And newly, it opened for Ty as well. She lifted Glory Be and kissed her forehead, smelling her milky breath. She promised her she'd protect her until the end of time.

That fall, Lillian tried out many of Celeste's recipes, taking notes in the margins on what worked and what she imagined she could improve upon. She was an eager student. One morning, Jess came in, leaning on the wooden beam by the sink, watching her work on the kitchen island. He asked her if she should really be called a granny since she was only twenty, but Lillian said she didn't know what else to call herself. She walked over and put her arms around him. And, feeling the movement of his heart against her cheek, she felt the glow of home all around her. They would make love that night and conceive a son and name him Carl Jess. He would be born without the cowl, leaving Lillian and Ty with much to discuss. There would be two more children beyond Glory Be and Carl Jess. Just as Celeste had predicted.

Jess converted the shed into a makeshift laboratory for Lillian, where she and Tyresius often spent afternoons reviewing tinctures, while Pete and Jess would piddle around the property. Ty would advise Lillian's own cooking at the stove while she read over Celeste's old notebooks, teaching her what she knew from her nearly eighty years of research. She'd sit in Lillian's rocker, her gigantic glasses low on her nose, and sip tea or a rare brandy, if Jess was in the mood to open the bottle. Ty would live another seven years before she joined her wife. For her last five years, she moved into the cabin with Jess and Lillian to assist with the children and brew full-time in Lillian's laboratory.

A week before the full moon one Saturday, Lillian spotted a small indentation in the bottom of the hope chest. She used her pocketknife to jostle it, revealing a secret drawer covered by a flat panel of cedar. In it, she found a treasure she had previously believed unwritten. Bundles of letters from Tyresius to Celeste. And beside them, letters addressed to Tammy. Sealed. Years worth.

The next day after services she sat quietly drinking tea at Ty's table. As Ty read over the pages, she nodded or chewed her lip or was silent. She removed her glasses, using her heavy apron to dab the corners of her eyes.

"I didn't have a damn clue," she told Lillian after a minute. Lillian bounced four-month-old Glory Be on her knee. The girl had Jess' eye color after all, but whenever she cried, Lillian could spot the cowl. No doubt about it. Southern.

Ty had said the letter had given her exactly what she had dreamed of hearing, things she fantasized about in the years after they had split, things she had assumed too absurd to have ever been true. It detailed the Changed Ones and their secret signals. The baby's desperate need. Her knowledge of what would happen if Ty would stay. Her false longing to get Ty to move out. To save her. It was all written right there in her tight script for Tyresius to see, to read over and over again if she liked, to balm her cold soul. Celeste had loved Ty. She sacrificed their marriage so Ty, so Tammy would live. In living, Ty's research would save so many more people. She saved Sugar, she saved Ty, Lillian, Jess, Glory Be. The baby growing inside of Lillian. Even Wendy.

"How could I not have seen this was a fiction?" she asked, holding the letter in her hand.

"I'm sure Celeste made sure you believed her," Lillian said, peering into the cluster of wet leaves in her teacup.

Ty leaned back in her chair and exhaled slowly. "If she had only told me," she said, the lines suddenly deeper in her face. "We could have worked something out, I'm sure of it."

"Maybe," Lillian said, marveling at her grandmother's selflessness. Surely, Sugar would never have had a chance at freedom in any capacity if not rescued. And it would have been impossible that she would have been born. Or Glory Be. "Maybe not."

They both looked out the window at the fire on the hillside, the highest point of the property line. The women of J Road would all have theirs lit every night until Christmas. For Marjorie.

Ty eyed her wife's granddaughter and great-granddaughter across the table and smiled sadly. "But then again, I suppose tinkering with things like that aren't always for the best."

"Some things are better left unrustled," Lillian agreed. "How's your heart feeling?"

Ty returned her glasses to her face. "You know, I spent the last seventy years working on a goddamn tincture for that vine, thinking, if I could only get something to win her back. That could do it. She could maybe love me again. And I sent my recipes in those letters you found. It was in the last one. She never opened any of them."

"I don't think she could have stomached it. I know I couldn't have," Lillian said, thinking of Jess, the way he held her tenderly about the waist.

Ty looked up, looking suddenly very old. "I wasted a lifetime thinking the love of my life didn't love me back."

Lillian reached across the table for Ty's other hand. "I reckon nothing feels as good as being wrong about that."

50

An unexpected cold snap in late October meant flu season came early for the children north of the Lick. With Marjorie and Celeste gone, the hill people had turned to Tyresius for their medicine. If she was booked, Lillian, her apprentice, whose treatments had expanded into general care, would take the case. Lillian had spent the early autumn treating toothaches, arthritis, and influenza. She had delivered three babies since having Glory that July, each time thinking of, longing for, her own midwife granny.

On Halloween evening, Lillian drove through the handful of farms dotting the landscape, passing clusters of children in costumes, their parents walking behind them, their flashlights lighting up the darkness. She saw a young girl dressed in a black robe and conical hat. On her face was a plastic nose on a flimsy string that kept slipping down. Lillian knew it was just a simple parody of what the city folk thought of the grannies, but it still stung a smidge. Celeste used to say she felt it risky that girls dressed like that, making jokes about such things, playing with spells to get even or to bewitch men. It was just so easy to dismiss as nothing or as too much. Lots of people think evil comes from a place or a time. Something like the backwoods hill country. But the thing to fear, Lillian knew, was in each of us. North born, south born. Good or bad. It's all our choice who we're going to be.

By the following week, along the waning gibbous, Lillian was called out every night. If it was a cough, she left the baby with Jess; if it was something not catching, Glory Be came along, slung to her back to watch her mother work, her odd eyes licking like flames everything they touched. Eugene came along too most nights, a silent apprentice. The first male granny, though Lillian suggested he call himself a Yarb in training. Eugene shook his head. Said he'd rather be called a granny.

Grannies weren't typically called for animals, but one afternoon, Lillian had been called up by Ty's neighbors in need of the removal of a screech owl that had somehow found its way inside the house. Ozark folk are superstitious about particular breeds of owls, so the errand was immediate.

Jess first offered to help, but since it was so close to the Lick, he stayed home with Glory. He hadn't been quite the same since that summer day, and Lillian knew the nocturnals well. She borrowed his calving gloves and took the Chevy the ten miles to J Road, turning off onto the familiar drive to the north end of the Lick. She found the owl tucked above a kitchen cabinet in a cluster of dust and feathers, more confused than dangerous. She had felt for its heart, soothing it with a low humming. When she felt it soften, she coaxed it forward with store-bought meat, gently covered its head, and carried it to the front door, where she released it into the start of the evening. It flew to the nearest timber, looked down at her, shook out its feathers to get bearings, then flew off into the forest.

In times like these, Lillian felt her feral nature nudging from within. The southern part of her, and her new knowledge of her shadowy family tree, made her feel a little dizzy. Though her scars had already begun to fade to pink, there were echoes of what happened that day. The Changed Ones. The beasts that wanted her milk. The watcher, coiled inside the body of her husband, his wanting to drag her back across to the south. Her husband nearly taken from her, her dead granny, her neck bent wrong, Wendy's pant in front of the baby, holding out until Lillian had returned home. She shivered at the memory.

Nerve damage from the bites lingered, phantom pain that woke her sometimes in the middle of the night, a needling reminder of what she had seen and what was inside of her. What lies inside of everyone if we aren't careful. The Lord had delivered them that day, but Lillian knew the darkness of the south would always lie adjacent to the light of the north, twins, always together, always inside of her.

Leaving that call, at the four-way stop between J and 7, she paused, looking up at the starting brightness of the half-lit moon, humpbacked in the sky, waiting on the end of day. Before turning, Sam's father, Brutus, pulled into the service station at the corner. He lifted a stiff hand without looking in her direction. She hadn't seen him since her wedding to Jess. She waved back before pulling onto 7 to head home to her husband and child.

Epilogue

Brutus idled at the four-way stop, his blinker clicking. The last light of the day cast long shadows on the chestnut-colored meadows to the west. He thought of the Black girl who had just passed him in Jess' truck, clean and polite compared to the hill people she came from. She'd be headed home to her man to cook his supper. He thought again of his Sam. His heart was still tangled up with sadness and anger, and his leg was paining him something fierce. There was nowhere to put all that he felt.

He parked his truck with a heavy sigh, then got out to pump his gas, leaning against his pickup as he watched a pair of Red Angus cows lumber toward their barn, finishing their grazing. A rooster waited on the fence, looking over his pasture. Behind him was a southern meadow, and he felt its dark pull against his back, despite his best intentions to ignore it. That land had cut up his boy, and still, there'd been no answers as to why or who. He kept his gaze forward, squinting petulantly into the distance until the nozzle clicked off. It had been months since Sam's death, since the quiet of his life had dissolved finally into absolute silence.

His family gone, his bloodline dead, his body aching.

Brutus walked inside to pay, finding Michael Monroe behind the cash register, the news blaring from a small, greasy television behind the counter.

"What's going on?" Monroe asked.

Brutus nodded curtly and pushed two twenty-dollar bills across the laminated counter. "Two packs of Reds," he said.

Monroe turned away from his newspaper. "Soft or hard packs?"

"Soft," Brutus said, eyeing the dog asleep behind the register. "Good-looking lab you've got there," he told Michael. "You ever take him out?"

Monroe slid the cigarettes across the counter. "This one's just for show. He's a lap dog if you want to know the truth. My wife made him soft." He fiddled with the register and slapped the change on the counter. "You still got your bird dogs?"

Brutus pocketed the cigarettes and shook his head as he picked up the coins, dropping the pennies into the take one, give one saucer. "Got a few left, but ain't got the time for training 'em up anymore."

"I hear you."

The men watched as low cloud cover started to overtake the sunset and were silent for a moment.

"Looks like a storm might be coming through."

"Looks like it," Brutus answered. "Well, you take care, Michael," he said as he turned.

"You do the same," the man said before the door and its bell closed off the conversation.

The first drops of rain fell on the windshield as Brutus waited at the turn at J and 7. Straight ahead, a blur, about thigh-high seemed to dart across the fence line. It was just a shadow of movement, but enough to catch his eye. He leaned forward, turning up the wipers, and the blur moved again, not twenty feet from the truck. Bigger than a coyote, smaller than a deer. Quick-moving.

Then, between the wipers, he saw it.

From behind a bramble, the body of a dog emerged. At first, he thought it was just old—its liver head covered in age, but it was too agile. Too lean. It was filthy, looking like it had been digging. It crept between the fence and the hedge, as though chasing something on the other side of the fence. Its broad shoulders made him think for a moment it couldn't be a dog, but it had pointer coloring. His pointers' coloring. Brutus squinted. The dog paced back and forth, as though longing to get closer to the road. When it stood parallel to the truck, it stepped into the last of the light, where its opaque eyes took him in. He could see its wasted jaw, covered in blood, its light, horizontal pupils as it panted in the air between them.

BJ.

Brutus gasped, despite himself. An old Pontiac honked from behind him. The dog darted westward. Brutus threw his pickup into gear, his heart racing as he turned left onto the highway just as the beast ran off with loping strides back into the southern tip of Lick Creek off J Road, toward wherever it had come from, toward whatever called it home.

Acknowledgements

Special thanks to April Gloaming Publishing, who gave this story a home, and to *Embark*, who originally published the first three chapters.

Though this work is entirely a work of fiction, the history of the folklore native to the Ozark region was derived in part from Vance Randolph, whose *Ozark Magic and Folklore* carried my imagination through hours spent wandering the forests of Camden County.

Many thanks to Dillon Wilfong who advised me on the pursuit of the White-Tail. Thanks, too, to Franklin County Deputy Sheriff Nate Wilson for answering my many questions on law enforcement.

And lastly, thank you to my husband, Chris Reed. I'll meet you under the bed anytime.

ALLISON CUNDIFF is the author of several collections of poetry, including *Snapshot* (Bottlecap Press, 2023); *Just to See How It Feels* (WordPress, 2018); *Otherings* (Golden Antelope Press, 2016); and *In Short, A Memory of the Other on a Good Day*, co-authored with Steven Schreiner, (Golden Antelope Press, 2014). Her first novel, *Hey Pickpocket*, was published in 2025 by JackLeg Press. Connect at allisoncundiff.net.

Similar April Gloaming Titles:

The House that Wasn't There
Andrew Forrest Baker

Ash Tuesday
Ariadne Blayde

The Eaten
Leah Saint Marie

All Things Holy & Heathen
Chelsea Jackson

At the Confluence
Christopher K. Doyle

The Peril of Remembering Nice Things
Jeffery Wade Gibbs

APRIL GLOAMING

View our full catalog at aprilgloaming.com

www.ingramcontent.com/pod-product-compliance
Lightning Source LLC
LaVergne TN
LVHW032007070526
838202LV00059B/6338